THE FLIGHT OF THE VALKYRIE

THE FLIGHT OF THE VALKYRIE

JAMES BECK

Primix Publishing
East Brunswick Office Evolution
1 Tower Center Boulevard, Ste 1510
East Brunswick, NJ 08816
www.primixpublishing.com
Phone: 1-800-538-5788

This is a work of fiction. Names, characters, places and incidents either are the product of the author's imagination or are used fictitiously, and any resemblance to any actual persons, living or dead, events, or locales is entirely coincidental.

Published by Primix Publishing: 04/08/2025

ISBN: 979-8-89194-398-8(sc)
ISBN: 979-8-89194-399-5(e)

Library of Congress Control Number: 2025900111

Any people depicted in stock imagery provided by iStock are models, and such images are being used for illustrative purposes only.

Certain stock imagery © iStock.

Because of the dynamic nature of the Internet, any web addresses or links contained in this book may have changed since publication and may no longer be valid. The views expressed in this work are solely those of the author and do not necessarily reflect the views of the publisher, and the publisher hereby disclaims any responsibility for them.

Contents

Dedication

Dedicated to J.T. Harley whose life in the shadows provided
pertinent insights for me

CHAPTER 1

Spring 1990

A clear pleasant day dawned over El Paso. The low humidity made the ninety-degree weather decent. Inside the Luftwaffe Headquarters of North America, located at Fort Bliss, Lieutenant Colonel Eric Schreiber was looking forward to a day off. His flight operations duties consumed an inordinate amount of his time. Although he still had a head of blond hair after two years, he was feeling drained. However, he was clearly marked for advancement, so even though he had arranged for a leave, he wanted to make sure that no last-minute developments had occurred that required his attention.

"Relax, Herr Oberst. Everything is fine," his aide, Captain Ritter, said. "We've checked the schedules more than once. Everything is going to be all right."

"I know. I just want to be sure."

"Sir, go out and enjoy the day and quit being so anal retentive. You'll feel better."

"I could have you court-martialed for that." Schreiber tried to appear serious, but a grin broke through his stolid demeanor.

At that point, Major General Paul Becker walked into the room.

"Eric, I thought you were supposed to be on leave today," Becker said with his distinct Bavarian guttural accent.

"I was on my way. Captain Ritter was pointing out my shortcomings."

"Such as?" Becker asked with a look of interest on his face.

"Basically, he says I have a tight asshole."

Becker laughed. "That's why I'm giving you some leave. A tight asshole, Captain Ritter, is sometimes a good thing in combat. At least that's what my father told me. However, the good colonel doesn't seem to know how to relax. In fact, I'm ordering you out. You will not enter this building again until tomorrow."

"Understood, Herr General." Schreiber shrugged. He knew Becker liked a person when the general bantered with someone. He had no use for incompetents, so the current needling was actually a compliment.

"By the way, what are you doing on your day off?"

"Alamogordo. I'm going with—" Schreiber never finished.

"I know who you are going with." Becker didn't say another word but with a nod of his head motioned for Schreiber to follow him. A shadow seemed to have come across Becker's face. He was no longer the jovial Bavarian. He now resembled the stiff-necked Prussians from past decades.

They entered Becker's office. It had pictures from the general's career. There were older pictures of a German pilot from World War II. Schreiber studied these as Becker opened a drawer and handed Schreiber a newspaper clipping from a New England newspaper.

"What's this?"

"Well, read it."

The clipping read, "Yesterday off the southern coast of Maine, fishermen recovered the remains of a submerged aircraft. Markings on the plane indicate that it was a long-range German floatplane. A local historian believes that it was one of the last Wiking flying boats. However, further information is not available. Although the historian pointed out that a few missions were flown to the United

States for reconnaissance, there is no record of one of these planes being flown on a mission to Maine."

"Well, Eric?"

"I had never heard of this."

"And you won't. I looked for further articles and found nothing. However, did you ever notice this picture?" Becker pointed to a particular photograph on the wall.

"No, I haven't."

"Then come around and take a look."

Schreiber had to bend down to examine the picture. He looked intently at the photograph. In the corner, someone had written Flensburg, May 1945 BV222C-09. In the background was a large Wiking flying boat. In the foreground were two German officers. One was dressed in Luftwaffe uniform, while the other wore the unmistakable dress of the Waffen-SS. He took a closer look at the SS officer and then at the serial number of the plane. A shudder went through him as he recognized the man with the Knights Cross with oak leaves at his throat and SS major's rank on his collar. His father had never mentioned being at Flensberg at the end of the war.

"I thought this plane was destroyed at Lake Travemunde in April 1945." Schreiber tried not to show his surprise at his recognition of the SS officer.

"That's what the history books say. But what does the picture tell you and newspaper clipping tell you?"

"I know a lot of strange things happened at the end of the war, but my father never told me about his activities during that time."

"Neither did mine until about a year ago. That's when he told me the story behind this picture before he went into a nursing home."

"Well, what was it?"

"Since you're going to Alamogordo, I think you're going to find out. As soon as you said you were going there, I knew whom you were going with. Let me walk you out."

Schreiber didn't ask anything else as they exited the building. He knew Becker's father had flown several clandestine missions for KG 200 during the war. Later he had been picked up by the CIA to continue long-range flights deep into Communist territory. For several years, he had been a pilot for Air America as cover for his covert missions. Now the man was in bad health. It must have been one hell of a story he had to tell his son.

"You must be wondering what is wrong with the old man today," Becker said.

"Not at all, Herr General."

"Well, let me give you a hint. Many of us who had family in the Wehrmact during the war have a past. Skeletons in the closet as the Americans would say. That is particularly true for those who had family members in the SS. If there is any doubt in your mind, have you ever noticed how senior officers may have looked at you in a strange way? And you wondered why? I see you recognized your father in the photo. Then you have a clue what you're going to find out."

The two men exited the Spanish-style headquarters. They strolled over to Schreiber's BMW. An older man was in the passenger seat. He had wavy white hair that bespoke his age; however, his complexion would have passed for a younger man's face. His firm build was evident under his clothes, and he had piercing blue eyes. He obviously took care of himself.

"Good morning, General Becker," he remarked pleasantly.

"Herr Schreiber, it is always good to see you. I was showing your son a photograph of you and my father in 1945. I didn't tell the whole story. I thought you would want to do that."

"How perceptive of you. Had you been around during the war, who knows what might have happened?"

Becker smiled at the compliment, while the younger Schreiber spoke. "Actually, he told me nothing. He just tantalized me."

"You just confirmed my impression of the general."

Becker laughed again. "Have a good trip, Paul. Herr Schreiber, it is always a pleasure." Becker nodded his head in obvious deference.

"I appreciate that since I was only a mere humble major."

"And a damn good one as my father said." Becker then walked back into the headquarters.

"That didn't take long," the older Schreiber said.

"I have a good adjutant."

"A good adjutant can be worth a whole platoon."

"Or a squadron."

Schreiber started the car and sped out the west exit of Fort Bliss. After a few minutes, he turned onto the entry ramp for Interstate 10 and headed for Las Cruces. He had timed his departure so that they would arrive during the noon hour. Schreiber was anticipating an excellent dinner at one of the restaurants. As they cruised along the highway, Schreiber surveyed the surrounding area. This was natural for someone who had chosen a pilot's career.

To his left lay the sprawling city of Juarez. Even from this distance, he could tell that there were few tall buildings across the Rio Grande. Less obvious was the extreme squalor that permeated Juarez and even reached across the river. To his right were the foothills of the Rockies. Everywhere else, there was sand. The barren landscape was broken only occasionally by sagebrush or even more rarely by a scraggly tree.

"I understand why the Americans call this God's country." Colonel Schreiber paused briefly. "God made it, God forgot it, and God damned it. If it wasn't for the fact that the open airspace here allows us to fly large maneuvers, I would personally lobby to abandon this place."

The older Schreiber laughed. "Sennelager was worse. Fortunately, I was there only a few months, thank God. It had sand dunes, low brush, and the worse terrain possible in Germany. Men sentenced to death were brought there to face the firing squad. It was the worse place to be if you were in the German Army. God could not have been very happy when he created Sennelager or El Paso."

"There are always posts that one likes better than others. Assignments are the same way."

"How true, Eric. At Sennelager, I heard about the 800th Special Transportation Company and left as soon as I could. Of course, it eventually became the Brandenburg Division. I still have fond memories of my younger days in the Brandenburgers. I also feel the same way about the days at Friendenthal with Skorzeny. We were young and idealistic and full of fight. We were ready to give our all for the Fatherland. Unfortunately, things turned out differently as our national leadership was lacking." The older man's voice trailed off.

They drove on in silence, with the older man in deep reflection. *He is reliving the war again*, the younger Schreiber thought. He refrained from asking about the picture at Flensburg that Becker had pointed out. *He'll tell me when he's ready*, he thought. He knew the look on the old man's face from seeing it on so many other veterans' faces. At times like this, it was best to remain silent.

Finally, they arrived at Las Cruces. Schreiber drove to the Old Spanish Square. The exteriors of the buildings were bone white from the constant bleaching of the sun. A fountain was in the middle of the plaza. Schreiber parked in front of it. The two men then headed for a restaurant on the north side of the square. The building was unremarkable on the outside and blended in with the other shops in the plaza.

They entered the restaurant and were seated. The interior was as elegant as the outside was stark. Gold-trimmed mirrors adorned the walls, while crystal chandeliers added elegance to the dining experience. They ordered their drinks and enjoyed their surroundings.

"I hope you're not becoming too soft, Eric." A twinkle shone in his eyes as he spoke.

"Not hardly. I've just learned to enjoy life when I can. I thought this would be tastier than the German Officers' Club back on Fort Bliss. After all, you can get all the German food you want when you go back home. Besides, too much shop is talked at the club. After all, who knows if we'll ever come through here again?"

"Let me give you some advice. Learn to appreciate every day. Many of my friends that were in their twenties when I was young are vague memories. Many died in their twenties. It does make you savor life when you do have time to reflect on it." He gave a deep sigh.

"I suppose it does."

The waiter interrupted the conversation. He had promptly arrived with the salads. The steaks soon followed. The older man nodded with approval at the efficient service. They ate silently for several minutes, while they enjoyed the fine meal.

The older man finally spoke. "I remember when we entered France in 1940. We thought we had gone to heaven—the food, the wine, the women."

"You never mentioned the women before."

The father smiled slyly. "I must be getting old to have let that slip. Of course, I never claimed to be a saint. I certainly think too much of your mother to have ever said that around her. But France was great for a German soldier in 1940. I still prefer French food to American or this stuff you call Tex-Mex. Still it beats the rations we were issued or the days when we had nothing. That happened more times than people realize."

"It seems hard to believe that all of that really happened. It's like another world you read about."

"In a way, it was. It's also good that it's gone. I hope you never see anything like it."

After an hour, they completed their meal. Schreiber gave the waiter a generous tip and departed. They returned to a considerably warmer BMW. They continued their drive up Highway 70 toward Alamogordo and the White Sands testing ground. The drive took about two hours. As they drove, Colonel Schreiber pondered the reason why his father had insisted on the trip. After all, he was the pilot with an interest in these things.

"Slow down." His father was alert now.

Colonel Schreiber slowed and pulled over. As he looked at his father, the man's face seemed exhilarated. He was reliving the war again.

"It seems almost like yesterday. Very little has changed."

"You didn't expect it too now, did you? Very little does in the desert."

"I am talking about July 1945."

"You were here? In July of 1945?" The son was incredulous. "I know the Americans brought the rocket scientists over to build the space program, but I would have never dreamed of them asking any Germans to be present when they were testing the atomic bomb."

"I didn't say that I was asked. I was sent here. The orders were so secret that even Hitler didn't know about the project. That's how secret it was."

"What are you talking about?" Colonel Schreiber was thoroughly confused. "Is this related to the picture on the wall?"

"Very much so. It's a long story. That's why I brought you here, or rather why I brought both of us here. I had to remind myself that I was here in July and August of 1945. I saw the first atomic blast. Now what I am about to tell you will be denied by any of the powers that be. If I were you, I certainly wouldn't repeat what I'm about to tell you."

"General Becker apparently knows. He said you had an interesting story to tell."

"He would since his father flew us over and had to remain." He paused and looked into the distance. "I swore an oath as a German soldier and officer to never divulge any of the secrets entrusted to me. Later I swore a similar oath when I worked for the Americans and then Gehlen. But I'm old now, and I paid my dues to the CIA and the BND. Because of that, I wasn't around much and not much of a father. I feel I owe you that much. I want to be honest with you for once. I am proud of what you have become. However, I wish that I could have been a bigger part of your life."

"That is all in the past. Don't say anything that might come back to haunt you."

"Who's telling? Anyway, if anyone does something, it would be a mercy killing. The doctors say I have chronic leukemia now. CLL is what it's called for short. Anyway, it is progressing slowly. They say I might not even die of the disease. No matter what, I'm on borrowed time. All of us are who fought in that war. That is why I have to tell you."

They walked along a little further. The older Schreiber walked slowly but deliberately. His face was aglow. His son recognized he was reliving one of his greatest triumphs as a soldier. A gust of wind blew dust into their faces. Colonel Schreiber shielded his face with his hand, but he noticed his father still staring ahead as if mesmerized by ghosts from the past.

"Are you okay, Father?"

"I feel fine. It was as if I relived my last month as a German officer. It seems only like yesterday. We had gotten it, and we were going to change the outcome of the war."

"What was it you had gotten?" Colonel Schreiber asked uneasily.

"An atomic bomb. We actually had one of their atomic bombs for three days, and we were going to change the course of the war. May 7th was going to be wiped out." His face was calm, but the voice was laced with barely suppressed excitement. His eyes blazed at the thought the memories elicited. "Let me start at the beginning. It's a long story, Eric."

Colonel Schreiber began having second thoughts about making this trip.

July 10, 1942

Dust swirled in the air as the engines on the Ford trucks kicked alive. Large red stars on the doors identified the vehicles as part of the Soviet Army. The occupants were dressed in khaki uniforms. A distinctive insignia of a sword and wreath was on the uniform's left sleeve, identifying them as members of the dreaded NKVD. The uniforms were meticulous as far as badges of rank and other uniform accessories. The commander of the unit had just checked each man's uniform to make sure it was within regulations. The officer might have been regarded as a martinet under other circumstances. However, the presence of a senior German officer carrying a sidearm gave away the true identity of the assembled men. They were all German soldiers, dressed in the uniforms of the enemy, and no mistakes could be tolerated. This was particularly true when one was posing as a member of the enemy's security service. In this case, they had chosen to don the uniform of the dreaded NKVD, as no sane member of Russian society, civilian or military, would question a person wearing the organization's insignia.

The men in this unit were no ordinary soldiers, and their commander was no ordinary commander. This elite commando unit was known as the "Wild Bunch." Many were veterans of the original unit, the 800th Special Duties Construction Company, and had remained with it since its formation in 1939. They had taken part in operations in the Low Countries in 1940 and in the Balkans the following year. During that time, they refined their ability to mimic the enemy. Now a regiment, the unit continued to add laurels to its name. Now known as Lehr-regiment Brandenburg, it was one of the most effective commando forces in the world.

The commander of the unit stood upright in the bed of the lead truck. He scanned the horizon while talking to the officer in German uniform. Baron Adrian von Foelkersam was well qualified to lead such an audacious mission. The Brandenburgers had learned that posing as an officer ran higher risks than posing as an NCO. Officers in most armies were expected to have certain social skills and a certain degree of military knowledge. The difficulty in posing as an officer was finding someone with the knowledge and language skills to withstand questioning should that happen.

None of this was a problem for Foelkersam. He was a Baltic German and the grandson of a Russian admiral who died with the Russian fleet that fought at Tsushima. In addition to fluent Russian, he spoke several other languages. Moreover, he possessed a cool head in difficult situations and so far had remained unfazed in adversity. In addition, he had trained the unit and had given it its nickname and earned the respect of its members. He would make full use of these qualities in the subsequent days.

"Remember, success depends on you," Colonel Alexander Pfuhlstein told the baron.

"So you have told me. We are ready."

"I know. I'm afraid that Ivan is also. He knows we need that oil."

"I'm aware of that. Still I think we have a good chance of securing the oil fields."

"Any questions then?"

"When do we leave?"

Pfuhlstein laughed. "Anytime now."

Foelkersam motioned for his men to move out. As they did so, he thought about the anticipated difficulties that lie ahead. The orders were simple. He was to drive across the Russian steppes and penetrate the Caucasus. He would enter Maykop, and when the Germans attacked, his men would seize the oil fields to prevent their destruction. Oil was the lifeblood of the German panzers. Without it, Foelkersam's superiors warned him that the German war effort would be in danger of collapse. Unfortunately, the Russians knew about the German's interest in Maykop. On April 28, 1942, Sergeant Hans Putzer had parachuted two hundred miles behind enemy lines to seize Hill 520, which overlooked the route to Maykop. This had been the first operation launched by Colonel Reinhard Gehlen of Foreign Armies East, and it had gone terribly wrong. Most of Putzer's men were captured, including his second in command. There was no doubt that the man talked given the persuasive means of Russian intelligence. Putzer, with the help of four Russian renegades who also escaped the debacle, escaped detection for several months before reaching friendly lines. It made a nice adventure story, but it also had alerted the Russians to German intentions and had given them months to prepare.

Foelkersam knew he did not have an easy task. Any attempt to take the fields by a coup de main would result in the fields' destruction. Subterfuge would be the only means possible. The main risk would be if someone recognized them as impostors. Worse was the possibility of a spy inside the Abwehr. Already, some disturbing incidents had happened to the Brandenburgers on the Eastern Front. There were too many unexplained ambushes similar to Putzer's experience. He had prepared the best he could, and if they were cornered, the "Wild Bunch" would fight. Everyone knew the penalty for fighting in the enemy's uniform if captured. If they were lucky, they would face a firing squad. Foelkersam shuddered at the thought of falling into the hands of the NKVD alive.

Minutes later, the convoy rumbled down a primitive Russian road. Some peasants were spotted leaving a village. Foelkersam stopped to obtain some local intelligence. The trucks squeaked to a stop. He motioned for one of the villagers to come over. A man hesitantly approached the truck.

"Are there any troops around?" Foelkersam asked.

The man hesitated. "Yes, comrade. Some deserters are on the other side of the village. They have taken a lot of our food. They do not want to fight either. We'll starve if they don't leave."

"How many are there?"

"Many. Several hundred."

Foelkersam had heard enough. He had already devised the strategy to get him into Maykop easier. He summoned his squad leaders. While he had only sixty men with him, he counted on the fear the NKVD inspired to keep the Russians in line. As his men assembled, he looked through his Zeiss binoculars and noticed smoke rising near the village. This indicated breakfast was being prepared. It was a perfect time to strike.

He spoke as his squad leaders gathered. "There are a lot of Russians in the village ahead of us. We are going to surround it and take them prisoner. We will use them in our plans. This is probably our best chance at success, so let's make the most of it. I want no firing unless necessary. If we do this right, what I am about to do may fit in nicely with our plans."

His men looked at him with a mixture of anticipation and unease. He was capable of anything. However, the current situation would have them on edge until the mission was complete. They all knew life was not dull under the baron. Many had been with him the previous winter when he led a devastating attack on a Red Army division headquarters. It had been particularly dangerous. However, Foelkersam had infiltrated the Russian lines with his usual finesse and gathered some important documents as well.

He spoke to his second in command. "Koudele, I want you to go south of the town with half the men while I drive north. That way, we surround them before they can react."

The "Wild Bunch" climbed into their trucks to carry out the encirclement. As they closed in on the town and Russian troops, it became evident that the Russians had no idea anyone else was around until it was too late. The Russians watched with trepidation as the men in NKVD uniform jumped down and proceeded to surround them. The Russians had decided to surrender to the Germans until Foelkersam arrived. As a group, they had seen the Red Army suffer one monumental loss after another. They were sick of the defeats and retreats, the wasteful attacks, and the needless dying. Now as they watched in fear, they realized that their turn might have come to pay the butcher's bill as the secret police insignia was recognized.

When Foelkersam approached, he had a hard time believing his eyes. Georgians, Chechens, Tartars, Ukrainians, and various other ethnic groups were present. Some of the troops even had camels for transport. Had he not known better, Foelkersam would have sworn he was back in time with Lawrence of Arabia. As he observed the cowering Russians, he noticed some gripping their weapons. The NKVD uniforms were producing the fear he desired, and anxiety started to spread through the ranks. Foelkersam noticed some Cossacks fingering their weapons. They were getting ready for a fight. He decided they would be removed from the group. The rest were beaten men, and fighting was not desired.

Foelkersam approached a sergeant and started questioning him. "Who are you and what is your name?" He spoke with a ring of authority that made the other Russians quiver.

The sergeant tried to remain calm. He obviously expected a bullet no matter what he said. "Sergeant Marensky. We are trying to retreat and avoid the Germans."

"Who gave you permission to retreat? Do you know the penalty for retreating without orders? Do you realize your predicament? You should all be shot cowardice, especially your officers."

"There aren't any. They all left and took care of themselves," a voice cried out.

Foelkersam was elated. Except for the Cossacks, these men would be easy to handle. He shouted to the Russians. "Gather round the truck." As he proceeded to climb onto the truck, he whispered to Koudele, "Surround the Cossacks and prepare to isolate them." He got on the roof of the truck and began a stirring oration that surprised even the men of the "Wild Bunch."

"Soldiers of the Red Army. Mother Russia is in a dire position. She is fighting for her survival and existence against the Fascist invader. The enemy is approaching and making great gains. The enemy has been very successful because of the stupidity of our own generals. But Mother Russia needs you, and Comrade Stalin needs you. Most of you deserve to be executed for your traitorous defeatism that you have shown. However, Comrade Stalin has great faith in you, and Mother Russia has faith in you. Right now, the enemy needs our oil fields and our crops. Will you not in the time of our country's greatest need unite and deny the enemy the victory he desperately needs? Unite and fight, and our homeland will yet remain ours."

The Cossacks were unconvinced just as Foelkersam had hoped. He wanted to exercise a carrot-and-stick policy for the edification of the assembled troops. A Cossack shouted, "What has Moscow ever done for us except rob us? If we fight, it will be for us, not for Mother Russia." Others started to shout agreement, and tension started to build. Foelkersam gave a nod to Koudele.

Koudele nodded in return. Suddenly, the Cossacks found themselves surrounded and staring into the muzzles of leveled submachine guns. They realized the futility of their position since none of the other Russian troops dared to support them.

"I hope that you all realize the seriousness of this situation," Foelkersam firmly remarked. "Take them into the woods," he ordered Koudele. The Cossacks were then led into the woods as a whole group. Koudele had them surrounded on all sides. Foelkersam accompanied the procession. Only a few of the "Wild Bunch" stayed with the remaining Russians. When they were out of sight, Foelkersam had his men fire several bursts into the air over the frightened Cossacks' heads. When the firing stopped, he approached the trembling Cossacks. "The German Army is three days away. Your comrades think that you're dead. Do you get the message?"

Understanding showed on the Cossacks' faces. They silently gathered their belongings and headed toward the German lines. The "Wild Bunch" watched them leave until they were out of sight to make sure that none returned to warn the other Russians. Foelkersam and his men returned to the main contingent of Russians. He found that his words and actions had produced the desired effect. Russian troops who had been willing to surrender and desert to the Germans only minutes before had discovered a new found loyalty to Mother Russia. They came forward gushing with enthusiasm about continuing the fight against Fascism. Foelkersam smiled inside as he realized that no one would suspect a unit wearing the feared NKVD uniform of being disguised Germans, especially when they were herding would be deserters back to the Russian lines.

Several of the Germans were equally confused since they did not understand the baron's thoughts. While Foelkersam was known to be innovative in the least, no one knew how he might seize an opportunity. Even Franz Koudele was unsettled as he was not sure what Foelkersam had in mind. He figured the Russians would be used as cover. Personally, Koudele would have headed straight for Maykop, as time was limited. However, Foelkersam had not enlightened him, but he was still in charge and that was that.

As Koudele was mulling over the events, one of his sergeants approached. He appeared completely bewildered by what Foelkersam had done. Max Schreiber was capable but young and still learning as was everyone else. Still Koudele suppressed a laugh as Schreiber approached. After all, Schreiber was a good man to have around. He had saved Koudele's life the previous year in the attack on the Soviet divisional headquarters. At home in German uniform, Schreiber sported an iron cross first class that he earned during the campaign in the Low Countries. Later, he added a close combat clasp and the army parachutist badge. He also had received one of the first German Crosses awarded to NCOs. Many in the unit felt he deserved a Knights Cross for knocking out five 34s and killing over thirty Russians singlehandedly while leading an assault on a vital bridge after his commanding officer was killed. However, a directive from the German High Command dictated that current recommendations for the Knights Cross were to be downgraded to the newly instituted German Cross in gold. Therefore, Schreiber ended up wearing Hitler's fried egg on his tunic instead of the Knights Cross that he had been cheated of.

"I hope he knows what he's doing," Schreiber muttered.

"Relax. I think he knows what he is doing. After all, the Russians don't have a lot of fight left in them. It will be all right."

"I hope you're right on both accounts. It makes me nervous." Schreiber left and went back to covering the Russians with his submachine gun.

Koudele watched Schreiber move back into position. Foelkersam approached, and Koudele stiffened. "I hope you know what you're doing. I assume you're using these men as some sort of cover."

"You've assumed correctly. Don't worry. They're beaten. Kaput! They still have no will to fight. Right now, they're enthusiastic because they don't want us to shoot them. In the meantime, we'll use them as our ticket into Maykop. No one is going to suspect us of being the enemy when we are wearing these uniforms and escorting this group of soldiers back to the lines."

Koudele noticed Foelkersam showed no expression other than of being in command. However, he knew the man was probably thoroughly pleased with himself. After all, he felt that the baron deserved the Knights Cross for the headquarters raid last year. The intelligence gathered had been instrumental in shattering a Russian offensive in the sector. It had been one of the few bright spots in the winter of 1941-1942 when the German Army was retreating all along the Eastern Front. Despite his stunning coup, Foelkersam's accomplishments were virtually ignored. The same thing had happened in Holland in 1940. Several officers and men were denied awards because of the high command's reservations about soldiers wearing the uniforms of the enemy to fight in. There were no reservations among the Brandenburgers, Koudele thought to himself. After all, it was the sixty Brandenburgers taking all the risks, not the smug generals in Berlin with their cognac to drink and carpet to walk on.

Later, as they prepared to move the Cossacks out, Schreiber approached Koudele again. "What's the plan?"

Koudele explained the brazen plan to Schreiber. If anything went wrong, he wanted everyone ready. Koudele knew Schreiber would get the word back to the other men discreetly.

Schreiber shook his head after he heard the plan. "The baron has really gone mad this time. If he gets us out of this one, he deserves a Knights Cross of gold."

Koudele laughed at that. As Schreiber left, life stirred in the encampment. In the middle of it was Foelkersam. The Russians were preparing for their trek to Maykop. They loaded up their lorries or saddled up their camels and horses. Foelkersam returned to his truck after the loading was started. He noticed Koudele and motioned for him to join him.

After they crawled into the cab, Foelkersam gave his instructions. "I want one truck in front and one in the rear of the convoy. The others are to be interspersed in between. That way we can herd them like sheep if we need to. Remember, they have to think we are NKVD. Even though we haven't shot any yet, they need to be reminded of the threat."

Following the discussion, Foelkersam climbed on the truck and motioned for the convoy to start moving. Minutes later, a cloud of dust marked the convoy's passage as it crawled across the land. Foelkersam remained in the lead truck. He had placed some of the Russians in the trucks with his men to allay their fears. Hopefully, some useful information would be gleaned from the soldiers as they talked to the phony NKVD.

The morning of August 2, 1942, was a typical Russian morning as the sun cast its amber rays across the clear sky. Foelkersam knew he was close to Maykop. He wanted to get into the town as soon as possible and thereby he could reconnoiter the area so he would be ready to strike when the German Army began its offensive in a few days.

Finally, the town came into view. As the convoy approached the town, Foelkersam noticed the oil derricks that were his objective. He did not have long to formulate his plans, but he would have to plan carefully or the oil platforms would be blown up. He was too well aware that the German Army could not afford to be deprived of the essential oil. As these thoughts ran through his mind, he turned his binoculars to the main road leading into town. He spotted the main bridge they would have to cross to enter the town. It was crowded with soldiers and civilians seeking refuge in the city. Foelkersam motioned for the convoy to keep moving. The column inched its way through the mass of humanity. Most of the Russians stepped aside when they recognized the NKVD insignia. As they reached the bridge, Foelkersam spotted real NKVD. The Russian security troops were directing traffic at the bridge. The baron gulped. Now was the moment of truth. He knew if there was going to be trouble, it would be now. Foelkersam gathered his wits and approached an officer in charge.

A harried lieutenant colonel was in charge. There was plenty of confusion between the civilian and military vehicles. The situation was compounded by the presence of both motorized and horse-drawn vehicles. The officer appeared to be having a difficult maintaining control as each vehicle or cart headed toward separate destinations.

Foelkersam approached. "Good morning, Comrade Colonel. I am Major Truchin from Stalingrad. On the way here, I rounded up several stragglers and deserters that I was tempted to shoot on the spot."

Before he could say another thing, the NKVD officer replied, "So you finally arrived. Well, I don't need you now. Please clear the way, Major. You can report to headquarters."

Baffled by the colonel's response, Foelkersam did not hesitate to make an unopposed entry into Maykop. Foelkersam was delighted by his good fortune and resolved to make the most of the opportunity. After stopping some junior NKVD men and asking directions, Foelkersam led his men to the Red Army headquarters. He brought the convoy to halt and went inside to report.

An aide was at an outer desk. He came to attention and stammered, "Comrade Major, how may I help you?"

Foelkersam replied in a matter-of-fact tone, "I am Major Truchin from Stalingrad. I have brought in several hundred deserters and others whose loyalty was wavering. I am here to report."

"Just a moment, Comrade Major." The nervous aide disappeared into an office. He was obviously leery of offending the security apparatus of the state.

Foelkersam was cooling his heels when a voice boomed out. "Major Truchin, please come in." The voice resonated with authority.

Foelkersam clicked his heels and strode confidently into the office. Behind a desk was an older man wearing the collar tabs of a lieutenant general in the Red Army. The face was round, jovial, and even flushed. *The man likes his vodka*, Foelkersam thought.

The aide spoke. "Major Truchin, this is General Persholl. Major Truchin has arrived to assist us and brought in a large number of ah wavering troops." The aide winced as he said the final words. "Several actually are deserters."

General Persholl walked around his desk and held out his hand. "Well done, Major Truchin. I'm not so sure I would have been so merciful. However, your example of the Cossacks should give the others some backbone."

"You already know about the Cossacks?" Foelkersam actually was surprised.

"Of course," Persholl replied. "I am supposed to know everything that goes on. Some of my local security people informed me shortly after you entered the town. I suspect you were sorely tempted to shoot the scoundrels. We still may need to shoot some of the moujiks for good measure." Persholl then shook Foelkersam's hand and slapped him on the back. "Thank goodness you didn't shoot all of them. I need every man I can get to defend Maykop against the Fascists beasts. Still, it may not be enough." Persholl coughed. He had not meant to make that last remark in front of a member of the NKVD. Any remark viewed as defeatist could have serious consequences.

"What I mean is that I am concerned about our situation given the rapid German advance."

Foelkersam caught the general's attempts to qualify his remarks. He also noticed Persholl's glances at his Zeiss binoculars. Persholl probably suspected that the field glasses had come from a German officer executed by the NKVD. He saw no reason to disappoint the man. "I agree with your concerns. However, Moscow has every confidence in your ability to handle the situation and inflict grievous losses on the Fascist invader. Perhaps he can create a surplus of materials for our men, like these binoculars that came off a late German officer who had no further need for them."

Persholl felt a chill run down his spine. Major Truchin was a man of obvious talent. He was also very dangerous. However, he offered no threat to Persholl, and his compliment of the general eased Persholl's mind. "I wonder if Moscow really knows what a talented individual you are, Major Truchin. I will be talking to them later today. I will make sure your superiors are informed. A villa will be found for you and your men to stay in. In the meantime, I must excuse myself. By the way, Major Truchin, do you have time for dinner tonight?"

"I would be delighted to make time."

"Excellent. Eight o'clock then."

"I will be there."

As Foelkersam left the headquarters, a young NKVD lieutenant was waiting for him. "Major Truchin, if you will follow me, I will take you to your quarters." He gulped. "May I say how impressive it was the way you handled those deserters."

Foelkersam realized news of his feat had spread rapidly. He was gracious in his reply. "Remember, you are capable or you would not be an officer entrusted with the security of the state." When the young officer said nothing in return, Foelkersam knew he had inflated the lieutenant's ego. *Make them like us*, the baron thought. *The more we ingratiate ourselves, the greater the surprise when we strike.* These thoughts ran through his mind.

"Follow me, Comrade Major," the lieutenant finally replied.

The NKVD officer got into a staff car. The rest of the convoy lined up behind him. Foelkersam noticed that the stragglers he brought in were being taken away by the local security troops. He had only the "Wild Bunch" with him now. Foelkersam motioned for the lieutenant to drive on.

They arrived at the villa fifteen minutes later. It was a neat, tidy building with a courtyard. The "Wild Bunch" dismounted and began stretching. Everyone was tired from sleeping on the ground or in the trucks. However, Foelkersam wasted no time in organizing his men. The NKVD lieutenant was thanked and dismissed. Foelkersam then had his men search the villa to make sure it had not been bugged. Once the building was secured, guards were posted, while the remainder gathered in the courtyard.

"I do not have a lot to say," Foelkersam began. "We have been together a long time and through this before. We know what happens if we fail and are caught, not only for us but for the Fatherland as well. We have our work cut out for us on this one. There are a lot of oil rigs we have to keep Ivan from blowing up. We have four or five days before our army gets here. We will divide up into teams of four and five. No one goes out alone. Find out where headquarters, supplies, fuel dumps, and communications are. In the meantime, the Russians need to keep thinking that we are the real thing. Take advantage. Remember to speak contemptuously of Fascist pigs with conviction. Good luck to all of you."

He then dismissed all but a few of his men. Koudele and Schreiber were kept back along with a few other key people. Schreiber's instructions were clear. "Max, Koudele, and I are having dinner with General Persholl tonight. I want you to personally look at the northwest part of the town. That is where the main attack will come. Get an idea what preparations are being made to destroy the oilrigs.

"It will be done, Comrade Major."

Foelkersam smiled. Schreiber was a quick learner. He turned to Koudele and said, "Let's go have a walk ourselves."

That evening, Foelkersam arrived fifteen minutes early for dinner. It was never good form to keep a senior officer waiting, especially a general. Most of the other officers on Persholl's staff had already arrived, and a few were already in the early stages of inebriation. Foelkersam whispered to Koudele to mind his own drinking and keep his eyes open. Hopefully, the vodka would loosen some tongues tonight.

"Ah, Major Truchin, the man of the hour. Come have a libation with my staff and me." General Persholl was obviously in a good mood.

"I could use one," Foelkersam replied. A glass brimming with vodka was thrust into his hand.

Persholl accosted the baron and introduced him to his staff. Koudele followed close behind to pick up useful information. Meanwhile, Foelkersam smiled ingratiatingly at the jovial officers around him. As the liquor flowed and tongues became looser, Foelkersam carefully elicited details from the assembled staff and filed them away for later use. He realized he would not get another chance like tonight to subtly interrogate the Russian leadership at Maykop.

Persholl finished the introductions and then turned to his officers. The room became silent as he raised his glass. "And now, Comrades, a toast to the incomparable Major Truchin, if only we had more like him."

If you only knew, Foelkersam thought while glasses clanged in the air.

"A toast to our glorious leader, Marshal Stalin."

Again, the clang of glasses rang through the air.

"To the heroic defense of our beloved homeland, Mother Russia."

Again, the glasses clanged again. Several more toasts were exchanged for the next few minutes.

"Let us be seated," Persholl finally commanded. The officers began to be seated. Persholl turned to Foelkersam. "Be my guest of honor tonight."

"You flatter me too much."

"Not at all. If anything, we don't reward talent enough."

Foelkersam didn't reply. If anything, the Soviets had rewarded talent the wrong way. He thought about the bloody purges that had emasculated the leadership of the Red Army in 1937 and 1938. *No doubt it will make our job easier. I just hope General Persholl is not a mind reader.*

Copious amounts of alcohol continued to flow. The mood was surprisingly jovial and even upbeat. One would not guess that an invading army was nearly at the city's gates. The officers continued their boisterous talk while anticipating the evening's repast and the upcoming battle. During a break in conversation, Foelkersam asked about the city's defenses.

"I would be delighted to show you the defenses myself," Persholl replied. "In fact, I would like your input on some matters. I will be ready at 0730."

"I am at the general's disposal."

Persholl grinned and turned his attention to another officer. Presently, dinner was served. It may not have been a dress dinner back in Berlin or even Moscow, but it was impressive for wartime. This was particularly true for a side that had been losing most of the time. Caviar was served even with fresh lamb. Even vegetables were available. *Nothing is too good for any general in any army*, Foelkersam thought.

As the meal progressed, the officers continued to loosen up. Foelkersam pricked his ears as the group discussed preparations in each sector. Foelkersam made a grim mental note that the engineers had nearly completed setting their demolition charges in the oil refineries. Others expressed their confidence in repelling the Germans at Maykop. Of course, they wouldn't say otherwise with the NKVD in their midst. None of them were that drunk. No doubt some of the talk was met to impress "Major Truchin" since he was obviously in such high favor. Several officers introduced themselves and offered to help him with the tour of the front in the morning.

Finally, the meal had been consumed. Persholl stood up and dismissed the assembled officers. "A long day awaits all of us tomorrow. I suggest we rest. We should not have any difficulty doing that. I will see most of you again in the morning with Major Truchin when we tour the front. Good night, comrades."

The officers rose and made their way outside. Foelkersam was glad he had refrained from more sips as several officers stumbled and had to be helped out the door. He noted that Koudele had partaken of perhaps more than he should have. Well, he would have a talk with his aide later. Grabbing Koudele by the arm, he led him outside. Once they were alone, Foelkersam chided him. "A little too much to drink?"

"Not as much as you think. Just part of the game," Koudele replied. Foelkersam noticed that his aide's gait had straightened also. Well, he had trained the man well. Hopefully, all of the others would be as good in the following days. They climbed into their truck and drove back to the villa. The guard posted at the front of the villa came to attention as Foelkersam and Koudele approached.

"Good evening, Major Truchin. My sergeant would like to speak with you when you have a moment."

That meant Schreiber wanted to see him. Well, there was no use in keeping the good sergeant waiting at this time of night. Anything he had to say would be succinct with no embellishment. He proceeded to the office Schreiber had made for himself. Schreiber stood at attention. Foelkersam motioned for him to be seated.

"Good evening, sir. I hope you had a pleasant evening."

"As well as could be expected with a bunch of Bolsheviks. What did you find out, Max?"

"Well, I had a look around. I rechecked the villa for any wiretaps. As clean as can be. Next, I went to the northwest as you instructed. I checked things out as well as I could in the dark. Looks like they have amassed a belt of strong defenses where we're likely to attack. There's a lot of artillery and tanks there. They had plenty of the T–34s and KVs. It will be a tough nut to crack."

"Maybe I can persuade General Persholl to crack part of it for us."

"Sir?"

"Just thinking, Max, just thinking. You can go now."

Foelkersam watched Schreiber leave and sat down. A unit

couldn't function without men like Schreiber. He didn't like the news Schreiber brought him, but that wasn't the sergeant's fault. Schreiber had done his job and confirmed much of what Foelkersam had picked up between glasses of vodka. *Well, time for sleep. The vodka needs to be out of the system in the morning so that I can think clearly*, he thought.

The morning came quickly enough. "Time to get up, Major Truchin. You have an inspection in one hour." Schreiber shook his commander awake.

Foelkersam sat at a table. The effects of the vodka still lingered as he still had a buzz in the head. Breakfast, consisting of eggs, milk, and coffee, cleared his mind. The coffee was particularly foul, and he tossed most of it into the courtyard.

"Time to go," Koudele stated.

The two officers climbed into one of the dusty trucks and made their way back to Persholl's headquarters. They arrived a few minutes early, but the building was already a hive of activity. There was a constant ringing of telephones. An army just could not function without the phones and the personnel to man them.

General Persholl stuck his head out during the commotion and greeted Foelkersam. "Major Truchin, please forgive the delay. I should be with you in a few more minutes. Then we can start the tour."

"I have nothing else planned for now, Comrade General. I will be here when you are finished."

Finally, Persholl appeared and broke free. "Let's be on our way." He seemed almost gleeful about escaping from the headquarters. He reminded Foelkersam of a small boy who is truant and knows he is not going to be punished. Persholl's ADC followed behind the general. The small group exited the building, and Persholl's staff car arrived. Persholl ignored protocol as he had Foelkersam sit next to him and his aide, a lieutenant colonel, sit in the front seat. Persholl seemed anxious to impress his visitor.

They toured the town first. Foelkersam noted the erected barricades. Most could be brushed aside by panzers with infantry support. They proceeded to the main defenses outside on the city's outskirts. Foelkersam suppressed a swallow. Schreiber had been right.

The Russians had put together a formidable defensive position to meet the German Army. T-34s and KV tanks were in abundance. In addition, several heavy artillery positions had been prepared. Unfortunately, these preparations lay in the path Foelkersam knew the Germans would attack through. If somehow these defenses could be dispersed, the inferior Mark IV tanks might stand a chance in the upcoming battle.

"Well, Major Truchin, what do you think? A rather potent force to meet the Fascist pigs with. I think we will cause there to be a lot of widows in Germany in a few days. Would you agree?"

Foelkersam remained the cool professional security officer with his reply. "It is a most impressive force, Comrade General. Our tanks are certainly much better. However, I am concerned about concentrating all of our defenses in one sector when the enemy still has many options in which to attack us. I am thinking specifically of what the Fascists did to us at Rostov and Taganrog. As you recall, they hit us on a broad front for which we were not prepared. You recall the consequences. They encircled us after piercing the weak points and rolled right over us."

Persholl mused over Foelkersam's comments. He also remembered what had happened to the commanders at both cities. They met the typical fate so many others had suffered for failure in Stalin's regime. Persholl had no desire to join them. Even though Stalin was responsible for many of the debacles that led to mind-boggling losses of men in several encircling actions, army commanders paid the price for his mistakes. Many times, the unfortunate general in question had been summoned back to Moscow and been shot the same day. The executions had resulted in a slight stiffening of the spine on the part of some commanders. Whether this would be enough was yet to be seen. Persholl also knew that he had a strong force at his disposal and could redeploy some of his forces to meet the German attack on a broader front.

Foelkersam bided his time but realized what Persholl must be thinking. He chose his next words carefully. "I do not mean to be presumptuous, Comrade General, but I am only too well aware of what has happened before when we allow ourselves to be surrounded."

"Not at all, Comrade Major. In fact, the same thought has been plaguing me. Now your opinion gives me added reason for carrying out the proposed changes. I will have forces redeployed immediately." Persholl seemed immensely relieved at having made this painful decision. No doubt he felt better that a respected member of the NKVD had made the recommendation. Thoughts of shifting the blame for any subsequent disaster lurked in his thoughts as well.

Persholl and Foelkersam continued on their tour while the general's ADC remained behind to ensure that redeployment was carried out. The tour ended on the outskirts of Maykop at the oil fields. Engineers were wiring the rigs with explosives. They were progressing rapidly, and the demolitions well placed, Foelkersam noted sourly. *The "Wild Bunch" would earn their pay this time if they pulled it off*, he thought.

"Moscow will be pleased with your preparations, Comrade General. I have never seen more thorough preparations made for denying our resources to the enemy."

"I would like to think that I am doing my duty for Mother Russia." Persholl was beaming in response to Foelkersam's compliment. "By the way, dinner again tonight?"

"I would be honored, Comrade General." Foelkersam suspected the tour was nearing an end.

Half an hour later, it was. Foelkersam learned the Russians at Maykop knew their business as far as preparations were concerned. The question was would they fight? Also, could they be tricked into not blowing the oil fields up? Persholl seemed to be sure of himself. Hopefully for the Germans, this would turn out to be misplaced confidence.

They returned to Maykop on the bridge that Foelkersam had entered on. As they returned to Persholl's headquarters, the general remarked, "I do hope that our preparations meet the approval of State Security."

"As I said, the results are impressive. I see that you are a man who knows his job. I am sure Moscow will be impressed with the results. I will mention how cooperative you have been. I am sure there will be no doubt about your loyalty."

"Thank you for your kind remarks, Comrade Major. We will meet again at dinner." Persholl then entered the headquarters, while Foelkersam returned to the villa.

"Thank God, that's over," Foelkersam remarked as he entered the villa. He was slightly rattled by the preparations he had seen. "They do seem to know what they're doing here."

Schreiber approached. "Is it as bad as I said?"

"Unfortunately, yes. It's going to be tough this time. I will have to think of a way."

"You usually do," Koudele replied. "It may be as tough as the attack on the headquarters last year."

"Perhaps so. However, we still have the element of surprise on our side. We'll have to make the most of it. I will work on a plan of action tonight."

That evening, Foelkersam met with his men and went over a layout of the city and its defenses. While formidable, the preparations had some weaknesses. He felt these could be exploited when the "Wild Bunch" went into action. He then went to dinner at Persholl's headquarters. The Germans had moved closer he learned, but there was no other useful information to be learned. The next few days would need to be used to pinpoint supply facilities, communication buildings, and other key locations. The routines of the troops assigned to these areas would be observed. Foelkersam continued to dine with General Persholl and refine his plan.

On August 8, Foelkersam was sleeping late when Schreiber shook him awake. He looked up groggily. "What is it, Max?"

"Thunder. Artillery anyway. It just started a few minutes ago."

Foelkersam stepped outside. He scanned the horizon. The roar of the guns was distant. The German Army would not arrive today. However, tonight and tomorrow would be decisive. He grabbed Koudele. "Get the driver. Let's go see Persholl and see what's going on. Tonight is probably the night."

Foelkersam sped to Persholl's headquarters. The scene was one of confusion. The staff scurried around amid a flurry of paperwork and ringing phones. Persholl tried to project an air of calm; however, the glistening sweat betrayed the turmoil he must be feeling. His face brightened when he saw Foelkersam.

"Good morning, Major Truchin. Things are not so peaceful now. The Nazi swine have finally made their move." He paused. "However, they do not seem to be attacking on a broad front as they have in the past." Persholl was clearly nervous now.

Foelkersam remained calm. "Let's make sure they die like swine. Where is the enemy now?"

Persholl's ADC laid a map on a table. "We made contact with the enemy here. Fighting broke out last night." He pointed to an area northwest of Maykop. So far, the enemy has not spread out. The panzers have been identified as part of General Herr's thirteenth panzer division. The SS Wiking division is thought to be on the right flank of Herr's division. However, we have not encountered any units from this division."

Foelkersam was relieved by what he saw. The Germans were following the original plan. Now he had to keep fooling the Russians. "It appears a little early for the Fascists beasts to begin an encircling movement. I would not expect them to launch an attack the same way every time. But their strategy of encircling an objective has remained fairly constant. We have yet to see the Nazi pigs attempt a coup de main recently."

It was as if divine revelation had occurred to Persholl. His relief was apparent to everyone in the room. "Once again, Major Truchin, you have eased my mind and reassured me that my plans are in order. Thank you for your timely advice."

"My pleasure, Comrade General. However, the work has been all yours. I'm sure that you will get the credit you deserve when this is all over. After all, the preparations are the best I have seen since the Fascist enemy invaded our beloved homeland. I'm sure the enemy will pay dearly for his temerity in thinking that he will have an easy victory here."

"I agree, Comrade Major. We are all ready to give our blood for Mother Russia. Your arrival here has been most fortuitous. Please stay in touch, Major Truchin. I may have further need of your advice. Now I need to get back to directing the battle."

With his dismissal, Foelkersam went back to the villa. He gathered the "Wild Bunch" in the courtyard. This was the final briefing. In the distance, they occasionally made out the faint roar of panzers. The booming from the artillery duels reverberated through the air and shook the windows. His words were to the point. He went over each team's assigned mission. His final words were concise as well. "This morning, the thirteenth panzer division was within twelve kilometers of the outskirts of town. We have to move quickly. We will now divide up into our teams. I will deal with General Persholl and the headquarters. Our next stop will be the communications center north of town. Koudele, you will take the telegraph office and send out false orders. The rest of you, get to the oil fields and stop their destruction. Any questions?"

"What about the bridge? Do we help Lieutenant Prohaska?"

Foelkersam shook his head. Prohaska would lead a disguised group to seize the bridge on the other side of the city. The baron wanted to help, but he was stretched thin as it was. "I am afraid he is on his own. We don't have the men. The bridge is not part of our operation. The oil fields take priority."

"When do we start?" Schreiber asked.

"About now," was the reply. "Let's go." There would be no turning back now. The baron looked at Schreiber again. "You seem ready to get into action. Sometimes I think you enjoy action more than leave."

"I'm just ready to break the tension."

Foelkersam nodded in agreement. He knew his men and trusted them implicitly. Still Schreiber seemed to stand out. "Let's go see General Persholl." He too was ready to end this. He felt it was amazing that their cover had not been blown as they began the night's activities.

Two truckloads of men went with Foelkersam to the headquarters.

As they tried to navigate their way, the trucks became ensnared in a morass of humanity, vehicles, and animals. Red Army troops and civilian refugees clogged the streets of the town. By constant honking and dire threats, Foelkersam's men moved forward. Finally, they arrived outside the headquarters. Foelkersam and his men got out of the trucks primed for action. The baron strode imperiously into the building. Only a few enlisted personnel were present. He stopped in front of a harried clerk speaking on a telephone. The man broke out in a sweat.

"Comrade Major."

Foelkersam cut him off. "I need to speak with General Persholl. It is most urgent."

The terrified clerk squirmed at his desk. He quietly said, "General Persholl is not here." He avoided looking into Foelkersam's eyes.

Foelkersam persisted. "I must see the general."

The soldier remained uneasy. Finally, he admitted the truth. With difficulty, he found his voice and told of General Persholl's departure for the rear without informing his subordinates. Persholl had left over three hours previously after deciding that Maykop could not be successfully defended. The clerk had been left to his own devices and told to manage as "best you can." The clerk was obviously unhappy about being left to his fate. In addition, the fact that he was on the staff of a deserting general was not in his favor. Meanwhile, the other Russians tried to remain inconspicuous.

Foelkersam hid his delight. Instead he commended the clerk. "You are to be proud of yourself for doing your duty. I see no value in your remaining here. Go attach yourself to a combat unit and help defend Maykop."

The clerk exhaled deeply. "Thank you, Major. I will go find a unit now."

"Go and fight well. I believe the soon-to-be-late General Persholl will have some answering to do," Foelkersam replied brutally. He turned to the other Russians. "I suggest you follow your comrade's lead and prove a better example than your commanding general has."

The Russians disappeared into the night. Foelkersam returned to the truck. This was better than he had hoped for. With its leadership gone, the Russian Army could easily fall prey to confusion. As they drove to the communication center, Foelkersam told the men what had happened.

Someone asked, "What do you think they will do to Persholl?"

"I don't even want to think about it. Better him than us."

The rest of the trip was made in silence. Finally, they recognized the building in the darkness. If this structure was knocked out, the Russian defense would be thrown into confusion since this building controlled the terminals for all of the field telephones linked to the front. This was in turn linked to a now deserted headquarters. As they approached the building, they were stunned to find that the Russians had posted only one sentry outside the building. Foelkersam led his men behind a low wall that ran along the side of the building.

Foelkersam gave his order. "Ger ready to blow the place up. When I whistle, everyone pull the pin and throw their grenade in."

They crawled along the wall. At the whistle, the pins were pulled followed by the sound of breaking glass. A huge explosion followed as the grenades went off almost simultaneously. Foelkersam's men rushed back to their trucks. When they looked back at the communications building, it looked like it had been hit by a large-caliber shell. No more messages would be sent or received by this location.

Foelkersam's team rushed to the front. Flashes lit up the sky as the artillery duels continued in intensity. They located an artillery battery. Foelkersam asked for the commander. A colonel in the Red Army appeared. Foelkersam feigned surprise. "You're still firing? General Persholl ordered a general withdrawal over four hours ago. I suggest you get moving before you get surrounded, but don't leave anything of value around to fall into enemy hands."

The colonel replied, "I had no idea this was going on. We'll withdraw immediately." He turned and starting giving orders to retreat.

Foelkersam returned to his truck and located another artillery position. He again asked for the commander. A lieutenant colonel appeared this time. He proved to be a tougher customer. Foelkersam asked him why he was still in position.

The Russian replied coldly, "I have no orders to withdraw."

"I suggest that you call your commanding officer."

"Indeed, I will," the Russian remarked suspiciously. He had Foelkersam accompany him to the tent where the field telephone was set up. The colonel ordered a sergeant to ring the headquarters. Naturally, there was no response. After several tries, the sergeant replied that the line was dead.

"I suppose that you get moving unless you want to be left behind," Foelkersam triumphantly remarked.

"Yes, I suppose I should," the colonel replied. He had no choice but to take Foelkersam's word.

While Foelkersam was persuading different Red Army units to retreat, Koudele had taken over the local telegraph office. He marched in and told the Red Army major in charge that the town was being abandoned. When the major tried to reach the communications center and then headquarters unsuccessfully, he figured Koudele was telling the truth. In no mood to be left behind or to argue with the NKVD, the major and his staff could not leave fast enough. In minutes, Koudele was in charge of a telegraph system serving most of the Caucasus. Soon messages were flooding in. A simple effective response was sent out to ensure panic. "You can no longer be connected. Maykop is being evacuated."

Soon all semblance of discipline and order had broken down. In the ensuing chaos, the Soviet troops panicked. Fear spread among troops and civilians alike, as no one wanted to face the Germans alone.

The remaining Brandenburg teams made their way to the oil fields and ordered the derricks evacuated. Demolition was stopped, as no one wanted to waste time to set the fuses and risk being left behind. Most teams were successful. Only in the suburb of Maksde was the "Wild Bunch" unsuccessful. The engineer in charge tried to contact the headquarters. Since he received no answer, he then contacted the telegraph office. After Koudele's men informed him that an evacuation was in progress, he used his own initiative and ordered the destruction of the oilrigs to commence. Engineers in the surrounding fields heard the explosions and assumed the demolition order had been given. Soon the surrounding fields were ablaze as the charges wreaked their havoc.

After stirring up as much confusion as possible, Foelkersam and his men headed for the telegraph office. There was nothing else to do but make sure the phony messages continued to go out to keep the enemy confused. Gradually, the other teams made their way back after making sure that the explosive charges on the derricks had been disabled. Outside the telegraph office, the mix of humanity was more panicked than ever. It was obvious that the Russian Army would offer no serious resistance now.

Finally, the rays of dawn began to lighten up the sky. The rest of the night had been uneventful. A disheveled crowd passed by outside. By now, it had thinned out considerably. Foelkersam stepped outside with Koudele and Schreiber. "It's hard to believe, but I think it's almost over now." There was relief in the baron's voice.

"I still wish we could help Prohaska." Schreiber seemed ready to seek more action.

"Haven't you had enough, Max?" Foelkersam was weary. "Forget it. We have not prepared for his mission, and he has. It's dangerous out there now. In addition, we're in the wrong uniform. In fact, we need to contact our forces. Sometimes this part scares me more than masquerading as the enemy. Franz, you and Max come with me. We're going to make contact with the thirteenth panzer division."

"I hope they haven't traded places with the Wiking division," Schreiber remarked.

No explanation was needed. Although it was one of the finest divisions in the entire Wehrmacht, the Wiking division was not known for its gentleness in battle. No love was lost between the opposing forces on the Eastern Front, particularly when the Waffen-SS was involved. The Brandenburgers always ran the risk of being shot out of hand by their own side if the mood of prospective captors was one of no prisoners, and running into the SS made that risk more likely.

In minutes, the three men had driven through the city toward the front. Only scattered forces remained. They passed a dog looking for its master, then they were on the outskirts. The truck slowed down. Foelkersam wanted to see the men of the thirteenth panzer division before they saw him. They heard the rumble of the Mark IV tanks before the panzers were visible. Finally, the baron spotted four of the metal beasts lumbering across the Russian steppe. They had accompanying infantry and obviously were on the lookout for antitank guns.

"Time to collect out pay," Foelkersam remarked.

They got out of their truck and headed toward the tanks. They hoisted a large white sheet. The lieutenant in the lead tank spotted the flag five hundred meters away and ordered his tanks for action. He was taking no chances with the vehicles and men under his command.

The infantry leader was aware of the Brandenburgers' activities. He climbed up and spoke with the panzer officer. "This could be some of ours. Remember the briefing about the Brandenburgers?"

"And they could be the enemy. I am not taking any chances."

Soon the two groups were within one hundred meters of each other. The tension was almost unbearable for Foelkersam. He advanced cautiously toward his own side. The infantry lieutenant approached with a private at his side.

Foelkersam spoke first. "I am Lieutenant Foelkersam of the Brandenburg regiment. We have largely cleared Maykop for you."

"We heard about you," the infantry officer replied. He was a little wary but knew this could be cleared up quickly. "I need to get you to the rear as quick as possible."

"That's fine with me. I would like to get my men out of Maykop and back into real uniforms before they are treated like the enemy since they are wearing the same clothes as I am."

"Understood. But I need to get you to the rear just to make sure."

During their conversation, a kubelwagen drove up. He noticed a senior officer in the backseat wearing the Knights Cross. Then he recognized him. Colonel Pfuhlstein had arrived. He got out of the car, walked over to Foelkersam, and to the astonishment of the uniformed Germans shook Foelkersam's hand. "Well done, my dear baron. We have started taking possession of the oil fields you saved. Soon you'll be wearing one of these." He pointed to the Knights Cross at his throat. "By the way, we are a little out of uniform, aren't we?"

Foelkersam shrugged his shoulders haplessly. "Just part of the job."

"What is the situation in Maykop?" Pfuhlstein was serious now.

Foelkersam described the night's events. He finally concluded, "Very few Russians remain in town. Resistance should be minimal. We saw plenty of individual Russians but no organized units. Most of them couldn't wait to get out of town once the panic started."

"Good." Pfuhlstein was obviously pleased. "Let's get your men out." He turned to the infantry lieutenant. "I want you to go in and get the rest of my men. Koudele can take the relief force in. Adrian, I need you to come back to the rear with me. I have something else in mind."

Within minutes, the relief force was on the move. The infantry climbed on top of the tanks as the group prepared to dash for the telegraph office. The panzer officer gave a sharp order, and the lead tank came to life. He climbed down into the turret. He told his gunner, "Now I have seen everything. They're ours all right."

In half an hour, they had stormed through the streets of Maykop and secured the telegraph office. Only scattered light resistance had been encountered. And this was easily brushed aside. The tanks stopped outside the telegraph office. The tankers were as relieved as the "Wild Bunch" at the ease of the battle so far. The panzer officer told Koudele, "This is the easiest town I have entered, and that includes Poland and France."

The Brandenburgers gathered their equipment and prepared to move out. Koudele noticed that Schreiber seemed to be deep in thought. "What is it, Max?"

"That we should be helping Prohaska. After all, I scouted that bridge after we arrived here. I think I could be of help."

"You heard what the baron said." Koudele paused. "After all, think how hard it will be to find him. It's utter chaos on the Russian side." He stopped. Schreiber was not interested in what he was saying. "All right. I'm going to get my butt chewed, but go ahead and see what you can do."

Schreiber did not hesitate and was headed to the bridge on a bicycle within seconds. Soon he was entangled in the rear of the Russian retreat. He looked desperately for other vehicles, as he knew Prohaska would be leading a platoon of tanks to secure the other bridge. Finally, he found a column that had stopped in front of a traffic control post. The lead vehicle had broken down. Schreiber pulled up beside it. Prohaska fumed as his driver tried to start the engine. Schreiber tossed a rock at Prohaska's head. The young officer looked up and opened his mouth and then closed it. He got out of the truck to talk with Schreiber.

"What are you doing here? I thought the Wild Bunch was finished."

"We are. However, I reconnoitered this bridge when we got here. I know it pretty well."

Prohaska looked around. "Get in the back. If we don't get this damned thing moving, we can forget about the bridge."

Schreiber got in back, and finally the engine started. The progress was slow in the crowded roads. However, the stirred-up-dust help obscure the iron crosses on the Mark IVs. Minutes later, the group had to stop at another crossroads. Here they had a close call.

The driver of the truck was a Russian renegade who had gone over to the Germans six months before. A Russian general was watching the withdrawal of his forces. When the truck stopped, he walked over to the truck and asked, "Who are you?" And then he recognized his runner who had disappeared in heavy combat. "It's you!" he exclaimed. "What happened? I thought you were dead. Tell me what happened."

The encounter reminded everyone who could hear the perils of being in the Brandenburgers and using renegade troops. Fortunately, the driver had been canny enough to have a cover story. "Comrade

General, as you know, the fighting was very heavy. I avoided capture by hiding in the swamps. Later, I made contact with the partisans."

It was time to get the column rolling again. The general cut him off. "Later, Comrade. You must move on if you want to avoid capture, but find me later and tell me the details. I could use a good runner. So come and get your job back."

"Thank you, Comrade General."

With a wave of his arm, the general motioned for the group to move on. He had no idea what he had let slip behind his lines. The convoy arrived at the bridge. If this bridge was destroyed, the engineers would not easily replace it. At the other end of the bridge, Schreiber spotted the guards. They were leaning against a fuel truck. They held their fire as they crossed the bridge. The Russians were completely surprised as Prohaska's men threw off their Soviet blouses and gunned the enemy troops down. Schreiber leaped out and began ripping the wires to the explosives. Two groups went to each end of the bridge as they waited for the tanks to catch up.

The firing baffled the crowd as the panzers crawled toward the bridge. Dust still obscured their features. They arrived soon after the bridge had been taken. The commander of the tanks held his fire as he did not want to give himself away until he wanted to. As they approached the west end of the bridge, they tried to move an abandoned limousine. The lead tank then stalled. Firing broke out on both ends of the bridge. Prohaska went back to see what the problem was. Schreiber followed right behind. They weaved their way between the now empty vehicles on the bridge. Finally, they reached the stalled tanks. Prohaska climbed up on the lead tank when he was suddenly thrown back. A crimson spray covered Schreiber. One look at the bullet wound in Prohaska's forehead told Schreiber that the man was dead.

Schreiber climbed up next. He found out what the problem was and organized the removal of the cars. Both ends of the bridge needed to be secured by the tanks soon. It took almost an hour to clear the bridge because of the fire. Finally, the bridge was clear, and the panzers clanked to the east end in time to beat back a counter attack. Despite the heavy fire, Schreiber remained unscathed. After both ends were secured, the Brandenburgers hunkered down until the main body of the thirteenth panzer division relieved them.

Schreiber thought about Maykop many times in the future. He had already been on several difficult missions and was highly decorated. When he thought about Maykop and the baron, he considered this the greatest commando mission ever until he was placed in charge of Operation Gotterdammerung.

CHAPTER 2

January 10, 1945

The air outside the SS Jagverbande headquarters was bone piercing cold, and snow covered the ground. The few guards outside were primarily concerned with staying warm. Inside the converted hunting lodge, SS Colonel Otto Skorzeny was conferring with his chief of staff, SS Major Adrian von Foelkersam. The building retained some of its grandeur from its days as part of the Kaiser's private domain. At least it kept one warm and was hidden from the rest of the world. The conversation drifted into reminiscing about the last year and a half. Skorzeny had gone from an obscure SS captain to colonel and been labeled as the most dangerous man in Europe by British Intelligence.

The period from June 1943 onward had been a whirlwind of plotting and covert operations. Many had been remarkably successful. His dubious label from the British had been earned the previous autumn with the kidnapping of the Hungarian regent, Admiral Horthy. Then Skorzeny had unwittingly terrorized the Allies during Operation Grief during the Battle of the Bulge. Skorzeny was still unaware of the full extent of the chaos his men had caused in the rear areas of the Americans. Four of his men captured by the U.S. Army had spread the fantastic tale that their mission was to kill

Eisenhower. Although unaware of his captured men's statements, he was still painfully aware of the healing shrapnel wound over his right eye, which he received during the battle. He rubbed it on occasion from discomfort. Skorzeny remembered that Hitler had wanted his personal physician, Dr. Theodur Morrell, to tend to his injury when Hitler saw his favorite commando's wound. Fortunately, some of the Fuehrer's entourage recognized Dr. Morrell for the quack he was and arranged for the competent Dr. Brandt to treat Skorzeny's wound, thereby saving the eye.

Foelkersam had been the guiding light behind most of these exploits. His vast experience had kept Skorzeny from being a victim of his own success after his rescue of Mussolini. Although II Duce's rescue was a spectacular coup, Skorzeny realized he was still a newcomer in this type of warfare in which Foelkersam was already vastly experienced. Fortunately, Foelkersam had left the Brandenburg division for Skorzeny's new organization. He had brought along a small cadre of talented officers and NCOs. One of them was Max Schreiber.

Finally, the conversation turned to current events. The two officers studied a map of the Eastern Front. Both knew what was coming. With little time remaining until the war was over, the German high command had little use for special troops of any stripe. Foelkersam lived for action. Although he had been with Skorzeny since Mussolini's rescue, the current job was a dead end given the current war situation. Foelkersam wanted a front-line job.

"So my Austrian charm has not convinced you to stay," Skorzeny said.

"You know this is a dead-end job," Foelkersam replied.

"Task Force East may be a dead-end job too, literally."

Both men were silent momentarily as they recognized the truth behind Skorzeny's words. Task Force East was being sent to shore up the defenses at Hohensalza against the Soviet offensive that erupted after the Ardennes offensive had simmered down. Hohensalza was the junction of several routes between Poland and East Prussia. Its importance was not lost on the Russians. Foelkersam would literally be defending his homeland.

After a few moments of reflection, Skorzeny somewhat resignedly spoke. "Well, I guess you had better go your way."

They proceeded to the building's entrance. Two men were waiting. SS Captain Max Schreiber and an enlisted driver were quietly pacing. The four men proceeded outside.

"I wonder if they will ever make it," Foelkersam said to relieve the tension.

"Who?"

"Scherhorn and his men."

"I hope so." Skorzeny sighed heavily. Scherhorn and his men had weighed heavily on Skorzeny's mind for months. Cut off deep in Russia, this stubborn commander did not know how to surrender according to the radio messages. He had gathered the remnants of a dozen shattered units and formed an ad hoc unit of two thousand. A radio was assembled, and contact with Germany was established. Scherhorn constantly pleaded for supplies and aid to be delivered. The man seemed to be doing everything possible to extricate his lost legion. Skorzeny had wanted to lead a team in, but Himmler had forbidden any such action. Skorzeny had in turn refused to let Foelkersam lead a team in. Several teams had parachuted in and been lost without a trace. A few finally made contact and were nudging the desperate group toward a location north of Minsk to a group of frozen lakes. Hopefully, air evacuation could be arranged from there.

The two officers looked at the forest around Friedenthal. Each man was thinking the same thing. There had been a lack of support for the endeavor to save the gallant Scherhorn. This was one of many reasons that Foelkersam wanted command of Task Force East. There was no longer any support for special operations. In addition, the baron would be fighting for his homeland.

They were beside Foelkersam's car. Schreiber got into the backseat with Foelkersam. Skorzeny thought how he hated losing Schreiber as well. He had been Foelkersam's right-hand man for some time since their days together in the Brandenburg division. He had followed the baron into Skorzeny's new unit. He proved himself a formidable fighting man, earning a battlefield commission and the coveted Knights Cross in the process. *I'm losing too many good men*, Skorzeny thought.

The two men shook hands. A handshake had been the traditional greeting between officers and their men in the Brandenburg Division. Skorzeny felt too close to the baron to make due with a mere salute. A strong bond had developed over the last few months between the two men. Skorzeny regarded the young baron as his best friend. Foelkersam had brought the Jagverbande to its current level of excellence. Now he was leaving, and Skorzeny had an awful premonition that this would be the last time they would see each other."

"Good luck, Adrian."

"Thanks, Otto. You take care of yourself."

The driver started the engine, and with a cough, the Kubelwagen came alive. A deep sadness came over Skorzeny as he watched as the vehicle left with two of the best officers he had ever served with. They had done so much in so little time. And still it had come to this. Germany was still fighting for her life. On top of that, it did not seem like any of them would make any difference. Still Skorzeny regretted losing two of his best men.

Foelkersam achieved his goal of being where the action was as Task Force East was soon involved in furious combat. Hohensalza had been named a fortress, which meant it was to hold out to the last man. Foelkersam had arrived with eight hundred men on January 18. The Russians made their presence felt immediately. Waves of Soviet infantry attacked the German positions with determination. Initially, they were driven back with ghastly losses. However, each attack left Foelkersam with losses that he could not replace. Soon the superiority in Soviet numbers began to be felt as Foelkersam's men were forced to make sacrificial stands. Often the tired and weary soldiers of Task Force East fought to the last man in bitter hand-to-hand combat.

On January 21st, the writing was on the wall. Foelkersam went to the communications bunker early that morning with Captain

Schreiber. Both men were bundled against the bitter cold. Inside the bunker, Schreiber loosened a scarf around his neck, partially exposing his Knights Cross. It had been earned along with his commission for action against the Yugoslavian partisans. He had followed Foelkersam to the Jagverbande shortly after Skorzeny's rescue of Mussolini. Schreiber continued to prove himself and rose steadily in rank. Now he was stuck in what was proving to be a deathtrap.

"Send the following message," Foelkersam ordered. "Position untenable." Foelkersam calmly spoke to the radio operator. It was apparent that his remaining men were about to be engulfed by a tidal wave of Russians. Even Foelkersam's thirst for action did not override his concern for his men. He somehow hoped that he could get the survivors out of their current predicament.

Back in Friedenthal, Skorzeny read the message with dismay. Although he was not surprised, he was still troubled by the message's contents. *At least Foelkersam is still alive,* he thought. The men still have a chance. Fighter that he was, Skorzeny knew there was a time to stop and override the powers that be.

"Send the following message to Task Force East. Break out tonight." Skorzeny was tired of senseless orders and was not about to suffer through another one. After all, Foelkersam had done all that could be asked of him, and nighttime offered a better chance of success for the proposed exodus.

A look of concern spread across the radio operator's face as he hesitated to send the message. "Obersturmbannfuehrer, Hohensalza has been declared a fortress. The Reichsfuehrer may disapprove of this action."

"I appreciate your concern," Skorzeny replied tartly. "Just let me deal with Himmler. You send that message now."

Back in Hohensalza, the officers looked at the message with both surprise and relief. At least someone in the rear had some sense. Foelkersam breathed a sigh of relief knowing that his men were not being asked to fight a futile last stand. A plan began formulating in his head.

Finally, he spoke, "Max, we break out after dark. Pass the word.

We break out on the west of town. Everyone, keep quiet and rest until then."

The two men split up as Schreiber gathered his lieutenants and NCOS and explained the plan. He went to the various outposts to check on the troops and encouraged them to conserve their ammunition for the breakout. He then dodged through sporadic shelling back to the ruins that served as a command post. He then received one of the greatest jolts of his life. Foelkersam's luck had run out. During his visit to the front, the baron had been struck in the head by shrapnel. He was partially conscious and in considerable pain. A medic was bandaging the gaping wound. The upper part of Foelkersam's jacket was dyed a dark maroon. Foelkersam looked up at Schreiber. He was in no condition to lead.

"Max, you are in command. It's the only command I'm capable of giving now. You may not be a Junker, but you're a better officer than most of them. Now get the men out of here. You can do it." Foelkersam slowly slipped into unconsciousness.

"I will," Schreiber choked out his reply. He could not believe it. Foelkersam had cheated death so many times he seemed indestructible. Now the baron was seriously wounded. Schreiber stood and gained control of himself. There was fighting to direct and a breakout tonight. To mask his feelings, he asked the medic quietly, "How is he?"

"He's out of it now, Haupsturmfuehrer. His pulse is fast but strong. His skin is cool. Early shock if you ask me."

"Take him to the assembly point. We're taking him one way or the other. There is a stone house with a cellar nearby. Take him there. He should be safe until tonight."

Schreiber went to the front to reassure the troops. A friendly pat on the back or letting a tired machine gunner smoke a cigarette while Schreiber took over for a few minutes worked wonders among the exhausted troops. No one panicked despite news of Foelkersam's injuries. Finally, dusk arrived, and the front began to shrink as the survivors of Task Force East made their way to the breakout point. They darted through the rubble-strewn streets and made their way through the ghostly hulls of shelled buildings. The last troops to withdraw maintained a steady stream of fire before withdrawing to mask German intentions for the night. Success was verified by no increase in Russian activity.

Dusk mercifully turned into complete darkness, and most firing fizzled out. Only an occasional rifle shot disturbed the eerie silence. What was once a full-strength battalion was now barely half a company. The pitiful group crouched behind a stone wall that afforded cover from the prying eyes of Soviet observers. They were surrounded and knew that escape was a long shot. Unfortunately, it was their only option.

Schreiber crawled along the wall. His words needed no explanation. "Once we start, keep moving. You won't be safe until you reach our lines. Don't fire unless you have to. Use knives to silence any sentries. Let's go."

Silently, the forward patrol moved out, then the rest of the once-proud battalion began its stealthy departure from the doomed city. Sporadic shelling continued from the Russian side. The explosions provided brief illumination as the survivors made for the woods. Foelkersam groaned as they proceeded. He had been placed on a tank recovery tractor with eight other wounded men for his comfort. A jabbering of Russian voices made the forward patrol halt for a few anxious moments. Finally, the Russians appeared to be moving on, and Schreiber's men resumed their walk to freedom. Schreiber silently prayed, "Dear God, let me survive this night."

January 30, 1945

One week after giving the order to Schreiber's group to breakout, Skorzeny received his own marching orders for the front. That morning, he received orders from the headquarters of the Reichsfuehrer SS to proceed to Schwedt on the Oder. Skorzeny decided to call Fuehrer headquarters. The news was not reassuring. During the night of January 28-29, Marshal Zhukov had sent his forces in the direction of the Oder. There was great fear in Berlin that Zhukov would cross the frozen Oder at Schwedt, which lay only sixty miles from Berlin. Worse was the fact that no one knew where the Russians were at now or what was going on in that vicinity. To compound the situation further, Himmler had been named commander of Army Group Vistula. Skorzeny had said nothing when this bit of disturbing news was passed on to him. The fact that Himmler, who had never fired a shot in anger or commanded a squad of soldiers in combat, would now command an army group was unfathomable to Skorzeny. He figured that many a German soldier from the lowest ranks on up would regret this decision. He also felt that there were dark forces and reasons behind Himmler's elevation to combat general.

The true reasons for Himmler's appointment would have filled Skorzeny with even greater dismay. No concern was given to the welfare of the troops when Himmler was given his exalted command. It was the result of a clever political trap laid in the Nazi hierarchy. Skorzeny had tried to avoid the high politics of the Nazi Party; but his boss, Himmler, was inextricably immersed in the intrigues between Hitler's satraps. At the top of the heap, Party Secretary Martin Bormann had become the second most powerful man next to Hitler by carefully worming himself into Hitler's confidence. His only other rival for power now was the Reichsfuehrer SS. All of Fuehrer's other minions had been reduced to impotence by Bormann's devious schemes over the years. However, Himmler's star had continued to rise during the war years and more so as the war situation had worsened. Part of his power rested in the hundreds of thousands of armed men under his control. The other power lay in his security organizations, the Gestapo and Sicherhietdienst (SD). While Himmler thought he had reached an accommodation with Bormann, like most of the other chastened party leadership, Bormann decided that the Reichsfuehrer's power should be broken and Himmler discredited in Hitler's eyes. There would be no need to relegate Himmler to some backwater post as Bormann had done to opponents who had not been brought to heel. Hitler would do that himself with Bormann's persuasion.

Bormann did not pick a head on fight. Instead, this sinister figure planned to let Himmler fall on his own sword. Bormann knew that Himmler had nursed ambitions of being a great soldier and earning fame as a battlefield commander. He deviously had already set Himmler up for failure. In November 1944, he had suggested Himmler for command of an army during the Ardennes. His performance had not been stellar, but his army had come close to taking Strasbourg and had given the Americans a considerable scare. Eisenhower had even considered abandoning the city, but he held at de Gaulle's insistence. While his offensive petered out, Himmler's performance was not entirely a failure.

Despite this mediocre showing, Hitler thought Himmler had some promise, and Bormann was not done with his Machiavellian schemes. When Hitler started casting about for a commander on the Vistula, Bormann knew just the man—Reichsfuehrer SS Heinrich Himmler. After all, Himmler had been named commander of the replacement army following the abortive July 20th bomb plot. Therefore, went Bormann's reasoning, who would be better able to command troops than the one who was responsible for recruiting and supplying replacements for the regular army? While the rest of the high command were aghast at this perverse reasoning, Hitler immediately seized upon the idea and confirmed Himmler's appointment. So for the second time in two months, Himmler had the opportunity to prove himself as generalissimo by fighting the decisive battles to come. However, the truth of the situation was becoming apparent to Himmler, and with considerable trepidation, he took command of the Army Group Vistula.

While Skorzeny knew he could have had a better commander than the one he had been saddled with, his dark feelings worsened as more orders flowed in. In addition to establishing a bridgehead at Schwedt, Skorzeny received an order to take the town of Freienwalde during his advance to Schwedt. Skorzeny took a look at the map and shook his head in disbelief—Himmler as military commander, what a cruel joke for the fighting men on the Eastern Front.

Skorzeny quit thinking about the command structure he had been subjected to and set about the work at hand. He called his ADC SS Major Karl Radl. "Karl, we have a new mission. No commando action this time. We're going to Schwedt. I want two patrols sent out in advance. I have no idea where the Russians are and neither does the high command. Tell them to be careful."

He then hung the phone up—so much to do and so little time. And he no longer had his best officer by his side. He could kick himself for letting Foelkersam go to Hohensalza, but that was over. He could only hope that the remnants found their way back to German lines.

The night of January 21-22 had gone better than Schreiber had hoped. They had managed to leave Hohensalza undetected and marched as far as they could during the night. At daybreak, they found a hiding place in the forest. The following day, they nervously watched as long columns of Soviet military vehicles drove by. Fortunately for them, the Red Army was more interested in its drive to Berlin than in an insignificant band of stragglers.

Schreiber stifled an urge to smoke a cigarette. The least misstep could bring unwanted attention to their position and doom them. It was obvious that they had to move at night as much as possible and hide during the day. At any time, they could blend in and escape detection. They had done it before.

He called the senior NCO over, Fritz Ziegler. "Fritz, we move out tonight. I want the Russian speakers up front. If there are any surprises, I want it to be Ivan who is surprised. Make sure our sentries stay alert during the day. Keep a sharp lookout for any of their security troops. If we see any of them in force, they could be looking for us, so stay sharp."

He gave Ziegler a clap on the back and sent him on his way. He pondered his group's dilemma. They had just escaped a situation where the enemy had forty heavy guns per kilometer. Now they were in the middle of a tidal wave of Russian armor and infantry.

As yet, the Russians apparently were unaware of their existence. Hopefully, it would stay that way.

Schreiber went over to check on Foelkersam. The baron was groggy from the morphine but alert enough to talk sensibly. "Where are we?" he asked Schreiber.

"Right in the middle of the Russian Army, except we are in German uniform this time."

Foelkersam smiled weakly. He recalled the days of covert missions behind Russian lines in Red Army uniform. They might have been better off now in Russian uniform given their current predicament. "It's a little late to change clothes now." Foelkersam seemed exhausted by the effort to speak.

"We don't have any of Ivan's rags to put on anyway." Schreiber paused. "Don't say anything. Just rest. We're going to move again tonight. That's our cover now.

Darkness came none too quickly that day for the tattered survivors of Task Force East. They came alive as dusk fell. They would try to get as far away from the main body of the Russian as they could. With luck, they might reach their own lines within a week.

"We'll follow the road. At least it leads to our lines. It's also our best hope for the wounded, especially the baron." Schreiber spoke plainly. "Keep alert. We want to spot Ivan before he spots us. Keep Russian speakers in the front."

The men moved out with the Russian speakers in front. Hopefully, they would supply some warning if a large contingent of Russians was met. Smaller groups would be ruthlessly dealt with. Contact with larger units would be problematic. Schreiber pondered these problems as the tractor carrying Foelkersam coughed to life and advanced.

The column proceeded west with the tractor in front. An occasional flash of artillery firing pierced the night. Intermixed with the sounds of battle was the whish of the dreaded Katusha rocket. Schreiber remembered the first time he had heard the rockets in Russia and the fear they instilled among the German soldiers. *At least we're not on the receiving end tonight*, Schreiber thought.

The small force made steady progress until midnight. Schreiber was forty feet behind the tractor when it inexplicably stopped. Schreiber proceeded cautiously forward to investigate. He discovered the answer before he had a chance to ask any questions. A junior officer of his was speaking loud enough for him to hear. The problem was he was speaking Russian. Schreiber stopped and listened to the conversation. As the conversation continued, Schreiber learned they had come upon the rear of a Soviet armored regiment. Another was supposed to be right behind them. They were traveling close together to squeeze any Germans between them. The Russians were looking for any survivors who had broken out. The unseen Russian had no idea that they had found the Germans or rather they had found him.

The German officer returned to find Schreiber. "Hauptsturmfuehrer, I need to report."

"No need to. I heard everything. It appears that we appear to be in a tight squeeze." Schreiber amazed himself on how calm he was.

"Hopefully, they'll take a fork somewhere down the road where we can separate from them." The junior officer tried to sound hopeful.

"Hopefully, but there's that other armored regiment of theirs that is moving behind us in case you've forgotten." Schreiber thought about hunting the Soviet commander of the column in front of him and providing some "useful advice." Then maybe he could deal with the unit coming up behind them. If he tried to withdraw, he might arouse the suspicions of the Russians ahead of him. He looked at the surrounding forest. The nearest trees were one hundred meters away. Schreiber made his decision.

"We stay here for now." He called Ziegler. "Get some machine guns in that tree line. Just in case Ivan finds out who we are, that will be our line of retreat." He pointed at the dark outline of the forest.

Schreiber walked back to the head of the column Next to the tractor was a two-man panzerschreck team. They carried an updated RPzB54/1 with blast shield. With a range of two hundred yards and the ability to punch holes through eight inches of armor, it was a formidable weapon in trained hands. Wooden boxes containing two rockets for the weapon were on top of the tractor for easy access.

Schreiber felt the men could be useful in the tree line if firing broke out. They were part of the army troops who had had been in Hohensalza prior to Task Force East's arrival. Schreiber barely knew the men. They were obviously good as evidenced by the tank destruction badges and iron crosses on their tunics. The two men, Klein and Gross, were known as the panzer crackers for the impressive number of kills they had amassed.

Schreiber approached the two men. His voice was authoritative. "I hope I don't need you two tonight. There is another Russian column coming up behind us, and we're going to be in a tight spot then. They may be looking for us from the sound of things. It may be up to you to buy us some time."

Neither panzer cracker spoke. Without a sound, Klein reached onto the tractor and pulled a box of rockets off. Gross did likewise. Each carried the boxes toward the forest and a depression to take cover in. After carrying of the all of the rockets to the site, Gross gingerly loaded a rocket into the panzerschreck.

Schreiber paced to the end of the column. He prayed for the Russian column in front of him to move. He paused there scanning the darkness. Other survivors milled around trying to stay warm. He saw nothing as he surveyed the frozen landscape. He was about to go the front of the column when he heard something. He pricked his ears. It was a low roar. Then it became more distinct. Finally, he could make out a black blur approaching his survivors. He finally made out the silhouette of a tank rumbling toward his men. He recognized it as a T-34. Just as he had feared, they were about to be caught between the armored fists of two Soviet tank units.

A soldier next to Schreiber asked, "Are they ours?"

"Hell no, they're not ours. You run to the front and warn the others." Schreiber gritted his teeth as the tension rose. He watched as the lead blob became more distinct. As it came closer, Schreiber recognized the snout on the turret. It was definitely a T-34 and not one of the Stalin tanks fortunately. Still it was small comfort. It was as an unpleasant sight now as in 1941 when Schreiber saw his first T-34. This metal monster had completely outclassed every German tank at the time. *Thank God the Russians didn't know how to use armor or most of us would not be here*, Schreiber thought. Even tonight its appearance was as unwelcome as it had at the beginning of the war in the east.

One of Schreiber's Russian speakers stood off to the side of the road. When the tank got close enough, the man yelled for it to halt. Schreiber approached the tank warily. He spotted the Russian tank commander standing impassively in the turret. A German soldier stopped in front of the tank with a panzerfaust slung over his shoulder. More of his men moved furtively alongside the tanks. They carried Teller mines to place on the tracks. There was a near certainty that there would be fireworks before the night was over.'

Schreiber was below the turret now and spoke to the tank commander. "Good evening, Comrade. It is a very cold night."

The T-34 commander replied caustically, "It's worse in these damned tanks. What unit are you with?"

Schreiber replied calmly. Thank goodness he had overheard the name of the Russian commander in front. "Colonel Yakov is in command of the regiment. We've come to a fork in the road, and he's trying to decide which way to go."

"Sookin sin!" The Russian commander spat out the explicative. "That fool will never make his mind up. We'll be here all night waiting." He then lit a cigarette. Meanwhile, his crew started arguing where they should be and then opened the forward hatch for fresh air. One of the crew turned on a flashlight and pointed it at Schreiber while trying to read a map. Schreiber was bathed in the light's beam long enough for the Russian commander to decide he didn't like what he saw. First he noticed Schreiber's MP43 submachine gun. Then he noticed the rank patches on the snow uniform. Finally, he caught sight of the SS runes on Schreiber's right collar. Finally, his brain connected to his tongue. He cried out, "Germanski! Germanski!"

Schreiber was ready for the moment. He swiftly swung his submachine gun up and nearly cut the Russian in half with a single burst. The commander fell across the turret. The soldier with the panzerfaust swung his weapon over and fired into the open hatch.

Schreiber dived for cover as soon as he saw what the man was doing. The tank exploded into a sheet of flames and glowing metal as its ammunition exploded. A rush of heat enveloped Schreiber and then passed. The soldier who fired the weapon was not so lucky. A piece of shrapnel had embedded itself in his thigh. Schreiber ran over to the fallen man. As he did so, other thunderous explosions rocked the night. Although he could not see it, Schreiber knew the men who had infiltrated the Russian lines had thrown grenades through open hatches now. Soon others would blow up as the T–34s moved and set the Teller mines off. As Schreiber knelt down by the soldier, he could see flames at the head of the column as well. A loud whoosh told him that the panzer crackers were already at work. *Make sure every shot counts, boys*, Schreiber thought. He then ran to the man on the ground.

'How bad are you?" Schreiber asked.

"I don't think it's an artery," the man groaned. "It burns like molten pitch from hell."

"We all may have that feeling if we don't get out of here. Hold still while I wrap it." Schreiber grabbed his own scarf and made a tourniquet to stop the flow of blood. The glow from the burning tank showed that he had been successful as the flow was reduced to oozing. As he looked up, he saw some of the men who had infiltrated the Russian column returning. "Help me with this man."

They stopped to assist. "We need to hurry, Hauptsturmfuehrer. Ivan has infantry, and he's sending it up. They'll be here soon"

"I'll give covering fire. Get this man into the woods now," Schreiber ordered firmly. "We'll give covering fire," he said to two others. After spotting a PPsh41 submachine gun that the Russian commander had dropped, Schreiber grabbed it and slung it over his shoulder. The way the night was going, he figured that he would probably need it.

The Russian infantry thought that there was only a small number of Germans to deal with in front of them. Anticipating a quick victory, they rushed past the stalled and disabled tanks. Instead of the quick mopping up, they found themselves facing a hail of submachine gun fire. Heavy casualties soon convinced them of their error in judgment. They paused briefly to regroup. Schreiber knew they would move up with tanks and infantry combined next time. Schreiber's men needed to move now, while the enemy was confused.

"Get back to the rest of the men," he shouted at the two men with him. "Tell everyone to make for the woods. It's our only hope." He continued to fire as his forces withdrew. Any lull might allow the Russians to surge forward and overwhelm his men. He could make out the movement of other T-34s through the flickering flames. The magazine in the MP43 emptied. As expected, the Russians detected a lull and rushed forward. He leveled the PPsh41 and gave the attacking infantry another stinging lesson in tactics as several white-clad figures tumbled over. Although crude and relatively inaccurate, the PPsh41 served its purpose at close range.

Schreiber gained enough time to rejoin the main body. The glow at the front of the column indicated that the panzer crackers had scored several hits on tanks. Fortunately for Schreiber, Ziegler had organized a fighting withdrawal as soon as fighting erupted. He had sent machine gunners to join the panzer crackers. Ziegler realized they would be in a desperate fight for their lives. As Schreiber approached, he knew that several had been wounded as several blood trails led to the woods. Other bodies were perfectly still.

Before Schreiber could ask Ziegler about the situation a soldier ran up to report that the Russians in front were trying to encircle them. It took no genius to realize the same thing would happen in the rear. Schreiber figured they had surprised the Russians, while the Russians were trying to surprise them. *We'll be surrounded by a wall of steel,* Schreiber realized, *if we don't break away now.*

"You know the routine, Ziegler. We start a fighting withdrawal now. Everyone takes turns providing fire.

"What about the baron?"

"What's going on there, Ziegler?"

"The tractor stalled. There's fighting all around it."

"Go to the woods. If I don't make it with any of the other officers, you're in charge."

"But, but…" Ziegler wanted to go with Schreiber to save Foelkersam, but he saw by the look on Schreiber's face that there would be no arguing.

Explosions racked the ground near the tree line. The T-34s had finally spotted the Germans in the woods and tried to catch them in crossfire. As Schreiber neared the front of the column, a few of his men still held their ground. A dark object rolled toward them. A bright orange tongue leaped out and engulfed his men in flames. They screamed in agony until the Russians gunned them down. Schreiber made out several figures darting around behind the Russian tank. He knew they were Russians, and he still was not near the tractor. A dull thumping sound came from the area of the Russian flame-throwing tank. A tremendous fireball illuminated the area as another rocket from the panzer crackers found its mark. It was the Russians' turn to be incinerated by their own tank as it exploded. Several writhed in torment on the ground as the flames burned down to the flesh. Schreiber ignored their screams as the smell of burning flesh irritated his nostrils.

Schreiber finally got to a point where he could see the tractor with the baron and other wounded still on top of it. It appeared that the tractor was on fire. A T-34 with supporting infantry passed by the tractor. Others were faintly visible behind the lead tank. Schreiber realized he could not reach Foelkersam. He looked back one last time at the man who had led him through so much as he knew this was the last time he would see the baron.

Schreiber dashed to the forest. He saw some dark objects on the snow. His men had placed Teller mines out for pursuing tanks. He reached the depression where the panzer crackers had set up. A MG 42 machine gun was providing covering fire. A few men had not fired their panzerfausts. Bitter fighting continued as the Soviet armor groped for its elusive prey. As they pounced toward the survivors, the mines cost the Russians eight tanks. Schreiber glanced at the scene of destruction through his binoculars. The view could have come out of Dante's *Inferno*. Another vehicle with volatile materials went up in a sheet of flames and cast an eerie light on the surroundings.

More figures ran around on fire. At this distance, they resembled sticks on fire.

The firing died down briefly as the Soviet columns met. Now all of the tanks were headed toward Schreiber's men. As Schreiber looked over his group, he saw that it had been whittled down considerably. The result was a foregone conclusion if he stood and fought the armored wave headed his way.

Some of his men wanted to stand and fight. They had plenty to be proud of. They had destroyed an estimated twenty-five tanks and killed scores of Russians. However, Schreiber pointed out that they were facing two armored regiments with at least a hundred tanks left and plenty of infantry left in support. He looked at the battlefield again. The shattered wrecks continued to burn furiously. The smell of burning flesh intermingled with that of burning oil reached him at this distance. It was an all-too-familiar experience on the Eastern Front.

Schreiber looked at his group. There were no more than forty survivors. The others had either perished or been seriously wounded, but no one would surrender to the Russians. Schreiber knew they needed to move. "Listen up. They think they're mopping up. If we don't get out of here, they will and soon. Get ready to move out."

"We'll stay as long as we can," one of the panzer crackers remarked. "We'll keep Ivan honest for as long as possible."

"Good luck. Do what you can, but get out of here when you're out of rockets." Schreiber ordered the survivors to withdraw. At the same time, the Russians were getting closer.

"There!" The panzer crackers were excited. The fires from the earlier fighting outlined the tanks as they advanced. Schreiber raised his field glasses and recognized the reason for the excitement. One of the tanks was fitted out with several antennae. That would be a commander's tank. If it was knocked out, the rest of the tanks would mill around like lost sheep and perhaps give Schreiber's men the break they desperately needed.

"Pick your target carefully," Schreiber calmly remarked.

The two men needed no encouragement. A whoosh and a deep

rumbling sound emanated from the command tank. A searing flame shot up as the ammunition inside exploded. The panzer crackers fired three remaining rockets. Three explosions that reverberated through the darkness confirmed success. Other explosions confirmed that some of Schreiber's men were scoring with their panzerfausts. Machine gun bursts kept the Russian infantry down. Schreiber watched as the firing bisected a Soviet officer.

"Run, for God's sake, run," Schreiber ordered. The tanks had stopped and decided to blast the area in front of them. A shell threw up frozen chunks of earth as it exploded at the ridge they had just left. Schreiber watched numbly as five men in front of him vanished in an explosion. Two more men fell from stray rifle shots. Schreiber watched as the wounded man he had helped earlier hobbled alone. Schreiber went over to help.

"Thank you, Haupsturmfuehrer. This leg is getting a little sore."

"Come on a few more meters." Schreiber was puffing hard now in the cold. His breath produced a small cloud. *Hope the Russians can't see that*, he thought.

A shell exploded in one of the trees, knocking the two men to the ground and dusting them with a coat of snow. Schreiber helped the wounded man up and summoned all of his strength to carry them deeper into the forest.

"Over here, Haupsturmfuehrer," a voice called.

Schreiber ran toward the voice. A series of explosions wracked the wood line behind him as he jumped into a small depression. Shrapnel flew over their head, and small turfs of frozen earth gently battered them.

"Gott in Himmel! That was close," the wounded man exclaimed.

"Too close," Schreiber agreed. "I think we've made it." Some of his men came over and helped the man up. The roar of the tanks indicated the Russians were not far behind. However, they were moving cautiously. As he looked back at what was probably the longest hundred meters he had ever run, Schreiber ordered his men to move again. Somehow he was still alive. Even though he was still being chased, Schreiber felt secure in the dark forbidding forest he was disappearing into. Although he had no more than twenty men with him, Schreiber was now in his element. He had been on so many partisan raids in similar terrain before. The Russians could now follow him at their own peril. They chose not to, and the sounds of battle became muted as the dense forest closed around them.

Skorzeny arrived in Schwedt the morning of January 31. His advance team was at the big Oder Bridge. What he saw depressed him and might have caused a lesser man to quit. All that Skorzeny found for a local defense force were three reserve infantry battalions and one reserve pioneer battalion. All four units were markedly under strength and consisted of sick and convalescing troops. To complicate things more, no one still had an idea where the enemy was.

Fortunately, the evening before at Friedenthal had been productive. Radl had organized a commando unit, sniper company, and assault company with light tanks. With these forces half an hour behind him, Skorzeny knew that he could do something, and something would be done.

First he needed to find out where the Russians were. Skorzeny summoned the other officer who had accompanied him. "I want you to go to as far east as Konigsberg, if you don't run into Ivan before then. Don't do any fighting unless you have to. I don't want to bring the Russians down on my head before I'm ready. Observe and report only. I need time to organize the defenses. You will tell me how much time I have."

The officer saluted and left. Skorzeny then walked through the streets of the city, pondering his many problems. Refugees including soldiers from shattered units were streaming through Schwedt to escape the hordes from the east. As he surveyed the mass of humanity passing by, solutions began to be obvious. The soldiers would be dragooned into the forces, defending the city, while the civilians would construct the defenses. Soon every able-bodied person was at work. Skorzeny had a glimmer of hope that he might just succeed as he watched a semblance of defensive positions take shape.

By the end of the day, Skorzeny's hopes had risen even higher. His reconnaissance team reported an area of no man's land for fifty kilometers around. A disoriented German was as likely to be encountered, as was an equally disoriented Russian. No organized Soviet units were detected. In the meantime, he had been able to construct the largest part of a ring of defense. After conferring with the commanders of the reserve battalions, a bridgehead was formed on the east bank of the Oder River. Around the bridgehead was a series of rifle pits and machine gun nests. Some artillery that Radl had conjured up and sent to Schwedt supported these. In addition, more soldiers had arrived, giving Skorzeny more men than he had ever dreamed of having.

As his first line of defense took shape, Skorzeny considered locations and the makeup for his second and third lines of defense. The second line would have containment trenches and hedgehog projections. The third and final rings would be centered on the bridge. With enough time, Skorzeny felt that he might save Schwedt from the Russians. As he surveyed the gingerbread houses, he wondered if it would still be known as the "Pearl of the Uckermark."

Dark was approaching quickly on that cold winter day. Soon the population would be settling down for food and rest. Skorzeny decided it was time to take a well-earned rest in the house he had commandeered for a headquarters. He had good reason to be pleased with himself. He had arrived to take charge of a nearly impossible situation and had made progress toward establishing a decent defense perimeter. While the situation was still shaky and would be for a week, he figured, the constant stream of warm bodies would allow him to consolidate his position. All in all, he was feeling good until a messenger arrived with orders from the Army Group Vistula.

"God damn, Reichsheini!" Skorzeny spat out the derogatory nickname with disgust. He had first heard Himmler's nickname in France from other Waffen-SS officers. Many in the armed SS had already lost their respect for him then. Skorzeny felt the same way as he reviewed his orders that Freienwalde must be retaken immediately. In addition, outposts were to be sent to Konigsberg if the Russians had not already taken it. *With what?* Skorzeny bitterly asked himself. He simmered at the idea of Himmler trying to command an army group when he couldn't even lead a Hitler Youth troop out of the mountains. Finally, Skorzeny cooled off and refused to be exasperated further by Himmler's military ineptitude and harebrained fantasies. Instead, he would ignore the orders to take Freienwalde as he had a few days ago.

Skorzeny leaned back in a chair. He decided it was a good time to rehearse in his mind his knowledge of Himmler. He recalled that some senior SS officers were content to mock the scarecrow figure of Himmler. Others were less restrained and more viscous in their scorn for Himmler, such as SS General Felix Steiner who called Himmler a sleazy romantic. Steiner had even dared question the sacred untermenschen policies in the east. When Himmler circulated an order for his generals to be National Socialist revolutionaries, most SS generals yawned and pigeonholed the directive. Those few who carried out the order became a laughingstock throughout the Waffen-SS. Even the politicians despised the man. Speer had called him a man from another planet, while one of the Strasser brothers had called him the "black Jesuit."

Unfortunately, Skorzeny's clout, while considerable, was not like that of Sepp Dietrich. When Dietrich had commanded the Leibstandarte Division, Himmler's power had ended at the barracks' gates as his orders were at best regarded as suggestions. More recently, Willi Bittrich had made some indiscreet remarks of sympathy about one of the condemned conspirators from the July 20 plot. Himmler had wanted to relieve Bittrich as corps commander. Bittrich refused to step down since the front was critical from the Allied advance into Holland. Moreover, Field Marshal Model backed Bittrich and forced Himmler to back down. Skorzeny knew of the letter Himmler sent to Bittrich, suggesting "that we talk." Somehow Bittrich never found the time to reply.

Skorzeny pondered his own position. While he had direct access to Hitler and enjoyed the Fuehrer's confidence, Skorzeny realized he had powerful enemies of his own. After all, he was not a general, and Himmler had made no overt moves against him that he was aware of while others had. Sure the Reichsfuehrer had chastised him a time or two, but that was to be expected. In addition, the man had been useful at times when Skorzeny had needed him. He realized while he had to be firm with Himmler, he had to also pick his battles with the man carefully. After all, Rohm had been close to Hitler and look at what Himmler ended up doing to him.

Skorzeny sighed deeply. He was exasperated by the kind of man he was dealing with. His main concern was whether Himmler would let him do his job. At least he had gotten off to a good start and had been unhampered by the Russians. He slowly stretched himself over a bed in his room. While lying in bed, he had not realized how exhausting the day had been. He stared at the ceiling briefly until sleep overpowered him.

The next morning, Skorzeny decided to send his patrols further east. The area of interest today was eight kilometers east of Konigsberg at Bad Schonfliess. Two platoons would enter and proceed further if there was no sign of the enemy. The platoons moved out just before dawn. Skorzeny shivered in the bitter cold as he watched the men climb into their vehicles and drive into God knows what.

He turned now to the problem of defending Schwedt. Most straggling soldiers still had their weapons. However, Skorzeny needed machine guns, tanks, and more artillery to make a stand. He also worried that the Russians could cross the frozen Oder with ease. His aide, Lieutenant Walther, solved that problem.

"Herr Oberst, We have solved that problem. I spoke with the pioneer commander. They can blow the ice today."

"Good. Anything else to report?"

"As a matter of fact, yes. We located some antitank guns. There is a factory in Frankfort on the Oder that is still producing the 75. They have forty guns we can grab right away. There won't be any problems on who gets the guns since Berlin has written them off. They're in range of Russian artillery."

"Get the guns and don't tell Berlin."

"Jawohl. I gave the orders last night to move the guns. Also, nearby the factory is an arms dump. They had a lot of the MG 42s with ammunition."

"I suppose they're on the way."

"Of course, Herr Oberst. We need those as well."

Skorzeny started walking toward the bridge. He thought how he wished Foelkersam were here now. He had no idea what the man was going through or if he was even alive after he ordered the breakout. Nothing more had been heard of from Task Force East. Fortunately, Walther was learning fast and performing admirably.

Explosions then caught Skorzeny's attention. Chunks of ice were flying through the air. He realized the pioneers had started blowing up the ice flows. They proceeded onto the defense works. The rudimentary defenses were more reassuring as he realized armaments were on the way. If only the artillery and machine guns could arrive today.

"The pioneers have an interesting idea. If we put some 88s on some of the chunks of ice, we could have sort of mobile artillery. It would be difficult for the enemy to pinpoint their location."

"An interesting idea, if we ever get some." Skorzeny put the idea in the back of his mind.

The two reconnaissance platoons entered Bad Schonfliess in the middle of the morning. The deserted streets gave the hardened Waffen-SS troops an eerie feeling. In the lead vehicle, Lieutenant Bauer surveyed the surroundings with unease. He crouched behind the 20mm gun in the SDK222 armored car. Nerves were on edge as they probed the outskirts. Finally, Bauer ordered his men out of the vehicles and to use the armored cars as cover. Too many of these men had experienced close calls with Russian snipers. With his troops alongside the vehicles, Bauer proceeded to the middle of town. Scattered rubble littered the streets but was of no size to hinder Bauer's progress. Occasionally, they spotted a figure dart between buildings. Still with no enemy contact, they proceeded to the east side of Bad Schonfliess.

It was there that they encountered their first real signs of life. A young blonde-haired girl was pushing a buggy with some of her belongings. Although a mere teenager at best, she seemed to have been aged by the traumatic events going on around her.

One of the troopers stopped her. "Have you seen any Russians?"

She lifted her right arm and pointed eastward. She was incapable of speech.

"Are they close?"

This time, she nodded vigorously up and down.

"How close?"

She remained mute. She was obviously afraid.

One of the SS troopers angrily kicked some rubble and muttered. "I bet Ivan got hold of her and had a good time with her. I'd like to get my hands on them."

Another trooper surveyed the quiet city and remarked. "Looks like these people have had it."

"We'll have had it if you don't keep your eyes open for Ivan. By the way, we're not a revenge squad either. We're here to find out where the enemy is. You'll get your chance at revenge soon enough." Bauer stood up in the armored car and gazed through his binoculars. It was too quiet. He was sure the girl was telling them the truth. Still he did not know how close they were. Bauer started back down into the SDK222. As he descended into the cramped space, a searing pain radiated along his right temple. Almost immediately, he heard the shot. A warm wet feeling spread across the right side of his face.

"That burns like hell!" Bauer roared.

"If you had moved a second later, you might have found out how hot," one of the crewmen replied. He mopped Bauer's face. "Just a flesh wound, Herr Leutnant. You'll be good as new. It won't get you any leave though. Here I'll dress it."

"Just pay attention to the fighting. I don't need anyone else getting shot."

"Our friend over there is inexperienced, or you would be dead. And don't worry about me. The firing will keep him honest."

Bauer's men dropped and swung into action as soon as they saw their leader fall. Some liberally peppered a suspected window from their firing positions, while others began to encircle him. The 20mm from Bauer's vehicle kept up a murderous fire. The action served to distract Bauer's mind from the pain of his wound.

"I see him. There in the window!" one of the troopers cried out.

The 20mm sprayed the area around the window. A white cloud hung in the air as debris flew through the air from the window's location. Bauer started to congratulate himself when he heard the sound of more submachine guns. They weren't German. Bauer saw flashes above a board fence and movement behind it. Bauer swung the armored car around so his gunner could have a better firing position. He reduced the fence to splinters. The firing died down. It was obvious that the sniper had been bait. With better troops the Russians would have done some damage to his men. Despite the eradication of the sniper and the infantry, Bauer was uneasy. It seemed the enemy knew where he was, but he still didn't know the location of Ivan. He wondered if the situation was going to get worse.

"Go search the bodies," Bauer ordered. At least maybe they could find out what they were up against.

The armored cars kept the men covered as they searched the khaki clad corpses for anything of value. Hopefully, there would be some identification papers or cards. Bauer watched closely as the men went about their ghoulish work. One of the troopers cut off a shoulder patch and brought it over to Bauer. Bauer recognized it as belonging to one of the guards' divisions. He carefully put it inside his blouse pocket. He surveyed the area again with his binoculars. The silence was ominous. Bauer realized that what he had run into was probably a probing action by the enemy. Still he wanted to know where the main body was.

"No one else around," a grizzled NCO reported back to Bauer.

"We'll keep moving east. Remember we have run into Ivan. There are probably more around." Bauer leaned back. His head throbbed horribly now. However, he needed to find the Russians' main body. "Send two foot patrols out ahead. We'll keep them covered. I want them to stay in sight."

The two patrols continued ahead. They darted between intersections and tried to make themselves as inconspicuous as possible. They were still wary of snipers. Fortunately, their white camouflage tended to blend in with the patches of snow on the ground.

They were almost out of town when Bauer saw one of the lead men gesturing wildly for the others to retreat. Bauer anxiously focused his binoculars to see the reason for the man's agitation. He heard the reason before he saw it. He picked up the sound of a distant rumble. Along a tree line, he discerned some movement resembling a caterpillar's. He focused again. Although it was camouflaged, he picked out a tank barrel out of the winter landscape. Finally, he made out the white hull of one and then five tanks. Since they did not have muzzle breaks, Bauer realized he had probably stumbled upon a Soviet reconnaissance in force. If it were the main force, more tanks would be following.

"Looks like our friends called in reinforcements," a crewman remarked.

"I doubt it," Bauer replied. "They probably found us like we found them." Bauer watched for a few breathless moments as his scouts returned to the column. He watched the tanks closely. They had the wrong shape for KV s. They were probably T-34s, but it was hard to tell at this distance. Bauer didn't think they were IS2s, but he couldn't be sure.

An explosion to his right caught Bauer's attention as it showered him with dirt and masonry. Although none of his men were killed, seven were injured. Ivan was trying to pay Bauer back for the earlier casualties. Bauer searched for the source of the firing. None of the tanks he saw had pointed their barrels in his direction.

"Mortars, Herr Leutnant?" the crewman asked again.

"Too big of an explosion. And there would have been more. Let's get out of here."

The column was barely moving when a shell landed at the spot Bauer had just left. More debris rained down on him. Bauer silently cursed. He would love to reduce the Russian numbers some more, but his priority was to observe and report. He directed the column to the center of town and set up defensive positions. He wanted to make sure the wounded were properly tended to before returning to Schwedt. An improperly dressed wound could be lethal in this environment.

His men disembarked and took up positions in surrounding buildings. The two medics were busy calming the wounded men and properly dressing their wounds. Bauer climbed out of his armored car and went to a second-story window to observe the coming skirmish. He suspected and secretly hoped the Russians would follow him into town. Street fighting neutralized the advantage that armor normally provided.

Bauer was not disappointed. He saw the shadow of the first tank before it turned a corner. By then, he had warned his men. Another followed behind it. Red Army troops were crowded on top of each tank. Bauer took a good look at the tanks now. He recognized them as T-34/76s by their hexagonal turrets. The tank commander in the first tank was looking for signs of Bauer's men. Like any commander, he wanted to get off the first shot. Bauer had his men hold their fire until the tanks were only meters away. Then the lead tank ground to a halt as a dull thud rang out. Smoke began billowing from underneath the metal beast. A panzerfaust had found its mark.

The Russians jumped off the tanks into a hail of lead. The SDK222 turned the comer and sprayed the street. Several Russians in a row collapsed as the large rounds passed through several bodies at once. The two lead tanks were now ablaze and blocking the street. All of Bauer's men were firing now into the scrambling Soviets and took a grim harvest of the infantry. Few of the tank crewmen survived to escape their smoldering hulks, but the Soviet infantry was strong enough despite its losses that Bauer thought it prudent to withdraw for good.

"To the cars. They'll have reinforcements swarming over us." Bauer planned no more delaying actions. His wounded were taken care of, and he had no need to stop.

His action was none too soon. The remaining Russian tanks halted and subjected the area to a methodical bombardment. Splinters and bricks flew in all directions as the shells found their mark. Clouds of dust rose and obscured Bauer's departure. His men shook in their vehicles as explosions rocked their vehicles. His men huddled down to avoid being targets and covered their noses to keep out the oppressive dust. Bauer watched in horror as one building collapsed onto one of his troop carriers. No one moved inside. Bauer motioned for the driver to keep moving. Otherwise, they would be encircled.

After what seemed to be forever, the bloodied group left Bad Schonfliess for the day. Everyone's nerves were in tatters. Bauer looked back to see a cloud of dust in the area where they had engaged the Russians. There was still firing. The dull boom of the Russian 76mm guns was audible at this distance. A louder explosion dwarfed the others. Bauer figured the ammunition in one of the burning tanks was going off. A fireball in the area confirmed his suspicion. Bauer began to breathe a little easier now. He lit a cigarette to relieve some of the tension. They had not done badly except for the men in the troop carrier. That incident showed how capricious war could be. It would have been understandable had they been killed while engaged in a firefight. But to be killed by a fluke of war while one was disengaging while out of sight of the enemy was a little too cruel. Bauer noticed his hands were shaking, and it was not because of the frigid air. He clasped his hands together to keep the shaking hid from the rest of men. At least he could tell Skorzeny where the Russians were now.

It was almost sunset when Bauer returned to Schwedt. Skorzeny greeted him and got the details he needed. "We don't have much time," Skorzeny said when Bauer had finished. "We need to get our defenses in better shape soon. I figure we have week at most. Bauer, you're going back into Bad Schonfliess tomorrow. This time, you're taking a whole company. You'll be looking for a fight this time. We must slow the Russians down. I hate sending you after you've been hit, but you already know the area."

"That won't be a problem, Herr Oberst."

"Good. Get some rest. You'll need it."

Lieutenant Walther appeared and updated Skorzeny on his weapons procurement. "We've got most of the 75s in place, and most of the machine guns have arrived as well. The rest should arrive tomorrow."

"Very good. We'll do final placements of the 75s in the morning. By the way, the Russians are at Bad Schonfliess now. Gather up anything else you can. I don't care how you do it. Just do it.

"Jawohl, Herr Oberst."

Schreiber had pushed his men until nearly four in the morning to put as much distance between his men and their pursuers. They were still unnerved by their close escape from the Russian armor force. Schreiber had an uneasy feeling that the Russians had information about his group's location. Unfortunately for the Russians, the attempted ambush had backfired in the confusion of night warfare. Of course, he couldn't claim that his men had fared better as there was only a small handful left. Now they were trudging for their lives through a dense forest that was hopefully devoid of any other humanity.

"Halt," Schreiber finally commanded. "We'll make camp here tonight."

"Shouldn't we keep going?" one trooper asked wearily.

"We will in the morning at daybreak. Now get some rest. We've just been through a lot. Two men on sentry duty at all times."

After two men were detailed for sentry duty, the other survivors carefully prepared shelters out of pine boughs. Most were utterly exhausted by their ordeal and sank into a deep sleep.

The next thing Schreiber realized was that he was looking at sunlight. It only partially penetrated the foliage. He had no idea what time it was other than it was well past sunrise. He slowly shook himself awake, as he was still groggy from lack of rest. Other men stirred in their shelters as well.

"What time is it?" Schreiber asked a sentry.

"0930, Herr Hauptmann," the man replied.

"I wanted up sooner."

"You needed the sleep."

"Liar. You needed the sleep."

The man smiled sheepishly while Schreiber bit his tongue. There was no need to be angry with the guard. His men were trying to take care of him. He remembered what his father had told him: "Your men will take care of you if you are a good officer, and you take care of them." So what if they slept a little late today? The man had been right. Schreiber had needed his sleep as well as everyone else. Instead of chastising anyone, Schreiber walked around to stretch and get the soreness out of his muscles. As he did so, he looked over his men. It was so strange. Not quite four hundred men had tried to break out two nights ago. Now he had less than thirty men deep in a thick forest, which in turn was probably surrounded by a ring of Soviet armor. With luck, they would find some breaks in the line and evade the Russians. *A lot of luck*, Schreiber thought.

A small fire was started. Somehow in these primitive conditions, they made some coffee. Several nibbled on their cold rations. A few tried warming the rations. Meanwhile, the distant sound of artillery reached their ears. This was somewhat reassuring, as louder booms would have indicated that a gun battery was nearby.

After consuming their meager breakfast, they renewed their attempt to reach home. For now, Schreiber did not know where they were or how far the Russians had advanced. While Schreiber's men were now in their element, he wished to avoid additional action until his men reached friendly lines. At least for now, any troops he ran into in the forest would be other German stragglers or lost Russians. The front-line Soviet forces would be concerned with maintaining their momentum. For now, Schreiber felt his force could escape detection.

By midday, they had resumed their trek west. They proceeded cautiously through the evergreens. Their ghostly figures were barely discernable as they moved about in their snow camouflage. They had made good progress through the afternoon when the point man motioned for everyone to get down. Schreiber dropped to his knees and brought his submachine gun to the ready. He crawled quietly up to the point man.

"What is it?" Schreiber quietly asked.

The man pointed. Schreiber made out four trucks with a red

star on their doors. The insignia seemed to taunt him. His blood started to boil as if he were being told, "Here we are, and you can't do anything." Then he realized the trucks might be his salvation. He scrutinized the area carefully now. It appeared the Russians had driven off a main road to spend the night. Schreiber tried to get an idea of how many Ivans he would be dealing with. There had to be a least four drivers. He looked for guards and saw none. He heard voices. Two Russians appeared and took a box out of a truck. No more appeared. Soon Schreiber could make out some smoke, and the Russians began singing some folk songs. They evidently felt secure enough not to even post guards. Schreiber decided they would be taught the error of their ways.

Schreiber crawled back to his men. Anxiety was written on their faces. Some were actually sweating despite the cold. "Listen up. We've got some Ivans in front with trucks. We're going to take care of the Russians and take off with the trucks. We surround them and kill them silently. No shooting if possible." He looked around to see if there were any questions. There were none. Instead, their eyes blazed with anticipation. Everyone had the same thought that this could be his ticket to home. Schreiber felt their anticipation and with a nod motioned his men into action.

Schreiber's men split into two groups as they encircled the Russians in the approaching darkness. They carefully avoided stepping on limbs and other objects that might betray their presence. When they were within five meters of the festive Russians, they lay in the snow and snaked their way behind the unsuspecting Russians. One Russian left the group to respond to the call of nature. He realized his mistake when a hand was clamped over his mouth. He caught a glint of steel as it was firmly slid across his throat. He swiftly lost consciousness and was allowed to slide to the ground by his killer. Schreiber's men continued their advance. One Russian moved over by himself. One of Schreiber's men pointed at him and indicated he would handle this Russian. The others nodded in agreement. Seconds later, six more Russians were expertly dispatched and slid to the ground. The Russian who had moved away saw what was happening and reached for a pistol. Before he could draw his weapon, a snow-clad figure was upon him and had knocked the gun out of his hand with an entrenching tool. The next swipe of the tool came down on the Russians head. As the unfortunate man collapsed into the snow, the SS corporal bludgeoned him until he was sure the Russian was dead.

Schreiber's men thought they had finished when a brown—clad figure approached with a submachine gun aimed at Schreiber. Before he could fire, he was jumped by a white-clad figure, and a fight ensued in the snow for control of the weapon. A short muffled burst was heard, and the white-clad figure stood up. Two other figures darted from the trucks for the woods. An expertly thrown knife brought one of the fleeing soldiers to his knees. One of the SS men was on top of the collapsing man and with a swipe of his entrenching tool all but severed the man's head from his trunk. The other Russian had evaded the knives and snow-clad figures and was in the open. He was on his way to freedom. Someone cried out, "Shoot that Russian bastard."

Schreiber gritted his teeth as he expected a rifle volley to advertise their position. Not a shot was fired, however. The Russian understood German and shouted back. "This is one Russian bastard you're not going to shoot. The men who had aimed their weapons hesitated and finally lowered them. Most of Schreiber's men were grinning or laughing by then. Schreiber thought about the insanity of war. They had gone in to butcher their detested enemy, and now they were letting one escape because of his wit. However, it also prevented any firing. It might be a long time before the lone Russian could spread the alarm.

Meanwhile, Schreiber surveyed the carnage his men had wrought. The crumpled heaps of the dead Russians lie in the middle of spreading crimson stains on the snow. His men's bloodlust had been temporarily satisfied. However, they needed to keep moving.

"No loitering," Schreiber ordered. "Check and see what they're carrying in the trucks. Ivan may leave us alone if we stay here, but I wouldn't count on it since one of them has gotten away. Now it's time to make good our escape." Schreiber pointed to some of his men. "Take off the Russians' overcoats and put them on. The rest of you, get in the back of the trucks. Cover the bodies. Then let's get the hell out of here."

Schreiber got into the lead truck after putting a Russian overcoat and in fifteen minutes had his small convoy on the road. Supplies had been left in the trucks. The explosives and food would come in handy. They looked for a well-used road. With luck, they would slip into a convoy unnoticed. Soon they came upon what appeared to be a main road. They paused to get their bearings. As they were stopped, Red Army trucks pulling artillery traveled down the road.

"We know which way to go now," the driver in Schreiber's truck remarked.

"Follow them," Schreiber ordered.

The four trucks slid in smoothly behind the artillery column and followed them through the fading light. Finally, the column pulled over. Schreiber did not care to join them and risk detection.

"What do we do, Herr Hauptmann?" the driver asked.

"Keep moving. Find a place a few kilometers down past them. I don't want someone ahead asking questions either. But don't go too far. I don't want to get shot up by our own side."

"I won't argue with you there, Herr Hauptmann."

They finally found a deserted area of road. Schreiber had the trucks driven behind some trees to make them less conspicuous. He planned for his men to rest better tonight. Tomorrow he wanted to get as near the front as he could, that is, if there was a front.

The next morning shone brightly. Schreiber waited for another convoy. Another artillery unit drove past, and Schreiber's group tagged along. The icy roads crunched under the loads of the trucks. Schreiber watched as large chunks of ice were flung off the trucks. Large units of infantry were passed. The manpower of the Red Army was unbelievable. Later they passed a field where dozens of T-34s and IS2s were parked. A dark foreboding came over Schreiber as he surveyed this array of armor. There was no way Germany could withstand the coming onslaught. However, that was not an opinion that one could voice out loud back home without risking execution.

Moreover, he still had his responsibility to his men. Still he felt ill when he saw what was aimed at his country.

They made steady progress until the afternoon when the column came to a complete stop. Schreiber cursed silently. It could be any number of reasons, but he was worried about the Russian who had escaped. *Had their security set up a roadblock?* Schreiber wondered.

"Can you see anything?" he asked the driver. "Can you tell what's going on?"

"Not yet."

Schreiber opened his door and got out. He noticed they were in a Ford truck. *Ironic,* he thought as he recalled how he had driven into Russia in a Ford and now he was trying to get away from the Russians in a Ford. He opened his overcoat, pulled out his binoculars, and looked ahead. He saw no reason for the stop. Then he noticed a staff car driving toward the end of the column. Schreiber got back into the cab to avoid attracting attention. He raised his binoculars and watched the car come closer. A Russian officer was in the front seat. Schreiber's heart skipped a beat. At first he wasn't sure. Now he recognized the distinctive insignia of the NKVD. Were these ubiquitous watchdogs onto his men? If so, Schreiber knew one thing: he wasn't going to be taken prisoner.

The staff car stopped alongside Schreiber's truck. The Russian officer viewed Schreiber's group with suspicion. Something didn't look quite right. Why were these trucks in the rear? They didn't seem to be part of the pattern to the NKVD officer. He got out of his car and approached the driver's side. His uniform was clean and well tailored. He obviously was no combat officer.

He immediately questioned the driver. "Where are you going? Are you part of this convoy?" His tone was imperious and menacing.

Schreiber maintained his composure. "We are part of a supply company. We're delivering grenades and machine guns. Soldiers can't depend on just artillery to win the war."

"I wasn't talking to you. Anyway, you're in the wrong place. I need your papers." The NKVD officer was getting angry. Something about Schreiber aroused his suspicions. He was used to running roughshod over senior officers. Now a lowly sergeant was talking back to him. NCOs might run the army, but they were more easily cowed than the officers except this one.

"I need your papers,' the officer demanded.

"I have them," Schreiber answered.

"I said I didn't ask you. Are you and your driver deaf?"

"He's a Chechen. He doesn't speak Russian."

Unfortunately, the NKVD officer spoke Chechen. He started jabbering at the driver. At the same time, Schreiber got out of the truck. This pest from the NKVD was going to have to be dealt with. He stepped in front of the truck where no one could see him.

"Do you want to see the papers or not. The language lesson can continue later. Some other sookin sin can do that."

The NKVD officer was stung by the impertinence—for a man of this rank to call him a son of a bitch. There would be absolutely nothing said if he drew his pistol and shot this man on the spot. First he wanted to teach the upstart peasant a lesson. He glared at the driver. "I'll be back." The driver grinned back. The officer marched a few steps over to Schreiber. Schreiber held papers purloined from the dead Russians out for the officer. The security man snatched them from Schreiber. "I don't know who you think you are, but your days in uniform are over." He started mumbling. Then he hotly exclaimed, "You are nowhere near where you are supposed to be."

"Yes we are, Herr Comrade."

A chill went through the NKVD officer when he heard the German term. He dropped his papers and prepared to draw his pistol. As he looked at Schreiber, a horrified look came over his face as Schreiber's overcoat came open and revealed his SS uniform. He noticed he couldn't move his right arm as Schreiber had already grabbed it. He realized too late that he had tangled with the wrong man as Schreiber plunged a dagger into his throat with the other hand.

Schreiber pushed the dying man against the grill of the truck and let him sink to the ground. Schreiber's driver looked anxiously at him and back to the Russian driver in the staff car. Schreiber motioned for him to remain still. He then strode over to the staff car and killed the driver almost casually with his knife. He wiped his knife blade on the dead man's jacket and then sheathed the dagger. He walked around to the front of the truck. The NKVD officer was in his final throes as he coughed up blood in attempt to keep from drowning in it.

Schreiber spit contemptuously at the man. "Comrade, you should have spent some time at the front where you would have learned a few tricks as these. Instead, you shot good officers on Stalin's whim when you ought to have been fighting." Schreiber then got back into the cab.

His driver nervously asked, "What do we do if more Russians come up and find them?"

"We kill them also," was the brutal reply.

The driver shook his head. At least the captain kept a cool head in difficult situations. Maybe he would get them out of this predicament like the baron had so many times before. At least they had gotten this far.

Low-flying planes distracted Schreiber's thoughts. An explosion in front of them threw frozen dirt and flaming debris in all directions. An ammunition truck had been hit. Pandemonium broke out in the convoy.

"Focke-wulfs," the driver cried out.

"Ground attack version." Schreiber recognized them by the fuselage. With its downward pointing guns, this version of the FW 190 was a formidable ground attack plane. Normally, this was a good thing, and Schreiber would have been glad to see them except for the fact his men were on the receiving end. Maybe Goering's much-vaunted Luftwaffe was not finished after all. Maybe, though, this was a way to get out of this jam. "Get moving," he ordered. "We're passing this convoy. I'm not going to be a target for our own side."

The truck pulled to the left. Schreiber motioned for the others to follow. The NKVD officer was ground into the mud by the other vehicles. Schreiber wanted to be on the move before the FW 190s could turn around and began another strafing run. This would not be a one-time deal with such a tempting target below. As expected, the FW 190s appeared again. Schreiber watched as they approached the rear of the convoy. He saw them open fire and kick up more dirt.

"Pull off now." Schreiber sharply cried.

The four trucks went up a slight rise off the road. They had barely missed being hit by the second strafing run. Beads of sweat formed on the two men's foreheads. The driver then got back on the road. They passed several wrecked vehicles on the road. Another spectacular explosion threw exploding shells into the air. Several vehicles were afire, but fortunately, the flames had not reached the gas tanks or ammunition. Other trucks had flat tires or were spewing steam after being hit in the engines. Bodies littered the road or were slumped in their seats. Schreiber's convoy ran over several bodies in their mad dash past the column. A foolhardy NKVD man tried to stop them. The driver just ran over him.

"Brakes aren't working too well on these Russian trucks," the driver remarked sarcastically.

"Just get us through this mess." Schreiber stuck his head outside and noticed the tires were stained red to maroon. He grimaced and scanned the sky again for the FW 190s. They were not long in coming. Without any Russian fighters to oppose them, the two FW 190 pilots were having a good target practice.

"To the left, here they come again."

The driver saw the dirt being thrown up and again narrowly avoided being shot up, He was sweating profusely despite the cold. "This gets hard on the nerves, Herr Hauptmann."

"Just get back on the road."

As they started passing the column, Schreiber decided to give the fighters some help. He pulled out a grenade and had the driver slow by a stalled truck with ammunition. With a flick of his arm, the grenade was in the middle of the explosives. Schreiber motioned for his men behind him to do the same to other trucks. In addition to destroying Soviet supplies, the explosions might give the FW 190s pause before resuming their attack.

Schreiber's driver was moving as fast as he could as the convoy erupted in a series of explosions. Frequently, he had to slow down to avoid large chunks of debris. However, Schreiber's tactic worked. Instead of continuing their strafing, the FW 190s veered up to avoid damage from the successive detonations. Schreiber watched with relief as the two planes peeled off.

"Looks like it worked." The driver was much relieved.

"We still need to make sure they don't come in from the side. Plus we need to get out of here before one of these trucks blows and takes us with it."

Finally, they came to the head of the convoy. The FW 190s had scored early in their attack. One truck and its artillery piece were lying in a ditch on their sides. No signs of life emanated from it. Another truck had come to a diagonal stop in the road. Schreiber's men passed it carefully. Two still figures were slumped in it. The driver's head hung outside the window. Blood was seeping from the bottom of the driver's closed door. Schreiber turned his head and tried to forget the terror of the last few minutes.

The road was now clear of any vehicles. Schreiber glanced back to make sure the other trucks were still with him. As he did so, he saw a large pall of smoke over the position of the column. He exhaled deeply as he was greatly relieved.

"Where are we heading?" the driver asked.

"West. Just keep heading west."

They approached a village near sundown. No other Soviet forces had been encountered. On the outskirts, they encountered a sickening scene. At first, they didn't recognize the frozen mass on the road for what it was. It appeared to be the usual debris of war that had been given a coating of snow and ice after being crushed by tanks. Only after they stopped did the full horror of the scene become apparent. One of the privates noticed the children's small hands. Finally, they realized they were looking at the remains of a group of refugees who had been overtaken by a Soviet armored unit and then run over as a terror tactic. Schreiber ordered his men back into the trucks. He did not want them dwelling on what they had just seen. The day had been bad enough.

"Drive on into town." Schreiber was weary and needed a break along with his men. They were all near collapse. He began to doze off.

"Herr Hauptmann, over there," his driver exclaimed.

Schreiber was instantly alert. Although it was almost dark, Schreiber could make out women and children cowering by a church. He felt his thirst for blood rising as he noticed a horde of Russians around them. *So this is how it is supposed to end*, he thought. He could not leave these civilians to their fate while standing idly by.

"Pull over." A chill ran through the driver. He knew what his commander was thinking. Although he was ready to mix it up with the Russians as well, to hear Schreiber's tone was unnerving. The driver felt like he was in the presence of a cobra.

They approached the group slowly. A Russian officer approached. "Don't do anything rash!" Schreiber ordered his men.

The officer stopped and was looking into Schreiber's eyes. "Report, Sergeant."

"Comrade Captain, Sergeant Pavlov reporting. We are delivering ammunition. We seem to be lost. We were strafed by the fascist pigs down the road."

"We saw the smoke and the planes" The man was convinced by Schreiber's play-acting. "I can tell you are lost, or you wouldn't be so near the front. There are strong German forces five kilometers from here."

Schreiber looked over at the women and children. The officer noticed Schreiber's look. "Don't get any ideas, Sergeant. We are not going to rape and murder these people like some of our undisciplined units do." The man's hand was on his holster. "One of our armored punishment regiments ran over a group of refugees outside of town. You probably ran over them as well. To spread terror as we are told. But let me tell you this, Sergeant. These people are not going to be hurt while I'm here. I don't know what will happen when we leave. I got to where I am by killing Germans, Italians, and Rumanians, not women and children."

"We're just trying to deliver ammunition to the front-line soldiers like yourself. Not all of us in the rear or such scoundrels, Comrade

Captain. I was in the infantry until I was wounded at Stalingrad. We don't have time or ammunition to waste. Do you need supplies, Comrade Captain? I like to see some get it that needs it."

The captain looked Schreiber over carefully before replying, "I don't think so. If I were you, I'd turn around before Fritz sees your group and decides to take a little target practice."

"We'll set up outside town, so if we get hit, your men won't have to worry. We'll still provide with supplies if you need them."

"I'll consider it in the morning. Good night, Sergeant."

The Red Army captain left. "Move on," Schreiber ordered his driver.

"Are we just going to let them have fun with the women and children?"

"You didn't understand what he said?'"

"I don't speak Russian."

"I forgot. He was protecting them... at least for now. A punishment unit ran over the refugees. The man threatened to shoot me if I tried to molest the civilians."

Both men laughed uproariously. "He threatened to shoot you. That took some nerve. I'm surprised you let him live. I can't believe it, a Russian I would like to hug."

"He won't survive the war."

"That's for sure. All of the good ones get killed off eventually. The shirkers, the parasites, those bastards will survive the war on both sides."

"Considering that we are still alive, we are two lousy bastards." Schreiber needled his driver mercilessly.

"We're just lucky so far. But what are our chances of surviving? Really, Herr Hauptman? Even if we get out of this pickle... You saw all the tanks. We're just delaying the inevitable."

"Perhaps. Right now, my job is to get all of you out of here. Pull over. This looks like a good place to stop for the night."

They stopped in front of a dark house. The men wearing Russian uniforms got out first and searched the house. Schreiber decided it would be a good place to spend the night after they found it was empty. Schreiber settled down after making it clear that the sentries were to be dressed in Russian overcoats at all times. He ate silently while his driver explained their earlier action regarding the refugees. This allowed Schreiber to think about his next move. If they were this close to friendly lines, he was willing to make a dash for freedom. By the time he finished eating, he had decided on his course of action.

"Start the engines at 0400. We'll try to cross over before daylight. Any questions?"

There were none. Schreiber went to a corner and made himself as comfortable as possible. The wounded man was put in a bed. Always take care of your wounded. Soon he was dead to the world, dreaming of freedom.

He was awakened by a kick in the legs. One of his men was frantically trying to wake him up. "Damn it! Is it that important? And what time is it?"

"Jawohl. It is important. It's not quite 0330."

"I said four, didn't I?"

"But we heard tanks, Russian tanks. We investigated, and it looks like a regiment of tanks are heading toward our lines."

"Why didn't you tell me earlier?"

"We just found out after doing a recon in the rear."

Schreiber gained control of himself. He knew to trust his men. "Are the trucks ready?" he asked in a more reasonable voice.

"They're warming up now. It appears the tanks are stopped for now, but we didn't think we wanted to get acquainted with them."

"Not hardly. Let's move out immediately."

The other men had been aroused, and the convoy slipped out of the unknown German town before 0400. Everyone was on edge now. They traveled with their headlights off to avoid fire from their own side. If one of the trucks went off the road, they would have to leave it. Progress was slow as they inched forward in the dark. After they covered three kilometers, they discovered the shells of five T-34s that were knocked out. One showered debris over the white landscape after suffering a massive internal explosion. The other four were still smoldering and had blistered the paint. They had been knocked out last night. All had been hit from the left side. The entry holes were the same size on the wrecked tanks. They had run into a tiger, possibly an antitank gun. *Looks like our side got its licks in first,* Schreiber thought. None of the turrets had turned, and the hatches were still closed on the intact tanks, indicating none of the crews survived.

Schreiber looked to the left. He suspected the tank or whatever was still there. A commander would loathe giving up a good killing ground. "Six of us are going over there. Be careful. They may be watching us now. I'd hate for our own side to kill us off now."

The squad was formed and set out. They darted from cover to cover. Occasionally, they stumbled across the fallen body of a soldier. It was impossible in the snow to tell which side the corpses belonged to. They stealthily worked their way to the wooded area they suspected held the panzer.

Schreiber motioned for a halt. He hit the ground. A light had flickered. Someone had lit a cigarette and had given away their position. Schreiber decided to work his way behind the position. Twenty minutes later, they were in position behind the probable tank. Soon they spotted movement. A solitary sentry was making his rounds. Unlike Schreiber's men, he was wearing a feldgrau overcoat. He came toward them, rubbing his hands. He was concentrating on staying warm rather than on his duties. A twig snapped loudly. He had slung his rifle over his shoulder and tried to lower it. One of Schreiber's men yanked it out of his hands. The scared man tried reaching for his dagger.

"Stop!" was Schreiber's sharp order. "If we wanted you dead, you would be dead. Now who's in charge here?"

The guard looked at Schreiber and noticed his Knight's Cross and SS runes. The significance of both was not lost on the guard. He started to salute but his arm was knocked down.

"No saluting here. I don't want to attract the attention of a sniper. Now who's in charge?"

"Follow me." The guard was still shaking from his close call and the bitter cold.

One of the troopers chided the young sentry. "We could have picked you off a kilo away when you lit that cigarette. Be glad we weren't one of Ivan's snipers. You would have been dead minutes ago."

"That's enough. Take us to your commander. I want to get my other men over without you shooting at them."

As he suspected, there was a tank. In fact, there were two vehicles. One was a king tiger, and the other was a jagdpanther. Either was a monster in battle and feared by the other side. Together they were a formidable team. A reinforced platoon of panzer grenadiers had dug in around the panzers. The position had been expertly hidden by the use of evergreen branches and snow camouflage. The tanks were nearly impossible to see unless one was right on top of them. It was a perfect location to deal with small groups of tanks. Dealing with an armored regiment would be another matter.

The commander was still asleep in the tiger. A banging on the hatch awakened him. *What is it now?* he thought. He badly needed some sleep. He opened the hatch and stared at the sentry. He probably wanted to report some inconsequential movement. He saw another man beside the sentry. He saw Schreiber's collar and became more alert.

"Herr Leutnant, some stragglers entered out lines. Haupsturmfuehrer Schreiber is their commander."

"Leutnant Schmidt." He dismissed the sentry with a nod. "I'm the commander of what you see. We formed rear guard hear two days ago until a counter attack can be launched. We didn't see much action except for those tanks you saw out there."

"We guessed you were still here since they're still warm. I hate to tell you this, but there are plenty more down the road behind them. The village we stayed in probably had a regiment enter it this morning. I guess they will advance at dawn."

"We'll be ready."

"Before you singlehandedly conquer the entire Red Army, I would like to get the rest of my men over. We took some ammunition trucks from Ivan. We broke out of Hohensalza a few nights ago. We are what's left of a group called Task Force East."

Schmidt raised his eyebrows. "That's some distance. You've been traveling since then?"

"Had to. We were caught between two armored units on our second night out. We shot Ivan up pretty good. He did the same to us. We went in with eight hundred men. Now we are barely the size of a platoon."

Schmidt tried to be hospitable. "Can I offer you something to eat? It's not much and it's cold."

"I'll take anything. We've also got some of Ivan's rations we'll trade with you. By the way, what are your plans?"

"I'm to remain here until our forces counterattack and reestablish the line."

Schreiber laughed. "There won't be any counterattack. If there's a line, it's far behind you."

"Those are my orders. You are also aware of the no-retreat policy"

"Yes, I am familiar with them. How long since you last heard from your superiors?"

"Twenty-four hours at least."

"You should have heard something sooner."

"I agree, but I can't leave."

"As senior officer now, I feel that a redeployment is in order. I am making that decision. If you stay here, you'll destroy a lot of tanks, but they will eventually roll over you. There are plenty of units out there begging for armored backup. I suggest we go find one. There is some safety in numbers."

By this time, the trucks had arrived with the rest of Schreiber's men. Daylight was beginning to break. Schreiber suggested that the panzer grenadiers ride in the truck or on the tanks. He felt they would have plenty of walking once they got into combat. Meanwhile, the two panzers came to life as they prepared to leave their hideaway.

"A rare honor, Herr Hauptman," Schmidt remarked casually.

"What, being here?"

"No, your Rritterkreuz."

"Oh, yes. You must excuse me, as I'm rather tired. That's a

souvenir from hunting partisans in Yugoslavia. I got my commission at the same time."

A sentry interrupted the conversation. "Over there," he pointed.

The two officers looked toward the village and wrecked tanks. The rising sun made visibility difficulty. Finally, behind the wrecked tanks, Schreiber spotted movement. T-34s were inching their way past the previous days' wreckage. "Damn," Schreiber muttered. "I hoped Ivan would be a little more considerate. It looks like we get to skirmish first."

Schmidt ran to his tank with Schreiber close behind. As Schmidt got in, Schreiber surveyed the approaching tanks again. He spotted what he was looking for, the antennae of a commander's tank. Knock it out and they might have a chance. He reached into the turret and pulled on Schmidt. "There's your first target at the rear."

Schmidt did not need to be told a second time. The turret of the tiger swung, and the 88mm gun lowered. Seconds later, a high-pitched blast was followed by a spectacular explosion at the rear of the approaching Russians. A second shot from the second panzer disabled the lead T-34. The remaining Russians stalled as they were now leaderless and as usual lost initiative. Two more blasts from the German side signaled the end of two more tanks, and the remaining T-34s withdrew.

"That should teach them a lesson!" Schmidt emerged from his tank exultant.

"Well done, Schmidt. However, before you break your arm patting yourself on the back, there are more of them, and they do have artillery. We need to get out of here before they shell us and send in infantry and armor. We won't be so lucky next time."

"I agree. We'll move out immediately."

Within minutes, the combined force was lumbering west. Everyone kept a watch on the sky. No one wanted to be on the receiving end of a fighter-bomber attack as they realized their little convoy would make a tempting target. After they withdrew, tremendous hunks of earth and snow were thrown up from their previous position. Schreiber and Schmidt looked back in awe at the results of the bombardment. Each trembled with the knowledge that they had escaped death by minutes, if not seconds.

"That was close," Schmidt muttered.

"Too close. I hope we are not too far from our side. Otherwise, we will have another fight on our hands when they catch up with us." Schreiber lit a cigarette. There have been too many close calls the last few days. He inhaled deeply as he needed to relieve his anxiety. Hopefully, this will end soon.

CHAPTER 3

The shaken men continued for a few more kilometers, with no further signs of Ivan. The jagdpanther led the way. A machine gun had been mounted on top of it. Schreiber was breathing easier when two figures appeared on the road. Schreiber saw the gorgets around their necks and recognized them immediately as feldgendarmeries. The field police were feared throughout the Wehrmacht as any soldier suspected of desertion or cowardice would be summarily executed by the military police. Schreiber had come across several high-ranking officers who had been dispatched on the Eastern Front by the police because they had no good explanation for heading to the rear. The jadgpanther slowed as the two military police blocked the road.

"Headhunters," Schreiber warned the men around him. "Be careful."

"Where are you from? What's your unit?" The pompous NCO who had planted himself in front of the tank seemed to be asking for trouble.

Schreiber jumped down and approached the two headhunters. His collar was open to show his Knights Cross and rank. He stopped in front of the arrogant NCO. The man repeated his question.

"Haupsturmfuehrer Schreiber. I am leading the remains of Task

Force East back to our lines. I brought along two panzers that were up the road about ten kilometers. We just outran a Russian column that will be here in the next thirty minutes. So if you want to be able to defend yourself, you just might ask us to stay and fight."

"I have to make sure that every man is fighting," the headhunter bleated back. "We're forming a battle group. We can't have men shirking when everyone is needed here at the front."

"Of course not. By the way, feldwebel, is not a salute customary for an officer wearing the Ritterkreuz even if he is Waffen-SS?"

The NCO stiffened to attention. Schreiber started to feel uneasy. He looked for tracks leading into the woods and wondered if there others around. Only months before, German Communists fighting for Russia had made the mistake of trying to apprehend some Brandenburgers. The renegade Germans had worn feldgendarmeries' uniforms. Unfortunately, they had worn some German decorations in the wrong place and had ended up dead. However, the incident provided the seed for Skorzeny's more recent adventure in the Ardennes. Schreiber wondered if the man in front of him was another renegade. It certainly would serve as a good excuse to shoot him if he did not back down.

The appearance of a white kubelwagen saved Schreiber any further trouble. It stopped in front of him, and out stepped a genuine army colonel. The colonel approached Schreiber while ignoring the other men around. He had the air of an aristocrat and appeared calm and collected. He was obviously interested in the two tanks.

"Haupsturmfueher Schreiber reporting. My men and I are what's left of Task Force East. We broke out of Hohensalza a few days ago. I came across Leutnant Schmidt's panzers and felt he could be better used somewhere else. We just broke contact with a Soviet tank regiment minutes ago." It seemed to Schreiber that the colonel had paid little attention to his words. The man was more interested in the tanks. *He probably doesn't have any as everyone has lost heavily. The man is forming a battle group with God knows what. He's desperate for anything, and then we show up.*

The colonel confirmed his thoughts and had showed he missed

none of Schreiber's words, "Hohensalza, that's quite a feat considering our current situation. However, you can tell me about you're little adventure story later. You know the Russians are coming right at me. Frankly, I do not have much to hold them back with. Now that you have showed up, I may have a chance. You are the only panzers I have along with a battery of 88s and some 75s as well. It's not the best of circumstances, but we need to hold here to buy some time. More defenses are being set up behind us. Are you up to it?"

"We are German soldiers. We'll do our duty."

"Good. Come get in the kubelwagen with me, and I'll show you where I want you. By the way, did you see many Stalin tanks in the forces that attacked you this morning?"

"None in that one. However, we passed several headed this way as we were making our way to our lines. We saw column after column of tanks headed west. It will get desperate, I'm afraid."

"I'm afraid you're right. But we must do what we can do for the others, if not ourselves. By the way, I do not believe that I have properly introduced myself to you. I am Colonel Weiss, and I have been charged with forming a battle group here to delay the Soviet advance on the Oder. I have to admit I was shocked and relieved to see you arrive. I have been praying for some panzers to come my way."

"Perhaps you should quit praying so hard. There are more on the way, just not from our side."

Colonel Weiss laughed. "I know. I was expecting them last night. Well, we are here."

The kubelwagen screeched to halt on the snow. The two officers stepped back out into the cold. Schreiber looked at his surroundings. An 88 battery was on a small dominating hill. The road itself ran under a small bridge. Machine-gun nests had been placed at each end of the bridge. Schreiber immediately had an idea for his troops' deployment.

Weiss pointed out the defensive features. Schreiber interrupted Weiss before he could assign Schreiber to his position. "Herr Oberst, if we place the two panzers under the bridge, we can catch the Russians in a crossfire. In addition, if one of our panzers is knocked out, it will block the road. Our infantry will dig in front to protect against their infantry."

Weiss nodded in agreement. "I see you know your job. Remember one thing. No retreat unless I order it. Good luck, Haupsturmfuehrer."

Weiss departed and left Schreiber in charge. Soon the two panzers were in position under the bridge. The infantry attacked the frozen earth with their entrenching tools to make foxholes. The Russian machine guns were unloaded and positioned. Schreiber sent some men with machine gun crews to protect the battery of 88s. Although his location was not ideal, Schreiber's position would be a tough nut to crack. His position was hard to hit from the air and ground. Attacking infantry would be shot to pieces, while the Russian armor would be caught in crossfire from the front and side. Unlike the breakout from Hohensalza, Schreiber would have the Russians between two fists for a while. He only wished that the men could build better positions in the frozen earth.

Schreiber's men had finished none too soon. Shortly before noon, the Russians sent a probing action to investigate. Schreiber's men waited anxiously as six T–34s approached without infantry. The tiger could take on all six with virtual impunity. Schreiber ordered the 88 battery to hold its fire, as there was no reason to give its position away this early in the fight. He watched until the lead T–34 paused. The turret began to swivel. Schreiber ordered Schmidt to fire. The lead tank erupted into a spectacular sheet of flame. The next T–34 in line tried to go around the blazing hulk and was disposed of by the jadgpanther. The third tank tried to pass on the other side and was reduced to scrap by the tiger. The remaining tanks attempted to withdraw. Initially, the smoke hid them from Schreiber's view. However, their withdrawal cost them the cover of the smoke, and each was knocked out in rapid succession,

Following the short skirmish, Schmidt exuberantly emerged from his tank. "That will teach Ivan to follow too closely." He paused to catch his breath. "They didn't even get off a shot. That was too easy."

"It was too easy," Schreiber replied evenly. "I didn't want them to fire. Next time, it will be different. They know we are here now. There will be a lot more of them the next time. And it won't be tomorrow." Schreiber lifted his field glasses. "This was easy this time, if they would give us a break."

The Russians came back quicker than expected and sooner than anyone on the German side cared for them too. Schreiber quit counting the string of tanks after he reached twenty. Things would heat up now as the Russians had IS2s along with T-34s. Schreiber grimaced as he spotted the larger tanks. Schmidt could not let them get as close as the T-34s. In fact, he had to shoot and hit first. Schreiber looked desperately for the command tank. If they didn't knock it out, the Russians might very well break through. Schreiber was also concerned that the Russians were sending their second rate troops in with such force. As he was wondering what the main attack would be like, he spotted the commanders tank in the middle of the column. It was also a Stalin tank.

Schreiber and Schmidt watched as the column headed their way. So far, the Russians had no idea that 88s were on their flank. If they could get the commander's tank, the attack could be broken, and Schmidt could have another thirty minutes of target practice. The converse was if the Russians knew what they were doing, they could sweep past Schreiber and the 88s. Schmidt looked up, anxiously awaiting the order to fire.

Schreiber noticed the two panzer crackers nearby. "Don't either of you start playing hero today. You're my fire brigade now. It's up to you to stop any breakthroughs." He turned to Schmidt. "I'll keep a watch for the Stalins. You see the commander's tank? Good. Remember, he and the other Stalins are looking for you. You've got to get the first shot in. Got it? Then fire when ready."

The 88 of the tiger coughed first followed by the jadgpanther's. Two explosions indicated success. The column was just starting around the wrecked T-34s when the action started. The lead T-34 was hit at the junction of the turret and hull. The explosion flipped the turret into the air and halted the tank. Targets were difficult to see from the smoke. It was time for the 88s to join in.

Although he could not see the results, the flames and explosions indicated that the 88s were finding their targets. No additional tanks were attempting to pass. However, infantry was spotted moving up the slope to assault the guns. Schreiber ordered Schmidt to move the tiger out and attack the infantry.

Schmidt was only too happy to oblige. The tiger moved forward with a crash. As Schreiber had feared, the T-34s were joining the assault against the 88s. Schmidt started picking off the T-34s as fast as he could. Schreiber was leading the infantry alongside the tiger when a large ping rang out. A T-34 hidden among the burning wrecks had fired into the tiger's turret. One of the panzer crackers converted the Russian tank into scrap with a shot from a panzerfaust. The dented tiger continued to advance.

The full brunt of the attack was being directed against the hill. The crews were firing as rapidly as possible. Some shells had fallen among the guns and inflicted numerous casualties. The machine guns had scythed down the attacking infantry. Schmidt was near the hill when Schreiber spotted more tanks heading toward them.

"Head toward them!" Schreiber yelled at Schmidt. "We'll take care of the hill."

Schmidt hurriedly turned his tank. If he was to survive, he needed his tank to meet the enemy head on with his strongest armor out front. It was a desperate bid, but if Schmidt could hold off the tanks and Schreiber save the hill, they might hold out. While Schreiber's men took care of the Russian infantry and knocked out the T-34s on the hill with Teller mines, Schmidt got the fight he had been looking for.

Schmidt focused on the command tank. He found it and knocked it out as it was preparing to fire. He proceeded to wreck havoc on the rest of the column. A shot hit a T-34, and nothing happened. The tank beside it exploded. Schmidt realized his shell had passed clean through the first tank and then fired into the turret. Schmidt then led his tank down the column to finish off any stragglers.

The Russians had enough. Schreiber's men broke the attack just meters outside the gun emplacement. The remaining tanks withdrew. Schreiber ordered a squad of men to join him and provide cover for Schmidt's tank. The moans of the Russian wounded rang in their ears as they passed over the killing ground. They stepped over blistering wreckage of war that had fallen in the snow and sizzled. The road was strewn with parts of tanks and bodies. The heat from the burning tanks contrasted sharply with the bitter winter cold. Several bodies lie alongside the tanks and roasted from the heat. A ghastly smelled of roasting human flesh irritated Schreiber's nostrils. Other bodies had been horribly dismembered. One figure had been bisected at the waist, with the two halves at ninety degrees to each other. Schreiber thought the color would have been pretty under other circumstances. Another, an officer, had been eviscerated and survived the initial injury. He had committed suicide judging by the pistol, hand position, and bullet hole in the head.

The squad came across a wounded Russian propped up against a smoldering tank. His left leg had been shattered below the knee. He was desperately trying to stop the flow of blood when Schreiber's men showed up. His rifle was several feet away, and he was completely defenseless.

His fear subsided when one of the SS troopers offered him a cigarette. Schreiber looked at the leg and ordered it bandaged. One of the troopers knelt down and cut open the trouser leg with his knife. A bandage and tourniquet stopped the flow of blood.

"Does it hurt?" Schreiber asked the wounded man.

"Nyet. Only numb," the Russian replied.

The man's cigarette died out. Schreiber offered him another one. "Consider yourself lucky. We're not the butchers you think we are."

"If I survive the next attack, I'll be lucky." The Russian took a deep breath. "A whole tank regiment is behind this one. There's a lot of artillery as well."

Schreiber thought about what the man had told them. The injured man might be bluffing, but Schreiber felt the man was telling the truth. Schreiber turned to a runner. "Find Oberst Weiss and tell him another armored regiment is preparing to attack. I request reinforcements." Schreiber stood outlined against the flaming carnage. Another push by Ivan was destined to succeed. The last attack had hurt him badly as it cost him half the guns and their crews. He gritted his teeth as he thought about the upcoming attack.

"Move the Russian out of the way. Find somewhere to hide him." Four of Schreiber's men carried the Russian off the road into the woods opposite the gun emplacement. He was placed in a small depression out of the line of fire. Schreiber went back up the hill and rounded up the ground crews, while Schmidt hid his tiger among the burning Russian tanks. Schreiber wanted the men busy so they would get over their shell shock. Empty shell casings and bodies were moved out of the way. Shells were moved from damaged gun positions and stacked by undamaged guns.

Schreiber had just reorganizing his defenses when someone called out, "They're coming again." Schreiber looked at the road and noticed a smudge in the distance. Schreiber raised his field glasses and discovered it was an IS2 with several others behind it. Obviously, Ivan was not calling it a day.

"Steady," Schreiber called out. He said it as much to calm himself as his men. He watched as the steel giants advanced up the road into range of the German guns.

"They're in range," a voice called out.

Schreiber looked for a command tank but did not see one. Finally, he ordered, "Pour it into them."

The lead tank went up in a sheet of flames. The next two tanks were soon engulfed in smoke. The other tanks spread out looking for their tormentors. As the lead tanks advanced up the hill, Schmidt went into action again. The Russians were caught in crossfire once more, but their superior numbers began to prevail along with some other help. Geysers of snow and earth were thrown up. Schreiber realized they were under artillery fire.

"Get back to the bridge!" Schreiber shouted. "That's artillery fire."

The survivors abandoned their position as the Russian artillery found its mark. Ground-attack aircraft joined in. Several explosions jolted Schreiber as the ammunition exploded on the hill from direct hits. The battery would torment the Russians no more. Schreiber continued sliding and crawling until he reached Schmidt's tank with a handful of survivors.

"The battery's gone. Pull back to the bridge," Schreiber ordered Schmidt.

Schmidt retreated slowly, still picking off advancing tanks. The sun was at his back now and made him harder to see. However, several of the IS2s had overrun the destroyed battery and were disappearing from view.

"They're going to encircle us. Let the other crew know,' Schreiber barked at Schmidt.

The tiger continued its withdrawal. As they neared the bridge, the jagdpanther had maneuvered into position to meet the expected attack. Schreiber briefly saw what appeared to be a commander's tank ascend the hill and disappear. He cursed silently at the missed opportunity. After what seemed an hour, the tiger reached the bridge.

Schmidt placed his tank at an angle so that he would receive glancing blows if fired on from the flanking attempt or an assault from the road. He had just positioned himself when the Russians crested a ridge parallel to the road. The weak underside of the T-34s presented targets that the Germans couldn't resist. The two German tanks along with the panzer crackers stopped the first wave of tanks with a volley that literally blew the tanks apart. The ammunition in each of the tanks exploded in massive fireballs. Three of the flaming hulks rolled down the hill. Some more T-34s appeared and were easily dealt with. Schmidt's tiger had shown that it was still king of the jungle as he vanquished a total of five attacking tanks.

The battle between the tanks died down as several explosions threw debris around the bridge. Several soldiers in the open were injured as metal fell on them. The two panzers repositioned themselves for another attack. Schreiber was numb from the tremendous concussions produced by the exploding tanks. As he lifted himself up, he watched a machine-gun nest by the bridge disappear in an explosion. If the Russians press home, their attack now we're done for, Schreiber thought.

A lull settled over the battlefield after the machine-gun nest was blown up. Schreiber ran to Schmidt's tank. He staggered over the frozen ground perplexed by the lack of a Russian attack. Schmidt stuck his head out of the turret. He had a headache from the shells that hit his tank and failed to penetrate. Both men looked at each other amazed that they were still alive.

"Pull back. I don't know why Ivan isn't hitting us now. He probably isn't coordinated. I won't stay and find out." Schreiber called his radioman over, "Contact Oberst Weiss and inform him we are withdrawing. Ask for a new position."

Schreiber rubbed his hands. His breath formed clouds in the frigid air. His heart was pounding from the ordeal he had just gone through. Now he expected worse from Colonel Weiss, probably a good chewing out and relieved of command, at worse a meeting with the field police after a summary court-martial. The look on the radioman's face was not good, and Schreiber prepared for the worse.

"It's bad. Tanks are overrunning Weiss. They're being obliterated, not breaking. He can give you no orders. You're on your own."

Schreiber swallowed hard. A chewing out would have been preferable to this news. His voice remained calm as he ordered, "Continue the withdrawal. We can expect no support from the others."

The battered survivors gathered up the wounded and put them in the two trucks not destroyed in the shelling. The able-bodied men climbed on the panzers or clung to the outside of the trucks. A light snowfall covered their retreat. As they did so, the Russians renewed their assault on the bridge. Artillery plastered the area initially. Then more tanks showed up at Schreiber's former position. An eerie glow in the gray sky illuminated the scene around the bridge. Schreiber hoped the Russians would stop for now.

"Hold your fire," he told Schmidt as he brought up the ear of the column. "I would like to avoid further action, if possible. How much ammunition do you have left?"

Schmidt shook his head. "Not much. I can't last through another fight like today."

"What I thought. Keep moving. We'll set up a roadblock three kilometers down the road and gather up any survivors."

The soldiers continued their miserable retreat. They silently walked past the fallen forms of their comrades. Most had been frozen in grotesque positions. The fact that they were unable to give their fallen comrades a decent burial added to the survivors' melancholy. Schreiber tried to ignore the shapes on the ground. At times, he closed his eyes. Nothing could remove the horror of the scene.

"Keep a watch for Ivan. If he catches up with us, we've had it." Schreiber spoke as much to distract his own mind as for their benefit.

Out of the falling snow appeared two figures. It was the panzer crackers.

"Where in the hell have you been?" Schreiber irritably asked.

"We took out the command tank at the bridge. We figured that would give us our best chance for escape."

Schreiber clapped each man wearily on the shoulder. "No more heroics today, you two. I need you alive for another day. Get on one of the panzers. How many rockets have you got left?"

"None."

Schreiber cursed silently. He was already down to five panzerfausts and needed to put some distance between the Russians and his men tonight. He marched them for three kilometers and set up a roadblock. He sent the wounded and the jagdpanther on ahead. Meanwhile, the explosions became more distant, but they served to remind the retreating soldiers that they were still in harm's reach. After the wounded left, survivors started arriving. Schreiber was determined to take anyone out who had survived this witch's cauldron. Unfortunately, no one knew what had happened to Colonel Weiss. Schreiber gleaned from the survivors that another armored regiment with plenty of infantry support had hit their sector as well. The initial assault was thrown back with difficulty. However, the worst was yet to come. Two armored regiments attacked next and cracked the German nut. The Soviet juggernaut had rolled over the Germans with ease. Fighting had been reduced to hand-to-hand combat. Schreiber noted that many of the survivors and their entrenching tools were covered with blood. The withdrawal did not have time to become a rout as the Russians' main force bypassed the small pockets of resistance and inflicted too many casualties. An easy mopping up was virtually assured for the Russians. Weiss had last been seen manning a machine gun next to a 75mm as a group of T-34s approached. He had ordered several of the survivors to leave while he and the gun crew held off the Russians.

Schreiber decided to move his survivors another kilometer. He did not want to find himself surrounded by a ring of Russian steel in the morning. An occasional burp from an MG 43 indicated that the Russians had stumbled onto some survivors. Schreiber wondered if it was the same gun firing. He crossed his fingers, hoping that the survivors would find their way back. He looked back at the glow where he had fought. Hopefully, no one would head that direction for salvation.

An hour later, Schreiber was preparing to leave when two figures appeared out of the darkness. Their presence was quite unexpected at this time. The sentry lowered his weapon, while Schreiber prepared for action.

"Halt!" Everyone tensed for action. The sentry nervously fingered the trigger.

"Can't a German officer at least be allowed to rejoin his own men?"

Schreiber stepped forward. It was incredible but true. Colonel Weiss had survived and brought one of his men along with him. Schreiber came to attention. "Mein Gott, Herr Oberst. How did you get out?"

"Barely," the taciturn Weiss replied. "There were just too many of them. I was knocked out next to a 75. This fellow pulled me away just before their tanks overran our position. We heard Russians all around us. We had to crawl several times to avoid their patrols. I'm sure we're the last ones out." Weiss was weary. "I see that you made it."

"We got out with both of the panzers. Good thing we had them, or we would not be having this conversation."

"We would be dead or enjoying Stalin's hospitality in Siberia." Weiss stared at the tiger. "Thank you again. We still have a chance."

"The MG 43 we heard?"

"I heard it too," Weiss sadly replied. "I haven't heard it for several minutes."

Schreiber swallowed. "Herr Oberst, if you will lead the men, I'll form a rearguard for us."

"Don't stay behind too long, Schreiber, We need the tiger."

After two hours, no more survivors appeared. Schreiber had dozed off on top of the tiger. Ivan did not appear to want to press his luck in a night engagement. One of his men shook him awake.

"Herr Hauptman, we have been here two hours. No one else has shown up."

Schreiber shook himself awake. The last few days had drained him. One of his soldiers steadied him, while he walked around. He needed to get the circulation going in his legs.

"Get moving," he ordered. "It will be easier to move tonight than tomorrow with Ivan's help." Schreiber was as alert as he was going to be.

Two hours later, Schreiber caught up with Weiss. Over the next two days, they retreated toward Czarnkow. During the day, they hid in the forest. An occasional Russian reconnaissance unit would drive by. No other German forces were encountered during this time. When they reached Czarnkow, the Russians were already entrenched. Colonel Weiss led the group around the town. Additional survivors from other smashed units were picked around the town. The trek seemed like it would never end.

At the end of two weeks, the battered group seemed no closer to German lines. By now, they had crossed the old Polish border. The group was settling down for the night when the western sky lit up from the flashed of artillery. Everyone gazed up at the sky with the same thought: the front must be close by.

Schreiber went to Colonel Weiss. "What do you think?"

Weiss looked up at the sky. "We are close. That is for sure. The question is do we try to breakthrough tonight? The men are so tired.

However, night is our best cover." Weiss rubbed the stubble on his chin. They were tantalizingly close now. Finally, he decided. "Have the men rest for two hours. Then we'll try to cross over."

Two hours later, the remnants of Task Force East and Battle Group Weiss were assembled. Few had rested in anticipation of breaking out and reaching friendly lines. Schreiber assembled his men. Tonight they would be marching to the sound of the guns. Weiss also checked the troops. He stopped and chatted occasionally to encourage the men. Several of Schreiber's men were thanked for their recent efforts. He finally made his way to Schreiber to confer before departing.

"This is it, Haupsturmfuehrer. We must make our supreme effort tonight to reach our lines."

Schreiber nodded in acknowledgement. "I suggest that my men go in front. They are good at this sort of thing."

"So I have noticed. Lead the way, Schreiber."

Schreiber conferred with Schmidt and ordered to have the panzers keep their distance, while Schreiber's men looked for Russian positions. Then the point men were sent out. An hour later, the point men motioned for silence. There was no question that the enemy had been detected. Schreiber went forward to investigate. Several loud booms suggested that they were near a Soviet artillery position. Schreiber looked the area over carefully. His binoculars froze his skin when he placed them to his face. He swiftly developed a plan, as it was apparent that the Russian position was newly established, with only sporadic firing occurring.

"We are going to demolish this position. If we leave it behind, it could cause us trouble later if they figure out who we are." Schreiber gathered his men together and gave them his plan. Schmidt was ordered to stay in the rear until he was needed. Schreiber then led his men behind the position. The sentries were dealt with first with daggers. Then when an artillery piece fired, Schreiber's men fired on the crew of an individual gun. The survivors realized something was wrong after a few volleys, and Schreiber decided it was time to bring things to a close. He led his men forward in a viscous charge that overwhelmed remaining gun crews. No quarter was asked or given in the ensuing brutal hand-to-hand combat. Schreiber charged a commissar and split the man's head open with his entrenching tool. The area was combed for survivors, and thermite grenades were used to disable the large-caliber guns.

Schreiber's men renewed their advance. The night continued to light up from the flashes of the artillery. An hour passed, and the flashes revealed some parked T-34s. Schreiber approached the tanks first since he spoke Russian. Schmidt was asked to come up quickly in case things got out of hand. Further flashes showed there were six tanks.

The Russians were not expecting an attack from the rear. Schreiber's patrol was alongside the stalled tanks before they were noticed. A sentry challenged them. Schreiber calmly asked then why they were stalled and lax with their security. The guard was flustered by Schreiber's question and stammered for a response. Meanwhile, other Russians gathered to enjoy their comrade's discomfort while Schreiber's men got in firing position. As the Russians started to laugh, Schreiber leveled his submachine gun and sprayed the tight group of Russians. As they were falling, the tanks were rushed, and grenades were thrown through the open hatches. Minutes later, the area was alight from the blazing hulks.

Schreiber's men continued their advance. The men under Weiss followed close behind. Schreiber wanted to get away from the burning tanks before they attracted attention from either side. Soon there were no other signs of life. They took a narrow road surrounded by forest. They reached a clearing after several minutes. Schreiber had his men slow down, as they would be perfect targets for anyone in the woods. He led his men into the tree line. One of his men took the point. After several meters, the man halted. Schreiber raised his field glasses. He thought he saw ghostly figures moving about. Probably someone in snow camouflage was over there. But he didn't know whose side. He had a runner go summon Schmidt up. Just in case Ivan was around, he might need to have the woods shelled.

Schreiber felt a chill run through him, and it wasn't from the cold. He had that feeling when he had hunted down partisans. He had to do something to clarify the situation. A tune came to his head. He approached the area he spotted the figures moving and started whistling "I Had a Comrade."

"Halt. Identify yourself."

Schreiber froze. Normally, it was good to hear German, but he realized any wrong move could be his last. In fact, he didn't have to make a wrong move. Hopefully, the man watching him wasn't too trigger-happy.

"Hold your fire. I am a German officer. I have a company of men coming down the road trying to get away from Ivan. I have two panzers, including a tiger."

Two men approached Schreiber and disarmed him. He was escorted to a cleverly hidden bunker. He walked down some crude steps into the interior. An oberleutnant was on the telephone. He hung the telephone up and approached Schreiber. He came to attention at the sight of the rank and decoration around the neck.

"Oberleutnant Meier at your service. This is quite a surprise. Where did you come from?"

"Hell, that's where."

Meier did not pursue the question. "I understand you have others."

"About a company and two panzers, including a king tiger."

Meier's eyes lit up at the sound of the tanks. "We could use some tanks. Meanwhile, we'll get your men safely through."

Schreiber sat in the bunker. He had done it. The men of Task Force East who had survived their terrible ordeal were home. Meier got on the telephone and contacted his superiors. Minutes later, Colonel Weiss appeared in the bunker. Meier was off the telephone briefly before it rang. Division headquarters was on the phone again. They were definitely interested in their visitors. Meier mentioned Weiss as the commander. He was also instructed to employ the two panzers as he saw fit.

"Jawohl." Meier hung the phone up for good. "Meine Herren, headquarters would like to talk to you about the Russian strength.

They still don't have a clear idea about what's in front of us. One of my men will take you there."

They followed a lance corporal who led them to the rear. They entered a much larger bunker and were put in a corner. Schreiber rubbed his hands to warm them.

"Are you cold?" Weiss asked.

"Aren't you?"

"We all are, I believe." The third voice was unexpected.

Schreiber and Weiss turned and found themselves face to face with a major general. They came to attention immediately. The general walked over to Weiss and shook his hand vigorously. They obviously knew each other.

"How long has it been? Two years?" he asked Weiss.

"A little less. We were last together on the Kuban peninsula."

"That long? Well, it's good to see you alive and well. We'll have to talk about what you have been doing since."

"Mainly staying alive, Herr General."

The general laughed at that. Then in a more serious tone, he said, "I do want to know about what you saw when you came through the lines. We get very little from the Luftwaffe anymore, and the last few days have been very chaotic in the least anyway." He walked over to a map hanging on the wall.

Weiss pointed out the route they had taken and what they had seen. Schreiber gave details of his observations before he met up with Weiss. It was all a very grim picture for the general. Weiss concluded, "I might add that we would not have made it without the timely arrival of Hauptsturmfuehrer Schreiber here. He and his men kept us from being completely encircled. In addition, they led the way through Russian lines. I might add that he was in the Brandenburg Division before joining the Waffen-SS." Weiss then supplied details of Schreiber's action at the bridge.

Schreiber blushed as Weiss recounted his exploits. The general spoke to conclude the night's business. "The Brandenburg Division, eh, a fine group of men. I see you have lived up to their reputation. Oberst Weiss, I want a full report. If this is true, I am personally recommending you for the oak leaves to the Ritterkreuz." A thoughtful look crossed the general's face. "I have not been a good host. I think we should have a drink to celebrate your safe return to our lines." He went to his desk and produced a bottle of wine. "This is the last of this, I believe, but it is very excellent. Like you, gentlemen, save the best for the last."

Schreiber's throat burned as he swallowed. It's more like the last of the best as he thought about his men. There were fifteen survivors from Task Force East with him out of the eight hundred who set out over two weeks ago. *They were definitely the last of the best,* he thought bitterly.

CHAPTER 4

After Bauer's first run in with the Russians at Bad Schonfliess, Skorzeny decided to be more aggressive. Right now, time was both his best friend and worst enemy. If he could buy some more time with delaying tactics, then time would be his good friend. He decided to make time his friend. The following day, Skorzeny sent Bauer back to Bad Schonfliess. This time, he brought a 75mm antitank gun in anticipation of meeting more armor. They passed by the wreckage from the previous day. Bauer was surprised to see no Russian forces in the town. The previous day's action had probably made the Soviets leery. The vehicles moved around the tangled forms on the ground that had been Soviet infantry and the burned out tanks that served as silent sentinels to the carnage. A light coating of snow gave a deceptively peaceful atmosphere to the place. The team proceeded east to look for Ivan. He would not give up that easily.

They found him a few kilometers east of the town. As many as twenty tanks were stopped. The 75 was wheeled around, and several shots fired into the tanks as mortar shells dropped to deal with any infantry. Bauer left before the Russians had time to locate his men. Although he was unsure of Russian losses, the event would remind the Soviets that the Germans still had some teeth in this region.

The following day, three teams were sent out to harass the Russians. Each force would draw blood that day. Every team came across Soviet advance columns. Fierce engagements followed each encounter. Sniper teams accompanied each team and claimed several Red Army officers. Every team also fired several rounds deep into Russian territory to give the impression that there were artillery batteries in the area to deal with. Each team would suffer several wounded as well.

On February 4th, the patrols went out again. This time, Ivan was expecting them, and the engagements were fiercer. The 75s could not be used up close this day. In addition, the patrols ran up against the armored might of the Soviet army as it advanced on Bad Schonfliess. Disengagement was carried out with difficulty as the superior Russian forces tried to overwhelm and surround each team. Skorzeny suffered additional fatalities this day.

The following day, the town of Bad Schonfliess was attacked. Patrols were unable to pass east of the town. Each team ran into a wall of steel. Skorzeny decided it was time to take a look at the situation himself.

The Russians had occupied the southern and eastern sectors of the city. Skorzeny entered the city from the west. Several seasoned veterans accompanied him, including some who had been with him at the Gran Sasso. A SDK 222 led the way since its 20mm gun could suppress any infantry that ventured in its range. Skorzeny followed in a kubelwagen with four men. An SdKF259 half-track with a dozen troops brought up the rear. Hopefully, the group could break and run if a fight developed.

Skorzeny was aware of the risk he was taking. However, he believed there was no substitute for leading from the front and not from behind a desk like Himmler. Only a year before, when he had been hot on the trail of Marshal Tito, Skorzeny had driven through partisan-held territory from Belgrade to an outpost in Zagreb. A few suspicious individuals had been encountered along the way. The local German commander was apoplectic when he learned of Skorzeny's trip. He informed Skorzeny that he and his two fellow officers were lucky not to have been killed or captured by Tito's men. Himmler later excoriated Skorzeny for his risk taking when he learned of the adventure. "A fine headline for the *London Times*. Skorzeny captured, and by the man you are supposed to capture. What would I tell the Fuehrer? You know the high regard he holds you in. This must never happen again."

Himmler's ranting left Skorzeny unmoved. All soldiers take risks, and Skorzeny had a convenient lapse of memory this day. He realized that Himmler's concerns were legitimate. Just last week, Oberfuehrer Herbert von Obwurzer had disappeared with his staff in West Prussia while inspecting the Fifteenth Waffen-SS Grenadier Division. He presumably ran into strong Soviet forces in Nakel. Skorzeny suspected he had been killed, as most officers in his position would have fought back. After all, every senior SS officer remembered what happened to Artur Phleps. Phleps had been the foremost mountain warfare expert in Europe and probably the world. The man had a distinguished career that had begun in the Austria-Hungarian Army. Following the empire's breakup after World War I, he had joined the Rumanian Army. After retirement, he was recruited into the Waffen-SS and distinguished himself again. Eventually, he became a full general in the Waffen-SS and was awarded the oak leaves to the Knights Cross. Phleps was not one to rest on his laurels and continued to lead from the front. His luck ran out on September 18, 1944, when he ran into Russians with his aide and driver. Three days later, the men were placed in front of a Soviet firing quad and executed. Skorzeny had no idea of how Phleps was abused prior to execution, but he vowed to never be taken alive and share Phleps's fate. He still was going to lead from the front.

As Skorzeny contemplated the fate of the two men, Bad Schonfliess came into sight. The convoy halted, and the infantrymen disembarked to begin their scouting. The gunner in the SDK 222 kept them covered as they patrolled the deserted streets. The town was eerily quiet, and the feeling was punctuated by the absence of any other signs of life. It was almost too quiet, but no shots were fired at them. They came across two civilians who had been shot and left in the road. The gray sky added a solemn feeling to the sortie as they pressed onward.

Finally, a civilian came out of one of the buildings. He was dressed in a worn overcoat and stared at Skorzeny and his men as if they were ghosts. "Are you really German soldiers?" he asked incredulously.

"Very much so," Skorzeny replied. "Actually, I'm Austrian though."

"I can't believe it," the old man exclaimed joyfully. He embraced Skorzeny much to the other soldiers' amusement.

Skorzeny gently tore himself away from the old man's ecstatic embrace. Skorzeny figured he was probably a World War I veteran, given his age. "What can you tell us about the Russians?"

The old man took Skorzeny's arm and led him to an intersection. "The Bolsheviks came in last night. They set up their headquarters at the train station." The old man spat in disgust. "They brought in dozens of tanks and have dug in. They're using the railroad to bring in supplies and troops. They are building up fast."

"Thank you for this information. You're welcome to come back with us when we leave."

"I would just be a hindrance," the old man said sadly. "Try to take some of the women and children before the Russians get hold of them. If this were 1918, it would be a different story. Then I was young and shouldered a rifle. Now I'm plagued with rheumatism and the likes."

"I suspected you had served then."

The old man came alive. "I was one of the ones in the Kriegsmarine who remained loyal and didn't raise the red flag." He spit again in disgust. "After the war, I served in the Freikorps at Munich and drove the red monsters out, that is, those we didn't kill. Now I am at their mercy. Take someone back with you who will be of use to Germany after the war. I won't be if I am still alive. If the Russians shoot me, then it's one less bullet they have to shoot at you with." He turned and shuffled back into his dwelling.

Skorzeny swallowed and motioned for his men to move on. He divided his men into three teams and sent two out, while he led the third to the train station. As they continued, he noticed that no other civilians showed their faces. He moved on, and as they got closer to the train station, a few civilians poked their heads outside their doors. Some came out into the street. His patrol came upon the partially clad figure of a strikingly pretty woman clad only in her blouse. She would have been desirable, except she was dead. "Raped," one of the civilians uttered. Skorzeny shuddered at the horror he felt inside. He maintained his composure and moved on. It was obvious the Soviet occupation was breaking the will of the people.

Finally, he reached the train station. Skorzeny led his men into a building overlooking the station to survey the scene. He looked through his binoculars at the Soviet buildup. He counted at least fifty tanks in the area. Most were the T–34/76 type. Several troops were milling about among the tanks. A large number of rocket launchers were present as well. Skorzeny lowered his binoculars: he had caught a glimpse of the armored fist headed for his bridgehead. He quietly ordered his men back to their vehicles. On the way back, two women and their children joined Skorzeny.

An hour later, Skorzeny's men were all assembled. All teams had confirmed the old man's story. The Red Army was firmly entrenched in the town, and it was obvious its next stop would be Schwedt on the Oder. Skorzeny returned to his headquarters, deep in thought. The Soviets would have to go through Konigsberg first; and, hopefully, they could be delayed there some more.

Once he was back in Schwedt, Skorzeny wasted no time. He ordered a parachute battalion and two volkssturm battalions to Konigsberg immediately. Walther was as efficient as usual, and the units were on their way in the early evening. The same evening, Lieutenant Schwerdt arrived from Friendenthal with a company of armored reconnaissance troops. It was none too soon.

The Russians struck within twenty-four hours with a vengeance. The paratroopers took the brunt of the assault on the east side of the town. The assault was stopped with heavy casualties on both sides. Armed with panzerfausts, the paratroopers forced the Russians back after knocking out over a dozen tanks and killing scores of infantry.

However, the paratroopers were badly mauled because of lack of armored support and had to be withdrawn.

The Russians renewed their assault after dark from the north and south side of the town. Fortunately, the volkssturm battalions had several World War I veterans, and their adhesion allowed them to give ground grudgingly. The units held despite a brief period of panic when the district leader and volkssturm commander ran away. The surviving paratroopers and some former Hamburg dockyard workers in the volkssturm brought the situation under control and held the front together. Skorzeny appreciated the irony of the dockyard workers, most of them former Communists, stopping the Soviet breakthrough.

Despite the incredible bravery of the dockyard workers and paratroopers, the Russian juggernaut was too powerful to resist. Skorzeny reluctantly gave the order to withdraw before his men were trapped by the onslaught. The small town of Nipperwiese was now indefensible, and it was ordered evacuated as well. Skorzeny had no idea how this would haunt him in a few days. However, Skorzeny wanted every man possible in the bridgehead when Ivan came knocking at Schwedt's gates. He knew it would come sooner than he wanted, but he was pleased with what he had accomplished with what he had been given. Schwedt on the Oder was about to begin its ordeal by fire, and Skorzeny felt that they would endure.

CHAPTER 5

The headlights of the black Zik sedan pierced the inky darkness of the Moscow night as it sped toward its destination. Two officers of the NKVD occupied the backseat. General of State Security Pavel Sudoplatov was seated next to his ADC Major Alexi Makarov. Sudoplatov had worked in Soviet intelligence since 1921 when he had been an apprentice to his older brother, a Cheka officer. Makarov had been with Sudoplatov since 1937, except for a brief period when he was investigating a then-obscure general in Siberia named Zhukov. The timing had been fortuitous as little suspicion fell on him during the bloody purges wracking the military and intelligence communities. Sudoplatov reflected how Makarov, a virtual newcomer to the world of espionage, was a prodigy in intelligence work. No detail escaped the man's eye, and he seemed to have an innate ability to distinguish between misinformation and the truth. Makarov produced concise, accurate, and to-the-point assessments devoid of ornamentation designed to enhance his own career. Sudoplatov was pleased to have had such a jewel fall into his lap prior to the outbreak of war. Sometimes he wondered how he had functioned without the man even before he joined Sudoplatov's staff. Thank goodness Makarov was in Siberia when Sudoplatov and everyone around him fell under suspicion and was nearly purged. During the war, Makarov's talents allowed Sudoplatov to concentrate on other areas.

"This is a far cry from three years ago," Sudoplatov ventured.

"Yes, indeed, Comrade General. For a while, we did not know if we would still be in Moscow," Makarov replied.

"Yes, indeed." Sudoplatov remembered how both men had prepared to leave in case the unthinkable happened and Moscow was taken. Boxes of sensitive information were ready to be moved so that the war could be continued. "Now we are at the gates of Berlin."

"The problem is will there be peace after Germany is finished?"

"I don't know. I just don't know," Sudoplatov softly replied.

Nothing more was said since the driver was with them. No one knew who might be working for Beria. Both men were thinking about the difficulties arising with the Western Allies. Already there was conflict in the air between the politicians. There was concern that there would be all-out war after Germany was crushed.

The sedan passed through the Spassky gate. The city was lit up compared with three years ago when darkness pervaded the capital. There had been complete blackout compared with the almost normal life of the city now. The sedan stopped at Ivanovsky Square by the Kremlin. The two men proceeded to the Kremlin for their appointed meeting. They stopped briefly as a guard checked their papers. They went inside and walked up a staircase. Once they arrived on the second floor, they walked down a long hall with thick plush carpet.

"The Scherhorn operation seems to be going well," Sudoplatov stated.

"It seems to be," Makarov replied. "There is no indication that the other side knows that we are playing a double game."

"Scherhorn is still ignorant of his role?"

"So far. He still is in a safe house here in Moscow under heavy guard. He suspects that something is going on, but we'll let him keep guessing. I still hold out hopes of getting Skorzeny, but I doubt that he'll ever be allowed to drop in. That would be too easy."

"We've done well as it is. Well, time for the big meeting. Are you ready?"

"Of course, Comrade General."

Their meeting place was a spacious reception room with three writing tables. Stalin sat behind one desk. Behind him hung a portrait of Lenin. On adjacent walls hung obligatory portraits of Marx and Engles. Stalin exuded confidence this evening. Despite the lateness of the hour, he did not seem to be even tired, although he was known to work long days. An aura of unyielding authority emanated from the man. His power was formidable, and he was a man not to be taken lightly as Trotsky, Tukhachevsky, and finally Hitler had learned. His powers of observation were not to be underestimated, and the two officers tensed as the conference began.

Stalin rose and greeted the two officers warmly as they arrived. He had an indescribable ability to make one feel right at home despite his ruthlessness. Both officers sat down and joined the other attendees. Finally, everyone had arrived, and the conference began.

Stalin opened the meeting. His speech was good-natured although coarse. "Comrades, we are on the threshold of victory. Over the last three and a half years, your tireless efforts have led us to this point. Soon Fascism will be a matter of historical interests only. At least the historians will have something to do when the Great Patriotic War is over." Several attendees chuckled at the last remark. Stalin himself was pleased with the effect he caused; now he became hard and firm, the man of steel. "However, the fighting will not be over when we hoist the Red Banner from the top of the Reichstag. A new war has already been started or renewed. The Western Allies have been double-dealing with the Germans throughout the war. Only by continued diligence and Comrade Beria's efforts have we thwarted peace between them and the Fascists. Otherwise, we would have been facing the invaders alone as many in Washington and London have wished. Comrade Beria will go into details of another threat now facing us from the west."

Stalin sat down. Beria spoke next. He did not have to ask for anyone's attention after Stalin's performance. His speech was harsh at first. "It has been known for some time that the Americans and British have been working on a weapon of mass destruction, an atomic bomb as they call it. In 1940, our scientists considered such a device theoretical. In 1941, our agents noted that the renowned physicists on the Allied side were being recruited for a secret project, among them several Nobel laureates, including Fermi. Also astounding to us was the fact that the Americans were spending 20 percent of their defense research in this area."

The last remark brought a whistle from one of the attendees. Others leaned forward at the mention of such a large number. A murmur arose as the implications started to sink in. "While no specific number of dollars is known, the amount of material that Russia received through lend-lease indicated that this had to be a very large sum of money, evidently, the Americans thought they were onto something."

Beria saw that he had everyone's attention. "Several episodes have confirmed our suspicions. One of our agents contacted Lise Meitner in Sweden, and she confirmed the feasibility of such a device. Another incident reinforced our concerns. When the British attacked the heavy water facility at Vemork, they did so without asking for our cooperation. Previously, they had asked for our aide in all other sabotage operations. Last month, one of our agents procured a copy of the design of the laboratories. We have been involved in a large-scale search for uranium as a result. Comrade Sudoplatov will provide more details on the American facilities."

"Thank you, Comrade Beria." Sudoplatov rose to deliver his information. "Our agents have discovered that the Americans have built tremendous structures to develop this new weapon. Under Comrade Major Makarov's direction, we have pieced together the details of this program. The Manhattan Project, as it is known, is a massive research program with unparallel funding. The man in charge, a general named Leslie Groves, oversees 130,000 workers at the Oak Ridge Plant alone, and there are several others. In addition, he has received over two billion dollars to develop the bomb."

Several gasped at the incredible number. Again, a murmur went up around the room. The impact was being made.

"Please continue, Comrade." Beria's voice was harsh. "We do not want to be here all night." The silence was immediate.

"The Oak Ridge facility is known as Camp 1. Camp 2 is located at Los Alamos, New Mexico. It is very isolated and is ideal for testing such a destructive weapon Security is tight, and access is highly restricted." Sudoplatov continued on for a few more minutes and sat down.

Stalin stood up thoughtfully puffing on his pipe. He had absorbed every word. He reiterated much of what he had said earlier. "The fighting that has nearly destroyed the motherland is almost over. You know what Russia has endured. However, I must be plain. Another war is beginning." Stalin stopped to gaze in the face of every man present. "We will have a victory march in Berlin. Our threat from there will be ended. The next war will not be with Japan. We will eventually enter it to reclaim some territory, but they are no threat as Marshal Zhukov demonstrated in 1938. Our war with the west has begun even while we are allied with them. This is an ideological war for now. That may change since we have not been invited to help in the development of this new device. There can only be one conclusion, Comrades. Russia will be its target once the Fascists are defeated. Comrade Sudoplatov, you are to be commended for your achievements. Comrade Beria has kept me informed of all of your developments. I expect more results in this area. All of the resources of the state will be at your disposal."

Beria then interjected with remarks about rounding up the German scientists involved in rocket and nuclear research. He mentioned that long-range rockets such as the V–2 might be useful in delivering a nuclear weapon. Stalin nodded his head in agreement. He enjoyed watching his satraps working so hard to please him and solve a problem of the utmost importance to him. The more successful they were, the more secure his position became.

Finally, Stalin adjourned the meeting shortly before midnight. Stalin shook hands with everyone as they departed. He expressed genuine thanks and gratitude to everyone as the left. He held Sudoplatov and Makarov back for special thanks for their dedication and sacrifice. He dismissed the two with a mention that he would personally be overseeing their work because it was so vital.

The two officers walked back down the stairs to their waiting car. They sat in the backseat, and the driver sped out the Kremlin gates.

"The boss seemed pleased tonight," Makarov said with a tired voice.

"Yes, he did, but there is so much left to do. Just when we thought we were near the end, we find ourselves behind," Sudoplatov replied wearily.

"We are working on it."

"I know. You've done well. Everyone knows that. We don't have to go through 1941 again." Sudoplatov decided to change the conversation. He was ready to leave work behind. "Let me have the driver drop you off at the apartment. I'll have you picked up in the morning."

"It's no trouble to go back to the office."

"Nyet. I insist. You deserve it. Consider it an order, if need be."

"If that is the way you put it, then I accept."

It was snowing heavily by the time they reached Makarov's apartment. He was glad he had accepted Sudoplatov's offer after all. The sedan stopped briefly as Makarov got out. Sudoplatov bade him good night, and then the sedan vanished in seconds into the snow flurries and Moscow night. Makarov went inside the apartment complex and tromped wearily to his second floor apartment. In the early years of the war, some of the factory girls would invite him into their rooms. Tonight, most had turned in early. Others avoided him because of his NKVD insignia. He had turned down most of the girls. However, one dark-eyed beauty had not been fazed by his membership in Stalin's security apparatus. Natasha stood in her doorway and batted her eyes at him.

"Long night at the office, Alexi?"

"Not tonight, Natasha. I have had a long day, and my boss is picking me up early in the morning."

She pouted with mock disappointment, and Makarov smiled. He paused and walked over to her and kissed her. She pulled her head back. He reached out and caught her with his arm. She laughed. "Now I have you."

"Not tonight, Natasha, the weekend maybe. How about—"

"How about tonight?"

"I could have you arrested for illegal possession of government property." He smiled a wicked smile. "I promise the weekend. I'm off, and I'll take you shopping." He then pushed her away and slapped her on her hips.

"Remember, you promised," she said as she closed the door.

Makarov opened his apartment and settled on a couch. The spartan quarters were strictly utilitarian. His other furniture consisted of a bed, table, and chair. He unbuttoned his tunic and poured himself a glass of vodka. At one time he could not stand vodka. Now he couldn't wait to have his evening's libation. After pouring his drink, he slumped back into the couch and reflected on tonight's meeting and subsequent moves. He lit a cigarette to steady his nerves. He had worked several days to assemble the material for the presentation that had been presented to Stalin. The enormity of what he had gathered started to sink in. He now had to think of what he would transmit back to his controllers in Germany and when he would do it. He knew Soviet counterintelligence was formidable, and although he was right in the middle of it, there were always unknown variables.

As the smoke curled and rose to the ceiling, he went back to when it all had started. His parents had been Baltic Germans who were murdered in an insurrection instigated by the Communists in Lithuania. They had been killed for owning a small shop and being middle class. He had sworn revenge as a teenager, and so when he became a young man, he eagerly went to work for the Abwehr when that organization contacted him. His excellent Russian served him well. Fortunately, he arrived in Russia before the Tukhachevsky affair. The Abwehr's rival for power in Germany, the SD, had provided forged documents to the NKVD, proving Tukhachevsky's treasonous actions. In return, the SD received thousands of Soviet banknotes. It seemed like a good trade to the SD except the wily Stalin had paid the Germans in forged banknotes that were easily traceable whenever they showed back up in Russia. Although Stalin never used the documents in his infamous show trials, he had the last laugh as several German agents were captured in the following months when they used the bogus notes.

Makarov had another close call after joining Sudoplatov's staff. Unfortunately, his new boss was being investigated after the fall of Yezhov. The man's bungling had cost the NKVD dearly, and it was fortunate for the Soviet Union that he was removed before war broke out. Sudoplatov had escaped imprisonment because a promotion order for Sudopaltov was left unsigned by one of the victims of the purge. Makarov had fortunately been detached to Siberia to investigate Zhukov. He vividly remembered the day when the shaken Sudoplatov had told him about the experience. Sudoplatov was later transferred to the Foreign Service Department as its head until the outbreak of war. Then with Makarov as his aide, he became the head of Special Tasks.

Makarov recalled the deadly games he had played in this area. He was always on the lookout for information indicating that the NKVD realized that it had a high level spy in its ranks. There were too many close calls. He cleverly exposed the only Gestapo officer to be recruited by the Russians. For weeks, he had played a deadly cat and mouse game before he pinpointed Willy Lehmann's identity. He had just managed to uncover the man's true identity before Lehmann exposed Makarov. Moscow was shocked by Lehmann's abrupt disappearance but was unable to come up with a suitable explanation. Makarov was asked to investigate; but, naturally, he had to apologize for not having anything definite but certainly a spy on the Russian side had to be considered.

He had gone on to help expose the Red Orchestra spy ring and send several members of the group to their deaths. Most recently, he had devoted considerable effort to identify the arch-traitor Werther. This man seemed to know every move the German High Command was making, and every detail usually reached Moscow within twenty-four hours. This man had probably cost Germany the war. Fortunately, Makarov was working under official orders on Werther's identity as Stalin personally had ordered Sudoplatov to find out who Werther really was.

There were setbacks and other minor operations he had not told Berlin in order to preserve himself. He had not mentioned the Scherhorn ruse. Although supplies were being dropped to waiting Russians instead of desperate Germans, Makarov had decided that this operation would not affect the war's outcome in any way. Meanwhile, Moscow was happy that the Luftwaffe was not providing supplies to the Ukrainian nationalist Bandera instead.

This concern with the atomic bomb was different. It was obviously important. He knew he could send the information back to Germany as Burgess had confirmed that MI6 had not penetrated the central headquarters of the SD. This could affect the war or even change its course if Germany had the bomb or had the time to build one. Meanwhile, the SD could arrange for the scientists in the Manhattan Project to be watched.

By now, the glass was nearly empty. A thin wisp of smoke hung in the air as the last ash from his cigarette fell to the floor. Makarov wearily stood up and walked over to his bed. He collapsed on his back. He turned his head and looked at a photograph of his family in happier times. He remembered the occasion well. They had been on an outing in the forest. His father had pointed out the different forms of plant and animal life. He particularly remembered the encounter with the ferrets. Maybe it was because it was such a fleeting moment but so thrilling. Although possession of the picture posed a risk in case someone recognized the individuals his luck had held. He had to admit the family portrait provided him some solace while he worked alone. In addition, it reminded him why he had joined the Abwehr and continued his risky work. The picture also served to remind him of his code name, the ferret. That is exactly what he had been for almost eight years as he ferreted out the secrets of the Soviet military. If he could now identify Werther and if this business of nuclear weapons was more than just a dream, Makarov felt he would have succeeded beyond his wildest dreams. Later, he would find the appropriate time to transmit the details of the American nuclear program back to Germany.

February 10, 1945

Lieutenant Colonel Gerhard Wessel was working late as usual when his aide knocked on his open door. The nearly empty desktop was a testament to the man's work and drive. Although exhausted from the day's work, he was dedicated to finding a solution to the Reich's problems on the Eastern Front.

"What is it, Hans?"

"A long transmission has arrived from the ferret."

The aide did not have to say another word. Wessel was instantly alert at the mention of the ferret. Normally, at this late an hour, Hans would have waited until the morning to pass on a message from an agent in the field to his boss, but the ferret was different. Anytime a message arrived from him, it was treated as if it was a piece of gold. Hans had been verbally reprimanded for not promptly alerting Wessel to the arrival of one the ferret's messages. He had not made the mistake twice. He also knew that Wessel's boss, Lieutenant General Reinhard Gehlen, would want to see the message as well.

Wessel picked up his phone and dialed Gehlen's number. "Herr General, we have a message from the ferret. Yes, yes, I will be there immediately." He hung the phone up. "Hans, make sure we are not disturbed. I will be with the general for a few minutes."

"Jawohl, Herr Oberst."

Reinhard Gehlen, head of Foreign Armies East, was seated impassively at his desk when Wessel walked in. A slight physically unimpressive man, his stature gave no clue to the massive intellect that made him a formidable intelligence chief. Wessel handed Gehlen the message. Gehlen examined the message carefully and reread it. Usually, he only needed to read a document once. This was unlike anything the ferret had ever sent before. In fact, it was information that he would not even act upon since Gehlen's sphere of operations was the Eastern Front and not against the Western Allies. Gehlen wondered at first if this was a trick. However, the message had the right call signs. There was no evidence that the man had been compromised or turned. It meant that the ferret considered this to be very big to have sent this rather than the movements of the different Soviet armies that Gehlen was always hungry for.

"What do you make of this, Herr General?"

Gehlen leaned back. "Interesting. It does not affect anything we are doing in our operations. I would rather know what Zhukov or Timoshenko is doing now rather than this. This does not concern us at all. However, I will have to talk to Himmler about this. He has taken over most of the weapons programs through Kammler. I know there has been research in nuclear weapons, but I am ignorant of the details."

Wessel winced his face slightly. He knew how much Gehlen despised Himmler. Both men would be happy if they never saw the Reichsfuehrer again. Wessel tried to help. "Couldn't we just send it by courier?"

"Most likely, we could and get away with it. However, I don't want it said in the future that we tried to hide or minimize a transmission of great importance. The fact is I will have to talk with Himmler since the SD is responsible for espionage in North America."

Wessel said no more as Gehlen was merely covering their tracks. Anyone of any rank in the army was wise to cover his tracks after the failed July 20th attempt on Hitler's life. In addition, Gehlen was not among Hitler's favorites because of his reports about overwhelming Russian superiority in men and material. Wessel knew, as Gehlen's subordinate, he could be considered guilty by association if anything went wrong.

"Set up an appointment tomorrow evening with Himmler."

"Jawohl, Herr General, I hope you are not putting your head on the block."

"My head is already on the block. I hope I am not handing him the axe to cut it off with."

The following evening, Gehlen and Wessel arrived at Himmler's headquarters for Army Group Vistula. Gehlen reminded himself to hold his tongue and provide only the necessary amount of information and no more. He hoped to avoid any provocation or confrontation in the conference. He tried to put out of his mind Himmler's remark about Gehlen's estimates of Soviet strength as being a gigantic bluff. That had stung. Worse was when Gehlen's beloved homeland was invaded by the Red hordes. Matters had been made worse by having an incompetent intelligence chief advising a demented warlord. Despite all his misgivings, Gehlen maintained a straight face as he entered Himmler's headquarters.

The two men were ushered to the waiting area outside Himmler's office. An aide announced the two men's presence. A mild-mannered voice replied, "Bring them in."

The aide ushered Gehlen and Wessel into Himmler's office. They gave the required Nazi salute with outstretched right arm. Himmler returned the salute. He was dressed in his black Reichfueher's uniform. It had an intimidation factor that Himmler liked to put to use in situations such as this. "Be seated," he ordered in his schoolmaster's voice. He noted with silent satisfaction that the two men were uneasy as they seated themselves. Both figured that his power was second only to Hitler's at this point.

Himmler affixed his signature to half-dozen documents and placed his pen down on the desk at the angle prescribed in writing classes. He carefully removed his glasses and folded them. He then turned his gaze on Gehlen. "More bad news from the Russian Front, General Gehlen?"

Normally, Gehlen would have thought that Himmler was mocking him. This time, Himmler seemed to be genuinely serious. Gehlen calmly replied, "I have nothing new to add to my previous reports, Reichsfuehrer. You are probably more in tune with the situation as army group commander than I am." Gehlen secretly hoped that Himmler was stung by the remark. "The reason I am here is because of an interesting transmission from one of our agents." Gehlen leaned forward with a typed report of the ferret's transmission. "A few days ago, our agent attended a high-level meeting of Soviet leaders. A considerable amount of time was spent discussing the American nuclear program. I felt this fell under your area since this is an American project and my responsibilities are against the Soviet Union."

Himmler placed his glasses on and read the transmission. "So you do have some news of interest." After reading the report, he asked, "Do you think this is feasible?"

"I don't know if a nuclear device is feasible. I am aware that we have conducted research in the area, and that is all. I will say that the ferret is one of the best, if not the best agent, that we have been able to place in Moscow. His reports are always accurate. I do not think he would have sent this unless he thought it was of the utmost importance."

"You do not think this is some sort of trick?"

"I doubt it. Obviously, the Russians don't have a bomb or they no doubt would have used it."

Himmler rubbed his chin. "I certainly agree with that. I still wonder about your source. How did he go from purloining army movements to stealing weapons secrets?"

"He has been in place for eight years. That has given him plenty of time to insinuate himself inside the NKVD. As far as him being trustworthy, he provided us the information that unmasked the Red Orchestra and Wily Lehman."

The last remark did sting, but Himmler did not show it. *No time for that now*, he thought. He stood up and dismissed the two officers. "Yes, indeed, it does appear that this man has provided useful service. General Gehlen, you were correct to bring this matter to my attention as promptly as you did. It does belong in our North American section. Perhaps they can make some use of it." Himmler then added felicitously, "I don't believe that we have fully appreciated the work that Foreign Armies East has accomplished. I look forward to hearing more from you. Perhaps you could join me for dinner sometime soon."

"I will have to look at my schedule before I can commit to dinner, Reichsfuehrer."

"Are there any more copies of this?"

"Oh course, the original that the radio operator wrote down."

Himmler replied, "I will have a SD officer pick it up. This is a very sensitive area that only a few people need to know about. You do understand the need for secrecy, of course?"

"Of course, Reichsfuehrer."

"All future transmissions from this agent should be referred immediately to me. Auf weidersehen meine Herrern." Himmler concluded the meeting, and salutes were exchanged. Himmler sat back down at his desk and resumed examining his papers.

Once Wessel and Gehlen were in the car, Wessel let loose. "I would just as soon as dine with the devil in hell."

"You may get your chance sooner than you think with the way things are going."

"Why would he want all of the copies of the transmission?"

"I was wondering the same thing myself. He obviously knew a lot more than he let on. And not just that we were coming."

"Are we that far along in nuclear weapon development ourselves?"

"Not that I'm aware of. However, since Kammler has taken over, I know very little about our secret weapons development. At least this is off our plate now. Now maybe he can do something besides make wisecracks about Foreign Armies East."

"Shall I schedule dinner for you?"

"Yes, sometime next year," Gehlen replied.

Both officers laughed as Himmler's headquarters disappeared behind them in the dark.

Himmler summoned an aide immediately after Gehlen's departure. "I need to meet with Skorzeny at four o'clock tomorrow. One of his battalion commanders withdrew without permission. I want a full accounting. Hopefully, the man in question has already been shot. In addition, another matter has come up that I need to discuss with him. I expect him to be on time." Himmler looked at the ferret's message again. "Sometimes we don't take full advantage of the opportunities presented to us. We must not let that happen this time."

"Yes, Reichsfuehrer?" The aide was giving Himmler a quizzical look.

"Just make sure Skorzeny is on time."

The following day Skorzeny led his men in ferocious combat with the Red Army. A determined assault was made against the first line of defense at Grabow. T–34s with infantry support hurled themselves against the stiff German defenses. Skorzeny's antitank guns took a generous toll of the targets that presented themselves. Skorzeny had been fortunate enough to scrape up some experienced gunners among the retreating soldiers. They had been dragooned only days before and were now proving their mettle. Others were manning the 88s he had placed on the ice flows on the Oder. They added considerably to the Russians' discomfort as they floated up and down the river. In addition, their changing positions confused the Russians as to the number and location of guns.

Skorzeny watched as the first wave of attackers was driven back. Over a score of battered hulks was sending oily black smoke into the air. Most were T–34s with a few KVs intermingled in the wreckage. Dozens of brown–clad bodies lay strewn among the tanks. The familiar smell of burning flesh made its way to Skorzeny's men.

Skorzeny winced as the smell of battle irritated his nose. He knew it was just the beginning of worse to come. He made his way along the front to check on his men. Fortunately, losses were light. This was partly because of the fact that the Russians had been packed tightly and incurred heavy casualties early in the fight. Most were killed long before they were in position to assault the German lines. While little damage had been done in the initial assault, a large amount of ammunition had been expended repulsing the Soviets. Several units needing resupply had sent runners.

An ominous lull settled over the battlefield. The silence was pierced by the occasional cry of a wounded Russian or exploding ammunition. On the German side, most of the wounded had been evacuated to the rear. Skorzeny noted with satisfaction that none of his antitank guns were knocked out. He expected more attacks, and every gun was priceless now.

As he was taking stock of his position, Skorzeny felt a tremor in the ground. The men around him were instinctively taking cover. Skorzeny dove for an entrenchment where one of the 75s was dug in. He had just positioned himself when the rockets and shells started falling. The Soviets had opened up with their dreaded Katusha rockets and heavy artillery. Skorzeny still felt a chill when he heard the whoosh of the rocket. Even though he had first encountered the Katusha three years earlier, the sound still made his hair stand on end as a bombardment from these missiles was a terrible event to endure.

A brilliant flash a few meters away indicated that a rocket had found a machine-gun nest. The MG 42 was thrown into the air as the ammunition went off with the sound of firecrackers. Debris fell around Skorzeny's position. He turned his head back to the front after he noticed that some of the ground around him was being stained crimson.

At the front, Skorzeny saw the source of the tremors as another Soviet assault unit as strong as the first advanced. The lead tanks wound their way through the wreckage and halted just outside the area of bombardment. Skorzeny knew exactly what would happen. As soon the barrage stopped, Ivan would rush his position. We've been hurt now, and they know it. This is going to get rough, and if we are lucky, we might hold.

Just as expected the Russians advanced as soon as the last shell had fallen. The Germans recovered and started picking off tanks. However, the fire was weaker, and the Russians immediately sensed this. Enough guns were out of action to allow the outer defenses to be breached. Opposing infantry opened up on each other at point blank range. Skorzeny watched as a machine-gun crew abandoned its position before one of the steel giants crushed the MG 42 beneath its treads. One of the Germans placed a Teller mine before retreating. After the explosion, the surviving gun crew gunned down the Russian crew. Soviet infantry closed with the survivors, and hand-to-hand combat broke out. While the Russians tried to impale the crew with their bayonets, Skorzeny's men fought back viscously with their entrenching tools in a desperate attempt to survive. One of the

Germans was obviously a veteran of this type of fighting as he split open the skull of one assailant and deflected the bayonet thrust of another before disemboweling the Russian.

Just as the Russians seemed to be about to make their breakthrough, Skorzeny's snipers went into action. The Russian infantry hit the ground quickly and left the tanks with little support. Each Russian thought he was in some sniper's scope and kept his head down. Meanwhile, a shell found its way to Skorzeny's position. Stunned briefly, he saw that the other crewmembers had been hurt badly. One man was bleeding profusely from a leg wound. Skorzeny stopped the flow of blood with his hand. A medic arrived and placed a tourniquet. An explosion in front of them threw up a cloud of dust. Skorzeny used the opportunity to drag two of the wounded out while the cloud concealed them from the enemy. He held his arms around the two, while he headed to the rear. A machine-gun nest was in his path. That would provide some cover until he could get them men evacuated. He looked behind as he led the wounded men into the dugout position and saw the Russians at his former position. After he got in, he pushed aside the bodies of the crew who had been killed by a shell blast. He then placed the bodies to provide some protection. He then leveled the machine gun and started firing short bursts. Several Russians fell, while the others found cover. For now he was safe until the tanks headed his way.

Skorzeny looked at the men with him. He ordered one of the walking wounded to the rear to find reinforcements. The man argued and wanted to stay. Skorzeny was firm. "I appreciate your loyalty, but it's more important that I get help now. Get moving!" Skorzeny fired a burst to cover the man, while one of the other wounded handled the ammunition belt.

Skorzeny was still firing when he felt Lieutenant Walther tapping him on the shoulder. "What are you doing, Herr Oberst?"

"What does it look like? Fighting!"

"But you are wanted at Himmler's headquarters immediately."

"Don't argue with me. If you would look out there, you'll notice the Russians are here. Now help me with the ammunition and get the wounded out."

"I can take over with the reinforcements, Herr Oberst."

"I'm not leaving. It's too critical. So do as I say."

By now, the tanks had appeared. Skorzeny opened fire to suppress the infantry. He wished Rudel were still flying. Hans Ulrich Rudel, the great Stuka ace, had been shot down only days ago and had lost a leg. His destruction of over five hundred Russian tanks had man him a legend on both sides of the conflict. Many a German infantryman had prayed "please let Rudel come" when facing an onslaught of Russian tanks. Now they could only pray that the man would fly again. Soviet propaganda had made much of Rudel's downing on February 9. This was the only time Skorzeny knew of when he appreciated Himmler's meddling. Himmler had pulled Rudel from General Schoerner's front to that of Army Group Vistula. Schoerner had protested bitterly, but to no avail.

The tanks were now closer, and Skorzeny heard his bullets pinging off their armor. The turrets swiveled as if looking for a target. So far, he remained hidden from view. Skorzeny broke into a sweat as the steel monsters continued their advance. If they located his position and fired, that would be it. On the other hand, if he remained, he might be ground into the dirt if his position was overrun. If he and his men ran, it would have to be soon.

At that moment, in answer to his silent prayers, a squadron of Ju 87Gs appeared over his head. Pandemonium broke out among the Russian tanks, as they had no antiaircraft guns with them. They had been caught in the open and knew it. Skorzeny breathed a sigh of relief as the scene unfolded. The T–34s drove around crazily as they sought to escape their tormentors. As the Stukas began their descent, they resembled a giant prehistoric vulture with their tapered wings and wheels that stood out like claws. Their dive reminded Skorzeny of a bird of prey trying to pick up its next morsel. However, it was the 37mm gun that was the dealer of death from this giant bird. Skorzeny saw a flash from one of the guns and watched as smoked poured from one of the T–34s. Skorzeny gunned down the crew as they tried to escape from their tank. He watched as another Stuka fired from four hundred meters as it approached the front of another tank. This was the distance that a Stuka had to close to within in order to achieve a kill. With a Stalin tank, the distance was down to one hundred meters. Skorzeny admired the skill of the tank busters as one had to look through a telescopic lens to zero in on the target while flying at the same time.

The Stukas had made a frontal pass and were preparing to attack from the rear. Several tanks were smoldering from the strike as the planes began another attack. Previously, the planes had fired at the point between the hull and turret. Now they were firing at the most vulnerable site of the tank. Several tanks exploded into flames as their fuel tanks were ignited. By now, the surviving tanks were withdrawing or crashing into buildings to hide from their hunters. The planes returned for another pass to look for any surviving tanks to destroy. The Soviet infantry had enough and withdrew as they valued the cover their tanks provided. The Soviet advance had been stopped cold but just barely this time.

Skorzeny realized that the next attack might very well crack the outer defenses. Serious casualties had been sustained among the gun crews. He grimly noted the upturned 75s and wrecked machine guns and knew those crews were likely dead. Large craters marked the former positions where other soldiers had fought. They would likely never be found. Walther was beside him as they surveyed the remains of the outer defenses.

"I need reinforcements up here now. The machine guns and 75s are urgent. These are all smashed." Skorzeny gritted his teeth as he surveyed the carnage. The Stukas had been a godsend; however, he could not count on miracles every day. In addition, the Stukas were vulnerable to fighters, and today's pilots were living on borrowed time.

Walther returned to Skorzeny's side. "Five antitank guns are on their way along with machine guns." Walther shifted uncomfortably. "One of Himmler's staff officers has arrived and wants to see you. You're being summoned to Himmler's headquarters."

That's all I need now, an imperial summon by Reichsheini, Skorzeny thought. "I'll be there shortly." He decided to let the toady from Himmler's staff wait. It would do him some good. Skorzeny stayed until the antitank guns arrived and supervised their placement. He then drove back to his headquarters to find Himmler's man waiting for him. The man saluted Skorzeny and asked him to accompany him to Himmler's headquarters. He gave no inclination of why Skorzeny was being summoned. He added that they were due at 1600 and most likely would be late now.

"Scheduled appointments are nice when you aren't fighting a war," was Skorzeny's testy reply.

"I am merely conveying the Reichsfuehrer's orders," the officer defensively remarked.

One of Skorzeny's men ran up. "Herr Oberst. The Russians are attacking in force again. They hit Grabow just after you left. The machine guns were arriving just as they struck. We're trying to keep the gun emplacements from being overrun."

Skorzeny ignored Himmler's minion. "Get the assault company ready. It looks like we are going to need it"

"Obersturmbannfuehrer, you will be very late." Himmler's staff officer tried to exert his influence one last time.

Skorzeny brusquely cut the man off. "You are dismissed until I return." Skorzeny nodded at a slightly wounded NCO who had been sent to the rear. "See to this officer until I return from the front."

The man understood and smiled. "With pleasure, Herr Oberst. Come with me." The crestfallen officer did as he was told. Meanwhile, Skorzeny led the assault company to Grabow. He knew there would be no air support at night. It would strictly be men and steel on one side versus men and steel on the other side. The trek took about half an hour to reach the front.

It was as bad as Skorzeny had feared. An armored regiment smashing the hastily reconstructed defenses and penetrating the outer ring had followed an artillery barrage. If the gap were not closed tonight, the middle ring would be the objective for the Soviet Army in the morning. The scene was unreal as flames flickered from the demolished armor and buildings. A sergeant showed them the new positions. Skorzeny noted with satisfaction that the surviving junior officers and NCOs had swiftly rebuilt a defensive line to contain the breakthrough.

"Get Schwerdt here," Skorzeny commanded. He wanted Schwerdt to know his plans for defense in case something happened. Skorzeny surveyed the battlefield. He still found it hard to believe that the Soviet Union had such resources. Numerous tank hulks were lit up, facing the German positions. Some were blazing brightly, indicating they had recently knocked out. As Skorzeny looked at the blazing wreckage, he noticed some American-built Sherman scattered among the wrecked T-34s. He knew he had not seen these in the earlier fighting. Skorzeny wondered if the Russians were throwing in their last punch for the day since the markedly inferior Shermans had appeared. As he looked over to the Russian positions, it appeared that the enemy was trying to dig in instead of pressing the attack. Instead of being mauled again, Ivan appeared to be consolidating his gains.

Schwerdt arrived with the fresh assault company, and Skorzeny decided that the Russians needed to be disabused of their notions of staying long in Grabow. Skorzeny knew each attack today had meted out terrible punishment to his men, and the Russians probably felt the Germans were too exhausted to pull off any surprises. However, the new assault company was fresh, heavily armed with assault rifles, grenades, and panzerfausts. Snipers stealthily crawled to good firing positions.

Skorzeny quietly led his men to their jumping off position. Within seconds, they were in place. He fired a flare into the air, and his men darted forward. The brilliant illumination caught the Russians by surprise as grenades were tossed into their positions. Following the explosions, the assault company overran the Soviet positions and gunned down the dazed survivors. Panzerfausts turned several T-34s into flaming scrap. The flickering flames combined with the bodies running about cast eerie shadows on the surrounding landscape. Flamethrowers turned men into living torches before they collapsed in agony as the counterattack continued its momentum against the poorly entrenched Russians. A few tanks were captured when the crews were unable to move their armor and fled for their lives. Finally, the force proved too much, and the Soviets broke, leaving Skorzeny's men the masters of the field this night.

Skorzeny decided he could indulge Himmler now. He returned to his headquarters to find Himmler's aide still waiting. Skorzeny kept his soiled uniform on instead of changing. The two men drove silently to Himmler's headquarters at Hohenlychen. Two nattily dressed SS officers in their black uniform greeted Skorzeny with the air of someone who had just received the sentence of death. Skorzeny recognized the senior of the two officers as Heinz Macher, commander of Himmler's personnel bodyguard. A combat veteran, he seemed to exude pity for someone who had been unfortunate enough to displease the Reichsfuehrer. The other minion seemed to take a delight in what he perceived as Skorzeny's rather precarious situation. Skorzeny ignored both.

Macher escorted Skorzeny to Himmler's study. The Reichsfuehrer was dressed in a black uniform for its full sinister effect. He was also in a foul mood and unleashed his venom at Skorzeny. "This is ridiculous what you have done tonight. Making me wait at my headquarters for four hours when you received instructions to be here much sooner. I should have you court-martialed and demoted. You, of all people, making me, the Reichsfuehrer, wait for four hours. It is completely unacceptable for you to treat me in such a manner. I will not tolerate such behavior and disrespect. You are an SS officer, and I expect you to act as such. Worst of all, I understand that you did nothing to the officer who evacuated Nipperwiese. This man should have been shot as soon as possible to set an example to others. His example will encourage others to avoid fighting when they can if this goes unpunished."

Himmler paused to catch his breath. Skorzeny used the opportunity to deliver his retort. "Reichsfuehrer, since I have arrived at Schwedt, I have received one nonsensical order after another, yet no one has thought about sending supplies or the manpower to carry them out with. I arrived at Schwedt with a battalion, not knowing whether or not I had as much as a Russian division facing me. Since then, I have built up a division of men retreating through the town from their shattered units. We located and commandeered our own 75mm antitank guns and food. My teams have been going as far as thirty kilometers behind Russian lines to cause havoc. None of the supplies for these actions came from up on high. We had to gather up everything ourselves. As far as the officer at Nipperwiese, forget about him. I gave the order for him to withdraw because his position was untenable. That is why he will not be court-martialed or shot by me. If anyone here thinks Nipperwiese is defensible, they can get off their arse and take a look themselves."

Skorzeny's rebuke jolted Himmler into sensibility. Himmler became more reasonable as he realized that Skorzeny was no longer the stumbling captain of eighteen months ago, feeling his way around as the Reichsfuehrer's new chief of SS commandos. He was now a seasoned veteran universally feared by the Allies. Kaltenbrunner had been correct to recommend him to Himmler. He was calmer when he replied to Skorzeny. "I'm afraid that I have not fully appreciated your situation. What you have accomplished is nothing short of a miracle. I know you were faced with an impossible task. The fact is you have done so much with so little in the past that we have come to expect it out of you. I realize that I should have paid more attention to your area. A Soviet breakthrough at Schwedt would have been catastrophic. As a result, the Russians have not advanced as far as we had expected them to. You probably deserve much of the credit for delaying them so much."

"It has not been easy, Reichsfuehrer, but if I had some reinforcements, I know I can hold indefinitely." Skorzeny relaxed as Himmler became more reasonable.

"My aide's report of tonight's battle indicates the quality of your men. You are right that your men need adequate food and ammunition. What do you need?"

"Antitank guns. We lost several today. We just barely held back an armored thrust tonight because of that."

"I will have an antitank battalion transferred to Schwedt immediately."

"That will be greatly appreciated. We will be able to hold with that."

Himmler asked Skorzeny about his material needs. Then in an effort to be affable, Himmler asked Skorzeny to join him for dinner. "I too have been delayed by various developments."

Skorzeny suspected that there was more for him being called here and invited to dinner. He immediately wondered about dark motives from others. He knew SS General Bach dem Zelewski would be trying to poison Himmler's mind. He was definitely a man to watch, as he had never forgiven Skorzeny for not letting him reduce Admiral Horthy's residence to a shambles with Thor. The giant mortar Thor had demonstrated its destructiveness in the Crimea. However, the huge cannon was out of place in Hungary in such a delicate situation. Hitler's orders were explicit: remove Horthy without forcing Hungary into Russian arms. As it was, Skorzeny's plan was carried out, and Admiral Horthy abducted with less than twenty dead on both sides. In addition, Hungary remained a German ally.

However, Bach dem Zelewski felt he had been upstaged and was known to hold grudges and settle old scores. During the Night of the Long Knives in 1934, he had his bitter rival, SS Colonel Freiherr Hohberg und Buhwald, gunned down in front of the man's teenage son. Following the brutal crushing of the uprising in Warsaw, he had SS General Kaminski summarily stood up against a wall and shot as a "potentially dangerous witness." In addition, Hitler had lauded the feat and regarded Bach dem Zelewski as the "cleverest of men." Even though the freebooter Kaminski probably deserved his fate, the fact that Bach dem Zelewski had killed Kaminski with virtual impunity testified to the man's standing and ruthlessness. Now Bach dem Zelewski was a corps commander in the Army Group Vistula. Skorzeny knew he would need to watch his back carefully and decided he would never be caught traveling alone in case a trap was set for him.

Himmler allayed Skorzeny's fears as they headed back to

Himmler's private dining room. They passed by Macher and the other officer. The junior SS officer was crestfallen at Skorzeny's apparent change in fortune. Skorzeny was offered a drink before he was seated. The meal, although simple, was quite delicious. Himmler was well known for being the perfect host when he hosted a diner at his house or headquarters. He certainly was living up to that reputation now. Skorzeny was actually enjoying himself, whether from the warm meal or his reversal in fortune was hard to say. He still couldn't get rid of the nagging feeling that Himmler had other ulterior motives on his mind.

Himmler asked Skorzeny his assessment of the front. The replies were honest and brutal: "Difficult, unpredictable, but it is not impossible for us to hold against the Russians, especially if Germany would coordinate her defenses better." Skorzeny used Schwedt as an example.

"When I first arrived there, the Russians could have taken the place with only a platoon. Had they arrived a few days earlier, they might already be in Berlin now. As it was, we organized, the people regained their confidence, and now there is a good spirit among both soldiers and civilians. No one is talking of giving up now." Skorzeny neglected to mention a district leader who had deserted and had been caught. That man would be dealt with later.

Finally, the meal was finished, and Skorzeny was offered some brandy. It burned his throat in a pleasant way. Perhaps his chances at Schwedt were going to be better than he dreamed. Himmler seemed to be coming around to his side.

"There is one more thing I would like to discuss with you, my dear Skorzeny."

Skorzeny had raised the glass to his lips a second time when Himmler spoke. He hesitated briefly before taking a sip. *This is it, the real reason I was summoned,* he thought. He braced himself for another fantastic mission dreamed up by God knows whom in the rear area. *Well, if it's too crazy, it will get the same delaying tactics like the nonsensical orders we were just talking about. Just remember to keep your mouth shut like Radl has told you to so many times in the past.*

"What I have to say is of the highest importance to Germany. It may be the most important assignment I have given you. What do you know about nuclear or atomic weapons?"

Skorzeny's thoughts went wild, while he maintained his composure. "I know that we have been working on them. So far, none have worked as far as I know. Most of this area is theoretical anyway from what little I've heard."

"Things have changed. A few days ago, General Gehlen's organization received a transmission from one of their most trusted agents in Moscow. The Russians appear to have deeply penetrated the American nuclear program. Of course, the information is relayed to Moscow where Gehlen's man is able to see it. The Americans have made tremendous progress in the last few months, and the Russians consider such a weapon feasible now. Such a weapon is thought to be capable of destroying an entire city. As a result, the Russians have started their own nuclear program to build such a bomb. They expect to come to blows with the Americans after Germany is beaten."

"If we had that at the beginning of the war, the fighting would already have been finished."

"Most likely. Certainly, the Allies are worried about our developing such a weapon. We must have been on the right track since they sent commandos to destroy our heavy water stocks in Norway. This would indicate that the Americans and British are very advanced in their development of such a bomb."

"And if they develop one tomorrow, we have nothing to counter with."

"Exactly, my dear Skorzeny. That is where you come in. We need to be prepared in case one is developed so that we can prevent its use against us. If possible, it would be desirable to obtain one for our own use should the situation arise."

"With our intelligence networks in shambles, how are we even supposed to know where to find a bomb should it arrive in Britain?"

"We do function in your absence, Obersturbannfuehrer. We still have a network in North America that Admiral Canaris set up to spy on American nuclear development. Hoover's FBI thinks the man is working for them. He is a defector as far as the Americans are concerned. He's sending us material that we know is fed to him by Hoover's men. However, the Americans are unaware that he is sending us a second set of messages that contains the information that we want. His input has been scattered, but the information he provides is good. It appears that we have had more difficulty penetrating the Manhattan Project than the Soviets have. Perhaps with the recent information from our Moscow source, our man in the United States can keep tabs on his Soviet counterparts."

"So when the bomb arrives in England, we land a force and snatch it."

"I even considered taking possession of the bomb in the United States and exploding it there to prevent its use against us."

By now, Skorzeny had decided that all of the talk about victory weapons was just that, just so much talk. However, he contained his disgust. "Such an operation would be very difficult just from the logistics. Then there is the problem of finding men who speak English without an accent and blend in. As you recall during Operation Grief, many of the English speakers we recruited were mediocre at best in their command of the language. It seems to be the reason why each person was captured that didn't make it back to our lines. They didn't have mastery of the language. If the original Brandenburgers were intact, we could draw from their ranks and expect a reasonable chance of success on such a mission. I am afraid that many of those are buried on the Eastern Front."

"Unfortunately, what you say is true." Himmler continued on in his schoolmasterly style. "Isn't it interesting how Brandenburgers who spoke English were sent to Russia and those who spoke Russian were sent to North Africa and the Mediterranean? At least the admiral is no longer in a position to thwart the Fuehrer's will anymore."

"Foelkersam mentioned that often. However, that still does not help us out on the English speakers. We do know how not to recruit. I'm still surprised that the Allies didn't pick up on Keitel's memo." Keitel's circular asking for English speakers to volunteer for a special mission had been distributed openly throughout the

Wehrmacht. Furthermore, the volunteers had been directed to contact Skorzeny's organization. Skorzeny had counted on Operation Grief being dead then and there. However, Allied intelligence had proved no brighter than Keitel, and the significance of the letter was not appreciated until after the Ardennes offensive started. Then after three of Skorzeny's men were captured, an embarrassed Allied intelligence almost panicked as it conjured up unbelievable plots following the men's capture, and Skorzeny's true goals remained elusive. Idiocy on one side was cancelled out by stupidity on the other.

"You will have time obviously. I do not expect you to have a team tomorrow. You must be careful in your selection for such a delicate operation of such magnitude."

"This would be perfect for Naujocks." Skorzeny was already thinking of a way out of doing this mission. He had heard rumors that Alfred Naujocks had disappeared and possibly went over to the Allies. There were whispers that Himmler was tying up loose ends, and Naujocks was one of the loosest ends around. Naujocks had done much of the dirty work for the SD until 1942. He had been responsible for kidnappings, assassinations, and sabotage when required. As such, he knew many of the Nazi Party's dirty little secrets, secrets that Himmler never intended to see the light of day. Naujocks had even taped one of Heydrich's romps with a prostitute in the Salon Kitty. In 1942, Himmler cashiered Naujocks for misappropriation of funds and sent him into the Waffen-SS as a sergeant. He had been watched after the July 20th plot. Unknown to Himmler or Skorzeny, Naujocks had received a letter warning of grave danger. In October 1944, Naujocks decided his situation was too precarious and made his way to the Allied lines.

Himmler did not know if Skorzeny was needling him about Naujocks but decided his head commando was ignorant of Naujocks's circumstances. "This will be more of a military operation than the intelligence operations such as the SD conducts. I agree the Brandenburgers would be ideal. However, we must make do with what we have. You must agree that you have done a very good job of that yourself. I want you to draw up preliminary plans and find a leader within a month."

Skorzeny bristled at the last sentence. "Reichsfuehrer, I am used to leading my men from the front. I never ask them to do something that I wouldn't. If there is anything major going on, my men expect me to be leading them."

Himmler was equally curt. "My dear Skorzeny, you are the most wanted man on the Western Allies list. Do you seriously think that you could pass yourself off as an American? I think not. You also stick out in a crowd. Someone will eventually put two and two together and figure out who you are. Someone else must lead this mission. Plus, you are too valuable here."

Skorzeny backed down, as he did not plan for this scheme to come to fruition. He had too many concerns going on like Schwedt. "One other thing, Reichsfuehrer. I am a little confused by all of this. Last October, the Fuehrer called me in when he was sick in bed, and we discussed nuclear warfare. I personally heard him speak of his opposition to such weapons. Specifically, the use of such weapons would herald in the Apocalypse. No group of civilized men could accept the responsibility of building such weapons. The strikes and counterstrikes would destroy civilization as we know it. Only the Amazon tribes and pygmies of Africa could hope for a chance of survival under such conditions."

"I believe he also said that he did not want to see our planet turned into a fire ravaged celestial body," Himmler interjected. "I am well aware of the Fuehrer's feelings on this subject as well. Having such a weapon does not mean that we will use it. It serves more as leverage. This will be particularly true if the Allies have several of these bombs, and the only one we have is one that we steal from them. You know the Fuehrer, Skorzeny. He did not want this war. He only wanted what was best for the German volk. This must go forth."

"Very well. I have a pretty full plate as it is with Schwedt."

"One month, Skorzeny," Himmler replied flatly. "You must

have preliminary plans by then. I'll see what I can do to replace you at Schwedt."

Following his dismissal from Himmler's presence, Skorzeny made a departure for Schwedt. The lonely burden of command was on his shoulders again. He had to strengthen his defenses more if he could. Hopefully, he would hold until Himmler's promised reinforcements arrived. Then there was the matter of the cowardly volksturm leader. First, he would need to get some rest.

The following day, a court-martial was convened for the leader of the volksturm. The wretched district leader made pitiful excuses for his conduct. However, his cowardice was common knowledge. No one could be found to speak in his defense among the former Communist dockworkers or seasoned combat veterans as the two battalions he had abandoned had suffered higher casualties than the surrounding units. The survivors of these units were ready to hang their former commander. That is exactly what Skorzeny decided to do with him. The verdict was a foregone conclusion. After finding the man guilty of cowardice and desertion, the court sentenced the man to hang. Skorzeny felt the man did not deserve the decency of a firing squad. As a district leader in the Nazi Party, he had a duty to set an example and had failed miserably. Skorzeny remembered the revulsion he felt when the man presented himself, claiming all was lost while his men fought desperately on.

Skorzeny wasted no time. A rope was thrown over a lamppost, and a box to stand on was all the necessary equipment. The man was forced on the box, and the noose was secured. Then without any ceremony, the box was pulled from under him. The district leader danced a jig of death for a few minutes and went limp. He was left hanging for the afternoon. Skorzeny took no pleasure in what was done. Too bad the man did not have any backbone, or a lot more of his men might still be alive as well as saving his own life.

What Skorzeny did not anticipate was the firestorm that resulted with the execution. Two days later, Skorzeny was directing the defenses against another Soviet attack when a runner came for him. Skorzeny could barely move because of the shrapnel and bullets flying through the air. The runner jumped into a hole next to Skorzeny as an explosion showered them with rock and dirt. The larger chunks stung as the debris landed on the two men.

"Herr Oberst, you are required back at headquarters." The man was clearly agitated.

"They will have to wait. There is a war going on in case you haven't noticed."

"Gauleiter Sturtz is there. It has to do with the swine we hanged the other day."

So a gauleiter was upset over a pipsqueak's death. Skorzeny knew he had tempted fate a few days ago during his meeting with Himmler. Now Skorzeny had stepped on a few toes by hanging a cowardly party official. Fortunately, he knew that Himmler secretly despised most of the top brass of the Nazi Party as well. He remembered Himmler grousing that for order to return to Germany every Gauleiter needed to be hung from a lamppost.

After the fighting had stabilized, Skorzeny returned to his headquarters. Awaiting him there was an obese man in the brown uniform and gold braid of the party hierarchy. His pressed, clean uniform contrasted sharply with Skorzeny's soiled crumpled uniform. Nicknamed "golden pheasants," the party functionaries were universally despised by soldiers and civilians for their haughtiness and arrogance. Skorzeny doubted that Sturtz would be an exception to the rule.

Both men exchanged salutes, each formally expressing "Heil Hitler" as they took measure of each other. Skorzeny decided to take the initiative and if possible maintain it. "I am Obersturmbannfuehrer Skorzeny, commander of the division here, and as you might not be aware, there is a war going on across the river. In fact, we are within artillery range of the Russians big guns if they chose to fire this far." Skorzeny hoped the fat bastard would squirm with that piece of information.

Sturtz shifted slightly on his feet, but either was unfazed or ignored the remark. Skorzeny decided he was too stupid to comprehend the basic facts of war. "Reichsleiter Martin Bormann has sent me to investigate the execution of Franz Kruger. Does the name ring a bell, Obersturmbannfuehrer?"

"Very well, Gauleiter Sturtz. He was hanged for cowardice two days ago."

"In case you are not aware, party members are not subject to the military courts. They can only be tried before party tribunals. Reichsleiter Bormann has been very clear on this before. Trial of a party member before a military court is totally and completely unacceptable." Sturtz concluded his blathering with a triumphant tone in his voice. He waited for Skorzeny to cave in.

Skorzeny eyed his opponent back. As he surveyed Stutz's waist, Skorzeny thought the man is as fat as he is stupid before he struck back. "The man was not tried as a member of the party but as a member of the armed forces from which he deserted. By the way, aren't treason and cowardice punishable in the party as well?"

"Of course," Sturtz bleated back.

"Then that should settle the matter. Otherwise, I will call the Fuehrer myself." Skorzeny was hard now. "I would like to know how the party deals with members who show no courage in the face of the enemy. Perhaps the rules have changed."

Sturtz went pale. "Perhaps we have a little misunderstanding."

"Any misunderstanding is on your part. I will not tolerate any person in command to desert his men, cause needless deaths, and go unpunished. I will firmly deal likewise with anyone who behaves similarly in the future. You may tell Reichsleiter Bormann my position on the matter. I hope it is perfectly clear."

"It is clear." Sturtz actually gulped nervously and made his way out. This was something that was getting to be over his head. Bormann would have to deal with this man. While Hitler might rave and rant about his incompetent generals, he still liked his individual soldiers. Even the all-powerful Bormann found this out early on. Sturtz vividly remembered Bormann's intrigues against Molders. After being decorated by Hitler, Molders had the gumption to ask Hitler to end the persecution against the churches. Hitler and Goring were deeply embarrassed. Bormann thought he had a green light to act against Molders and began building a case against the famed flier. Much to everyone's surprise, Hitler turned on Bormann. Sturtz could still hear the Fuehrer dressing down Bormann. "If Molders has the courage to speak his convictions, I can only respect him for it." Hitler had actually screamed at Bormann. "You leave this decent German soldier alone!" Bormann had been a pariah for days afterward. Although firmly entrenched in power, it was a sobering experience for someone as exalted as Sturtz. Skorzeny was a Hitler favorite, so let Bormann fight this battle.

"Trouble, Herr Oberst?" Walther stepped in after Sturtz left.

"Just unnecessary meddling." Skorzeny was letting his exasperation evaporate. "Let's get back to the front."

"I had anticipated that. I have a car waiting."

Skorzeny got up and walked out to the car. He wondered how he had managed without Walther all these months. *It's because you had the baron*, he reminded himself. He also figured that he probably was not through feuding with Bormann. There would be repercussions of some kind after the exchange with Sturtz. He had counted on that. After all, it was with good reason that Bormann was thoroughly hated by those who came into contact with him. Various leaders had warned him about the man. He had gained compete control of Hitler's court by smashing all rivals and reducing them to irrelevance except Himmler.

His second brush with Bormann occurred a few days later and from an unexpected quarter. Walther was waiting for Skorzeny to return from the front. Walther was holding a message. "What is it now?" Skorzeny asked him.

"A message from Bormann." Walther smiled.

"About the execution?"

"No. It's about certain 'important state papers.' It appears that some party members were evacuating Bad Schonfliess and left them behind."

"Any idea where these papers are now?"

"No information was provided other than that which I have just given you, Herr Oberst."

"I am not sending patrols out to look for a bunch of papers that maybe here, there, or yonder. Also find out what these papers really are. Something does not sound right."

"Right away, Herr Oberst."

"Take your time. Tomorrow will be fine."

Skorzeny was still at the front the following evening when Walther hunted him down. They withdrew to a less exposed area. Skorzeny could tell Walther was delighted with his knowledge by his bemused look.

"It seems like you found something amusing. Let's hear it."

"I found out some more details about Bormann's papers. The so-called state papers are actually Bormann's personal papers. He does not want the Russians to get hold of the papers."

"I am getting less enthusiastic about this search as time goes on."

Walther continued, "Two party officials were driving the papers out of Bad Schonfliess when they ran off the road and got stuck in a ditch. They abandoned the truck and made no attempt to destroy the papers."

"I would like to see what Bormann has to say about dereliction of duty," replied Skorzeny sarcastically. "Inform Bormann that I need the two members of the party to come here to help us locate it. More than likely, the Russians have already found it and are using the papers for the toilet paper they need."

Walther grinned back broadly. "With pleasure, Herr Oberst."

Skorzeny was eating alone that evening when Walther interrupted him. "What else is new about the papers?" Skorzeny knew it could be nothing else.

"The two illustrious members of the party do not consider it necessary to present themselves in the search for the papers." Walther smirked as he reported the latest reply from Bormann.

"Tell them I will not send one soldier out to look for the papers without anyone to guide us. He obviously does not know that Ivan has had control of that area for almost a week now. I could send ten patrols out, get them wiped out, and still not find the papers because we don't know where to look." Skorzeny figured he had more important things to worry about such as defending the bridgehead.

The next day, Radl arrived from Friendenthal. Skorzeny had kept him there to run things in Skorzeny's absence. Radl had chafed at being left out of the action, but that is where he was needed. Skorzeny decided to let him out for a day. In addition, he wanted to run Himmler's mad proposal by him. He needed Radl to do the legwork on devising a feasible operation on paper anyway.

Radl arrived when Grabow had been struck a second time by the Red Army. By now, the enemy outnumbered Skorzeny's men fifteen to one. Skorzeny was preparing to hit the Russians from the flanks in a preemptive strike. Skorzeny was anxious as the attack assembled. The situation was becoming critical.

Radl was wearing a crisp uniform when he arrived. The second Russian attack of the day had been beaten back. Skorzeny was huddled over a map with his aides when Radl arrived. His concern was obvious to the unflappable Radl. "Well, Otto, I see that you have things under control as usual."

"I'm glad you're in such good spirits," Skorzeny responded. "Sit down. We need to talk."

"If it's replacements you want, I am about all there is left. You've been sent everyone else."

"I wish you could conjure up some more troops." Skorzeny paused briefly as an explosion rocked the headquarters. Radl's crisp uniform took a mild dusting. "Himmler's come up with another crazy idea."

"Something like Magnitogorsk?" Radl asked.

"Close to it."

"Well, what is it?"

"The Reichsfuehrer wants a commando team to be sent to America and steal a very secret and powerful bomb if it is developed."

Radl roared with laughter at the apparent ridiculousness of the whole situation. "You've got to be serious. We don't have that many English speakers to pick from. You remember the difficulty we had during Operation Grief."

"I reminded Himmler of that."

"We'll have a hard time finding anyone to speak decent enough English, let alone an American accent."

"I already know that, Karl. And Himmler wants someone else to lead it. I am too recognizable according to him."

Radl was still amused. "Is the man completely crazy? We can't just teach the men to say eat a fucking egg when they are challenged or asked for identification papers in America. That may have worked for Operation Grief, but it won't work here."

"Too bad Foelkersam isn't with us. This would have been perfect for him."

"It certainly would have been perfect for the Brandenburgers. It's a waste to see them reformed into a panzer grenadier division. No one remembers what they accomplished earlier. Now they are so much fodder for the Eastern Front."

"I wish I had never given Adrian command of Task Force East. He was our best man."

"I know. We've probably seen the last of him. Schreiber last saw him surrounded by Russians. By the way Schreiber just called in this morning. He led fifteen survivors out and met up with some other remnant of our invincible armed forces. Evidently, he had quite a journey back. He's been recommended for the oak leaves."

Skorzeny leaned back. "Schreiber. He's back. He was a Brandenburger, wasn't he?"

"From the beginning, he was Foelkersam's right-hand man. He was at Maikop and…"

"Okay, I remember. He speaks English too, doesn't he?"

"Flawless. In fact, he was born in St. Louis right after the last war. His father emigrated there. Evidently, an uncle had political strings and got his brother over to work in the family business. However, Schreiber's father was too restless and returned to Germany to join one of the Freikorps. Max grew up as a child in the United States, while his father was saving the Fatherland."

"I think we have our team leader."

"You're not serious, are you?"

"As serious as I was about Magnitogorsk."

Radl smiled. He remembered the technique well. "I'll draw up a suitable plan."

"This may seem like child's play to you, but I suspect that Himmler may have his own agenda. Last November, the Fuehrer himself told me of his opposition to nuclear war. I don't see any good coming of this."

"We'll use the Magnitogorsk technique with deftness this time. Meanwhile, if you are summoned to the Fuehrer headquarters, I'm sure you can let the Fuehrer inadvertently know about Himmler's latest project."

"I had planned on that. You have to admit that was one good piece of advice Schellenberg gave us on dealing with Himmler and the high command."

Radl roared with laughter again as he recalled Skorzeny's encounter with the head of the SD. Himmler had ordered Skorzeny to destroy the blast furnaces at Magnitogorsk. Skorzeny was about to tell Himmler the plan was insane. Sly baby-faced Walther Schellenberg had managed to intercept Skorzeny and gave him advice that had been useful ever since. "The more absurd a proposal that your superior gives you, the more rapturously you should receive it. Showy preparations should be made. Then gradually insert seeds of doubt that unanticipated difficulties may arise as time goes on. Eventually, the originator of the idea will lose faith in the concept if he hasn't forgotten it already." It had taken nine months to shelve the Magnitogorsk raid, but it had been accomplished using the technique. Radl and Skorzeny also noted that sleek young Schellenberg had become an SS general in his early thirties by ingratiating himself with Himmler in the same way.

After Radl finished laughing, he replied, "I'll get to work on this. I'll need to get information from the SD on information they have on the project and other areas of interest to us. It may take some time between the bombings and downed lines to get everything together."

"Get it together when you can, Karl. Oh, get Schreiber back with us. He deserves a break after what he has been through." Skorzeny rose, and Radl knew he was being dismissed.

"I'll make it look good so we can avoid Himmler's padded cell," Radl said.

"It could be worse, so let's watch ourselves. I need to see how the front is holding. Let me know how things are going."

Both men left the building. Radl got into his kubelwagen and started the engine. Skorzeny headed to the front. He was expecting his defenses to be breached at any time. The reinforcements were just not enough to overcome the superiority of the soviets opposing him.

Despite Skorzeny's pessimism, the lines did not break under him. After Radl left, Herman Goering had arrived at Skorzeny's headquarters. Skorzeny had to indulge the fat man's appearance at the front. At least the man had the guts to go where the fighting was. Goering had been especially pleased at the sight of the knocked out T-34s when he learned that Luftwaffe flak crews were responsible. On top of that, Goering had promised Skorzeny a fresh battalion of the Herman Goering Division, which arrived within twenty-four hours.

Skorzeny thought things had been going good when he received a phone call on the evening of February 27th. It was from Himmler's headquarters. Skorzeny was being relieved of his command in the morning. It was time for him to go back to being Germany's top commando. In addition, he was being summoned to a meeting with Himmler and Colonel Baumbach, commander of KG 200. The meeting was to be this week as soon as Baumbach could break free from his other duties. After he hung the phone up, Skorzeny realized that there were other problems brewing for him to be relieved. The atomic bomb project came to mind.

In the morning, a Waffen-SS officer wearing the collar patch of a standartenfuehrer in the Waffen-SS entered Skorzeny's headquarters. Colonel Hans Kempin had been sent from the army's 547th Volksgrenadier Division. He wore the iron cross first class with the second class ribbon in his buttonhole. He greeted Skorzeny warmly.

"It is good to meet you, Colonel Skorzeny. You have quite a reputation."

"It does appear that way. Please come in and have a seat."

Kempin took off his cap and had a seat in front of Skorzeny. Skorzeny unfolded a map to point out salient features. Skorzeny then took his replacement on a tour of the front. A few shells whistled overhead. Neither man flinched as soldiers scurried around. The 88s coughed a few times. They were still on ice flows in the river and by moving around were next to impossible to find. Snipers also remained on the flows to harass the Russians. Fortunately, the front was rather quiet compared with previous days as Skorzeny escorted Kempin around the defenses.

Kempin was suitably impressed and said so. "No one expected you to do what you did. I had a similar experience with the 547th. It is amazing what older troops can do with proper training."

Skorzeny prepared to take his leave of Schwedt. He gave orders for his Jagverbande troops to return to Friendenthal. He hated to take the best troops from Kempin, but if he was going to conduct commando operations again, he needed commandos. Skorzeny was sick of the notion in the high command that a commando operation was little more than a glorified Indian raid. His operations required as much meticulous attention to detail as did large extended campaigns if they were to have a chance of success.

Walther was waiting for him back at headquarters. Walther started the engine as soon as Skorzeny appeared. He had matured fast like everyone else who had survived, Skorzeny thought He could not resist needling the young officer though. "Anxious to get out of Schwedt?"

"I'm trying to keep you out of trouble with the Reichsfuehrer. I took a call from his headquarters in your absence. Your meeting is at 1700 promptly. Don't be late like you were at your last meeting."

Skorzeny gritted his teeth at the last remark. It wasn't Walther's fault. If only Himmler would let men like him fight the war. Instead, that pedantic ass calls him up to remind him not to be late for a meeting that would probably come of no good anyway "Very well," he mildly replied. "Call Radl and ask how he's doing on getting Schreiber back." He then got into the car and drove off.

Colonel Werner Baumbach was at his desk early on February 28,

1945. He had been placed in command of KG 200 in October 1944. He lit a cigarette as he shuffled through a stack of papers on his desk. He seemed to have one in his hand constantly after taking over his current assignment. A thin cloud of smoke floated above his head and almost blended in with his pale blond hair. His ice-blue eyes were as cold as the winter day outside. He wore a leather bomber jacket, although he only flew desks now and fought his battles with a succession of bureaucrats instead of the British and Americans. His decorations, however, were evidence of his mettle. Foremost among these was the Knights Cross with oak leaves and swords that dangled at his throat. He had been the fourteenth person in the entire German armed forces to earn the rare and prestigious award from Hitler on August 16, 1942. He had earned the decoration for his dive-bombing exploits in the Arctic regions flying a Ju 88 against the convoys bound for Russia. His award was even more special since most of the higher awards went to fighter pilots instead of bomber pilots. His skill in the big planes as well as his leadership qualities had earned him a transfer to command of the mysterious and shadowy KG 200. Because of the nature of the unit's operations, Baumbach was unlikely to get the highest decoration to the Knights Cross, the Diamonds. By now, medals were only so many baubles to him. He had to command a unit that operated under difficult circumstances. His headquarters was a beehive of activity as missions were planned and scrubbed, and his office constantly fought with party higher-ups and different intelligence agencies. Each group claimed its mission had priority over the others. Some insignificant functionary was always invoking the name of some higher insignificant functionary, threatening dire consequences if their mission was not flown out promptly. Baumbach had always ignored the threats, and the dire consequences had never materialized. After all, given the backdrop of short supplies and a decreasing number of planes and pilots, he could only do what was possible and no more. He certainly was not getting replacements as attrition took its toll on KG 200 as well as on any other unit of the Luftwaffe. He would have been a bundle of nerves if not for his nicotine and the fact that he did not care what his superiors thought.

An aide with a worried look on his face knocked on the door and entered quietly. Baumbach was invariably considerate of his officers and enlisted men. However, his tongue would let fly when provoked by idiotic proposals from his superiors. His short fuse ensured that he would not make general during the war despite his organizational and flying skills.

"What is it?" It was obvious that something was bothering the man.

"Himmler is on the phone." The aide stood stiffly and waited for an outburst. While the harangue would not be directed at him, the aide preferred not to be around when his boss let loose on superiors. He certainly did not want to hear things not meant for his ears.

As expected, Baumbach exploded in rage. "What in the hell does he want so early in the morning? If it's about Scherhorn, we can't fly when the weather won't let us. Also, we're low on fuel." Baumbach simmered down. "Put Himmler's lackey on the phone."

The aide practically whispered. "It's the Reichsfuehrer himself."

Baumbach was unimpressed and motioned for the aide to leave while he picked up the phone. "Oberst Baumbach here. How may I be of assistance?"

"How good of you to answer so promptly." The schoolmasterly voice gave no hint that Himmler had heard any of the outburst. "I am having a meeting with Obersturmbannfuehrer Skorzeny this afternoon at five to discuss a matter of great importance to the state. Your presence is required as we need your input for this most delicate operation."

Baumbach's face reddened even more. If this was about Scherhorn, he was going to bring it to a head now. To hell with a 1700 meeting. It was bad enough that Skorzeny thought that KG 200, including Baumbach, was under his supervision. It was time to dispel both men of that notion. After all, Goering was Baumbach's boss and still Hitler's heir apparent. "Reichsfuehrer, if this is about Colonel Scherhorn's group, I can already give you an answer."

Himmler casually cut him off. "I am interested in Colonel Scherhorn's rescue. However, I did not call you to discuss such a trivial matter. Such things are best settled between you and Obersturmbannfuehrer Skorzeny. What I have to discuss is of the highest importance. I expect you to be there."

Trivial matter! Baumbach barely contained his rage. He and Skorzeny had moved heaven and earth to get supplies to Scherhorn. Then a chill ran down Baumbach's spine. Himmler's choice of words was enough to make anyone with any insight run and hide. A matter of the highest importance meant learning a state secret, possibly one that could come back to haunt him later. Baumbach was not worried about his career. However, when people disappeared, that was another matter. "I'll be there on time," he conceded.

"I look forward to a productive meeting. Heil Hitler." The line went dead.

Baumbach held the receiver and then dropped it into place. He broke into a cold sweat. His aide poked head through the doorway again.

"Is everything okay, Herr Oberst?"

"Fine. Everything is just fine. I just have to meet with Himmler tonight about a matter of the highest importance. Whatever that means, make sure my driver is ready to pick me up at 1600 hours." Baumbach then went back to his paperwork.

CHAPTER 6

Skorzeny and Baumbach arrived at Himmler's military headquarters just prior to the appointed time. As Baumbach proceeded into Himmler's lair, the SS guards came to attention. Baumbach responded with a correct military salute. He hoped this would irritate the SS as the military had been required to give the Nazi Party salute after the July 20th bomb plot. He noted with satisfaction that the guards seemed awed by his decorations. He did not regard the SS and Himmler as highly as they regarded themselves. In addition, he was relieved to be at Himmler's military headquarters instead of the main SS headquarters in Berlin.

While Skorzeny and Baumbach cooled their heels, Himmler was deep in discussion with another man from the shadows of the SS. When he finally invited the two men into his office, Himmler appeared calm and in self-control. Neither man was aware of the inner turmoil that was troubling Himmler.

During his association with the fringe elements of society, Himmler had become a believer in astrology. He feared that his star was setting now. This feeling had flowered after Zhukov drove back a flanking attack in the Schmeidemuhl. Even though Himmler had used his best Waffen-SS troops for a spearhead, the attack failed miserably. Now Himmler began to stay in bed longer and made frequent visits to the SS hospital in Hohenlychen. Himmler was at his headquarters a few hours each day now.

Himmler was fighting for survival, and he knew it. His political survival was immediately at stake. He slowly comprehended the elaborate trap his archrival Bormann had prepared for him. In addition, Himmler's personal survival might be at stake if Germany lost the war. Already, Walther Schellenburg, the head of the SD, was attempting to negotiate immunity from any war crimes prosecution through his contacts in Stockholm.

The army was already scheming to slide Himmler out of the way as army group commander. Guderian had planned one last offensive against the Soviets with Army Group Vistula. He envisioned an attack in the Arnswalde area, which might lead to the clearing of the Red Army from Pomerania. The German Army could then reestablish contact with West Prussia. To plan the attack, Guderian wanted General Walter Wenck as chief of operations. Guderian had presented his plan on February 13th to Hitler who immediately saw that the goal was to remove Himmler from control of the army group and a shouting match ensued.

Himmler had been forced to watch the two men argue over his qualifications or lack of. He had been humiliated and embarrassed when Guderian presented the plan. Predictably, Hitler exploded, but Guderian held his ground.

"This is insane. Himmler does not need General Wenck to do his planning for him."

Guderian replied just as hotly, "Wenck must be placed in charge of the planning, or the attack will surely fail."

Hitler violently replied, "Don't tell me the Reichsfuehrer doesn't know how to do his job."

"The Reichsfuehrer does not have the training to plan such an attack. Wenck must plan it."

The wrangling continued for two hours. The two stubborn men resembled roosters at a cockfight as each refused to give ground. Finally, Hitler stepped in front of Himmler and said sarcastically,

"General Wenck will plan the attack. The general staff has won another battle this day. The conference will continue."

Things did not go as planned. Wenck was injured four days after the conference, and the attack did not achieve its objectives. The efforts continued to unseat Himmler as commander. Most galling to him were the efforts of his own Waffen-SS generals to get rid of him. The generals were turning out to be among the most vocal of his critics now, and there was little he could do as they had the backing of their army colleagues. He was looking at the prospect of his reputation being serious tarnished by his failure on the battlefield.

He had to admit that there was a certain poetic justice to all of this. He had refused to believe General Gehlen's estimates of Russian strength. Yet the greater irony might be that Gehlen had given him the information to extricate himself and Germany from an otherwise impossible situation.

Himmler hid these thoughts and reflections from his visitors. He projected a quiet air of confidence. Himmler stood to greet the two men as they entered his office and offered them refreshments. Baumbach had to grudgingly admit that Himmler was the perfect host. Baumbach was thinking of how to approach the conflict over Scherhorn when Skorzeny arrived. He noticed Skorzeny stiffen when he saw the fourth person in the room. Baumbach turned his gaze back to the person that had been in the room with Himmler earlier. The man appeared to be in his early forties and wore the rank of an obergruppenfuehrer in the Waffen-SS. Baumbach thought he looked familiar but could not place him. Skorzeny obviously knew who he was, and this likely meant that Scherhorn's battle group probably would not be discussed.

Skorzeny recognized General Hans Kammler immediately. He knew his presence tonight could only mean one thing. Himmler was serious about trying to steal the atomic bomb from the Allies if they developed one. Kammler was in charge of all secret weapons projects in the Reich. In the last six months, the rocket program had finally come under his control, and he had ensured that production remained steady at the costs of thousands of lives of slave laborers.

He reminded Skorzeny of what he had heard about Heydrich, good-looking, ambitious, and utterly ruthless. His feeling was that by going from the clutches of Bach dem Zelewski to those of Kammler's that he was replacing the devil with Beelzebub.

Himmler finally spoke. "Oberstleutnant Baumbach, I believe you already know Obersturmbannfuehrer Skorzeny." Both men nodded. "Gentlemen, if you don't already know him, I would like to introduce you to Obergruppenfuehrer Kammler. He is in charge of our secret weapons programs. There are some important matters of discussion that we need his input on. Please be seated."

All four took their seats. Baumbach noted that Skorzeny rubbed a fresh scar over his right eyebrow. *He didn't have that the last time we met*, Baumbach thought. Evidently, he is on the hot seat tonight. He had to admit that a certain grudging respect had developed between the two men over the months. Baumbach knew Skorzeny had torpedoed some of Himmler's harebrained schemes. If this was another one of those projects, then let the SS argue among themselves. The presence of Kammler suggested that this about using the Mistels to knock out bridges. That was KG 200's responsibility, but why involve Skorzeny? Baumbach relaxed as somehow he did not figure that he would be the major player tonight.

Himmler began his exposition softly. "The war has not gone exactly as we had hoped for the last year and a half. As you know, we are now fighting on our home soil. We are outnumbered on all fronts. However, there are some recent developments in weapons technology that we should try to avail ourselves of." Himmler paused and looked into the faces of the three officers. They looked back stolidly. He continued. "Of course, we will continue with other projects at hand to the best of our ability. For example, if we can get Scherhorn's men back to Germany, the psychological import would be incalculable. Imagine the effect on the German people."

Baumbach held his tongue. Fortunately, Skorzeny spoke. "I agree it would be a great propaganda victory and morale booster. However, two thousand men rescued from behind German lines are not going to win the war at this stage."

"Of course not." Himmler seemed slightly annoyed by the interruption. "My dear Obersturmbannfuehrer, that is why we are having this meeting tonight. If the war does not end with the desired outcome, then we should try to be in a position to reverse or moderate the terms."

Skorzeny and Baumbach both noticed that he did not say terms of surrender. It galled the two officers that a man in Himmler's position could not or would not speak openly. Skorzeny spoke again. "Perhaps it would help if we talked about what is planned as I only have the sketchiest details myself about this operation. I'm sure Oberst Baumbach is wondering what this is all about as well."

"I certainly am," Baumbach replied.

"Well, Skorzeny, I am glad you have given this project some thought," Himmler replied with a touch of sarcasm in his schoolmaster's voice.

"As much as I could while being a divisional commander," Skorzeny firmly replied.

Himmler ignored the reply and turned his head toward Kammler. "Perhaps, Obergruppenfuehrer Kammler, you can enlighten these gentlemen on the latest in weapons.

Kammler stood up to deliver his lecture. He obviously loved to hear himself speak. "We have received information that the Americans have made startling advances in the development of a nuclear bomb. Such a device could theoretically destroy an entire city."

Himmler interjected. "As Oberstrmbanfuehrer Skorzeny knows, the Fuehrer does not believe in nuclear war. There would be no winners. However, the Allies call for our unconditional surrender, leaving us little choice, particularly if they are building one."

Kammler continue, "In addition, the Japanese have requested supplies of uranium and other rare materials whose only use could be for a nuclear weapon. It appears that they have made progress as well. After all, they were privy to information from the Spanish TO ring."

"What is the TO ring?" Skorzeny asked.

Himmler responded, "It was a Spanish spy ring headed by Angel Alcazar de Velasco. They penetrated the Manhattan Project and were active until the middle of 1943. They provided information to the Japanese and us. We suspect that they provided a lot more to the Japanese."

Kammler concluded, "Such a weapon is still theoretical. However, the information we have shows such a device is likely to be tested by the Americans in six months. I feel that based on the technical data that we have acquired that their tests will be successful."

Himmler spoke, "I doubt that the Allies would hesitate to use the bomb. We are familiar with Hamburg in 1943 and more recently Dresden. The political leaders on the other side of this war do not see things the same way as our glorious Fuehrer. It is my proposal that we be in position to take control of such a device should the Americans succeed in making it."

"If it is made," Skorzeny concluded.

"So we are going to put men across the ocean to capture a bomb if it is made. If the Americans fail, then our men are stuck until or unless we pick them up." Baumbach was incredulous at the concept.

At least Skorzeny is showing some enthusiasm, Himmler thought. "We have to face the fact that the war may end on terms less favorable than those we received in 1918. Germany may be at the mercy of particularly vengeful victors unless we have some leverage."

Which means we are likely to have unconditional surrender forced down our throats, the two combat officers thought. Each was wondering what planet Himmler had finally stepped off of to finally head back to Earth. Not that he was exactly there yet. The looming defeat seemed to have finally brought him back to some sense of reality.

"Excuse me, Reichsfuehrer. We are looking at transporting two to three men across the ocean for a mission of dubious significance. KG 200 is already stretched to the limit." Baumbach was slightly exasperated now.

"It could be more men. That will depend on what Obersturmbannfuehrer Skorzeny decides what is necessary."

"Several trips to deliver a handful of men at a time would take us from carrying out other missions, perhaps several, for the time it would take to fly a plane to America and back." Baumbach thought he was trying to be reasonable.

Himmler continued on like an adult correcting an errant child. "My dear Oberst, possession of such a weapon would make our enemies think twice about imposing harsh terms at the war's conclusion. Have you forgotten Casablanca? Good. Then you will recall that the Allies demanded our unconditional surrender. You do know the meaning of that term? Then would you have our beloved Fuehrer taken by his foreign enemies and held up to ridicule? I don't think so. In addition, Reichmarshal Goering will support this mission as well."

The meaning was clear to Baumbach. Himmler had the goods on Goering and was prepared to use them to get his way. "Could U-boats be used to send more men?" Baumbach mildly asked.

"Too risky. The Americans and British as finding our U-boats too easily, usually from the air. I would like to remind you of what happened to the Abwehr during Operation Pastorius. Six of the eight agents were executed, and the Americans found all of their supplies. It was a tremendous waste of effort. Frankly, I do not envision this as a mission for only two or three men. This could easily involve a platoon. By the way, you do have all of the long-range flying boats under your command as I recall."

"Yes, but as you recall, those are being held in reserve to fly the government leadership off in case of capitulation." Baumbach had fumed at these planes being held in reserve for the golden pheasants. This was a good time to throw this back at Himmler and the party. "They are supposed to be flown to Greenland to hide out."

"I don't believe that the party leadership has always had their priorities straight." Himmler showed no emotion as he continued. "They can get there by ship, U-boat, or swim as far as I am concerned. They are not essential for the successful outcome of this war."

Baumbach thought he was going to fall out of his chair. He had heard that there was an estrangement between Himmler and the party hierarchy, but he had not expected a statement of such complete contempt to come from the Reichsfuehrer. Baumbach began to feel uncomfortable and wished he were somewhere else.

Meanwhile, Skorzeny shifted uncomfortably in his chair. Himmler's remarks had caught him off guard as well. He knew that Himmler would like to summarily hang most of the party leadership in public. He had not expected Himmler to express that sentiment to an outsider. Skorzeny sensed difficulty in shelving this operation.

"How many people do you plan to transport?" Baumbach asked. "Skorzeny?"

"I don't know for sure. Probably a squad at least. As many as one or two platoons. It depends on what we need and whom we can find that meets our requirements. I have already discussed the difficulties that I foresee with my ADC already. I need a good leader with a good second in command just in case. An explosives expert will be needed. And several people with knowledge of the United States would be useful."

"Very well," Himmler replied. "I think that a Wiking flying boat could handle that."

"So it is to be by plane," Skorzeny stated.

"I think that would be best," Himmler concluded. "I believe Oberst Baumbach is very capable of handling that." Turning toward Baumbach, he paid the famed pilot a compliment. "My dear Oberst, I wonder if anyone has told you of the excellent job you and your men are doing. It is unfortunate that you did not take command of KG 200 sooner. The Fuehrer himself has praised the job that you are carrying out under such arduous circumstances."

The conference continued another hour. The problem of Battlegroup Scherhorn was discussed briefly. Further commando attacks were discussed as well as the insertion of agents. Himmler finally adjourned the meeting. "Gentlemen, that is all that I have on my agenda. Thank you for a productive evening."

The three officers summoned for the meeting filed out of Himmler's office. Baumbach and Skorzeny then swiftly strode out of the building to smoke. Himmler was adamant that there be no smoking in his presence. Both men felt relief as the nicotine entered their bodies.

As they walked to their cars, Baumbach decided to feel Skorzeny out more. "I noticed your enthusiasm exceeded mine slightly for this project. Do you really want to send men to steal this big bomb?"

Skorzeny did not waste words. "It's one of Himmler's madcap ideas. What in the hell he is thinking is beyond me."

"It's a waste of resources for me. I could carry out two or three missions for this one flight across the ocean."

"I agree. I'm in the same predicament as you are with dwindling reserves. Trained commandos just don't walk off the street to join my unit. They need a lot of training to be good at what they do."

"And I can't replace planes once they're down or lost. Parts are hard to come by. Some flights have to be cancelled because of fuel shortages," Baumbach said bitterly. "Worse, everyone thinks their mission is the most important one, and their flight should be the next one. It doesn't matter if the area is fogged in or a plane is down, or if I lost a pilot the night before."

"I know the feeling. I just lost eight hundred men in East Prussia at a position that was declared a fortress. I ordered the survivors out when it became obvious that they were about to be overrun. Fifteen came back."

Baumbach whistled in admiration. "That took some balls overriding a Fuehrer order. So what do you plan to do about this proposed waste of men?"

"Shelve it. Discreetly, of course." Skorzeny paused and then told Baumbach how he had dealt with the issue of sending a team into Magnitogorsk. "It took me nine months, but I haven't heard anything else."

Baumbach laughed at that. "Well done, Otto. There is more to you than I had ever guessed, my dear quintessential SS officer. Well, I'll do my part in the spirit you propose."

Skorzeny became serious. "Tread very carefully on this one. I think Himmler is serious on this one. I would make sure all of my paperwork is in order. He just didn't bring Kammler for the hell of it. You noticed that Schellenberg wasn't around either."

"Now that you mention it, I did. Very interesting."

"Also, I was relieved of divisional command to become head commando again. With what, I don't know. I lost most of my best men in East Prussia. And I'm sure you noticed his not-so-subtle remark about putting leverage on the Reichasmarshall. We have to be careful on this one. I suspect that the Fuehrer is ignorant of this affair."

"That would not be a first, I suspect. Well, KG 200 will be ready for whatever is proposed. You don't think I'm still here because I can't play these games as well. Good luck on your part."

Skorzeny was at his car when one of Himmler's aides came running for him. "Obersturmbannfuehrer Skorzeny, Major Radl is on the phone."

Skorzeny cursed silently and walked back into the headquarters. He smiled inside, as he knew that Radl's use of army rank instead of the cumbersome SS rank was sure to irritate some in this building, including Himmler. Skorzeny absentmindedly lit up another cigarette as he entered the building. He walked over to the receiver and picked it up.

"What is it, Karl?"

"Schreiber. We are having difficulty getting him back to Friedenthal. He is practically under arrest. The local commander says he is too valuable to lose."

"And he is too valuable for me to lose. After losing Foelkersam, he's our best officer and most experienced. I'll deal with it in the morning and pull what strings I can then." Skorzeny curtly hung the phone up and found himself face to face with Himmler. He swiftly put out his cigarette against the table, as there was no ashtray.

"A filthy disgusting habit, Obersturmbannfuehrer Skorzeny." Himmler's disgust was obvious. "Can't you refrain at all from one cigarette? I still wonder about your ability to command with such an apparent lack of control. Please come back into my office."

A beet-red Skorzeny followed the black-clad figure back into his office. The aides had scarcely concealed features of glee as Skorzeny was apparently going to his doom this evening over such a trivial matter. *Let them think whatever they want to,* Skorzeny thought.

Himmler motioned for Skorzeny to have a seat. "Tell me about Hauptsturmfuehrer Maxmillian Schreiber." He then folded his arms like a schoolmaster awaiting a student's presentation.

Skorzeny was caught off guard. It was as if the previous private court-martial had never taken place. Skorzeny collected his thoughts and spoke, "He's probably my best man right now, especially since I lost Major Foelkersam."

Himmler opened a file and began leafing through it. Skorzeny realized it was Schreiber's. "I see that he was born in the United States and grew up there."

"His English is flawless and with no accent. During the Ardennes offensive, some American prisoners asked him where he grew up in the United States." Skorzeny looked at the folder and thought, *Does the bastard have ears everywhere?* He knew Radl would not have mentioned the possibility of Schreiber leading the mission. Had Himmler had their offices bugged?

Himmler read on, speaking some of his thoughts aloud. "He was with the Brandenburgers from the very beginning. He took part in the campaign in the low countries."

"He followed Foelkersam over to my unit in 1943. The baron always considered him his best soldier, his right-hand man."

"As you may know, he is being recommended for the oak leaves.

"I'm sure that he deserves them. He is a good man."

"As good as you, Obersturmmbanfuehrer?"

"Possibly better. He has been on more commando operations than I have. Most of them involved the use of enemy uniforms. He is something of a legend in our unit."

"Perhaps if we had heard of him before, he might be in your current position instead of you. I take it you were considering him for command of this operation we discussed?"

"Yes, that is correct. He's perfect for the job."

Himmler continued examining the file. "I see that his father fought in the Freikorps in the east around Lithuania. The commander was Harold Alexander. Interesting. The current British field marshal?"

"Yes. Alexander was detached from the British Army as an observer. Evidently, he did not think too highly of the Communists and took a more active role in things. The elder Schreiber was aide to Baron Rahden, Alexander's German ADC."

"Most remarkable. The whole family. The other siblings were in Norway after the war. The older siblings went there after the last war to keep from starving. It is unfortunate that we were not able to get the Norwegians to see things clearly and had to invade."

"It's certainly not the best way to repay a favor."

Himmler ignored the remark and summarized Schreiber's career from the file. "Born in late 1919 in St. Louis and lived with an uncle. Arrived back in Germany at age ten. The usual progression through the Hitler Youth. He joined the 800th transportation company just before the war broke out. Received Iron Cross, second class in Poland and first class in France. Clasp to Iron Cross in Greece. German Cross in gold in Russia."

"That should have been a Knights Cross," Skorzeny interjected.

"Which he finally received in Yugoslavia along with his commission." Himmler paused over some sections on training and continued with more of Schreiber's exploits. "Also Partisan badge for his actions around Dvar, infantry badge, and close combat award. Wound badge in gold for six wounds now." Himmler closed the dossier and shoved it over to Skorzeny. He continued in his methodical voice, "Of course, his file is not complete."

"Excuse me, Reichsfuehrer?"

"His recent destruction of over sixty Russian tanks on his escape back to our lines will be another glorious entry into his record as well as in the annals of the Waffen-SS."

"I did not know the details, but I certainly agree with your assessment."

"You are sure that his English is good?"

"He was an English instructor for Operation Grief."

"Very well. I think we have our man. I wish to speak with the two of you later this week about this mission. It appears fortuitous that you ordered him out when you did. His loss would be incalculable now."

"It does appear that I am going to have a hard time getting him back. The local commander is talking about him being too valuable to leave."

"So I heard. That will be rectified, Obersturmbannfuehrer. By the way, do you have any ideas for a codename for this operation?"

Skorzeny rubbed his eye again. His recent wound throbbed again. Finally, he blurted out, "Gotterdammerung."

"An interesting choice."

"It seems appropriate under the circumstances."

Himmler eyed Skorzeny coldly. "Is there something bothering you about this mission?"

"Yes, there is. I still cannot get over the Fuehrer's abhorrence of nuclear weapons. Now we are to steal one if it is made and possibly use it. Does the Fuehrer even know about this operation?"

"No, he doesn't."

"Then why not?"

Himmler decided to play his cards. He needed Skorzeny's full support. He took his glasses off and almost whispered as he spoke. "What I am about to tell you cannot leave this room. There is a high-level Soviet spy in the high command. He is very high. He has been giving the Russians details of our operations from the day we first invaded Russia in 1941." Himmler sighed. "He is known as Werther. Unfortunately, he has been very clever as we have been unable for four years to pinpoint his true identity. He has given away valuable information on all of our operations. Our victories might have been greater and our defeats only dreamed for by Stalin. Werther probably cost us the battle of Stalingrad. Had we won there, we would have knocked Russia out of the war. These are only a few examples."

"Could Canaris be Werther?" Skorzeny was stunned by the revelation.

"I wish that he was. However, information is still getting back to Moscow from Werther. I hardly doubt that our guards are giving the good admiral a transmitter as well as information to transmit back to Moscow. We have sadly confirmed that the flow of information continues."

"And if you tell the Fuehrer about the proposed operation, you are afraid that he will let this Werther inadvertently know."

"Exactly. You do see my predicament. Look at how good Werther is. He escaped our round up of the Red Orchestra two years ago. Our spy in the Kremlin who provided the information about the bomb has been unable to discover his identity."

Skorzeny stood up and slammed his fist against the wall. "So we have been betrayed from within. Of all of the rottenness I have heard about, this is the worst. How much of what we have done has been in vain?" His face was red with rage.

"A lot, Skorzeny. And it will continue. We are still trying to locate Werther, but I can tell you nothing new. You understand why I have chosen this route about stealing atomic weapons. Also, understand that the Fuehrer is counting on you even if he doesn't know it. All of Germany is."

Skorzeny looked back at Himmler. "It's Schreiber that you are counting on if he goes. He'll be doing all of the hard work."

"He must be aware of how important this mission is. You must prepare him thoroughly." Himmler stood up and shook hands with Skorzeny as he dismissed him. "You must not fail. Auf weidersehen, Obersturmbannfuehrer."

Skorzeny turned and left the office. He heard Himmler ordering an aide to contact the head of the SD, Walter Schellenberg, immediately. Skorzeny had the feeling that Himmler had not disclosed everything there was to know about the bomb and about Werther.

As Skorzeny suspected, Himmler had not confided all of his secrets to his top commando. He had a very good idea who Werther was since Schellenberg ran a very efficient spy service. When he penetrated the Abwehr, Schellenberg found that Admiral Canaris had solid evidence that Werther was Martin Bormann. Schellenberg had then independently confirmed the admiral's findings. Bormann had access to a transmitter and was the only person with access to all of Hitler's notes, including his military decisions. Unfortunately, Hitler would not have believed anything that Canaris produced at that point. On top of that, he would not believe anything derogatory about Bormann from anyone. The bearer of such evidence could present it to Hitler only at great risk to his own life. Even Himmler's exalted position could not guarantee his own safety if he attempted to bring down Bormann. In addition, Bormann might very well be aware of Himmler's flirtations with the Western Allies. And now Himmler's failings as military commander did little to enhance his status in Hitler's eyes. Himmler had considered having Bormann poisoned by the secret Gestapo unit entrusted with such matters. However, Bormann ate the same food as Hitler when in the leader's presence, and so that idea was tossed out as unfeasible. Other means of assassination were dismissed as nonviable as well.

Himmler considered his situation as his aides located Schellenberg. There would be no more military glory in this war. If his plan worked and Schreiber stole the bomb, then Himmler's star would be ascendant. He would be the savior of Germany, and the SS would be preeminent and then he could deal with Hitler's Iago. He would not need to convince Hitler of his traitor's infidelity with Stalin, and so Hitler's absolute faith in Bormann would be irrelevant. No matter what means he would need to employ, Himmler would do as he acted then. Hitler and Goering could be retired, and Himmler would emerge as the new Fuehrer. That was an appealing thought.

Finally, Schellenberg had been located, and Himmler spoke to him. "Reichsfuehrer Himmler here. Mueller hasn't given you any more problems, has he? Good. Listen, I need you to have Haupsturmfuehrer Schreiber brought back to Friedenthal tomorrow. His army commander will not let go of him. I suspect the army will not say anything to a pair of SD men coming to pick him up." Then as an afterthought, he said, "Send Sturmbannfuehrer Dietz to see me tomorrow." Himmler hung the phone up and resumed signing his paperwork.

Schellenberg hung the phone up with great relief. The head of the Gestapo had arrested him earlier in January, but Himmler had ordered his immediate release. Tonight's phone call showed that

Schellenberg was still in Himmler's good graces. The mention of Dietz only confirmed his thoughts. Whenever Himmler summoned Dietz, the reason was usually an important one. He would ensure that Dietz was promptly at Himmler's headquarters in the morning.

Skorzeny arrived back at Friedenthal later that night. Radl was still up. "Ah, you're still up, Karl," Skorzeny said wearily as he entered.

"Couldn't sleep. Plus, I wanted to hear what our great leader the Reichsfuehrer had to say. Anything important?"

"The usual. Baumbach was there along with Kammler. Interestingly, he had Schreiber's file. How did that happen?"

"I certainly didn't tell them he was a consideration, although some of the SD have been snooping around lately. I did mention to one how much trouble we were having getting Schreiber back. The SD man did ask some questions about Max, and I told him he was now our best man. He offered to help, and interestingly, I haven't seen it since. I guess I opened my big mouth."

"Don't worry as long as we get Schreiber back. Still we will watch ourselves on this one. Himmler confirmed my suspicion that the Fuehrer is ignorant of this affair. Ostensibly, Himmler has not told him because of a highly placed spy in our high command. I still am not sure that Himmler has told us everything."

"I would be surprised if he did," Radl resounded with jovial sarcasm. "He certainly didn't tell you everything about Schwedt, did he?"

"He didn't know what he was doing at Schwedt and still doesn't," Skorzeny spat out.

"This whole operation still may take a while to organize," Radl continued cheerfully. "There still may be a way to avoid one of Himmler's padded cells. Of course, Schreiber may be the lucky one."

"If this is delayed enough and we keep him from the front line, he may actually survive the war."

"He deserves to, but so did Adrian."

Skorzeny shook his head. He was tired now. "Do what you can to get Schreiber back, just as long as he gets back. I'm going to bed, Karl."

CHAPTER 7

The following day, Himmler convened his war council for Army Group Vistula. After two hours, Himmler concluded the conference and let his professional military men finalize the details. He returned to his office to find a SD officer with the rank of sturmbannfuehrer waiting for him. He wore awards for both classes of the Iron Cross and German Cross in silver. His green service dress uniform while uncluttered with decorations was immaculate in appearance. He appeared to be in his midthirties except for his thinning blond hair.

"Greetings, Reichsfuehrer."

"Oh, Dietz, I'm glad you're punctual. I'm very busy today. Please sit down."

Sturmbannfuehrer Konrad Dietz, a shadowy man in shadowy organization, made himself comfortable. "How am I to employ my nefarious talents in your behalf today?"

Himmler detected a slight mocking in the man's voice but ignored it. "There is an important matter for me to discuss with you. How much do you know about nuclear weapons?"

"Mainly that they are on the drawing board. No one has made one as far as we know. I am familiar with conventional explosives.

This theoretical stuff that the scientists come up with isn't of much use to me. It doesn't help me blow up a building or assassinate some premier. I have to have real materials to do my job."

"Understandable. What if I told you that the Americans are building such a weapon?"

"It would be nice to make sure it never got dropped on Germany."

"Agreed. Even better if we could get hold of it."

"What are we supposed to do with it if we did? Transporting large bombs is not my specialty. Blowing them up is."

"I was thinking along the lines of leverage. Blackmail, if you prefer."

"How's that?"

"You may have noticed that the war has not been going favorably for us."

"So I have. I believe our last notable victory was at Arnheim."

"You also know what the Allies are calling for, unconditional surrender. You know what that means."

"Only too well."

"Obersturbannfuehrer Skorzeny is preparing a team to steal this device when it is made. It would make the Allies think twice about using it if we have one ready to explode in, let's say, New York City. Also, we might arrive at a negotiated peace or make the peace terms less onerous."

"Exactly where do I fit in?"

"You will have the names of the operatives who are still active in the United States. I also want you to be sure that the mission goes as planned."

"I gather you have some concerns?"

"I'm not sure how enthusiastic Skorzeny is about the mission. I'm sure that he will come up with a team. He has already picked a promising leader. Officially, you will take orders from the man in charge. You will work on your own, if necessary. I doubt that you will need to explode the bomb. However, if you need to destroy a city to make our point, then you will do it."

"Do you have any targets in mind?"

"Not yet. However, an explosion in New York or Washington DC should get their attention. You may have to make that decision on your own when that time comes, depending on the circumstances."

"I appreciate your continued confidence in me."

"You have demonstrated your ability in the past. Here is some information on your new commander." Himmler slid Schreiber's file to Dietz. Himmler filled in some details of Schreiber's secret missions.

"Quite a character," Dietz remarked slowly. "If anyone can pull this off, he can. He sounds better than Skorzeny."

"My thoughts exactly. By the way, how is your English?"

"Tolerable now. It was better a few years ago."

"I suggest you refresh your knowledge of it."

"Yes, Reichsfuehrer."

"I will summon you when I need you again. Please have a safe trip back to Berlin."

Konrad Dietz stood up, smartly clicked his heels, gave the Nazi salute, and departed. After he left, Himmler breathed a sigh of relief. He sat back exhausted from his tenure as army group commander. He then reflected on Dietz and his activities over the years. Himmler wondered now what was true and how much embellishment had taken place over the years. Dietz himself gave no clue about his exploits and let others do the talking. There was plenty to talk about. Dietz joined the SD in 1934, and so he did not get to stain his hands at the expense of the SA during the Night of the Long Knives. His hands had become crimson enough over the years. Himmler recalled that Dietz had been involved with Operation Canned Goods, which ignited the war with Poland. There, Germans convicted of crimes had been dressed in Polish uniforms and then shot to simulate an attack on German soil. Besides the possibility of Naujocks, Dietz was the only man alive who had participated from the SD. All of the others had conveniently disappeared over the succeeding years, as Himmler did not like inconvenient witnesses running around.

Diets had continued to work as Naujocks's right-hand man for several years. He had traveled to the Iberian Peninsula and generated reports that led to the recall of the heads of German consulates in

Spain and Portugal. The replacements were more conducive to the requests of the SD than the original diplomats had been. Dietz had returned to Germany in time to aid Naujocks in the abduction of the British agents Werner and Best at Vento. After the fall of France, he was back on the Iberian Peninsula as the SD plotted to kidnap the Duke of Windsor.

When Churchill recalled the duke before the plans could be finalized, Dietz had moved on. Himmler thought his next appearance had been in Rumania. The SD had plotted to remove Marshal Antonescu and replace him with Horia Sima, who commanded the Iron Guard. When the coup failed, Dietz smuggled Sima out of the country and into Germany. This was fortunate because of the political fallout that followed. The SD had acted counter to the policy of the Foreign Office and Himmler's rival power there, Foreign Minister Joachim von Ribbentrop, had worked Hitler into a frenzy. Hitler had shouted at Himmler that he would smoke out the black plague if it did not shape up. Himmler and Heydrich had been shaken by the outburst and had kept low profiles for weeks afterward. That did not keep Dietz from pursuing other duties that Himmler deemed essential. Himmler had placed Dietz on detached duty with the secret Gestapo unit Section A-4 charged with carrying out the discreet assassinations of party officials who were embarrassing and guilty of treason or of other actions that Himmler felt made them not fit for living. This unit had been formed to avoid the spectacle of a public trial for prominent officials and therefore tarnishing the party's image. On top of that, following the demise of the person in question, Goebbels was able to put on an extravaganza by staging an elaborate state funeral. Poisons had been developed which did not leave any traces that could be picked up by current medical tests. Dietz had made liberal uses of the chemicals at his disposal, and if that wasn't enough, there was always an accident waiting to happen.

Himmler almost had to rein Dietz in immediately after his first accident. In 1942, Fritz Todt's plane had crashed immediately after the takeoff at the Fuehrer's headquarters of all places. Even though Todt had privately irritated the Fuehrer by saying the war was lost,

Hitler had ordered an immediate investigation into the disaster. Fortunately, the SS handled the subsequent inquiry, and Dietz's role remained undetected. Himmler later recalled with delight when Viktor Lutze, Roehm's successor as head of the SA had died in an accident on the autobahn in 1943 after obtaining some eggs on the black market. Lutze was trying to regain the power the SA lost in the blood purge of 1934. His accident put an end to those ambitions. Dietz had also gone to Spain as the SD attempted to replace Franco with someone who would bring Spain into the war on Germany's side. Their candidate, General Munoz, had been commander of the Spanish Blue Division in Russia and enjoyed the support of several right-wing officers. He was a willing conspirator and made preparations for a coup. However, Franco's intelligence was as adept as the SD, and the plot was discovered. Franco chose not to execute the popular general or even bring him to trial but instead recalled Munoz and promoted him to an important-sounding but largely ceremonial office where an eye could be kept on the scheming commander.

In February 1943, Dietz had traveled to Bulgaria and assassinated General Christo Loukov when Loukov started to voice pro-Russian sentiments. Loukov had been shot outside a theater in Sofia. Best of all, Dietz arranged for the pistol to be found in the possession of a member of the Communist National Liberation Organization. Later, when King Boris III didn't see eye to eye with Hitler about Bulgaria's future role in the war, Dietz happened to show up shortly before the king collapsed and subsequently died. Recently, in 1944, he had gone to Budapest where he assisted Skorzeny in the abduction of Admiral Horthy. More recently, he had been in Stockholm keeping a watch over negotiations between Schellenberg and the British to make sure that there was no outside interference.

Himmler recognized that Dietz was a very dangerous man, perhaps the most lethal in his employ, to think that British intelligence considered Skorzeny the most dangerous man in Europe. It was nice to know he had kept some things secret from MI6. However, Himmler realized that Dietz harbored ambitions of his own, and

Himmler had decided that Dietz must never be allowed to accumulate the power and position that Heydrich had. Of course, the matter of Dietz's half-Jewish wife was a useful piece of leverage in keeping the man in line. On further reflection, it occurred to Himmler that Canaris might have had such information on Heydrich. After all, Heydrich had never made any serious moves against the admiral despite their rivalry. At least Himmler held the secrets on Dietz. The man was perfect for the mission. He was ruthless and capable, and the motivation regarding his wife could always be discreetly alluded to.

Himmler rubbed his head. He was tired, and under these conditions, it was hard for him to maintain his front for his men. He decided that maybe he needed to go to the hospital again that evening. His abdominal pains were getting worse during his tenure as army group commander. He called his aide and had an appointment made. He then retired to bed.

Schreiber was hunkered down in his bunker trying to stay warm. Fortunately, fighting had died down in his sector. He and the other survivors of Task Force East rested as well as they could in their cold, primitive conditions. They were munching on their rations when a messenger arrived.

"Hauptmann Schreiber, you are required back at headquarters."

"Anything special going on?" Schreiber asked.

The messenger stammered briefly. "Nothing that I know of, but two SD officers showed up and strutted into the general's quarters. A few minutes later, Oberst Weiss was yelling for me to report immediately. He told me to find you at once."

"Enough said. I get the idea. Let's go."

Schreiber got up and walked through the frigid air to the headquarters. What did the SD want with him? he wondered. Was he in trouble for leading the break out from Hohensalza even though he was following orders? If so, he had no regrets, even though his previous encounters with the SD had not been particularly pleasant. The last time had been during the Ardennes offensive when he and other Waffen-SS officers had tried to get the SD to release some villagers that the security forces had rounded up. The SD had brushed of all attempts to reason and summarily shot thirty men.

Schreiber arrived at the headquarters fairly quickly. A sleek black Mercedes with a driver was parked in front of the general's quarters. The SD evidently did not plan to remain long as the engine was still running. He walked inside and spotted two SD officers immediately. They were dressed warmly in dark green overcoats with their distinctive black diamond on the left sleeve. Their highly polished black leather boots contrasted sharply with Schreiber's muddy worn combat boots. Although the senior SD officer outranked him, Schreiber decided to ignore him until they forced the issue. He started looking for Colonel Weiss when the two officers intercepted him.

"Hauptsturmfuehrer Schreiber?" the senior officer asked.

"That would be me. What's this about?"

"I'm Sturmbannfuehrer Mohr. We have been asked to pick you up and take you back to Friedenthal. Evidently, you are needed there urgently by Obersturmbannfuehrer Skorzeny."

"That's news to me." Schreiber was suspicious of these men.

"That's all we know. Schellenberg called last night and ordered us to get you out of here. Evidently, your superiors here would not let go of you easily."

Schreiber looked around the room. Everyone else was pretending they did not hear the exchange. Several personnel had disappeared into the cold. He looked back at the two officers. "Well then, I'm ready. I would like to have one more nice meal and bath before this war is over."

The two SD officers said nothing, and the three men walked out to the waiting car and sped off. They traveled in silence. Even the driver gave no hint if something sinister was up. Finally, the warmth of the car lulled him asleep, and he forgot about his concerns.

An arm nudged him. Mohr was waking him up. "We're here."

Schreiber shifted in his seat and blinked his eyes. He blinked again. He couldn't believe it. They were diving up to the main building at Friedenthal. He wasn't in trouble after all. An uneasy feeling told there was a catch to all of this. However, he kept his thoughts to himself as he got out of the Mercedes and thanked the two SD officers for returning him. He then walked toward Skorzeny's office.

He found Skorzeny at his desk with Radl. Radl looked up and quipped, "The prodigal son returns."

Skorzeny looked up. "Mein Gott, Max, you actually made it."

"Of course, I did. Did you just expect me just to disappear without saying goodbye?"

Skorzeny and Radl stood up and clapped Schreiber on the back. Schreiber knew their elation was genuine as frontline troops rejoiced when their comrades returned safely from combat.

"We were worried about you," Radl blurted out. "We thought we wouldn't see anyone form Task Force East again."

"You almost didn't as not many of us made it," Schreiber replied somberly. "Only fifteen of us made it out, as you may know."

"I know. You've been recommended for the oak leaves for your actions. I know that's small recompense for the men you've lost."

"Can you tell them to keep it? I've got enough decorations."

"We all do," Skorzeny replied. "I know how you feel, especially after losing Foelkersam. Any idea what happened?"

"We were all hurt. I think the fight went out of a lot of men when they realized the baron was gone. It seemed like the Russians planned to trap us between the two columns. If it was an ambush, it was nearly perfect. Fortunately, each column thought we were the other columns since we had our Russian speakers at both ends. We were able to get the first blows in, but the Russians recovered quickly. We had Adrian on a tractor. When I last saw it, the Russians were all around it. There were too many by then to break through. The preparations we made just before the fight were enough to get the survivors out. It was awful."

"That's enough. Fill out a report later. How do you feel?' Skorzeny asked.

"Frankly, I could use some leave. The last few weeks have taken a lot out of me. By the way, what was the deal with the SD bringing me in? The army men thought I was a dead man when I left."

Skorzeny sighed. "I wish that you weren't right, but you are. An especially important mission has come up, and I need you to lead it."

"An especially important one for the high command to get rid of. What have the generals come up with now?" Schreiber cynically remarked.

Radl laughed loudly, and then Skorzeny burst out as well. Radl had come up with the phrase in the early days at Friendenthal when the German High Command would get rid of troublesome tasks by giving them to Skorzeny to deal with. Invariably, the tasks would be described as "especially important." Radl had decided that the tasks were especially important for the high command to wash their hands of. The recent attempts to extricate Scherhorn were a prime example of the generals' ways of dealing with unwanted problems. Let Skorzeny handle it.

"It's not the generals," Skorzeny finally said when he quit laughing. "It's worse. It's Himmler's project. And even better, the Fuehrer doesn't know about it."

Schreiber whistled. "So I presume he has his own agenda. What is it anyway?"

"Basically, you are to lead a team into the United States and steal a certain secret weapon that the Americans are developing, somewhat similar to your expedition with Foelkersam into Maikop. You will be wearing American uniforms to penetrate the American's security."

"It may take more than uniforms. Things like ID cards, for example."

"I realize that. We're just getting started."

"Sounds pretty heady. What am I supposed to be stealing?"

"Ever heard of nuclear weapons?"

"Not really. What is it?"

"Right now, it still is in development in the laboratory. Most of what I've been told indicates that we are still in the theory stage. I know for a fact the Fuehrer is opposed to these kinds of weapons so that may account for our lack of progress. However, our intelligence has good information that the Americans have made tremendous strides in this area and may be able to test such a weapon in a few months. Such a bomb is thought to be able of destroying an entire city."

"That's some bomb. What am I supposed to do after I get the bomb?"

"Hold it in reserve for future use as leverage, blackmail, or whatever you want to call it."

"This sounds like it could be complicated. What if we get over there and they can't make the bomb or we can't steal it? What then?"

"Then you try to get back. I'd go through Mexico."

"Aren't we at war with Mexico?"

Radl answered this time, "Officially, yes. Mexico declared war on us in 1943 under pressure from the United States. However, we found out that Mexico had no intention of prosecuting the war since it is unpopular. To date, no Mexican troops have appeared in Europe."

"Anything else?"

"Plenty," Skorzeny answered this time. "I'll give you details as far as locations, contacts, etc., later. You will probably want to use your contacts with your old Brandenburg friends and find some English speakers."

"I thought we had scraped the barrel for those during Operation Grief," Schreiber muttered.

"We may have. However, I think you want as many English speakers as possible. After all, not too many people came over to us from the Brandenburg Division."

"I'll try to jog my memory."

"Before you do that, why don't you kick your heels up for a day or two? If possible, I will get you some leave. You've earned it."

"Thanks for throwing me back into the fire," Schreiber mumbled.

"Don't give up hope. I have thought about using the same technique on this as we did on the Magnitogorsk project."

Schreiber smiled as he realized that things could go in any direction. He would just wait and see. Right now, he would follow

Skorzeny's advice and relax. It might be some time before he did that again.

The first week of March 1945 was hectic for Colonel Baumbach. He did not know if Himmler's scheme would come to fruition, but Goering's arm had certainly been twisted. When Baumbach approached the Reichsmarshal, he had been informed to aid Himmler in any way that was needed. Baumbach reluctantly contacted Captain Peter Stahl, commander of Detachment Olga. Currently, the detachment was based in Frankfurt Main and was the KG 200 unit originally responsible for flying clandestine missions in Western Europe and Iceland. After Stahl took command, Detachment Carmen was disbanded and absorbed into Olga. Stahl's responsibility now included Italy and North America. Considerable effort and resources were expended to supply agents and equipment in these enemy territories.

It wasn't as if KG 200 and Baumbach had nothing to do. Baumbach had received orders to "oppose all Russian crossings on the Oder and Neisse rivers." Baumbach had decided to use the HS 293-guided bomb against the captured bridges. He had fought a bitter fight with the Luftwaffe Operations Staff over the use of the modern bomb. It had been previously forbidden to use the device against land targets for fear that the enemy might be able to reassemble the weapon from its debris; therefore its only targets had been ships. Fortunately, Hitler's backing had ended the lunacy or Baumbach would not have been able to meet with Stahl.

Stahl was busy himself with plans. He currently was scheduling a flight into Belgium and Paris to drop off agents. In addition, he was looking for another base because of the advancing Allied army. He had been visiting airfields in his Ju 188 and thought he had found a base at Echterdingen to transfer Olga to.

Baumbach strode imperiously into Stahl's office. Stahl came to attention, but Baumbach motioned him to stand at ease. "Forget the formalities, Peter. I am busy and in a hurry."

Stahl mumbled, "I had no idea that you were coming. I thought you were occupied with the bridgeheads."

"Well, I had no idea until Himmler dropped another delightful operation in my lap." Baumbach's voice was tinged with sarcasm. Stahl smiled thinly as neither man had a high regard for the Nazi elite.

"Sounds serious if it came straight from Himmler, and you've taken time from busting up bridges."

"It is. Worse, Hitler may not even know about it. Anyway, the mission is as follows: Skorzeny is to organize a commando team that will enter the United States and steal a top-secret bomb that is capable of destroying an entire city. Himmler wants to get hold of the weapon in case the war does not turn out as we desire."

"This sounds a little bizarre. What are we supposed to do with the bomb after it's stolen?"

"It gets even better. Hopefully, we will have the bomb as leverage. But the Americans haven't even made the weapon. They have made tremendous progress in the bomb's development, but testing is supposed to take place in about four months."

"This is insane. We don't have four months. The war will be over by then."

"I wouldn't say that too loudly if I was you. Of course, this means this gets dumped on you since Olga is your department."

"This is just great. Just as I'm looking for another airfield to move to before we get overrun. It's too bad our wonder weapons haven't materialized."

Baumbach nodded in agreement. "If only we had developed the Me 262 two years ago or the guided missiles. Well, at least select a crew, make a flight plan, and so on. Pick an out-of-the way location to drop Skorzeny's men off."

"So we are going to carry this out?"

"Just make the preparations on paper anyway." Baumbach practically whispered. "After all, the weather could change, planes are damaged in air raids, and accidents and other unforeseen events could happen." Baumbach gave Stahl a knowing look.

Stahl smiled again. "You know I'm behind on our missions. I'm already having trouble because of fuel and parts shortages. Moving won't help any."

"Well, you're in charge of Olga, and that's why I picked you— you get things done. Of course, the problems you are experiencing were taken into consideration. We still expect you to accomplish the impossible, I'm afraid. Frankly, I'm surprised at what you have done given your resources. I certainly have no complaints about what you're doing. By the way, if any of the golden pheasants give you too much trouble, give me a ring. I can give Goering or Himmler a call or even Hitler since he has personally entrusted me to destroy the Oder bridges."

"Any idea of the size of the group? That will determine which aircraft we'll use."

"Not yet. Skorzeny is still getting his men together. He's going to have trouble finding English speakers. I feel certain it will involve more than one squad of men, possibly a platoon."

The two men walked out to the airfield. Stahl told Baumbach of his planned move. He was told not to get lost.

"Good luck on the bridges," Stahl remarked as he left.

"And you on your crazy assignment."

Baumbach climbed into the waiting Storch and closed the door. Within minutes, he was airborne. Soon his plane was a speck as it disappeared from Stahl's view. Stahl then returned to his office to complete the final arrangements for Olga's transfer to a new home.

CHAPTER 8

March 9, 1945: Supreme Allied Headquarters

General Everett S. Hughes, special assistant to the supreme allied commander, was at his desk when his phone rang. He picked up, listened, and said, "Yes, sir, I'll be right there." He got up from his chair and headed for Eisenhower's office. Hughes was known for his discretion and as result was confidant to many of Eisenhower's deepest thoughts and secrets over the last few months. The tall, quiet general knew his boss had been brooding for a few days following the revelations coming out of the concentration camps. The horrors had hit everyone hard, and it was obvious the scenes had affected Eisenhower deeply. Eisenhower had already developed a deep revulsion toward the Germans. After the Axis powers had been defeated in North Africa, Eisenhower told General Marshall that he wished more Germans had been killed. In August 1944, he told the British ambassador in Washington that the officers of the German General Staff should be liquidated. Ike had said on numerous occasions that he was ashamed of having a German name. On top of everything else, he was under tremendous pressure to bring the war to an end.

Hughes entered Ike's office. His boss stood up and flashed his famous grin. Hughes noted his smile was did not seem as warm as it usually was, but he did not feel Ike's dark feelings were directed at him.

"Have a seat, Everett."

"Thank you, sir."

Ike folded his hands in the air and rested his head on them. "There is something I want to run by you." He looked as if to make sure no one was listening. "You know how I feel about the Germans. They are utter savages. Look at what they did in Poland and Russia. Now look at what we're finding in the concentration camps. We couldn't begin to imagine the things they were doing in these places. I never realized that a people could fall to such depths. Now we are taking large numbers of German prisoners, and we're having trouble feeding so many mouths. Not that I really care. They need to be taught a lesson. I want the status of Germans taken after the capitulation changed. Once Germany surrenders, I propose that prisoners be classified as disarmed enemy forces. This would relieve us of the responsibility of feeding these people as they would not be covered under the Geneva Convention."

Hughes trembled inside at the implications of Ike's words. "Have you run this by anyone else such as General Marshall?" Hughes was careful with his words.

"Not yet. I'm sending a draft to the combined chiefs of staff tomorrow. Take a look at it."

Hughes took the piece of paper and read it carefully. In his memorandum, Ike addressed the chaos that was likely to result with Germany's surrender along with the inability of the German authorities to feed their own troops. Ike did not want to feed prisoners better than the civilian population. At the end of the paper, Ike made his proposals and requested the joint chief's approval. Hughes had an uneasy feeling Ike wanted to starve the Germans. He knew his boss well enough to know how evasive Ike could be and that he preferred the indirect method to solving problems. That was why Hughes was Ike's special assistant; he knew the man, his peculiarities, and what he really meant when he spoke.

"What if they starve?"

"Then they starve. They created this mess, and now they need to live with it. I don't have any sympathy for them in their current situation. They need to suffer for their crimes, and we shouldn't have to answer for letting them reap their just desserts. What I've seen makes me wish I never had a German name." Ike was irritated by the time he finished.

"Well, be careful. I would be sure to get approval from above before proceeding," Hughes cautioned. "I'll also feel out certain people in London the next time I'm there. No need for you to get stuck to a tar baby at this stage. After all, look at what happened to General Patton for running his mouth off."

Ike smiled at the last remark. "I'll keep your advice in mind. For now, this is between the two of us."

"Understood," Hughes replied.

"Take care, Everett. I'll keep you advised of developments."

Hughes saluted and left the room. The following day, Ike sent his cable to the combined chiefs and awaited their decision.

Skorzeny's plans were now being dictated by the course of events. Catastrophe in one theater seemed to be followed by unrelenting disaster in another. The most recent problem was now at Remagen. The Americans had captured the Ludendorf Bridge after the demolition charges failed to detonate. The Americans were pouring supplies and men across the bridge at an alarming rate. The Luftwaffe had attacked the bridge repeatedly without success. The army brought in a 540 mm cannon and bombarded the bridge until the gun jammed on the fifth round. As a last resort, Hitler had demanded Skorzeny's involvement, and so Hitler's head commando began drawing up plans for attacking the bridge during the first week in March. He decided to send in frogmen. His usual team of frogmen under Major Otto Beck was trapped in Hungary, so Skorzeny looked for others to take their place. As he recalled, Schreiber had training in underwater demolition. Skorzeny decided that they would have to do, and he would worry about Himmler later. He summoned Schreiber and was pleased to see that a week's worth of leave had worked wonders for Schreiber after his harrowing adventure behind Russian lines.

"How are you feeling, Max?"

"Much better, Herr Oberst. I did not realize how exhausted I was. I thought about some of the men I would like to take with me if this scheme of Himmler's goes any farther."

"Later, Max. Right now, I have a more pressing problem. The Americans have captured the bridge at Remagen."

"We didn't blow it before they crossed?"

"I'm afraid not. Anyway, the Americans are rushing everything across as fast as they can. The bridge needs to be blown as soon as possible. Repeated attacks by the Luftwaffe have failed to destroy the bridge. Since you have some training as a frogman, it's up to you to lead an assault."

"How will this go over with Himmler? I don't mind leading the attack, but I hate to see you in trouble with him if something happens."

"I'll worry about that if something happens. Right now, there's a bridge to be blown."

"Jawohl. When do I lead the attack?"

"Tonight at dusk"

March 16, 1945

That night, Schreiber led his men into the dark cold waters of the Rhine. Despite their wetsuits, the chill penetrated to their bones. The small group drifted downstream with just their heads above water. The explosives were floated on a small raft draped in black. They used their feet to direct them to avoid any splashing. As they approached the bridge, they kept their heads down even lower as the bridge and surrounding area was lit up with searchlights. The Americans were determined to protect their prize. Schreiber's men worked their way to one of the bridge's support beams. Their placement of the charges was agonizingly slow as their fingers were thoroughly numb from the cold.

As they proceeded with their deadly work, Schreiber caught sight of another bridge alongside the Ludendorf Bridge. As he focused his eyes, Schreiber realized that it was a pontoon bridge. He decided to go after it as well. He took another swimmer with him and swam stealthily to the second bridge. They were placing charges when rifle fire rang out. The American sentries had spotted his men at the main bridge and opened fire. Five of his men were hit. Schreiber watched helplessly as two sank beneath the water to never surface. The other comrades held the three wounded up as they floated downstream to their pickup point. As gunfire peppered, the water around them several explosions lit up the night. Debris flew through the air and in the water nearby. Firing ceased momentarily as the stunned Americans ran for the safety of land. Schreiber looked back with disappointment to see the bridge still standing. However, he still had his men to lead to safety, and the survivors paddled on furiously during the lull granted them. The bridge gradually receded in the distance; and, finally, they reached the rendezvous point. The wounded men were pushed ashore, and then the half-frozen survivors were pulled out of the water. Schreiber made sure all of his men were ashore before he allowed himself to be dragged out of the river. Although he knew the bridge had not been destroyed, Schreiber was only interested in getting his men and himself warm. The bridge could always be assaulted again.

On March 17th, the mighty bridge collapsed and killed several U.S. Army engineers who were trying to repair it. Although Skorzeny knew his attack had not brought the bridge down and refused to take credit, the OKW swept his objections aside as Skorzeny was lionized as the man of the hour.

Skorzeny's supposed accomplishment was one of the few bright spots for Himmler as the Soviet juggernaut continued its inexorable advance west. Although Baumbach knocked several bridges out, the Soviets were past masters of building smaller underwater bridges to continue their momentum. In addition, the Soviets possessed an overwhelming numerical superiority that was difficult to overcome even with modern weapons.

By now, Himmler's failure as a military commander was apparent to everyone and, most painfully of all, to the Reichsfuehrer himself. He continued his frequent trips to the SS hospital to see his old friend, Dr. Karl Gephardt, for treatment. Himmler had arranged for Gephardt to take command of the hospital for his own benefit. The immense pressure he was under was taking its toll on Himmler. He continued to sleep long hours, and his abdominal pain continued its severity. In addition, several of his key officers were defecting and transferring their loyalty to Bormann. Kaltenbrunner, Fegelein, and Wolf had each reached an understanding with Himmler's rival. Himmler found himself exercising little control over his unruly satraps.

In addition, Guderian continued his efforts to get rid of Himmler as army group commander. Guderian's purpose was less self-serving than that of Himmler's minions: he just wanted a competent military commander in charge so that the Army Group Vistula might have a chance to accomplish something of military value. Finally, Guderian decided to go to Himmler and ask him to step down as commander.

On March 18th, Guderian arrived at Himmler's headquarters and was greeted by Himmler's chief of staff, Brigadefuehrer Heinz Lammerding. Himmler had already retired to bed with a bout of coughing. The two generals exchanged pleasantries as Guderian exited his Mercedes. As they walked to the headquarters, Lammerding asked Guderian, "Can't you get rid of our commander for us before he ruins everything?"

Guderian replied, "That's what I'm here for. How bad is it at the front?"

"It's indescribable. Himmler has no concept of what a field commander's responsibilities are. He stays in bed most of the time, while our men are dying and bleeding in their foxholes."

The two generals were now at the entrance. Guderian continued on, and one of Himmler's aides took the legendary panzer general to Himmler's sick room. Himmler broke out into more coughing as he recognized his visitor.

Guderian decided to help Himmler convince himself to ease out of his current predicament gracefully. "Reichsfuehrer, I see that your duties seem to overwhelm you."

"General Guderian, I believe you are right. There is so much that has been ignored, while I've been here at the front."

"If you keep going on like this, Reichsfuehrer, you will be of no use to anyone."

Himmler looked up at the remark. "What should I do?" He coughed out.

"Perhaps you should relinquish some of your responsibility. Like here, for example. There are plenty of experienced generals who could take over the Army Group Vistula while you could tend to your vitally important duties of tending to the Reich's internal security. After all, command of an army group is a small matter compared with all of your other responsibilities."

Himmler realized that Guderian was offering him an honorable way of stepping down. He considered this a wise move as power was slipping out of his hands. He coughed some more. "What will the Fuehrer say if I step down? He will at least be disappointed."

"Allow me to speak to the Fuehrer on your behalf. I'm sure he'll be reasonable. After all, he can't afford to lose his top policeman because you didn't take care of yourself."

"I suppose you're right."

"Very well. I will speak to the Fuehrer today," Guderian continued soothingly. "I'm sure the Fuehrer will appreciate the wisdom of your decision." Guderian straightened up. "Good day, Reichsfuehrer. If I can be of further assistance in any other way, let me know."

"Thank you, General. I will keep in touch."

On March 20th, Hitler agreed to replace Himmler and readily assented to the appointment of Colonel General Gotthard Heinrici as commander of the Army Group Vistula. On March 22th, Heinrici arrived at Himmler's headquarters to assume command. After exchanging pleasantries with Himmler, Heinrici then listened to a report on the Army Group Vistula's current situation. Himmler then departed without ceremony to Berlin. On his way back, Himmler reflected on his failure as military commander. If only it was 1940 or 1941. Victory had come so easily then, and Himmler knew he would not have failed then. His thoughts turned from being a great military leader to cunning savior. He knew Schellenberg's talks were still tentative in Sweden, and Himmler always liked to keep as many options open as possible. He would need to talk with Skorzeny when he got back. Skorzeny would be summoned to SS headquarters tomorrow for an update. Perhaps Gotterdammerung would succeed. Then he would be in a position to deal with Bormann. First he would rest and regain some of his energy. He would do a little work when he got back into Berlin. Then he planned to take the rest of the afternoon off. Tomorrow his nerves would be better, and his mind would be clearer when he talked with Skorzeny.

On the morning of March 20, Major Makarov was winding his way through the maze that formed Lubyanka prison. He was headed toward Block Two where VIP prisoners were kept. The area was deceptive, as the cells resembled hotel rooms rather than prison cells. The food for these prisoners was much better than the usual prison fare. Adding to the deception was the presence of the Kommendatura on Block Two. This was the office of the NKVD charged with carrying out executions on block 2. Today, the Kommendatura would be dealing with a captured German agent who had been on the block since February. He was supposed to make contact with the "ferret" but had been captured almost as soon as he entered Soviet territory. Fortunately, he did not know Makarov's true identity. However, the agent's interrogation had alerted the Soviets to the presence of a high-level spy in their midst. Makarov had wondered if the man had been sent by Werther to unmask him. If so, Werther had failed at the expense of the man Makarov would see for the final time today.

Makarov arrived at Block Two and went to a super secret cell called the spetsialmaya laboratornaya kamera. Makarov maintained his composure as he entered the room. The captured agent was seated in a chair. A man in a long laboratory coat was filling a syringe, while another huge four-hundred-pound man stood beside the agent. The man in the coat, Professor Grigori Maironovsky, carefully squeezed the last air out of the syringe. Maironovsky explained he was trying to avoid an air embolism. Makarov suppressed a shudder at the presence of the gorilla, Bogdan Kabul. Kabul was Beria's chief torture specialist, and Makarov realized that only a matter of luck kept him out of the clutches of these two men.

Makarov watched as a tourniquet was applied around the agent's right arm. He was mesmerized by Maironovsky's calm performance of his duties. Makarov had watched the good doctor perform several executions over the years, and it amazed Makarov how Maironovsky remained emotionally detached as he dispatched his victims. Perhaps it was because the doctor had experimented with various poisons in cancer research and had seen too much death already in his field. However, his experience earned him a transfer to the NKVD's secret unit for toxicological research. There was never a dearth of subjects to try out his new concoctions on. As a result, Makarov was able to transmit several of the infernal formulas back to Germany. He had no idea if any had been put to use.

Maironovsky inserted the needle into a bulging vein and slowly injected his lethal chemical. The agent looked up at Maironovsky with questioning eyes but did not speak.

"Keep your arm straight," Maironovsky commanded as he finished the injection. "You should feel better soon."

The agent continued to look up. He tried to say something but was unable to speak. He stated to raise his arm but dropped it. A look of understanding came over his face before he slumped in the chair. His eyes rolled back and glazed over.

"He's dead. Take him away." Maironovsky then turned and left the room.

Makarov followed behind the doctor. Kabul pulled the body up and slung it over his shoulders. Soon the corpse would be at the Donskoi crematorium to be reduced to ashes. Then the ashes would intermingle with those of Yezhov, Tukhachevsky, and other notables of recent Russian history. Makarov trembled slightly as he left the place of execution. Only by carefully covering his tracks had he avoided being in the chair as the recipient of one of Professor Maironovsky's injections. He was relieved to know that the SD had suffered no deep penetrations from MI6. At least that was what Philby's reports indicated.

However, as the war drew to a close, it seemed the past might come back to haunt him and Sudoplatov. It seemed to Makarov that he was more likely to be the victim of an internal purge than he was being exposed as a German spy. Makarov recalled a dinner he and Sudoplatov had with the Bulgarian ambassador in July 1941. Since Bulgaria represented Germany's interest in the Soviet Union after war was declared, the Bulgarian ambassador was approached to see what peace terms might be obtained. Now that the euphoria of approaching victory permeated headquarters, such embarrassing events were not fondly remembered. Although they had been acting on direct orders from Stalin, Makarov realized that he and his boss could be purged in the future if a campaign developed to rid the secret service of personnel who made illegal contact with the enemy. A charge of treason could easily be leveled against the two men, and then a visit with the good doctor would erase all memories of the clandestine meeting in 1941.

Makarov made his way back to his office. Sudoplatov was at his desk when he saw Makarov pass. "How did it go?"

"The usual," Makarov replied. "The man had no idea he was going to die until it was too late."

There was a brief silence before Sudoplatov spoke again. "At least we've rounded up everyone we can. I wish we could have gotten more information out of that agent before Maironovsky injected him."

"I don't think that he had anything to give. His errand was one of desperation on the enemy's part, a fool's errand at best. Unfortunately, it gives us no clue to his contact."

"I agree." Sudoplatov walked around deep in thought. "Still he was to meet someone who evidently is well placed. Check our intercepts again. There may be something obvious we're overlooking. By the way, what's the latest on the Scherhorn project?"

"Good. The Germans still do not have a clue this is a Russian operation. We continue to capture supplies and well-trained troops. Some of the men we've captured indicate that Skorzeny would still like to take part in one of the drops. We are hedging our bets on that one."

"I'm glad that's going well. Don't be too successful, or we'll be out of a job. However, this atomic bomb project may keep us busy for years, so be ready to switch gears in the future."

"You may be out of a job, but I suspect I'll still be employed."

Both men laughed, although Makarov was pained inside. He had tried to let Berlin know that the whole Scherhorn operation was a Soviet deception without success. Finally, Makarov had finally decided that Scherhorn was not worth the risk of having his cover blown. That could still happen at war's end if the NKVD-captured German files and found records relating to him.

"One other thing." Sudoplatov was serious now. "You have a new aide. A fresh one, I think." Makarov was on guard as his boss continued. He had expected more help to come on board because of the workload, but Sudoplatov was trying to tell him something. "Comrade Beria has noticed the excellent work you have done. He feels others would benefit from your example. Captain Alexian Korotkov will be joining you in a few days."

"I hope I am as good as Comrade Beria thinks."

"Better in my opinion," Sudoplatov replied.

Makarov took a silent, deep breath. It was obvious that his boss did not want the new man. Naturally, Sudoplatov would have preferred to have his own man to help Makarov. Evidently, Sudoplatov felt the man was being sent to keep a watch on them. Captain Korotkov, if that was his name, might just learn a few things about Department S if he lasted long enough. Sudoplatov's manner indicated that he wanted to be rid of Beria's eyes on them, and Makarov thought of how that might happen. Even Beria might learn something from this as Makarov smiled inside. There was no doubt that the man was a spy for Beria. For four years, Beria had not seen the need to give them any help as they ran sabotage operations behind German lines. Nor had he apparently seen the need when Department S was formed two months ago. Somehow Makarov would find a way to discredit the man. Korotkov would not even have to be executed. Spending the rest of his career as a border guard in Siberia would be fine as long as Korotkov was out of the way.

Darkness was approaching, and Makarov decided he had seen enough for one day. "Comrade General, I am going to call it day. Days like today depress me."

"Go right ahead." Sudoplatov had meant to give his faithful aide more time off. "Be careful," he added.

Makarov knew his boss was not referring to the Moscow traffic. Evidently, dangerous times were looming in the future. Well he would deal with Korotkov first. If they struck first, Beria might decide he was fighting a losing battle. At least Korotkov would not be in a position to bring Makarov and Sudoplatov down if he was swiftly removed. Makarov pondered on a solution as he walked back to his apartment.

The night of March 20th found Himmler in severe physical torment. Although Guderian had gracefully eased Himmler out of his command, Himmler's sense of failure gnawed at him. In particular, he feared Hitler's displeasure. As a corollary, he feared Bormann's next move as he sensed an additional decline in his power. As a result, his abdominal pain returned with intensity that only his masseur had been able to relieve. Now he desperately needed the man to assuage his torment.

Himmler went to bed early that night. His coughing intensified after Guderian left. Himmler summoned his aide. "Do you know anything about Kersten? Where is he?" Himmler implored. "I need him now."

"Kersten was called before noon, Reichsfuehrer," the aide replied. "Travel is difficult to say the least."

"I don't care. I need him now. After all, he has a pass from me to go just about anywhere."

The aide did not reply. Himmler was completely unreasonable under such circumstances. Hopefully, Kersten would arrive soon and relieve Himmler's pain. Once Kersten arrived and sunk his fingers into Himmler's muscles, the Reichsfuehrer was like putty.

Around eight o'clock, Felix Kersten arrived at Himmler's residence. Himmler was sleeping lightly. His groaning betrayed his discomfort even in his sleep.

The aide started to wake Himmler, but Kersten stopped him. "I'll wake him myself." Kersten walked into Himmler's room and announced himself. "Guten abend, Reichsfuehrer. It seems your work has taken its toll on you again. I see that you need my fingers again."

"Thank God you have finally arrived," Himmler said with great relief. "I've needed you for a long time."

"So it would appear. Then I suggest that you undress, and I'll work my magic."

"Please do," Himmler groaned pitifully as he painfully got out of bed.

In minutes, Himmler lay sprawled as Kersten's fingers kneaded Himmler's flesh. Soon the tormented man's pain was gone, and Himmler headed toward a deep peaceful slumber. A fat jolly man, Kersten had supreme confidence in the power of his fingers. He had learned his trade in the 1920s in Finland. He had profited handsomely afterward from his ability to relieved patients' suffering. In 1928, his reputation was such that the Dutch Royal family acquired his services. By then, there were no doubts about Kersten's abilities. In 1939, he acquired his most dangerous patient when another patient, August Rosterg, introduced Kersten to Himmler. Even then, Himmler had endured chronic pain for several years. Several physicians had been consulted over the years without success. After a few minutes under the capable masseur's fingers, Himmler's pain had completely resolved. Himmler was incredulous at his sudden, almost-miraculous relief.

"Please be my physician," Himmler had implored Kersten. Soon Kersten was almost completely at Himmler's side. Kersten soon found that his fingers exerted a power over his patient that ended only where Hitler's began. Over the years, Kersten made clever use of his fingers to cast powerful spells on the monster with bloodstained hands.

Kersten first used his hands for humanitarian purposes. He initially secured the release of individuals from the concentration camps and Gestapo. He wrangled permits for others in disfavor to leave Germany. Later, he arranged for the departure of the Scandinavian Jews into Sweden. Other concessions had been assiduously obtained by careful manipulation of Himmler's flesh.

Later, Kersten would venture into the political arena. More recently, he had been urging Himmler to break with his beloved idol, the Fuehrer. Kersten had learned of Schellenberg's insidious attempts to wean Himmler away from Hitler, and together they had nearly weaned Himmler from his god. Already, Schellenberg had secretly negotiated with the Swedish envoy, Count Bernadotte, to move the remaining inmates of the Scandinavian concentration camps to Sweden. Schellenberg had hammered Himmler to make use of Bernadotte to negotiate with Eisenhower to end the war. Finally, Himmler had agreed for Schellenberg to utilize Bernadotte to contact Eisenhower.

However, tonight, Himmler was only interested in relief of his dreadful pain. Within minutes, Kersten had worked his magic. As Himmler drifted off to peaceful sleep, he considered his options again. Perhaps Kersten was right: instead of killing the Jews, use them as a bargaining chip. Himmler had already signed a decree in October 1944, halting the execution of the remaining Jews in the concentration camps. As he relaxed, it occurred to him to use the carrot-and-stick approach that had been perfected by Heydrich. Himmler recalled the epitome of this strategy in Czechoslovakia. Heydrich began his rule as protector with prominent bloodletting. He had struck on a weekend by arresting Alois Elias, the Czech premier, on a charge of treason. The unfortunate man was tried and executed by the following Monday before any other German official had an idea of what had occurred. The Czechs had been stunned even further as Heydrich crushed all resistance. Then in a hundred-and-eighty-degree turn, Heydrich emerged as the benefactor of the Czechs. He patronized the workers, raised the fat ration, released shoes, and requested hotel rooms for relocation.

That is what I will do, Himmler thought to himself. *The Jews will be the carrot. The Allies will found out that I am the man to negotiate with, especially when we get the bomb. That will be our stick. It will be obvious that we can and will use it. That will work. Germany will emerge unvanquished, after all, and the SS will continue as the dominant force in the Fatherland. Then I can deal with Bormann at my leisure.*

"About the Jews"—Kersten brought Himmler out of his slumber—"there is some trouble with Eichman."

"Eichman will have to be reminded that he is not in charge of the SS. I am. The Jews will be spared." Himmler was sharp in his remarks.

Kersten continued his massage. Himmler had kept his word before. He knew Himmler would have his first peaceful sleep in a long time tonight. He would apply more gentle persuasion later. However, Himmler's dismal performance did not endear him to the Fuehrer. Kersten knew that he would be able to wrangle more concessions in a few days.

The "magic Buddha," as Himmler called Kersten, had performed his magic again. The next morning, Himmler awoke refreshed and full of confidence again. After breakfast, a courier brought him a copy of an agent's report. Himmler read and reread the contents of the message. It described the contents of a draft Eisenhower sent to the Joint Chiefs of Staff. He read with interest Eisenhower's proposal to treat surrendered Germans as disarmed enemy forces rather than as prisoners of war. The significance of the document was not lost on him. It meant anything could be done to surrendered forces without any protection under the Geneva Convention. This is what the Germans expected from the Russians, not the British and Americans. The document convinced Himmler that there was still a divine purpose to recent events. It explained why he had failed on the Oder. Germany was not meant to win her salvation on the battlefield. He was being released from his military duties by Providence to save Germany by another means. Operation Gotterdammerung was obviously that means. He would meet with Schreiber and Skorzeny soon and push the mission forward. The latest information should provide the proper motivation.

Himmler summoned the two officers the following day. Schreiber and Skorzeny arrived at Himmler's office early in the morning. Himmler was as usual preoccupied with paperwork. He looked up at the two officers when they entered his office. Himmler paid particular attention to Schreiber. Schreiber had already sewn on his new rank of sturmbannfuehrer. Neither he nor Skorzeny were wearing the oak leaves, although Hitler had approved the award the award for both men.

Finally, Himmler broke the silence. "Guten morgen, gentlemen. I trust that you had a good trip."

"Not difficult. Fortunately, we did not have to evade any fighters," Skorzeny replied.

"Sturmbannfuehrer Schreiber," Himmler said, gazing intently at the young SS officer, "I understand that you had a narrow escape from Hohensalza."

Schreiber stared back impassively. He was not fazed by Himmler's exalted rank. "Actually, two narrow escapes, at Hohensalza and Remagen."

"Oh, please explain yourself, Obersturmbannfuehrer Skorzeny." Himmler was obviously irritated.

"Sturmbannfuehrer Schreiber led a group of frogmen against the Remagen Bridge. The order was most urgent from the Fuehrer's headquarters." Skorzeny stiffened as he awaited Himmler's tirade. It began immediately.

"My dear Obersturmbannfuehrer, I thought I had made it clear that nothing is to take precedence over this operation. You needlessly risked the one man who can carry this off. As I recall, you have Captain Harmel under your command. And he wears the Knights Cross for bridge destruction. Use him next time or one of the others. Schreiber has one mission to devote himself to. Is that understood, Obersturmbannfuehrer?"

"Yes, Reichsfuehrer."

"Good. Read this. Then you will understand my feelings on this.

I have the man available who deciphered the signal if you want to talk to him," Himmler replied in a calmer voice.

"That won't be necessary," Skorzeny replied. He still stung from Himmler's chastisement. He took the paper from Himmler and read the contents. He mumbled some until he came to the words "disarmed enemy forces." He looked up. "This changing from prisoner of war status to disarmed enemy forces is chilling. Am I reading this right? If so, our men will have no protection under the Geneva Convention in the west. This sounds like something Stalin would have come up with."

"Precisely. I know we all expected better from the Western Allies. This is what we expected from the hordes of the east. Of course, we had warning at Casablanca when they called for our unconditional surrender. If this proposal is adopted, then our troops can be whipped, starved, and mistreated in any way with no recourse under the Geneva Convention. Now you understand my preoccupation with Gotterdammerung."

Schreiber and Skorzeny grimly nodded as they stared back at Himmler. Skorzeny recalled that when the big three had called for Germany's unconditional surrender, many of his countrymen had been reinvigorated to fight on. No reasonable German could accept such terms.

Himmler continued, "I am trying to open contacts in the west to bring about a favorable end to this war. None of us wants to be subjugated by the untermenschen from the east. As much as I despise that repulsive levantine Goebels, I suspect that his speech in February about an iron curtain spreading across Europe from the east may only be too accurate. Schreiber, you must succeed. You must be aware that you don't have any choice. I don't think it is an accident that the fates have been kind to you."

"That will depend on whether there is a bomb," Schreiber replied.

"Our information indicates that the Americans will start testing soon on this weapon. I believe they will succeed, and then you will succeed. Remember how fortune has smiled upon you."

Schreiber was going to reply when Skorzeny nudged him with his boot. He replied simply, "I will do my duty."

"Of course, you will, as will your men. Have you picked out a team yet?"

"Not yet. I have been going through the records of the Brandenburg Division. There are some men I would like to have if they are still alive. I hope to have better luck with finding English speakers than we did during the Ardennes offensive."

"Very well. I want to see the two of you in a week to discuss your progress. Also, Skorzeny, I want you to talk with General Gehlen about developing the werewolf program more. If Germany is occupied by foreign powers, they need to know that there will be a price to be paid. You are dismissed. Heil Hitler."

Skorzeny and Schreiber replied likewise and exited Himmler's office. As they departed, Schreiber whispered, "So he's still going to try to pull this off?"

"You are going to try to pull this off, maybe."

"Well, maybe. Sorry if I placed you on the spot by bringing up Remagen."

"Forget it. It isn't the first time I've been chewed out by a general officer."

They continued on to a staff car. As they drove back to Friendenthal, Schreiber flatly remarked, "I can't guarantee success."

"I know. On top of everything else, the bomb may not work, in which case you have to find a way out of the United States. That's why I'm not enthusiastic about sending you across the ocean to start with. However, we will have to play the game. Have you picked out anyone to be on this adventure?"

"As I told Himmler, good English speakers are rare. And you know better than me of our experiences during Operation Grief. However, I think some men are still around who were involved in some the Brandenbergers' secret African operations. Their desert experience may come in handy if we operate in the American southwest."

"What about a second in command?"

"I haven't even thought about that one."

"Well, get some names together. I at least want to be able to tell Himmler that we have a team. I personally have doubts about the whole operation, but I want things to look good on paper as long as Himmler is looking over our shoulder. Events may overtake us yet. By the way, how long has it been since you saw your wife?"

"I saw her a few days after I returned from Hohensalza. None since then."

"How about a three-day pass? To rest and think things over. Take some files with you and work on this at home."

"Are you serious?"

"Absolutely."

An hour later, Schreiber had his signed pass. He was hassled briefly by the field police at the railway station, but his Knights Cross and SS rank dissuaded most from asking any questions. Finally, he boarded the train and found a place to stand. As the train pulled out, Schreiber realized this was the first time in months that he had a real break. He intended to make the most of it.

After Schreiber and Skorzeny departed, Himmler made arrangements to meet with Count Bernadotte. Himmler had now regained his energy and was like possessed man. Mainly, he was concerned about saving his own skin. The magic of Kersten's fingers and Schellenberg's tenacious badgering were pushing Himmler to the precipice as far as breaking with Hitler. To strengthen his hand, Himmler was going to push ahead with Gotterdammerung and the werewolf program. If Germany could emerge intact after the war, then his power would be unmatched, and the Wagnerian flavor of the projects would appeal to Hitler, that is, if Himmler decided to allow the Fuehrer to stay in power.

After making his arrangements with Bernadotte, Himmler summoned Dietz to his office. Dietz had made some discreet inquiries about the progress of Gotterdammerung prior to the meeting. He arrived promptly and was impeccably dressed in the green service uniform. His highly polished boots gleamed in the light.

Dietz entered Himmler's office. He placed his cap on a chair.

"How was your trip, Dietz?"

"A little wearisome after looking out for allied fighters."

"Of course. What have you found out?"

"Skorzeny has sent Schreiber on a three-day leave."

"That's interesting."

"Seems like it's a working leave. Schreiber took a large number of files with him."

"I suspect he will have some names ready for me within a week. He does seem to be conscientious about his duty. I want you to supervise rounding up the names of the soldiers he provides. While I expect all SS officers to be that way, I suspect that there are many who just like to wear the uniform and nothing more."

"Anyway, Dietz, I want to fill you in more on your role, specifically your contacts. You will have the name of our main contact, not Schreiber. The Abwehr recruited the man you will meet before the war. His placement was a brilliant stroke by Admiral Canaris, if I may say so. Canaris sent the man over to investigate any nuclear weapons projects. As part of his cover, the man turned himself into the FBI. He turned in his transmitter, money, documents, and so on to convince Hoover's men of his cooperation."

"How do we know we can trust the man?"

"The man had another transmitter of course. He worked for us in the last war and really never stopped spying for Germany. When he transmits for the FBI, he uses code that begins with certain letters that lets us know that he is transmitting what they have prepared for him. Sometimes that information is useful since we know that the enemy has prepared it. There is a different code when he is transmitting the information we really want. It is almost always accurate. Schellenberg scrutinized his messages closely, and so far, there is no reason to think that the Americans have discovered that the man really works for us."

"Sounds like dangerous work."

"Canaris assumed the man would be under intense surveillance for months. It was six months before he transmitted one of his legitimate transmissions. We think that he recruited a spy ring right under the nose of Hoover. I have good reason to believe that one of his collaborators may be Alfred Wehring."

"The real hero of Scapa Flow? I thought he had been discharged afterward. There was some story of how hard it was to attack a country that one had lived sixteen years in. I assumed that Canaris wanted to keep the man happy and quiet."

"I suspect that is what Canaris wanted us to believe, somewhat like his fiction of being related to the Turkish Admiral Kanaris when his ancestry was actually Italian. I would be shocked to see someone like Wehring actually retired. Canaris was far too crafty to let go of someone like that. Of course, the man's English is also excellent. Here are other reasons why we believe he is still active in the United States, but that is not important for now."

Dietz laughed. "That Canaris was a fox."

"Indeed he was. However, the fox was finally caged," Himmler said reflectively. "I believe the old fox has about outlived his usefulness. That is another matter I will deal with soon."

Dietz shuddered inside. He immediately realized that Canaris was a dead man. The old admiral would probably soon be led out of a cell to have a noose placed around his neck and left to dangle. It was still difficult for Dietz to imagine such an exalted figure as Canaris coming to such an ignoble end. Dietz felt his neck muscles involuntarily tighten as he contemplated Canaris's imminent fate.

Himmler interrupted Dietz's thoughts. "Messages have already been transmitted to our agent in America. He knows he may be required to assist you and Schreiber. He has penetrated a NKVD ring, which in turn has penetrated the Manhattan Project. Of course, you may need to do some espionage of your own. I'm sure that you won't necessarily believe everything that our man tells you. You can take with you whatever you need to ensure the success of this mission."

"Which is to make sure that we get the bomb. Afterward, what is my role?"

"Protect it. Explode it if the Allies do not come around to our way of thinking. You will be in contact with us for instructions as things progress."

Dietz stood up. He knew Himmler was almost done with him. "Very well. If Wehring is involved, then he'll have procured some interesting information. I'll be delighted to meet such an agent."

"I'll wish to meet with you before you depart. By the way, how is your wife?"

A shadow crossed Dietz's face. "She is well, Reichsfuehrer."

"I am glad to hear that. Such an elegant and cultured lady. Give her my best. Heil Hitler."

"Heil Hitler." Dietz saluted and strode out of Himmler's office. He knew very well what Himmler was getting at. His unspoken threat was clear. Your family will suffer if you fail. Whatever Dietz's loyalty to the SS, he also loved his wife. She was exactly as Himmler described her, elegant and cultured. She was also a mischling, a half-Jew. Because of Dietz's early involvement with the SS, he had been able to protect her for this long under the exemptions that existed for her category. Himmler's remark was a not so subtle reminder that things could change. It was the carrot-and-stick approach applied to Dietz.

After Dietz left, Himmler continued with his paperwork for another thirty minutes. He then attended a meeting with his top aides to prepare for transferring the headquarters of the SS. The development of safe houses for high-ranking SS officers to hide at in the event of capitulation was also discussed. Himmler as usual intended to have more than one option open in the event of surrender.

Schreiber sprang up in bed with sweat pouring off his body. His heart was racing as he felt his blade enter the Russian's body. Then he awoke.

"Max, snap out of it." Greta was shaking him.

"I was… ah… having a bad dream."

"It seems more like a nightmare the way you were thrashing."

"You're right it was." Schreiber hung his face in his hands as he calmed down. Baby Eric started to cry, and Greta picked him up. Her lullaby calmed the baby. Schreiber calmed down as he realized he wasn't running for his life from the Russians. He had relived his retreat with Colonel Weiss for the previous minutes in intense detail. He had hoped to live that episode only once.

"My poor Seigfried, was it bad?" Greta stroked her husband's hair as Eric drifted off to sleep.

"It was horrible. I wish I could forget."

"Why don't you tonight?"

Schreiber looked at his wife. She was wearing a fine lace gown he had picked up for her in France. It outlined her figure nicely, he admitted to himself. He watched as she placed the baby in his crib. She then began nuzzling him, and he let her lead him back to the bed. He picked her up and placed her in the middle of the bed. He then pinned her with his legs, and she tried playfully to get away, but not too hard, he noticed.

"It seems like I need to do my husbandly duty."

"It's about time you got the idea."

Schreiber gently grabbed her by the back of her hair and brought her face to his. Their lips slowly touched. Their embrace became more passionate. He held her close to him.

"Please don't ever let me go, Max."

"I wish I didn't have to."

They continued their lovemaking for an hour. After finally consummating their passion, Max lay on his back, while Greta curled up against him. He fell asleep peacefully as he had finally forgotten about the war.

The following morning after breakfast, he pulled his files out and raked his brain. There were so many far-flung operations that had gone on. The problem was so many of the men who had carried these missions were dead captured or otherwise unaccounted for. He concentrated on the operations carried out in Africa, Iraq, and India. The snatching of the Indian Nationalist leader Chandra Bose particularly fascinated Schreiber. He noted that a Sergeant Pohl had been involved in Bose's escape from British house arrest. In January 1941, Pohl was part of the team that slipped Bose out of Calcutta and escorted him to Peshawar. The group had posed as Muslims and eventually made across the border to safety. The rest of Pohl's official record was murky, but Schreiber knew the man had not rested on his laurels. He also had been alive when the Brandenburg Division was reorganized.

Schreiber kept thumbing through the files, looking for other potential recruits. He came across reports of Lieutenant Leipzig's trek into the middle of Africa. Three different patrols under his command had surveyed northern Africa. One patrol had headed south in an attempt to find a suspected east-west railroad that the German High Command thought existed. In addition, there was a cryptic note about the patrol trying to reach the Belgian Congo and its uranium mines. Unfortunately, there were too many Free French troops barring the way, and Rommel could not spare additional troops for a sideshow. Sergeant Oskar Rahn had been on this patrol. A highly decorated NCO, Schreiber knew he had been alive recently as well.

Schreiber continued his review of the files. He needed an explosives expert. He looked carefully at the files on the Coastal Raider Battalion. Schreiber quickly zeroed in on the name of Lieutenant Kohlman. Kohlman had been responsible for scuttling and disarming many small ships. His expertise had branched into aerial bombs so that he would be more versatile. His presence would be a welcome and needed addition.

Finally, he had a list of names that he wanted as part of his team. There were twenty-six in all. He thought about calling Skorzeny but decided against it. He had two more days of leave and decided against it since Skorzeny was not particularly interested in bringing this operation to fruition. Besides, he was just now realizing how much he needed the rest.

The three days went by quickly enough. *Too quickly*, Schreiber thought as he boarded an early train in the dark. Greta had accompanied Schreiber with Eric. He realized this could be the last time he saw his family. He suppressed his feelings with difficulty. Two of the field police checked his papers and moved on to harass someone else. Schreiber was relieved the "hero snatchers" had left him alone. The train arrived, and it was time to go. He handed Eric back to Greta.

"Max, please come back."

"I plan to."

"I made this for you." She handed him a scarf she knitted for him.

"I don't know that I'll need this considering where I'm going."

"Where are you going?"

"I can't tell you. You know that."

"It's another mission, isn't it?"

Schreiber nodded. "I'll take it anyway. It'll give me something to remember you by."

He took the scarf and boarded the train. As the train pulled out, Schreiber and his wife kept their eyes focused on each other. Soon Greta was out of sight, and Schreiber found a seat. Soon he would be back to war.

Skorzeny was waiting on Schreiber when he returned from leave. "How was leave, Max?"

"Not long enough, Otto."

"It's always like that, I'm afraid. Have a seat. We get to meet with Himmler tomorrow. I hope you've got some names ready."

"Actually, I do. Several African veterans stand out. Here let me show you."

For the next two hours, they went over the men's files. Skorzeny noted they were high-quality men. The NCOs had at least one Iron Cross first class. One had the German Cross, as did the one officer. All were veterans of undercover operations behind enemy lines. Thank goodness all had been spared this long. Kohlman and the NCOs spoke excellent English. *Schreiber knew his men*, Skorzeny thought.

As they finished, Skorzeny complimented Schreiber. "After today, I could actually see this operation succeeding. You've done well. Now we get to go see Himmler tomorrow."

"I thought we had a few more days?"

"I guess you didn't know, since our last visit, he has moved his headquarters out of Berlin, just in case."

"Where's it at now?"

"At Ziethen Castle, near Wustrow."

"Sounds like he doesn't have much confidence in the final outcome."

"I agree. That's an opinion I would keep to myself if I was you."

"It's a little late for me to be scared, but I'll watch my mouth."

"Good. I would like to keep you around for a while, especially since one of us will have to watch the sky while the other one drives."

"I'm refreshed. I'll drive."

"Just get us there in one piece," Skorzeny said.

They arrived at Himmler's headquarters the next morning. It was hard to imagine that a war was going on because of the quietness surrounding the castle. The SS guards demonstrated that this was an important structure and not because of an historical value. A junior officer led the two officers to Himmler's new office. It was spacious and spartan. Schreiber suspected this was because everything had not been moved from Berlin. As they entered the room, Schreiber noticed an SD officer of the same rank as himself standing next to Himmler. He also noticed Skorzeny flinch slightly when he saw the man. Obviously, Skorzeny knew the man, and his body language told him that Skorzeny was leery of the man. Schreiber tensed up as the meeting began.

"I trust you had a good trip, gentlemen?" Himmler seemed to be in a good humor this morning.

Schreiber and Skorzeny nodded back politely.

"Good. Sturmbannfuehrer Schreiber, I assume that you have come up with a team?"

"I have some names, twenty-six in all. Many were still in the Brandenburg Division when it was reorganized. Hopefully, they are still alive." Schreiber handed Himmler a list of names along with files.

Himmler read the list and then flipped through the files. He asked for occasional details on each soldier. Finally, Himmler reached the last one, and after a few questions about the man he placed the folder on top of the others.

"A rather impressive group of German soldiers, Sturmbannfuehrer. Each man is essential?"

"Absolutely," Schreiber was adamant.

Himmler turned his gaze on Skorzeny. "What is your feeling about this?"

Skorzeny bluntly replied. "If Schreiber says they are needed, then there is nothing to discuss. We need them. With these men, this operation actually stands a better chance of success than I thought possible. Without them, I recommend that this mission be given no further thought."

Himmler eyed Skorzeny. "Interesting. I'm glad to see that you have some enthusiasm about this mission at last."

"As much as I can for one that I won't be leading."

"And that is not a matter of discussion either," Himmler blandly replied. "By the way, Skorzeny, I believe you already know Strumbannfuehrer Dietz."

"How could I forget? Back in August in Budapest."

"I believe some guards were drugged," Himmler interjected.

"And a few other things," Dietz replied. Schreiber looked at the man. His thin smile seemed to be mocking them. *What was there to this man?* Schreiber wondered.

"Dietz," Himmler continued, "Sturmbannfuehrer Schreiber here is one of Skorzeny's finest officers. He will be adding the oak leaves to his Knights Cross soon."

"Impressive," Dietz replied.

"I thought so too," Himmler replied. "That is why he has been selected to lead this mission into the United States. That is, if Obersturbannfuehrer Skorzeny decides not to waste his talents on another bridge."

"That has not happened," Skorzeny testily replied.

"Good. I'm glad that you have finally learned to obey orders. If only some of my senior Waffen-SS officers would do the same. It's amazing how they love the sound of general in front of their name instead of their SS rank." Himmler gave a sigh of exasperation. "They just don't understand that the SS is more than a military organization." Himmler looked back at the list. "I wish I had been called about this. These men could have been rounded up or at least we could have checked to see if they were still alive."

"I did not think that we wanted to discuss such matters over the phone," Skorzeny replied.

"We don't have to make reference to the operation if we need something or someone my dear Skorzeny." Himmler paused. "There are some details that Oberst Baumbach is working out, but he feels that he will have a plane on standby to deliver Schreiber's men to North America. As you may have guessed, Dietz will be accompanying the team as well. He has some special communication skills."

"And some others," Skorzeny grimly noted.

"Yes, he does." Himmler was matter of fact in his reply. "That is why he is going with you. I might add he trained under Naujocks. Fortunately, Dietz was prepared when Naujocks had to be dismissed for financial irregularities."

"What about our contact?" Skorzeny did not like the sound of things.

"Dietz will handle that as well. It would be better that way. If his cover is blown, then perhaps Schreiber and his men can remain undetected if Dietz maintains he is operating alone."

Schreiber and Skorzeny did not buy any of that at all. Schreiber decided to put Himmler on the spot. "I will be leading this mission, and it is dangerous when you are on the enemy's soil wearing his uniform. I would feel better knowing this was not a waste of time, effort, and men."

"I think that is reasonable." To everyone's surprise, it was Dietz who responded. "Some background would be reassuring. I certainly would want some if I was in Schreiber's position."

Himmler was briefly off guard but quickly recovered his senses. "Perhaps you are right. The whole project got started by accident and for the wrong reasons. A businessman named Hohlhaus noted a marked increase in helium production during a tour of a plant in Amarillo before the war. Hohlhaus had a limited understanding of physics, but he surmised that the Americans might be serious about developing a nuclear weapon. It was thought that helium might be a necessary material for building such a weapon. It turns out that we know the helium was for the dirigibles of the American Navy. However, Hohlhaus submitted his report to Colonel Joseph Schmidt who was then chief of Luftwaffe intelligence. He conferred with Colonel von Roder at the Bureau of Ordnance and concluded that the Americans were serious about building a nuclear weapon.

Himmler continued disdainfully. "The Abwehr nearly blew the whole operation. Not until 1942 did they send a man, agent 2232, to penetrate the Manhattan Project. This man is the first agent to be devoted to being a nuclear spy. We think he actually has a ring gathering the information for him. That information along with that from other sources indicates the Americans will definitely be ready to test their bomb in four months or less. Remember you have plenty of incentive to carry this out. Eisenhower's proposal to deny our men protection under the Geneva Convention means you must succeed. That could mean waiting until after peace has been made if the terms are not favorable to Germany. Gentlemen, I wish to see you again next week if not sooner. For now, I must busy myself with setting up my headquarters here at Zeithen castle. That is until Berlin is out of danger and becomes the capital of a glorious new Germany. Dietz, would you remain behind? Heil Hitler."

With a flourish of salutes, Schreiber and Skorzeny left Himmler's office. After they left, Himmler turned toward Dietz. "I hadn't expected you to take their side on things."

"They're frontline soldiers, and I will have to work with them closely for who knows how long. They don't need to feel that I'm a threat so early in the game. I'm sure their suspicions are aroused already."

"Dietz, you are to make sure this mission is carried out, and the bomb exploded if need be."

"In which case, I am a threat if Schreiber's men fall in love with America and want to back out of the mission. They should feel I'm merely there to assist like any good intelligence officer."

"You do make a good point," Himmler conceded.

"I personally have some questions about Koehler myself. How

well do we trust him? That was a matter I didn't want to bring up in front of the others."

"I appreciate that. I trust Koehler as much as I do any of our agents. He's not without fault. He was one of our agents in the first war. He went to the United States after the war and set himself up in business again. All the while, he was still controlled by the remnants of our intelligence service. As you know, he was asked to account for financial irregularities in 1940. The Abwehr didn't exactly clear him, but he was needed. Canaris tapped him to be our man in the Manhattan Project so he underwent a crash course in physics. Of course, you know about the charade he went through to get back into the United States. He was watched closely when he approached the American Embassy in Madrid for a visa. Of course, he showed them the spy equipment as ordered. The FBI swallowed the whole story. They started to play the game of funkspiel against us."

"After reaching the United States, he started transmitting messages. Of course, the first were under the direction of the FBI. We knew those by the letters at the beginning of his transmission and when he transmitted normally at eight o'clock Saturday or Sunday mornings. However, on Friday nights, his real messages come in. These are the ones Hoover knows nothing about. Of these, at least three out of four have been correct and possibly more, but our scientists have been unable to verify all of the technical details."

"That's pretty good for an agent in the field." Dietz seemed convinced.

"Schellenberg agrees. The question is someone else involved, particularly Captain Wehring. I would like that checked out, if possible. However, Schreiber's mission comes first."

"Of course, Reichsfuehrer."

"Make sure it succeeds, Dietz."

"If the Americans have the bomb, I will get it. However, if the Americans fail in their attempt, what am I to do then?"

"Then you are out of a job, it would seem. However, our scientists are convinced that the Americans are likely to succeed.

Obergruppenfuehrer Kammler concurs that success is within the Americans grasp. Make sure it is in ours when the time comes."

"As I said, I'll get the bomb if they make it."

"Very well, I will see you when I need you. Heil Hitler."

Dietz saluted and made his exit. Himmler sat back and slumped in his chair. The others had been unaware of his mental agony. Hitler had given him a dressing down for the perceived poor performance of the Waffen-SS units in Hungary and ordered Himmler to chastise the units by having them remove their unit armbands from their uniforms. The Leibstandarte Division was particularly incensed when they received the order. Some of the officers suggested returning their decorations to Hitler in a chamber pot with a ribbon worded Goetz von Berlichgen tied around the pot. As much as Himmler wanted to bring his generals to heel, this episode only weakened his standing as he feared Hitler still but could not afford to alienate his generals.

Just as worrisome as the dressing down was the order to eliminate the inmates in the concentration camps. If that happened, Himmler would lose a valuable bargaining chip in his negotiations with the west and most likely such a course of action would seal his fate. As much as he hated to admit it, the Fuehrer was breaking his hold on Himmler as Schellenberg and Kersten were.

The result was the return of Himmler's abdominal pain. As the pains intensified, Himmler decided he needed Kersten back. Meanwhile, he would contact Schellenberg and see what progress had been made with the safe houses and in Stockholm. However, he intended to preserve the Jews for his own reasons. Whether or not Hitler chose to remain in Berlin was the Fuehrer's prerogative. Himmler intended to survive. He would also manage everything from Zeithen castle. A transmitter would be put in so that he could monitor Gotterdammerung personally. He would also call Baumbach to make sure a plane was available to fly Schreiber's men out when the time came.

Skorzeny pulled Schreiber aside after they left the castle. "I don't like this at all."

"I gathered you didn't like the SD fellow too well," Schreiber responded wryly.

"As much as I like a cobra. The man has a reputation. Death seems to follow him everywhere he goes. I know he was involved with Naujocks at Venlo. There were rumors about him and the death of the Bulgarian Minister of War and even King Boris. He also assisted when I brought Horthy back as a guest of the Fuehrer."

"I hope Horthy likes his accommodations," Schreiber cracked.

Skorzeny laughed. "Horthy better be glad that Dietz's orders were not more severe. The man is rumored to have been involved in some rather interesting 'accidents.' Viktor Lutze comes to mind."

"I don't see Himmler coddling someone like Lutze after the Night of the Long Knives."

"Evidently, the party has a way of dealing with its undesirable members. I've heard rumors of a secret Gestapo unit created for that purpose. Poisons have been developed that don't leave a trace. Some formulas were also stolen from the Russians. Anyway, if someone gets to be too big of a problem, someone like Dietz is sent in, and the next thing you know, the person has dropped dead from a heart attack. That way, no embarrassing party tribunal is held, and the party is not tarnished."

"And there's probably a nice state funeral at the end."

"I would suspect so. They want to keep up appearances. Anyway, keep an eye on Dietz. I suspect Himmler has saddled you with him for him to keep an eye on you. I suggest you do the same with him."

"Sounds like a charming person. Doesn't sound like he's endeared himself to you."

"Nothing in him to do so. He seems like a cipher to me. Did you notice his mocking grin? It's like he's got another agenda."

"Maybe he has," Schreiber ventured. "Uncle Heinrich is certainly not the most benevolent person around."

As they prepared to leave, Dietz pulled up in a black Mercedes. He called out to Skorzeny, "So we are teamed up again."

"Not exactly. Himmler won't let me lead this one. He says I would be too conspicuous."

"You certainly don't blend in too well at your height. Problem is, you are still responsible for this mission." He then drove on.

"What was that all about? Letting you know you're going before the brick wall if this thing fails?"

"Perhaps." Skorzeny was nonplused. "Not that it's going to worry me. I've been threatened plenty of times before. Remember, you're the one who has to deal with Dietz. It may have to be discreet." Skorzeny stared at Schreiber to make sure he understood. "Remember, you are in charge. You make the call. Dietz is only to assist. Make sure that is all he does."

"I understand perfectly. If things don't go well or the bomb doesn't work, what then?"

"I would go to Mexico. Hide out for a while. Then make your way back to Germany. I will make sure you have a transmitter to communicate with me. That way, you can act independently if needed. And if Dietz gets in the way, you know what to do."

Without another word, they got into their vehicle and began their long drive back to headquarters. Each was deep in thought over the events overtaking them. Both felt powerless in the drama that was unfolding. Each wondered if this would really make any difference. Despite their misgivings, Himmler had a point. Hundreds of thousands of German POWs would be treated like animals if they didn't have the protection of the Geneva Convention. Although Schreiber and his men might be operating outside the bounds of the convention, it wouldn't make any difference if it was not going to be applied to regular soldiers.

As they approached the guard post to leave, a SS captain stopped them. "My apologies, but I've been told that there is a change of schedule for you. You are to catch a flight to Furstenfeldbruck."

"This is awfully convenient," Skorzeny sarcastically replied.

"I'm sorry. That's all I know. Himmler's direct orders. There is an airfield four kilometers from here. You are to go directly there." The captain then gave them directions.

"Just great." Skorzeny was not amused. There were plenty of things he needed to discuss with Radl. However, that apparently was going to wait. After they had driven a few meters, Skorzeny piped off, "If the plane crashes, Himmler has found a way out of this and doesn't want us around."

"It would beat freezing in Siberia."

The airfield came into view. A Ju 52 was warming its engines. As they approached, they caught a glimpse of Dietz. "Somehow I don't think the plane is going to crash with him aboard," Schreiber muttered.

"Let's see if he has a parachute and we don't," Skorzeny replied.

"You really like this man, don't you?"

"As I said, as much as I do a cobra."

The two officers climbed aboard the plane. Although noisy, the Ju52 was revered as the "Auntie Ju" because of its reliability. Thousands of paratroopers had jumped from the plane in earlier campaigns. Schreiber had made several jumps from the plane behind enemy lines himself.

"I thought we had gotten away from you, Dietz." Skorzeny was still a little ruffled from having his plans changed,

"No use for civilized company, Skorzeny?" Dietz had his mocking grin on his face.

"I would use a different term." Skorzeny noticed that Dietz did not have a parachute nearby. "I suppose we are to make this flight safely. I see you don't have a parachute either."

"I see no need to help the Allies out. Their fighters can knock this plane down without my help. Besides, getting rid of you, Skorzeny, would require an order from the Fuehrer to me personally. I'm careful at what I do. I am not as much of a loose cannon as you may think. Dangerous but not loose."

Skorzeny finally grinned. "It's reassuring to know that I am held in such high esteem."

Schreiber broke in, "Who would have to order my elimination?"

Dietz coughed. He did not want to answer that. Although the question was partly in jest, part of it wasn't. Skorzeny was still in rare form and answered. "Probably Himmler's aide or more likely his dog."

All three burst out laughing. Even Dietz could not contain himself. "I have to admit, Skorzeny, you are very perceptive. Is that part of your Austrian charm as well?"

"Comes from years of experience."

The flight was short and uneventful. No Allied fighters had been encountered or they would have made quick work of the Junkers. After the plane landed, it was quickly moved to a camouflaged position to hide it from prowling fighters. After the plane stopped, the three men disembarked.

As they stepped down, Dietz looked around. "This isn't where we're supposed to be."

A Luftwaffe lieutenant approached. "Meine Herren. Welcome to Flensburg. You are to come with me."

Dietz commented, "Well, if this isn't interesting."

"I thought you would know what was going on since you're the one with the black diamond on your sleeve." Skorzeny couldn't resist needling Dietz.

"Believe me, I haven't been told a whole lot more than you have."

"Normally, I would find that hard to believe. For once, I actually believe you, for now. However, I wonder what your agenda really is." Skorzeny decided it was time to feel Dietz out.

"To help you get the bomb," Dietz replied straight-faced.

Before Skorzeny could say anything else, he spotted Radl coming toward him. "Greetings, Otto. I thought you might be needing me after I heard you were being diverted here courtesy of Himmler and KG 200."

"Karl, if I didn't know any better, I would think that you are working for the SD. Is there anything you don't know?"

"I'm just well informed. As far as working for the SD, I wouldn't dream of contaminating myself with them. It's bad enough being in the presence of one of them." Radl said his words with such a cheerful countenance that even Dietz chuckled.

"You are well informed, Major Radl," Dietz said. "What is going on?"

"Unusual to know something the SD doesn't," Radl replied back.

"The main thing is the Wiking flying boats are here at Flensburg or will be. Some are to be flown here to avoid capture. Schreiber is going to need one to get to the United States. A Ju 290 would have got him there, but he would have to parachute in. Second thing was to start looking for American equipment. We can't very well send these men overseas, expecting to pose as GIs when they're carrying Maussers. I felt that I could gather jeeps, weapons, and uniforms if I were closer to the western front. Plus, if we are already here, we can lay claim to the big planes before the party big shots do. I guess they may have to find a different way to Greenland."

"It would do the golden pheasants some good to exercise. I believe Himmler said they could swim," Skorzeny said bitingly.

"Well, we want to give them a fighting chance," Radl continued.

"How sweet of you," Schreiber replied.

"Your best interests are my heart's desire."

"Liar," Schreiber retorted. Dietz snickered.

Even Radl was having trouble keeping a straight face. "Listen, we all have doubts about this, I know. But I want you to get ashore and then survive and evade detection."

"Karl, you are sounding more like a lawyer rather than my ADC."

Radl continued despite the laughter. "Seriously, I want to get everyone on the ground and moving before the Americans realize that anyone has landed. Remember that Operation Pastorious was blown from the outset. One team was detected as it landed. Of course, one agent betrayed the rest. Six men went to the electric chair as a result."

Everyone had a serious look on their face. Radl continued, "If you land by plane and get moving without being detected, the Americans probably won't have a clue. Someone else has betrayed every spy that we sent to the United States. In 1942, one member of the Pastorius group who collaborated with the FBI was a former SS colonel. Of course, one of the teams ran into a sentry on landing as well. After they let the man go, the game was pretty much up."

"What's your proposal?" Schreiber asked.

"With the flying boat, we can land a fully armed platoon,

including jeeps and motorcycles. Once you land, you look for a road, and then you're off. If you land at night, hopefully, the waves will wash away most of the tracks by morning. Plus, with the flying boat, you can be unloaded in minutes even with vehicles. You could be heading out within thirty minutes."

"If everything goes right," Schreiber replied.

"Exactly. Unless you land in front of a naval vessel with lights, you could claim you were on maneuvers and just landed in the wrong place. Hopefully, you will find a deserted spot to land at."

"We still need men," Skorzeny reminded Radl.

"I'm having a search made for the men Schreiber listed. They should arrive in the next few days. I'm having them brought here."

"Make sure they are in the dark until they get here," Skorzeny ordered.

"I had already figured that out."

"Get ready for some unhappy customers, Max," Skorzeny cautioned. "I'll let you handle them. Let's take a break, gentlemen. I'm starved. Let's go over some details this evening."

Detachment Olga was still at Echterdingen when Himmler called. However, the long-range flying boats were based at Lake Travemunde. Captain Stahl took the call from Himmler. He was a little exasperated by the time he hung up. The Americans had just strafed the flying boat at the lake.that he planned to use. Although the ground crew had not destroyed the badly damaged plane preparations were under way. Himmler had suggested having the plane listed as destroyed, but he wanted the plane brought to Flensburg. Stahl wrung his hands in exasperation. It was no wonder that Baumbach had aged so much over the war years.

Meanwhile, the other members of the Brandenburg Division that Schreiber had requested were being located by the Reich's security system. The bewildered men were pulled out of the front lines, sometimes out of combat, and were told to report to their new assignment. The SD men were unable to provide answers other than that they were following orders.

Captain Stahl had just landed at Furstenfeldbruck and minutes after leaving his previous headquarters at Echterdingen thirty minutes before as the Americans rolled into town. The airfield was a shell of itself from previous years. Once it had been bustling with activity with planes all over the airfield, but only a few scattered hulks of planes were immediately visible. The intact planes would be hidden in the trees or in camouflaged pits. Now he was trying to relocate his command here. He spotted a pair of B-17s from KG 200 and taxied his Junkers 290 over to the parked planes. As he got out, one of his NCOs came running over to him.

"Sorry, Herr Hauptmann. I don't think we are wanted here." The man paused to catch his breath. "You better report to the general in charge."

"Relax. The worse he can do is tell us to leave."

Stahl then dismissed the man with a wave of his hand. He walked toward the headquarters building with some foreboding. Surely, they won't run their own people off. After all, the last few days had been ones of extreme chaos, and Stahl needed a chance to regroup. He checked to make sure he still possessed the secret red card authorizing all citizens of the Reich, civilian and military, to assist him in any way possible in carrying out his secret state assignments.

He knocked on the general's door. "Come in." And Stahl opened the door. He faced a general who appeared to be in his thirties. He was certainly youthful. Only flecks of gray hair betrayed the strain the man had been through during the war. Stahl then noticed the Knights Cross at the throat and stiffened to attention.

"Captain, what am I supposed to do with you? I have my hands full already. And if the Allies see your B-17s, they'll realize KG 200 is setting up shop again and will give us some unwanted attention."

"Herr General, I already have had their unwanted attention. I left Echterdingen just as American tanks entered the outskirts."

"Is that so?" The general leaned back and gave Stahl a hard look. "You were at the Battle of Britain, weren't you?"

"Jawohl. I flew Heinkels at the time. Later, I got to fly Ju 88s, a nice, versatile plane." Stahl paused and proceeded carefully since familiarity had been established. Stahl now vaguely remembered the general who as a fighter pilot had risen through the ranks. "You flew with JG 53. You saved our bacon on Eagle Day."

"Actually, I was with JG 52. But you're right. We did save your bacon that day. I started with 109s.Then I flew 190s. Now I fly a desk." The general looked at Stahl's decorations. "Looks like you've been around yourself."

"That's part of the territory when you're in KG 200. I have flown in the Arctic, Russia, and the Mediterranean at some point."

The general noticed the red paper. "What's that, your secret orders?"

Stahl shrugged his shoulders. "Basically, yes."

The general took a look at it. "What? I thought I've seen this before. As far as I'm concerned, you can just wipe your arse with it. It won't carry any weight around here. Do you still have any fuel?"

"A little."

"Then disappear while you can. You might try Oberpfaffenhofen. It's a Dornier airfield, and your red card may carry more weight there than here. All that will happen here is you'll lose more planes. Good luck, Captain."

Stahl saluted and walked back to his plane. Within minutes, he was airborne for his new destination. The flight was a short one, and Stahl was on the ground again. The Dornier people weren't any happier than the general had been to him, but the red card worked its magic here. For now, Stahl had another base of operations.

Stahl had barely settled in for an hour when a messenger arrived. He handed Stahl some orders. They were simple and direct. A pilot was needed for Gotterdammerung. The man was needed in Flensburg tonight. Stahl folded the piece of paper and placed it in his pocket. *This is crazy,* he thought. The idea was as ridiculous as the plans to fly the Nazi bigwigs out at the end of the war to hide in Greenland. However, he had to at least go through the motions of complying.

Stahl knew whom he would send. The list of names was small anyway after all of the attrition. One man stood out. It would have to be Oberleutnant Becker. He had the most experience with long-range flying. The man had flown several long distance missions deep into Soviet territory. He had also flown the arduous trips to Japan with much-needed war materials. One flight had been the northern route over the Siberian peninsula. Because of Japanese concerns about Russian views on such flights, the northern route was never flown again, and all official references to the flight were thoroughly purged. Becker had spent some time altering his logbook weeks after the flight was made to make it appear that he had flown over Southeast Asia.

In addition, Becker, more than anyone else in KG 200, could keep his mouth shut. His uncle, General Becker, had been the first head of the German rocket program. As a result, secrecy had been a vital part of the younger Becker's military personae. The man never said much anyway, and his discretion made him perfect for such operations.

Stahl had to wait for Becker to arrive later that day. Flying in the daytime was hazardous for any German pilot even if he was as good as Becker. It was evening when Becker landed. Stahl finished some paperwork and then looked Becker up in the building that functioned as an officer's club. When Stahl walked in, Becker had managed to locate a bottle of beer and was sipping on it. As Stahl looked around the room, he couldn't help but think how this was a far cry from the early war years when every club he entered was very comfortable or even opulent. Now everyone had to make do in whatever was to be found. Stahl sighed briefly and then got on with breaking the news to Becker.

Becker had hid out in a comer by himself. He lay stretched back, his eyes surveying the ceiling. He seemed to be without a care in the world. *Hope it stays that way*, Stahl thought.

"Don't get too liquored up. You've got some flying to do tonight."

"Oh, not tonight. We've just got settled." Becker straightened himself in the chair."

"Can't wait. Himmler is breathing down our necks on this one. Even Baumbach has limited say so on this one."

"It's that important. What is it then?"

"You've got to fly to Flensburg tonight. Eventually, you're to fly a team of Skorzeny's men into North America.'

Becker looked up incredulous. "You've got to be kidding. The war is almost over. What are they going to accomplish now except probably get caught? We've never even dropped anyone by air into North America. In addition, we don't even know what to expect."

"It's not my call or Baumbach's. You're the best I've got. You may not like dropping these men off. But if they're going to be deposited like this, I want to give them the best chance they've got, and you are the best I've got anywhere."

Becker got up and walked over to a window. He looked at a wall of low-lying clouds. "That explains why I feel so bad. Fohnwall."

"You actually believe in Fohn disease?"

"I'm not sure. My father is a doctor, and he didn't early in his career. He felt lazy people used it to justify their lack of action. Then he developed the symptoms one day and decided it actually existed. He couldn't bear the thought of being considered lazy. Well, so much for my plans to end the war peacefully on the ground."

Both men laughed at that. "Well, you didn't want to turn belly up now without a fight, did you now?"

"I guess I don't have much choice."

"I'm afraid not." Stahl was serious now. "You're the man for this. Whatever else you say about the men you will be flying, they are brave. I can only do my best by giving them the best pilot for the job. You go to Flensburg tonight."

"I agree. But will it matter in the end?"

"I don't know. I just don't know. Well, good luck." The two officers then shook hands. They omitted any goodbyes, even though both knew there was a good chance they would never see each other again. Stahl then walked off to check out the remainder of detachment Olga. He had not opened the door when Becker had started packing his gear for the flight to Flensburg.

Captain Fehler, commander of U-234, stood passively in the coning tower of his vessel on April 15th. He and his crew were finally going to start their voyage to Japan. Fehler had known this voyage was going to be different when Lieutenant Commander Langbein had come aboard with a list of material that U-234 would transport to Japan. Langbein was the representative of the Marin Sander dienst Ausland and as such was responsible for gathering the transported items. Hitler had decreed that the Japanese were to have access to the latest German technology, and Langbein was the man to whom this responsibility fell. Earlier in March, Langbein's adjutant arrived to supervise the loading.

Fehler's second watch officer, Ernst Pfaff, determined the placement of the items aboard U-234. As Fehler observed the loading of his vessel, he had to admit he was impressed with the items he was to deliver. A dissembled Me-262 fighter and V-2 rocket were crated aboard. Then there were the crates marked U-235. Only Fehler and some of his officers knew the U stood for uranium. The rest of the crew felt that there had been a mistake or that the Japanese couldn't get their numbers straight. Fehler did not bother to correct this misinterpretation when he learned of it. In fact, he would be carrying 1232 pounds of U-235 on U-234. The uranium was placed in ten cube-shaped containers and stored in the vertical mine shafts.

On March 25th, they had departed for Norway. Prior to leaving, U-234 had picked up some important guests as well. Several German military personnel with detailed technical knowledge boarded in March. In addition, two prominent Japanese military officers, Colonel Shoji Genzo of the Air Force and Captain Tomonaga Hideo of the Imperial Navy, joined the list of passengers. The Japanese had been the last to arrive and board.

Fehler had immediately sailed for Norway. The voyage was marred when U-1301 rammed U-234. A full-ballast tank had been torn open, and a considerable amount of fuel was lost in the collision. Despite the enormity of the damage, Fehler was able to nurse his stricken vessel into Norwegian waters for repairs. While there, more distinguished passengers joined him, most notably Lieutenant General Ulrich Kessler of the Luftwaffe. He was slated to be the German Air attaché to Tokyo.

The presence of so many important people aboard his U-boat

made Fehler slightly nervous. Fortunately, none tried to throw their weight around, and Fehler performed his job unhindered. Some of the crew was uneasy about the bad luck that presaged their final departure. Although the men remained quiet, Fehler knew their thoughts. He had quietly exhorted them to go about their duties, and no difficulties had arisen.

Finally, on April 14th, preparations had been completed, and Fehler received his orders to put to sea the following day. An overcast sky was a welcome sight that morning as the crew made ready for their departure. Allied aircraft were not likely to spot them under these conditions while they were surfaced and heading for diving stations. As soon as everyone was below, Fehler gave the orders for departure. Lieutenant Pfaff joined Fehler as U-234 departed Kristiansand. Spray from the wind and sea stung their faces. For several minutes, they traveled in silence.

"Seems like so much so late," Pfaff finally remarked.

"Perhaps," Fehler softly replied. "We will still do our duty."

"Of course, Captain. I didn't… ."

"No need to apologize. The war hasn't exactly gone according to plan, has it now?"

"No, sir."

More silence followed. Fehler thought about his days aboard the Atlantis. Then, they had survived by avoiding enemy warships, while they hunted merchantmen. Now he was to avoid all enemy ships again. He looked at Pfaff. The man was nervous but putting up a good front. Well, he has a right. U-boat losses are too high. We'll all be lucky to survive.

"We'll want to be submerged for two weeks. By then, we should be outside the range of the enemy's patrol planes. May 1 should find us in the Atlantic. Then we can relax a little, but just a little."

Pfaff had straightened up at the captain's remarks. "Of course. We would all like to survive this war."

"So would I. It's time to go down."

Pfaff nodded his head and descended. Fehler followed and closed the hatch above him. Fehler gave the order to dive. Fifteen minutes later, U-234 was beneath the waves with her deadly cargo. Now she and her crew needed luck and a lot of it to survive.

While U-234 made the dash for the open sea, the regime she served continued to implode. Himmler was still torn between his oath to Hitler and his own fantasies about Germany's future and his own. His minions held no such illusions especially at the lower ranks. Sepp Dietrich's SS Waffen-SS officers under his command remained incensed over their treatment in Hungary. The break with their Fuehrer had already occurred, and the motto on their daggers "Meine ehre heist treue" no longer held special meaning. Some still wanted to return their decorations to the demented tyrant in a chamber pot.

Still Himmler maintained vestiges of loyalty. On April 19th, Schellenberg was still endeavoring to break the eerie hold on his boss and replace it with his own influence. Schellenberg still hoped to have Himmler depose Hitler and abolish the Nazi Party and People's Courts. Hopefully, these would provide for negotiated surrender terms. To further his case, Schellenberg had Norbert Masur, the representative of the World Jewish Congress, flown to Templehof Airport.

Himmler had decided to be with Hitler on his birthday on April 20. It also gave him the chance to set the stage for more tying up of loose ends. He realized that he would still have to deal with Bormann. Now was not the time. However, as he was driven to his last meeting with the Fuehrer a plan took shape. It occurred to him that he didn't need to have a showdown with Bormann personally. Himmler knew who to talk to, plant the seed, and then let events take their course. Himmler knew Bormann wanted to be near Hitler constantly in order to dominate the leader. However, if Hitler stayed in Berlin and died, then Bormann would not be in a position to give further orders. Already spearheads of Zhukov's Second Guards Tank Army had reached the outskirts of Berlin. To the south, Koniev sliced toward the capital city in a race with Zhukov. Relief of the capital simply was not feasible. Without Hitler's protection, Himmler would not be the only top Nazi that Bormann would need to watch. That moment seemed nearer with each advance of the Red Army.

By the time Himmler reached the Reichs Chancellery, his mind was relaxed. All he had to do now was give his perfunctory greetings to Hitler and then set his trap. As he arrived at the building, he noticed the façade was relatively undamaged from the allied bombing. His SS guards were still vigilant in their black uniforms. Following his inspection by the guards, Himmler proceeded to the Court of Honor. There Hitler received the congratulations of his paladins. Most urged the Fuehrer to leave Berlin. Hitler remained noncommittal. He greeted Himmler frostily. The recent setbacks had been too much for Hitler. Their parting was cold, and Himmler made his way from Hitler as inconspicuously as he could.

Himmler still had to get his cards ready to play. He searched out the man he felt would deal with Bormann when the time came. All he needed to do was provide the proper motivation. Within minutes, he had cornered Hans Baur, the Fueher's personal pilot. Baur had been Hitler's pilot since the early thirties and was utterly devoted to his boss. Himmler knew the appeal to use. Also, since Baur and his crew were members of the SS, Himmler felt he had some leverage to use if needed.

Baur was drinking some champagne from the party when Himmler found him. Himmler approached him. "Good morning, Gruppenfuehrer."

"And to you as well, Reichsfuehrer."

'How are things with you?"

"Good, thank you."

"It appears that the Fuehrer is determined to stay in Berlin despite my suggestion and that of others."

Baur sighed in resignation. "He has not said for sure, but everything he does now seems to have a finality to it now. I think he has given up."

Himmler bowed his head as in reflection. "I am disturbed to hear that. I feel that we could still fight on even if Berlin falls as long as the Fuehrer is leading us. Without him, I see no hope of a successful outcome."

"I certainly am willing to follow him wherever he goes. As long as he is willing to fight, I am right behind him."

"I know you are. I know the regard he holds you in. I wish that everyone that our beloved Fuehrer thought highly of was so deserving."

"What in the world are you talking about, Herr Reichsfuehrer?"

"There is a man so highly placed that has been betraying us from day one. This man, this traitor, has been giving our secrets to the Russians from the start of the war. All of our moves and well-laid plans were all passed on to the Russians before a single soldier moved into position. This spy that we know as Werther may have cost us the war."

"Why don't you arrest the man? If anyone deserves to be hanged, this man does." Baur's face was red at this revelation from his boss.

"Because if I did, the Fuehrer would not believe me. Most likely, he would turn on me."

"How could he doubt you with all of the intelligence service at your disposal? If he would believe anyone, it would be you."

"Normally, I would agree with you, but this is one person I can't touch."

"Tell me, and I'll bring it to the Fuehrer's attention."

"More than likely, he will not believe you, and I would not want to act against you if the Fuehrer ordered me to do so. However, I might not have any choice."

A look of bewilderment spread across Baur's face. About that time, he caught a glimpse of Bormann in the distance. A sudden shudder went through Baur. Himmler noticed this and nodded his head. Baur swallowed hard as understanding came. "I think I understand now."

"As you realize, even I can't move against Werther. It sickens me to think that he might survive our Fuehrer and become more powerful than before. It is the worst treason of the war I know of, and I am completely powerless. In the meantime, I will do the best

I can to arrange decent terms for Germany after the war. Take care of the Fuehrer as best you can."

Baur gritted his teeth as he shook hands with Himmler. "Don't count on Werther making it out. Some of us have strong feelings about the man."

"Take of yourself, Gruppenfuehrer. Germany will live on."

Himmler then departed the Reichs Chancellery and headed for Kersten's estate at Hartzwalde. Although he showed no outward emotion, he was thoroughly pleased with himself for the seed he had planted in Baur's mind. If Hitler made his last stand in Berlin, Himmler felt that Bormann would not long survive him. Now he needed to salvage what he could of the Third Reich.

As his Mercedes arrived at Kersten's estate, he spotted the masseur waiting for him. "Ah, there you are, Kersten. Have you made any contact with Eisenhower?" Himmler was visibly relieved to see his "magic Buddha."

"No, Reichsfuehrer."

"Would you be willing to negotiate with Eisenhower for me?"

"Perhaps Count Bernadotte would be better. After all, he is a trained diplomat." Kersten considered his remarks carefully.

Himmler turned toward Schellenberg. "Get me in touch with Bernadotte immediately."

"The count is at Hohenlychen. I asked him to be there in case we needed him."

"Very well. It will just as easy for us to go there as it would be for him to come here."

Himmler walked with Schellenberg and another SS officer back to the Mercedes. Before he seated himself, he turned and held his hand out to Kersten. "You don't know how thankful I am for your care. You alone of men have eased my pain and suffering." Himmler's eyes were moist. Somehow he knew that he would never see Kersten or feel his magic fingers again.

After parting with Kersten, Himmler proceeded on to Hohenlychen. Despite the deprivations of the war, Count Bernadotte had thrown together a fabulous smorgasbord. As Himmler exited his car, Bernadotte noted that the Reichsfuehrer appeared utterly exhausted.

"Good morning, Reichsfuehrer."

"My dear Count Bernadotte." Himmler then shook hands with the count.

"You had a pleasant trip, I hope."

"Actually, it was very wearisome. However, that is not important." Himmler stared hungrily at the feast Bernadotte had prepared. "My dear Count, you must be hungry yourself this early in the morning. Please eat."

Count Bernadotte was used to bread and coffee and so took little of the food. He sat quietly as the others ate greedily. Himmler seemed very nervous as he repeatedly tapped his fingers on the table.

"Surely you must be hungry," Himmler repeated as he tried to induce the count to eat.

"I am a simple man with few needs, Reichsfuehrer. Breakfast is a light meal for me." Bernadotte decided to get down to business. "I hope you have considered releasing the Polish-Jewish women at Ravensbruch. I think that I can arrange transport by the Red Cross if you do so."

"Very well then. The women will be released." Himmler continued to eat ravenously.

"Also, the women prisoners at Neuengamme."

"I see no difficulty with their release." Himmler made no attempt to hide his hunger as he drank a cup of coffee. "Surely, you are hungry." Himmler pushed a plate toward Count Bernadotte.

"My dietary needs are simple at this time of day, Reichsfuehrer." Inwardly, Bernadotte breathed a sigh of relief. Perhaps this was the beginning of better things to come.

The conference ended as Himmler finished eating. Bernadotte had obtained the release of all prisoners discussed. However, Himmler neglected to bring up peace negotiations with Eisenhower. Himmler parted company with Schellenberg and Bernadotte and drove off separately. Schellenberg drove the count back to Berlin. On the way, Schellenberg suggested to Bernadotte that he meet with Eisenhower and set up a conference with Himmler. Bernadotte replied that any initiative must come from Himmler. On reflection, Bernadotte told the head of the SD that Himmler did not realize the reality of his position. "He should have taken over Germany after our first meeting," was the count's blunt assessment.

April 20th would find KG 200 flying its last mission to the supposedly beleaguered Scherhorn battle group. Two Arado 232As took off to drop supplies. However, one plane developed mechanical problems shortly after takeoff, and the other encountered severe weather that forced its return before reaching the drop site.

The failure of KG 200 to deliver the promised supplies was duly noted in Moscow by Major Makarov. So far, his identity as a German spy had remained safe. However, Captain Karotokov was definitely shadowing him. General Sudoplatov had been right about the man. Makarov turned his attention to the failed drop and thought of a way to turn the occasion to his advantage. Something would have to be transmitted back to the Germans inquiring about the cancelled airdrop. Makarov devised a plan to rid him of Karotokov once and for all based on the day's events. Beria would have to find another way to keep tabs on him.

As the war was winding down, Karotokov had been put in charge of the Scherhorn project. What Makarov had never foreseen was how this would play into his hands. Since he had heard about failed drop before Karotokov, he had time to come up with a plan that he felt Karotokov would fall for and cause the man to be hoisted on his own petard.

"Captain Karotokov, would you please report?"

Seconds later, the unsuspecting captain stood before him. "How may I be of help, Comrade Major?"

"You are aware that the Germans did not drop the promised provisions to our Scherhorn group."

"I became aware of that only a few minutes ago."

Markarov sniffed the air suspiciously, probably talking to Beria instead of doing his job. "I assume you are going to send a suitable inquiry back to Berlin?" Makarov asked innocently.

"Of course, Comrade Major."

"What are you going to say?"

"I was going ask why the drop was not made given the desperate situation."

Makarov smiled thinly. "Of course, you will. I can't tell you what to say. But remember these are desperate, starving loyal soldiers of the German nation. If you were the commander, would you not be upset at the lack of commitment from the Luftwaffe?"

"Of course, Comrade Major. I suppose a commander in such a situation would be very upset. Thank you for your input. I will send a message to Berlin, expressing great disappointment in today's events."

"Remember, I can't tell you what to say. However, General Sudoplatov and I have confidence in your abilities. Remember, it is better for us to get the supplies rather than have the arms going to Bandera or other criminals."

"Of course, Comrade Major. It will be done."

Later that day, as Makarov was drinking a cup of coffee, he came across the reply that Karotokov had composed. As he sipped, he nearly dropped the cup in surprise. This was better than he had hoped for. This was far different than any previous messages that had been sent to the Germans. If the other side did not pick up on this, then they were truly a bunch of dunces, no better than the moujiks that he worked for now. Makarov went to a chair and sipped his coffee with a deep satisfaction. While no one could relax if they were members of the Soviet security apparatus, Makarov was pleased at thwarting another potential threat to himself. Things might turn out well after all.

Makarov read the message again in disbelief. The German High Command was castigated for writing off the Scherhorn operation for starters. The transmission continued on in the same vein. Makarov put his cup down. He and Sudoplatov would make sure that Beria found out about Karotokov's blunder. Karotokov was going to learn a painful lesson about the world of intelligence if he was lucky. If Beria were merciful, Karotokov would end up doing border duty in some thankless outpost in Siberia. Makarov lit a cigarette. He watched the smoke curl to the ceiling. Another threat neutralized for now. He realized that others might develop if the Russians captured any of the Abwehr files. However, for now, that could wait as he silently savored his victory.

German intelligence was not as dense as Makarov feared. The SD officer in Berlin groaned as he read the transmission from the Scherhorn group. The implications hit hard as he realized that they had in reality supplied the Red Army for the last nine months instead of German soldiers who desperately needed everything they could get. With a heavy heart, he picked up the phone and cancelled all further flights to Battle Group Scherhorn.

In Flensburg, Schreiber organized his men. Radl had worked miracles in cooperation with the SD in obtaining American uniforms and equipment. He checked the American uniforms that he had been supplied with. American jeeps had been commandeered along with some motorcycles. As he went about his duty, Schreiber often thought about his early days in the Brandenburg division. Inspections would be held with the men dressed in the uniform of a foreign army. Everything would be accurate down to the tags on their underwear.

Schreiber and Skorzeny had thought about the identities the men would use. They quickly decided that they would be disguised as military police. They had found out that the ruse caused untoward confusion among the Americans during the Battle of the Bulge. Until one of their jeeps wrecked and the true identity of Skorzeny's men ascertained, the SS commandos had virtual immunity from questioning during their forays behind American lines. The two men felt that in the United States a group of military policemen was unlikely to attract a lot of questioning. No sane German military was going to question a feldgedarmerie about his credentials. In addition, it was apparent to German intelligence that the American MP was not the brightest soldier on the other side. Everyone hoped that this might help with any language difficulties that might arise.

As he inspected his men, Schreiber had reason to be pleased. The equipment was all American, and the uniforms were American down to the bootlaces. American cigarettes had been procured as well. Schreiber again recalled that during the Bulge jeeps, weapons, tanks, and other equipment could not be located when requested. He remembered the attempts to disguise a Panther tank as a Sherman. Schreiber felt sick as he recalled the episode. The mission had not been taken seriously by the high command. This time, Himmler was in charge; and, evidently, the word had gotten out that the events of December 1944 would not be tolerated again. The SD and secret field police had been given orders to confiscate any captured American articles and rank be damned. If an unfortunate German soldier was caught wearing American uniform pants to supplement his clothes, the field police would still confiscate the pants. The soldier would then go on his way unless he wanted to know more about the German intelligence service than he wanted to previously. Few did, and those few learned quickly they hadn't wanted to after all.

Schreiber finished his inspections proud of his men's abilities even at this stage of the war. He was reminded of the early days of the Brandenburgers. In 1940, he had been disguised as a Dutch soldier. Since then, there had been several missions. The culmination had been at Maikop. Now he was on something bigger. He felt that the mission might actually have a chance of succeeding, that is, if the Americans were able to build the bomb. He felt his men could pull this off since they were better than he had originally hoped for. Not everyone spoke English fluently, but the poor speakers would be kept in the background once they were on enemy soil.

Schreiber scrutinized his men closely during these inspections. He wanted to make sure he missed no details that would alert the enemy. He remembered an enemy spy caught in German uniform because he had sewn the corporal's stripes on the wrong shoulder. He also recalled that a German operation was blown in North Africa because an operative was smoking German cigarettes. As a result, the British shut down a secret KG 200 base. As least German intelligence had found out the reason. Schreiber was determined that no stupid oversights like that would occur on this mission.

Dietz usually tagged along on these inspections. He wore the rank of a first lieutenant in the United States Army. Schreiber wore captain's bars as he was in command. Dietz had accepted the lesser rank with grace, but Schreiber kept Skorzeny's words of caution in the back of his mind. Kohlman had to make due with a second lieutenant's rank, although he was second in command. However, he was often absent as he was brushing up on his knowledge of explosives. Certain physicists were briefing him on the theoretical concepts of atomic weapons.

Near the end of April, after one of the inspections, Dietz complimented Schreiber on his progress. "Well done. They do look and even act like Americans. This might actually work."

"If there's a bomb and if we get flown over," Schreiber quietly replied.

"I know. Too bad we have to hope they finish the thing."

"Only to force a negotiated peace and to make sure our POWs are treated well after the surrender. We thought the Russians were bad, but now for the Americans to follow the Russians' lead, at least Eisenhower anyway."

"Strange that our main opponent is of German origin," Dietz continued.

"Maybe that's why he hates us so much."

Schreiber was feeling relaxed despite Dietz's presence. Schreiber had to admit that he had developed a grudging but wary respect for Dietz. He was about to say something else when he noticed some activity around the giant floatplane. Several Luftwaffe mechanics were working to repair the badly damaged plane to make it fit for flying. A Mercedes had arrived and disgorged some dignitaries. As he looked closer, Schreiber could make out the brown party uniforms. Their gold braid even at this distance suggested their exalted status.

Dietz had noticed the unwanted visitors. "Major Schreiber, may I suggest that we get the men—"

"Out of here." Schreiber finished the sentence for him. "We don't need these clowns fowling things up." They immediately started shouting at the men and ordered them back to the barracks and to get rid of the American uniforms now. Soon the field was empty of soldiers, jeeps, and motorcycles. A squad of SD men soon arrived to surround the barracks to quarantine the men during the golden pheasants visit.

"What in the hell is this all about?" Schreiber hissed at Dietz.

"I know as much as you do," Dietz calmly replied. "The presence of the party is never a good sign though, especially on something like this. They either want to give us unwanted advice or push their own pet projects. There is a secret plan to move important party officials to Greenland if Germany capitulates. I can't imagine Himmler telling anyone about Gotterdammerung."

"So we can expect trouble."

"I would believe so."

They noticed a Luftwaffe lieutenant walking toward their barracks. The SD initially denied him entry until Schreiber appeared on the scene. He recognized the man from previous encounters at Flensburg and ordered the SD to stand down. He confirmed their worst fears by the look on his face.

"Herr Major," He stammered briefly, "there's a problem."

"We can tell," Dietz caustically replied. "A certain party official, I suspect."

"Yes, Herr Major, a Gauleiter Gesele. He wants to requisition the Wiking floatplane. He wants to institute some plan to fly party members out of Germany. He wants the current mission for the plane canceled."

"Does he know what the planned mission is?" Dietz demanded.

"I don't think so. At least he didn't give any indication of it. I know I certainly don't. Well, anyway, the golden pheasants have interfered too much the last few weeks. Somehow he found out about the plane, even though we kept quiet about it. He wants our people working on it twenty-four hours around the clock, if necessary. Anyway, I just wanted to give you some advance warning. Currently, he's chewing the colonel's ass out."

"Thank you, Herr Leutnant. Dietz, let's go meet this Gauleiter Gesele."

"Perhaps we shouldn't," Dietz interjected. "There are other ways."

"I want to head this off now."

"I suggest—" Dietz stopped as watched Schreiber's eyes turn ice-cold blue. *Not a man to provoke*, he thought. *Like it or not, I have to work with him for some time.* "Very well," he conceded. "Let's see if these people can be reasonable for once."

The two officers headed toward the Luftwaffe colonel's office. They could tell before they entered the building that the colonel was being thoroughly harried. The Gauleiter's voice boomed through the closed door. As they entered, the colonel's adjutant sat outside the office, studying the ceiling. As he glanced down, he noticed the two officers and came to attention. Gesele's voice was easily understood now despite the closed door.

"Whatever Himmler wants is secondary to the party's needs. As a senior party representative, I have authority to override the Reichfuehrer's petty schemes!" Gesele was shrieking at the colonel now.

The colonel tried to explain in a voice barely audible to those outside. Schreiber decided it was time to intervene. Without knocking, he flung open the door; and, motioning the aide aside, he entered. Dietz followed right behind and took up position to Schreiber's right as Gesele started roaring at the colonel. He was now in the colonel's face, shaking his finger at the frustrated man. The colonel made another halfhearted attempt to reply when he stopped midsentence as the two SS officers intruded. He stuttered, "Meine Herren, may I help you?"

"I should think that we may be of help to you," Schreiber replied, ignoring Gesele.

"I am preoccupied now."

"Not too busy to discuss cancellation of our mission, I hope. I understand that is what is at stake here." Schreiber remained cool for now.

Gesele turned his gaze on Schreiber. He had a smug look on his face from his confrontation with the colonel. He thought he had more easy meat in front of him. He became irritated as he saw

Dietz with the SD badge displayed prominently on his arm. Gesele directed his wrath at him.

"Let me tell you, Hauptsturmfuehrer, that the party does not do Himmler's bidding, does not answer to Himmler, and does not take orders from Himmler. What you are doing can't possibly be as important as saving the party leadership from the Allies."

As Gesele caught his breath from his blustering, Dietz retorted, "What we are doing is not as important. It's more important. We are trying to save the German nation, and my rank is Sturmbannfuehrer."

Gesele turned beet red. Another junior party official in the room walked to Gesele's side. Pure malevolence was on both their faces. "I see that you have not learned your place," Gesele screeched. "I'll personally see that you learn it. Whatever Hitler Youth outing you have planned, you can cancel."

"At least several of the Hitler Youth are fighting and dying for their country. How many gauleiters are?"

Gesele's face underwent contortions as he fought to find words to express his anger. He was incredulous as well as furious at such back talk. This had never happened. At last his brain connected to his tongue. "You little shrimp. I'll have your head. Wait until I speak to Bormann. You're finished. You'll be lucky to end up in a concentration camp."

"I've been in far worse," Dietz replied. He then walked out the door. He did not give the required Heil Hitler. Schreiber went after him.

"That was a rare performance considering I was supposed to stir up trouble. I feel we still have a problem."

Dietz smiled thinly. "No, we don't." There was hidden menace in the answer. He proceeded to the office of a junior SD officer. "I need the use of this phone," he brusquely announced.

"Of course, Herr Sturmbannfuehrer. Is there anything else I can do to help?"

"Yes. Get out. Now. Stay out until I'm finished.

Schreiber entered the room after the junior SD officer left. "Now what?"

Dietz picked up the phone. "Dietz here. Give me the Reichsfuehrer." Dietz turned to Schreiber. "You might not want to hear this."

Schreiber decided that he didn't want to be part of the discussion. It was obvious that part of the reason Dietz was attached to his team was the man was a damned good troubleshooter. He was also not a man to cross.

Himmler came on the phone. "What is it, Dietz?"

"A certain Gauleiter Gesele is interfering with our operation. Somehow he found out about the plane and is trying to requisition it. He wants to cancel our operation in favor of flying the party bigwigs to Greenland. I believe you are more familiar with Gesele."

"Oh, that nonsense." Himmler was obviously irritated. "Well, Gesele is no important person in the scheme of things. He is an embarrassment to the party and the Aryan race. He is worse than Julius Streicher. The Fuehrer should have given directions regarding him a long time ago. By the way, do you have some of Professor Maironovsky's chemicals?"

"Of course, Reichsfuehrer. I have always kept a supply of his chemicals around. I have found them to be very handy."

"What a pity the good professor doesn't know the true extent of his work. How ironic that a Russian scientist has provided us the means of dealing with troublesome party members. I do not expect to hear any more about the problems Gauleiter Gesele is causing."

'I don't think I'll have to bother you again."

"Good." The phone went dead.

Dietz hung the phone up. He leaned back and let out a deep breath. Gotterdammerung would go on. Gesele had vastly overestimated his own importance. Now he would pay for his miscalculation. Dietz considered the course of action that he would take. It took him only a few minutes to decide, and then he was on the phone to the local SD officer in charge.

As Dietz was perfecting his schemes, Schreiber walked over to the makeshift officers club. Just as things seemed to be going well, the party had to interfere. Now he wondered, How was he going to end the war? Would he end up in one the squalid American POW camps? He thought about not surrendering and trying to make his way out of Germany at the end of hostilities.

As he sipped on some beer, Gesele strutted in with his lackey and demanded a drink. Schreiber felt his blood starting to boil. The arrogant fat bastard had nothing on his uniform to show he had ever been shot at. The younger party member's uniform was also devoid of any combat awards. At least Dietz had an Iron Cross and Wound badge. Gesele was obviously dodging military service through his party connections. He was one of the rear area swine that Hitler raved and ranted about.

Gesele sat down at a table and slammed his hand down. "Can't we get any service here? What kind of place is this?"

The young NCO serving as bartender replied, "If you would come up to the counter, I would give you what you want."

Gesele exploded. "Come up to the counter! You can come out and wait on me. The whole military needs to learn proper respect for the party leadership."

The flustered NCO went over to Gesele and took the drink orders for the two men. As the man departed, Gesele spotted Schreiber and loudly exclaimed, "At least the Luftwaffe seems to know its place. The SS will learn its place."

Schreiber tried to hold his tongue. "I started out in the army, the Brandenburgers originally."

"Oh, that bunch of drones," Gesele sneered. "At least if you had stayed in the army, you would know your place after July 20th."

Schreiber gripped the edge of his table. Enough was enough. He was looking for something to throw at the arrogant Gauleiter when Dietz walked in. The SD man strode to the counter in a nonchalant manner.

Gesele noticed him as well. The black patch with the letters SD seemed to taunt him. "So the black plague has returned. Hitler should have smoked you out when he threatened to after your little caper in Rumania."

"I wasn't involved too deeply, or there would have been nothing to talk about."

Gesele was about to explode when the NCO spoke to try to break the tension as much as anything. "Your drinks are almost ready."

"Good. Perhaps some pleasantness can be obtained despite the presence of the SS." Gesele remained in a foul mood as he gave Dietz a look of disgust.

A shadow seemed to come over Dietz's face. He remained at the counter. As the NCO came around the counter with the drinks, Dietz stopped him. He took the tray from the man and headed toward Gesele. The NCO breathed an audible sigh of relief. He had enough of the pompous party official. If the SD man wanted to bear the brunt of the Gauleiter's wrath and sarcasm, so be it.

Schreiber watched semi-amused as Dietz brought the tray over to Gesele and his companion. For a second, it seemed like Dietz made some strange motion with his right hand, but Schreiber wasn't sure.

"Oh, so the SD is trying to be civilized. It will take more than an officer's uniform to do that for your crew." Gesele was remaining true to form.

"Maybe with a little alcohol aboard, you'll be quiet."

"You'll only wish for a concentration camp when I'm done with you!"

Dietz ignored him and walked over to Schreiber's table. Schreiber remarked, "You're more patient than me. I was looking for something to hit him with when you walked in."

Dietz smiled slightly. "I didn't come in to save him from you. Just watch what happens."

Schreiber felt his hair prick at that. Dietz was up to something, but what?

He didn't have long to wait. A crash of glass focused Schreiber's attention back to Gesele. The man was clutching his chest. He was breathing heavily. A blob of white froth came out of his mouth. "Help me!" the desperate man cried out. He then slumped into his chair and then rolled onto the floor.

"Get a doctor," his companion cried. "Help is on the way," he said to Gesele to reassure him. Looking at Dietz and Schreiber, he cried, "Come help us."

"He needs a doctor, not the black plague as he put it," Dietz replied coldly.

The young party official looked up surprised by Dietz's remark. A cold chill ran through him as suspicious thoughts crept into his mind. He decided he better remain quiet for now.

Soon medics arrived with a kubelwagen to transport Gesele in. Two medics barged into the area with a stretcher. They cleared the area around so they could work. By now, the man was in extremis.

"What happened?" one of the medics asked.

"He was having a drink when he grabbed his chest and couldn't breathe." The younger man stuttered out. He was still in shock over seeing his benefactor rendered impotent.

"Probably a heart attack. Let's get him out of here. We can't do anything here." The medics heaved him onto the stretcher and took him outside. The young party man wanted to say something but closed his mouth as Gesele was carried outside. The young toady followed his boss, hoping for the best.

"I wonder if he'll make it?" Schreiber asked.

"No," Dietz replied.

Schreiber suspicions had already been raised by Dietz's seemingly polite actions in bringing Gesele his drink. He decided to press Dietz for more information. If Dietz had done what he suspected, Schreiber knew that Dietz would be proud of his coup, given his history.

"How did you know which glass to put it in?" Schreiber tried to sound jovial over the episode.

"I didn't," was the cool reply.

Schreiber persisted. "Just an educated guess, I suppose."

"Call it what you will."

Schreiber didn't ask any more questions. However, the look on Dietz's face betrayed the brutal truth. Dietz wanted to say so badly what he had done. Underneath Dietz's cool exterior, there was unbounded glee in the way he had dealt with the troublesome party member. Schreiber watched as Dietz continued on. This isn't over yet as he thought about the junior party member. The man was in deep trouble and didn't know it. Schreiber suspected he would be unable to extricate himself from whatever fate Dietz had in mind, and Schreiber was sure that Dietz would not be long in tying up this loose end as the day was not over.

As he thought about Dietz, he wondered about the man's true role in coming along. The ostensible story about knowing the SD contacts did not hold water. Schreiber had never encountered nonsense like that with the Brandenburgers. Was Dietz being used as a commissar was in the Soviet Army? Perhaps he was carrying out a hidden agenda on secret orders from Himmler once or if the bomb was acquired. Whatever the reason, Dietz bore watching.

Schreiber's attention returned to the present as he noticed Dietz talking to other SD men. Meaningful nods were exchanged among the group. Dietz turned his face briefly. It was that of a conspirator. A junior SD man nodded vigorously as Dietz obviously gave some orders.

Schreiber decided to needle Dietz some more. He knew Dietz was proud of his little exploit but was obligated to remain silent. He waited until Dietz was alone again.

"Planning the little bootlicker's wake? Can't say that I blame you."

A stony stare greeted Schreiber. "I'm merely tying up some loose ends."

"I sometimes wonder if I'm a loose end in the grand scheme of things."

Dietz stared at Schreiber hard for a moment and then couldn't contain himself. He broke out laughing. "You're more like a loose cannon, a very important loose cannon, I might add. Otherwise, you would not be alive or have been picked by Himmler for this job.'

"Skorzeny picked me."

"But Himmler approved you, which means I move against you at my own risk. I thought you would have figured that out by now."

"In that case, I guess I can count on living another twenty-four hours unless the British bomb us tonight."

"Probably longer."

Both men fell silent. Each recognized a grudging respect for the other even if there was no love lost. Each considered how useful the other could be if Gotterdammerung actually got off the ground. A certain amount of cooperation was essential.

As they were absorbed in their thoughts, a black Mercedes drove up. Gesele's aide was at the wheel. The man's face betrayed a mixture of fear and anger. He got out and approached the two men. He tried to project his previous cockiness, but the tremor in his hands betrayed his fear. Both officers noticed this.

"The pipsqueak returns," Schreiber muttered.

Dietz smiled faintly. "Not for long."

The party man approached. "Gauleiter Gesele is in serious shape and unable to make any decisions. However, as his deputy, I will remind you two gentlemen that the plane will be used to fly the party leadership to Greenland." As he continued his blustering, he regained more of his self-importance. "By the way, should Gauleiter Gesele expire because of his illness, an autopsy will be arranged by me." He hoped to inspire fear into the officers.

Dietz was not easily intimidated. "To show what? That he had a big tongue and little brain. That really would be amazing now, wouldn't it?"

The party man grimaced. "I see that the party needs to clarify the role of the SD in the party. A particular emphasis needs to be placed on its subservience."

"Your place will become clear enough."

"Is that a threat?"

"A statement of fact."

"I'll see that you are broken yet."

"I think not, Herr. What was your name again?"

"Drexler. Anton Drexler. I will personally report this matter to my superiors."

Schreiber interjected now. "If it is so important, why don't you call it in?"

"This is far too important to be discussed with narrow-minded military officers. Good day, gentlemen." Drexler went back to his

Mercedes. Gesele was right. Hitler should have smoked out the black plaque a long time ago. If the SD had poisoned Gesele, then heads would roll. Drexler would see to that. The SD bully and his sidekick only thought they were doing something important. Well, they would learn that the party decided what was important.

As Drexler fumed on his way out of the compound, Dietz gave a nod to another SD man. He returned Dietz's nod and went over to a telephone. As Drexler's vehicle faded in the distance, Schreiber noticed two camouflaged vehicles take off behind it and follow Drexler from a distance. Somehow Schreiber knew that Drexler would never make his report.

Schreiber approached Dietz. "How long has he got?"

Dietz hunched his shoulders briefly. "Thirty minutes or less."

"I hope he didn't make any calls."

"He couldn't. All outgoing lines were down."

Schreiber whistled in admiration. "No loose ends then."

"No loose ends."

At that time above Flensburg, two RAF Spitfires were flying a routine patrol. They were looking for any objects of opportunity to strafe as the Luftwafffe had been virtually cleared from the skies. Wing Commander Douglass Young was about to return to home when he called out to his wingman Sergeant John Morris.

"Johnny, I think we've come up empty again."

"Roger that, sir. Seems like there's nothing to do anymore."

"Just make sure that we don't get hit by any ack ack."

Morris took another look along a road and thought he spotted movement. "Sir, I think there's something moving."

"Let's take a look."

Drexler was preoccupied with wreaking vengeance on the SD that he had not paid attention to the skies. Most vehicles had two occupants anymore as someone always needed to watch for enemy aircraft. Strafing had claimed too many lives of those who had been careful anyway. Drexler did not know that he was being tailed until bullets shattered the rear windshield. One grazed his right arm, while another blew out a tire. The car started to swerve out of control.

Drexler grabbed the wheel to avoid hitting a tree. He swerved finally into a wooded area. His face slammed into the steering wheel as the Mercedes came to an abrupt stop.

Above, the two Spitfires made another pass. All they saw was dust where Drexler went off the road. The trees protected Drexler for now.

"I think we got him, sir"

"I agree. Let's call it a day and tea time."

"Roger that, sir."

Drexler sat half stunned in his car. Blood poured out his nose. He was sore but could still move. He pinched his nose, still somewhat dazed. A car drove up behind. Drexler heard footsteps approach. He lifted his head. At least someone had seen what had happened and could help him.

"Help me," he cried out.

There was no response, but the footsteps came closer. Finally, a figure appeared in the side mirror. Too late, Drexler recognized the letters SD in a black diamond. His brain became more alert as two grenades were thrown through the shattered windshields and landed in the passenger's seat. Drexler cried out in terror.

His cries ended with the explosions. Both doors were blown open, and Drexler was thrown out with the blast minus some of his body parts. The explosions nearly eviscerated him, and his right forearm was missing. The flesh hung in tatters from his right leg. As he looked up, Drexler saw three SD men around him. He tried to beg for help, but blood gurgled in his throat. Drexler was obviously a dying man.

"Shall we finish him off?"

"No, we'll let the swine bleed to death. That way, he can suffer a little more. He's caused enough trouble. He doesn't deserve to die nicely. Too bad we can't leave him to rot."

The SD men returned to their vehicles and began to smoke. They had no worries, as they knew that the Spitfires had turned for home. Minutes later, they returned to Drexler's body and flung it into one the camouflaged vehicles. Then they made the drive back to Flensburg.

That evening, Schreiber joined his men for a round of drinking. He still had not disclosed to them the nature of the mission. As Germany collapsed more each day, the likelihood of the mission proceeding faded. In fact, many of the details would have to be worked out once in the United States. All that intelligence had provided for now were vague references to locations. Nothing was definite. He walked over to the building his men had gathered at.

A carefree attitude was evident. Many were smoking. Several card games were in session. Underneath it all was a tension waiting to rise to the surface. Schreiber recalled that often the hardest part of a mission was the waiting. Once things happened, the tension disappeared.

"Hey! Let me see that hand again.'

"Think I'm cheating?"

The two men started to rise when Schreiber appeared. They quickly took their seats.

"No need to fight over this money. It will be worthless soon anyway." Schreiber was mild but firm.

"Major, it's been a while since we've had a good bar fight."

"Save it for the enemy. That chance may come soon enough."

A hush fell briefly over the group, but soon the games resumed and the smoking continued. The incident was swiftly forgotten. Schreiber's attention was soon turned elsewhere as he heard some giggles. Someone had brought some females into the makeshift club. Schreiber was concerned that someone might talk just as Dietz appeared on the scene. Schreiber motioned for him to join him.

"Pretty girls. Where did you find them?"

Schreiber quietly replied, "Slipped in. I thought your security men were keeping a tight wrap on things."

"So did I. The untersturmfuehrer in charge may be a little excited after today's events. I will have a little talk with him."

"I hope it's at least fatherly."

Dietz snickered. "I won't be too hard on him. By the way, you heard that Gesele didn't make it."

"I'm not surprised."

"Neither did Drexler."

Schreiber raised his eyebrows. "How?"

"British fighters spotted him. Strafed him. He went off the road, and the car blew up. Rather messy, I'm afraid. He should have checked with the Luftwaffe. The RAF usually flies a sortie that time of day every day."

"How unfortunate."

"Or fortuitous."

"Tell me, Dietz, if your connections are so good that they involve getting the RAF to do your work, how come I'm coming along?"

Dietz laughed. "Don't overestimate me. I have my limitations too."

"Well, I certainly don't want to underestimate you. That could be fatal."

Dietz had his faint smile. "Perhaps." He turned serious. "The girls. I think you're right. We need to get them out of here." He walked out to speak with the SD lieutenant.

As Dietz left, Sergeant Fouts started playing an accordion. Schreiber vaguely knew the man but had asked for him because of Fouts's experience with Sergeant Rahn in Africa with the Brandenburgers. His unit had gone on a secret expedition to locate a railway that was thought to cross Africa. Fouts had grown up in the American west. The unit of course found no such railway. However, considerable desert experience was gained, and Schreiber felt such experience would be useful in the American Southwest.

Much of the noise died down as Fouts entranced the audience with his playing. He was a virtuoso with the instrument. Schreiber stopped and listened to the first melody. Everyone recognized Lili Marlene, of course. Soon the whole room was singing the lyrics. Memories flooded back as the song continued. Many a night he and his comrades had rounded up a radio to hear Lale Andersen's rendition of the tune on Radio Belgrade. It was always a favorite whenever a musical instrument could be found.

As Fouts's fingers danced around the keyboard and the 120 buttons on the left side Schreiber was transported back in time. "Vor der Kaserne, vor dem grossen Tor, stand eine Laterne und sheht sie noch davor," reminded him of how he had met his wife when he was an enlisted man. She was the sister of one of his comrades and romance blossomed soon after their first meeting. Until then he had been carefree without a concern in the world.

"So wollen wir uns weidersehn bei der Laterne woll'n wir stehn" was equally poignant for him. *How many times she waited for him and he for her?* Schreiber thought. Now her wait may be a lot longer. Forever. Schreiber shuddered and tried to forget that thought.

Finally, the words "Lili Marlene" signaled the end of the tune. Schreiber was absorbed in his thoughts as the song ended. He noticed Dietz at the door with some SD behind him. He too seemed wrapped in his own thoughts as the song ended. Dietz walked over to Schreiber.

"Have a change of heart, Dietz?"

"Sort of. For some reason, it seemed to touch me."

"Me too, for some reason. I'm glad you didn't empty the room yet."

"I wasn't here yet. I'm sort of glad I was late."

"About the girls. Maybe I should leave them. After all, no one but you and me know the real nature of the mission."

"True. But they will suspect something. With all this training in English, they'll know this isn't just a drill."

"Yes. But remember a lot of disinformation can result as well. That is not so bad as well."

"I'm not sure I follow." Dietz appeared puzzled.

"Remember the Ardennes. Some of our men who were captured told the Americans they were supposed to kill Eisenhower. It was pure nonsense, but the Americans fell for it. It caused panic and confusion as they suspected each other of being infiltrators."

"Perhaps you are right. We'll let the girls stay."

Meanwhile, a hush had fallen over the crowd. The song had

reminded everyone they were still alive. Hopefully, the next few days would mean an end to all of the sacrifices if only they could survive the following days.

However, Fouts did not remain silent long. His fingers began dancing on the accordion again. His next tune was "Die Lorilei." Following that, he struck up a polka to dance to. Schreiber and Dietz listened briefly and stepped outside. Dietz dismissed the SD men.

"Have you heard any updates?" Schreiber asked.

"The pilot is on his way. He should be here tonight. He's flying from the south and has had to evade the Americans several times. Detachment Olga has moved its headquarters at least twice because of the American advance."

"It had better be soon. Things like this don't remain a secret forever. I am especially worried about our plane. Some Allied fighter may see through the camouflage yet."

"We are keeping a close watch on everyone here. However, we can do nothing about the planes." Dietz reminded him.

"I'm not worried about the men. It's the powers over us I'm worried about."

"You're thinking about Canaris, aren't you?"

"Not specifically, but yes. I was on too many operations that were ambushed because of treachery. To think that a colonel was passing on information to the Russians."

"Well, Oster paid dearly for that."

"I suspect he wasn't the only one. Plus, there's always someone you miss. I just hope this is soon if we're going to do it."

"Don't worry. It may come faster than you want."

Meanwhile, Himmler had nearly completed the break with the man he had nearly viewed as a god. His mind was on the future now, and it was clear that Hitler was not going to be part of that future. He had seen to the release of the female Ravensbruch prisoners as promised. Finally, on April 22nd, he asked Bernadotte to present to Eisenhower an offer of surrender. However, to maintain the illusion of loyalty, he phoned Hitler several times, urging the Fuehrer to leave the doomed city. He still wanted the dictator's acceptance as one of his minions for now. In addition, he tried to distract Hitler from thoughts about his loyalty after SS General Felix Steiner had refused to attack a vastly superior Russian force with his diminished force. Hitler had ranted and screamed over the stalled attack against Zhukov. Hitler sobbed that even the Waffen-SS was letting him down now.

To placate Hitler, Himmler sent six hundred men of his escort battalion to assist in Berlin's defense. Hitler calmly accepted the offer and had personally placed the men on arrival. However, Himmler continued his negotiations with Bernadotte.

On the night of April 23rd, Himmler met with Bernadotte again. Himmler was exhausted and nervous. Only with difficulty did he remain calm. He was only partially reassured that he had more freedom of movement with Hitler's decision to remain in Berlin. He did feel comfortable enough to ask Bernadotte to convey to Eisenhower an offer to surrender to the Western Allies that included Norway and Denmark.

However, Britain and the United States would not consider dealing with Himmler because of his dark reputation. Churchill and Truman swiftly dismissed the idea. Stalin was promptly informed of the offer and refusal, and then the news of the secret negotiations was made known to the Reuters News service. Soon the whole world knew of the Reichsfuehrer's attempts to broker a peace behind Hitler's back.

The news soon made its way into the Fuehrer's bunker on April 28th. The radio operator trembled as he wrote out the message. With great unease and trepidation, the message made its way to Hitler. The demented dictator exploded with rage as the contents of the broadcast were read to him. His face became contorted with rage, turning from red to purple as the full extent of treachery and villainy was now exposed.

"This is the worst treason I've experienced. This is worse than Rohm or July 20th. To think it was all engineered by the man I called 'der treue Heinrich.' Now I know why Steiner's attack failed. Himmler was behind that. That is why Himmler failed on the Oder.

He had started his treason then. That evil intriguer was determined to remove me from power."

Hitler walked along the bunker, showing his staff the message. "Can you believe this? Himmler of all people." Inevitably, everyone gasped in shock or shrieked as they read the poisonous document. Behind him hovered the sinister Bormann, egging Hitler on. In Germany's hour of despair, Bormann was enjoying his hour of triumph over Himmler once and for all. Just hours before, Goring had made a poor grasp for power and had been thwarted by Bormann. The former Reichsmarshal had been dismissed by Hitler and was placed under arrest. At least Goring had asked Hitler fumed. However, Himmler had crossed a line that Hitler was not prepared to forgive. Bormann would make sure he did not forget.

Hitler finally settled down from the shocking news. Bormann continued to foment discord from another angle. "Mein Fuehrer, may I remind you about General Fegelein? Surely he knew about Himmler's negotiations. Why else should he have deserted when he did? Surely as Himmler's representative from the SS he knew what was going on."

Hitler's face lit as he fastened onto Bormann's words. Hitler was anxious to get his revenge on Himmler. "A traitor should never succeed me as Fuehrer, and his henchmen should not live to enjoy Germany's fall. Of course, Fegelein was involved. Otherwise, he would not have deserted us when Germany is fighting for her life. Have him thoroughly questioned, and we'll deal with him later."

Later Fegelein would face an SS firing squad for his infidelity. Meanwhile, Hitler summoned Ritter von Greim, promoted him to field marshal, and ordered him to fly out and arrest the arch-traitor Himmler. Hitler was adamant that the Reichsfuehrer be stopped at all costs. In addition, Hitler signed an order demoting Himmler to a private in the SS.

Bormann continued his scheming deftly. "Mein Fuehrer, you must decide now about a successor since Himmler and Goering have proved so unworthy."

"Yes, I know. Still I have difficulty believing that my top aides have proved to be so unreliable. Goring at least asked, but Himmler, that is the ultimate betrayal. Both are to be expelled from the party for their actions. In addition to my successor, a new Reichsfuehrer will need to be appointed."

"Of course. However, for now, your successor must be decided upon in order to forestall any of Himmler's moves. I'll see to it that the expulsions are carried out."

"Good. Still someone of undoubted loyalty should fill my shoes."

"Few men are left that could be described as truly loyal."

'Particularly in the army. The army has let me down too many times for me to choose a general. Plus, they led the July 20th attempt. Nor will anyone from the SS succeed me now Himmler's treason has been going on for so long, and no one told me about it. Don't tell me his generals knew nothing about this."

"What about the Luftwaffe?"

"No. They have let our cities and factories be destroyed. The pilots have not fought hard enough."

"The navy."

"I must admit I did not pay enough attention to the navy. They have suffered incredible losses. The U-boats could have done so much more if there had been more of them at the start of this war. The navy has shown that it knows how to fight to the last man. If only the army had learned the same thing early in this war."

"What about Donitz?"

Hitler paused in thought. "Donitz has proven himself immensely loyal both to me and National Socialism. If only I had listened to him earlier in the war, things might have turned out differently. I listened to Goering, and look what happened. I had plenty of planes built for the Luftwaffe and pilots trained that wouldn't fight. He failed me at Dunkirk, with Operation Sea Lion, and finally at Stalingrad."

"No need for that, Mein Fuehrer. I know that you have done everything possible to bring this war to a successful end."

"I have tried. However, for now, I think that Donitz is the ideal successor. He should be the next fuehrer. Please send a message to him informing him of my decision.'

"At once, Mein Fuehrer. I will send a message at once to Doenitz. He will also be notified of Himmler's and Goering's treason and will be advised to take appropriate action."

"Good. A good German must succeed me as Fuehrer. Nothing less will do."

"It will be done, my Fuehrer." As Bormann departed from Hitler's presence, he felt immensely satisfied in engineering the fall of his two closest rivals. Goering was already under arrest and hopefully soon to be executed. Once he notified Donitz of Hitler's decision, Himmler would be in a similar position. What Bormann failed to take in account was that he was trapped in Berlin, while Himmler was free and close to the new seat of power with plenty of armed men at his disposal.

Himmler, of course, was not aware of the changes being ordered by Hitler. On April 30, Himmler was returning from a late meeting with Donitz. Both men had assumed that Himmler was the heir apparent in case Hitler could not carry on. As of yet, Donitz had not received Bormann's message. It was dark when Himmler reached his headquarters. Awaiting him was a summons to return immediately to Doenitz's headquarters. Himmler grew agitated as he read the note. He immediately summoned Heinz Macher. Macher appeared almost immediately. A much-decorated combat officer, Macher was ready for any possibilities.

"Macher, something has happened since I left the Grand Admiral's headquarters. Something is wrong for me to be summoned back so soon. I want you to bring some men with me, just in case."

"I will have a platoon of armed men ready in half an hour, Reichsfuehrer."

"Good. When you are ready, let me know. I do not want to go back to Doentiz's unprepared."

As Macher assembled his men, Himmler went to his office and picked up the phone. "Himmler here. Find Sturmbannfuehrer Dietz at once.'

There was a pause, then a familiar voice. "Yes, Reichsfuehrer."

"Is everything ready for Operation Gotterdammerung to proceed?"

"The pilot arrived last night. The plane is being fueled tonight. That is a rather tedious process partly because the engines require fueling in a certain sequence."

"You can spare me the details, Dietz. Will the plane be ready in the next twenty-four hours? We can't wait much longer."

"I think so. The plane is the main concern since it was so badly damaged by strafing. Otherwise, Schreiber has done a good job in getting his men trained. He feels that there is a good chance that we can pull this off provided the Americans succeed."

"That is out of our hands. I am glad to hear that Schreiber feels so confident. Have you heard from your wife lately?"

"No, Herr Recihsfuehrer. Is something wrong?"

"There was heavy bombing last night. I have been unable to contact several of my men as a result. Anyway, my best wishes for your success."

After hanging up, Himmler was notified that his escort was ready. It was still dark when they reached Doenitz's headquarters. The small convoy slowed and then stopped as they approached the headquarters' entrance. Macher got out and scouted the area. Several sailors were spotted hiding behind the trees. *Poor dumb bastards,* Macher thought. *We'll kill them all before they realize what is happening.*

However, Macher was thankfully spared from shedding his countrymen's blood. A naval officer appeared in the headlights. The Knights Cross at his throat commanded instant respect. He called out to Macher, "We've been expecting you. Captain Cramer at your service."

Macher came to attention. "I see. I spotted some of your welcoming committee."

Cremer smiled. "I'm afraid some of our younger officers are either too enthusiastic or easily spooked. Anyway, these matters are best left to the professional infantry, not sailors pretending to be infantry. Would you not agree, Major?"

Macher relaxed. He felt he could trust this man. "Of course, Captain. Show us the way."

Minutes later, Himmler was in Doenitz's office. Himmler had dismissed Macher who along with other SS officers joined their brother officers from the Kreigsmarine in drinking some fine brandy. However, the rest of Himmler's escort remained vigilant.

"Read this," Doenitz commanded after the door was closed.

Himmler picked up the paper. It contained Bormann's instructions to the grand admiral. Himmler's fingers trembled as he studied the contents. He was pale when he put it down and addressed Doenitz. "May I congratulate the next German Fuehrer?' Himmler paused as he struggled to find words. "May I say that my negotiations were for the benefit of Germany? You know yourself that Hitler could not manage things in Germany when he refused to leave Berlin. I felt that I had to do something to alleviate the current situation."

"That may be, Reichsfuehrer. The message is clear. I am the next head of state, as far as your position is concerned."

"If you would allow me to be the second in you government, I would be deeply honored. I could bring much needed experience in security and police matters."

Doenitz thought about that one. *Is he sincere, or is he telling me he still has control of his forces and is willing to use them? Furthermore, he's right. I do need someone to maintain control. There is too much chaos as it is. However, I do not need to make him feel to secure in his position.* "I'm not sure I need a policeman more than anything else. What I need is a statesman, not some fool politician like Ribbentrop to make things worse. I just don't know of any good credible diplomats that the Allies will listen to."

"I do have contacts."

"Of course, with Bernadotte. We may have to see where that leads. Perhaps, Reichsfuehrer, the German nation has not fully appreciated your service. We still need order maintained."

"My security forces can do that."

I'm sure they can, Doenitz thought. He was still wary of Himmler. At least the man did not seem inclined to usurp Doenitz's new position. On the other hand, Himmler seemed relieved that the grand admiral was not going to have him arrested. Both recalled days before when both assumed that Himmler would be holding the reign of power. They had reached an understanding on the delegation of power when Bormann's message had changed everything.

Doenitz decided at one thirty in the morning that it was time for a break. He sent a reply back to Berlin. He still did not know that Hitler was dead at his own hands. In his message, Doenitz reaffirmed his loyalty and pledged to fight on.

Doenitz and Himmler continued their discussion behind closed doors while their aides continued to sip brandy. Finally, at dawn, Himmler walked out of Doenitz's office. He joined Macher for breakfast. After eating, Himmler prepared to leave with his escort. On the way, he ran into Ritter von Greim and Hannah Reitsch. They proceeded to castigate him openly for his treachery.

"You are a traitor of the worse kind!" Reitsch spat at him.

Himmler calmly replied. "My dear Fraulein, I have acted in the best interests of Germany. This is not treason. This should have ended a long time ago. Hitler wanted to shed the blood of every last German to satisfy his pride and honor. This bloodbath should have ended a long time ago."

"You have no right to speak of pride and honor when you don't even have an Iron Cross to show for bravery. Hitler died a hero in Berlin. You and Goering will be infamous from now on as the worst traitors imaginable. Millions would have died for Hitler."

"Millions already have. I acted so that millions more won't have to. I have tried to stop the shedding of all German blood and salvage what is left of our country."

With that, Himmler headed back to his headquarters. He was upset briefly by the exchange with Reitsch. However, by the time he arrived, he was in better spirits since he had not been arrested. The wily Schellenberg was waiting for him. They discussed the events with Doenitz and Schellenberg's continued intrigues with Bernadotte.

May 1st found Himmler in control of himself again. He realized how much Doenitz needed him to maintain control of the deteriorating situation. Otherwise, the evacuation of refugees from the east might break down altogether with more people left to the mercy of the Red Army than anyone wanted to think about.

On May 2nd, Himmler and Schellenberg joined Doenitz for lunch as they continued their wary courtship. However, the meal was interrupted by the news that British tanks had broken into Lubeck. A hasty departure was imperative as the enemy was only thirty miles away now. Doenitz decided to move his headquarters to the naval cadet school at Flensberg. As the evacuation was being prepared, Himmler decided he would call Dietz, that is, if he hadn't left.

"Dietz here."

"Why have you not left?"

"Some last-minute mechanical problems. The plane was heavily damaged, as you will recall. However, the maintenance crews feel they can have her ready for takeoff tonight. The men have done well on the repairs. After all, the plane is officially listed as destroyed, and it very nearly was in actuality."

"Yes, I know, Dietz. However, the British are in Lubeck now, and Doenitz, our new Fuehrer, is moving his headquarters to the naval cadet school. I would like for you to be out tonight."

"That's a little close. I didn't realize the British were moving so fast. We'll make a supreme effort to fly out tonight."

"I would prefer not to hear about any more delays."

Later, Dietz located Schreiber and gave him the news. "It looks like tonight is the night."

"Even with Hitler dead?"

"There's been no cancellation."

"If we have to go, I'd like to go tonight. This plane makes such a big target. Some allied fighter is likely to spot it soon even with the camouflage."

"Well, unless there is another mechanical problem, tonight's the night."

Schreiber walked on until he ran into Sergeant Fouts. "Fouts, I want you to pass the word. We load up tonight." He then left to notify Kohlman as well.

Fouts passed the word. In half an hour, all twenty-eight men of Schreiber's team knew they were headed across the ocean. They began making preparations, and soon the air was filled with noise of clanging boots and groaning men. They wanted to get the plane loaded in daylight when they could be sure that the vehicles were properly tied down.

As the men worked, there was the feeling of excitement, something contagious as the men prepared. It began as the jeeps were rolled up the ramp followed by the motorcycles. The men were excited. Even though Schreiber had given them the barest details regarding the mission, the men knew something big was in the air. The veterans that had been Brandenburgers recalled Maikop. They knew Schreiber had been there. To some, it seemed he had taken the baron's place. They had never known always what Folkersam was getting them into, but they always trusted him. This mission and its preparations had the markings of something the baron would be leading if he were still around. They also recalled that while the baron had not made it back after the last mission, Schreiber had and the men who had followed him after the ambush had.

The loading went without a hitch. The vehicles were thoroughly checked to make sure they were fastened down. Weapons were brought on last. Now all that remained was for night to fall so that they could depart.

When dusk arrived, Schreiber's men lined up behind the gigantic BV 222. The plane was fueled and repairs complete. Although he had been on the plane before for clandestine operations, Schreiber still marveled at the size of the craft. At least it would get him to his destination, and with the vehicles, they had a chance to get away from their landing undetected.

Schreiber walked up to the ramp and stood off to one side. His men lined up for boarding. They were fully dressed in American uniforms except for one major item. Most wore SS jackets. The few who had been scavenged from the remnants of the Brandenburg Division wore army issue. If they were surprised on landing and captured, they could claim POW status under the Geneva Convention. Once they had landed and were sure they were undetected, the German clothing would disappear. Only then would they be in full U.S. Army uniforms.

Schreiber looked his men over. He knew they would have to improvise on some things. For example, not everyone spoke good English. Schreiber decided then that every jeep driver had to be fluent in English, as they would most likely be doing any talking. Schreiber and Dietz would ride in the two forward jeeps, as their English was excellent. Kohlman would be in the jeep behind them. Schreiber was sure there were other things that would come up. However, he was a past master of improvising, as were any Brandenburgers. Their biggest hurdle would be getting inside the Manhattan Project. Hopefully, the agents in America would provide some ideas.

The pilot appeared at the top of the ramp. Becker was ready to go. "Are you ready now? It's dark now"

"We are ready whenever you are," Schreiber replied.

"Good. I would like to get airborne as soon as possible and get into the Atlantic before the Allied night fighters get up and start nosing around. This plane makes a nice big juicy target. I would like to avoid any medal hungry pilots from the other side."

"I would too. Men! Line up and prepare to board."

Within minutes, twenty-eight men had clambered aboard. The only noise was the tramp of boots on metal. They seated themselves and secured themselves and any loose gear. A Luftwaffe crewman closed the ramp making the interior of the plane almost pitch black.

In the cockpit, Becker turned the switch that brought his plane to life. With a cough and whiff of smoke, each engine sputtered on. Soon the six large propellers were rotating in unison. Slowly, the mammoth plane began moving ponderously down the runway. As it picked up speed, the nose rose followed by the rest of the plane. They were airborne, and Becker turned the plane west. Minutes later, they had cleared the Jutland peninsula and were over the North Sea. The flight continued uneventfully. Most of the men were asleep by the time England came into sight. The only person stirring was the flight engineer. He walked the catwalk between the big engines to check fuel levels. He started his first check thirty minutes after takeoff and then made hourly rounds. By then, many of the men's snoring was competing with the steady drone of the engines in making the most noise. *At least if they're sleeping, they won't be so nervous,* Schreiber thought. Soon he was in dreamland himself.

CHAPTER 9

April 30 in Berlin found the Fuehrer's bunker in considerable agitation. Hitler's suicide and the nearby fighting drove home to the occupants the seriousness of their position. Those not contemplating immediate suicide began making preparations for escape. Hans Baur tried to avoid Bormann for now as he made preparations for departure. Baur fumed that Bormann and Goebbels had not let him see to the cremation of Hitler and Eva Braun as requested by the Fuehrer. Himmler's last words also remained etched in his mind, and Baur watched the sly Bormann out of the corner of his eye.

Baur approached one of the doctors, Professor Haase, and asked for some Tarnjacken and packs off wounded soldiers. Baur realized his own leather coat and boots would hinder travel and make him a target for any Russian sniper watching. The jackets were soon secured, but no packs were available. Baur offered the doctor his shirts and underclothes in exchange to help the wounded. A haversack was obtained later, but it had no straps. Baur made use of one of Bormann's suitcase. Finally, he burned his ID cards and tied a large sum of money around his neck.

Several officers asked Baur to shoot them. Baur refused, even though he was too well aware of how vindictive the Russians were. If they wanted to die, they could shoot themselves. Baur was now ready to leave, but information on how to get out depended on General Josef Rauch. Rauch was currently with his men, directing the defense of Charlottenburg. Meanwhile, an attempt by General Krebs to negotiate a surrender that would end the worse excesses failed, and he was left with no choice now but escape or death.

General Rauch did not arrive until 11:00 p.m. He reported that the Havel Bridge was still defended by the Waffen-SS. He recommended that escape should be attempted the following night. On May 1, Rauch attempted to rejoin his division at dawn. He returned a few hours later, unable to do so, and reported that the Russians now completely surrounded the city center. It was decided that the breakout would be tonight at nine thirty.

The strain was intense as the survivors waited for the appointed time. Plaster and dust filled the underground air as shells rocked the bunker. That day, the Goebbels decided they could not go on and took the lives of their children and then their own. Three other members of Hitler's inner circle committed suicide that day as well. Other survivors, including Bormann, started drinking heavily to relieve the tension. Meanwhile, the commander of Hitler's bodyguard, SS General Wilhelm Mohnke, and his staff made the plans for the breakout.

Finally, it was dark and time for the breakout. Eventually, the groups would make their way northwest to Doenitz's headquarters, it was hoped. The departures did not start until 11:00 p.m. Ten groups with about four armed soldiers to accompany them had been formed and were scheduled to leave every thirty minutes. Baur's group was the third. He still had mixed thoughts about Bormann as he could not forget Himmler's words, but Hitler had specifically ordered Baur to get Bormann to Doenitz's headquarters with some important papers.

Originally, they had planned to leave by the underground chancellery garage. However, gunfire erupted close by, and the group decided to leave at the main entrance on Vosstrasse. At the appointed time, the group ran for their lives to the Kaiserhof subway station. Even Bormann who was overweight and quite drunk made it with his group in less than two minutes. They swiftly slid down the staircase to the platform. A group of frightened refugees were gathered on the platform. Baur ignored the terrified group and proceeded into the railway tunnel. Their progress was slow as only a few men had flashlights, and no one knew what terrors might lurk ahead in the darkness. They cursed as they stepped over the rails. By now, this group of older men was breathing heavily, and their steps were heavy as they crunched along on the gravel.

After an hour in the darkness, they realized they had missed a turn to the north. They decided to exit at the Stadmitte station. When they reached the entrance, the street was ablaze. The armed soldiers were placed in front and in the rear of the column. They proceeded single file through the carnage along the Friedrichstrasse and headed north where they crossed the Unter den Linden Boulevard and continued until they reached the Weidendamm Bridge. It was barricaded and had been the scene of savage fighting. Burning tanks casts their eerie light on the bodies of scores of soldiers and civilians. They soon had to take cover as the Russians started firing on the bridge again.

As Baur's group took cover, they came across members from one of the earlier groups. They too had taken a wrong turn. As Baur crouched beside a wrecked vehicle, he placed a handkerchief over his nose. The crackling bodies in the burning tanks gave off a terrible smell.

Baur looked for a way out. He dragged Bormann with him to a ruined hotel. They watched sweating as a group of Russian soldiers approached. A shell hit the ruins, sending up a tremendous cloud of dust. Baur ordered the group to keep moving. Suddenly, he heard the roar of tank engines. Several tiger tanks from the Waffen-SS Division Nordland materialized out of the chaos and charged the bridgehead. They broke through the barricades, and Baur's group raced across the bridge behind the tanks.

As they crossed the bridge, several of the men got lost. Baur found Bormann sitting on steps with a dead Russian beside him. Baur nudged Bormann to his feet and looked for a way out as the Russians were shelling the street now. At first, Baur could not find a way through the ruined streets. They decided to work their way up the Schiffbauerdamm. They decided to meet at the Lehrter S-Bahn station if they became separated.

The group followed the street for another thirty minutes without incident. Then all hell broke loose. A tiger fired its 88 in front of Baur. It was so close that Baur's face was burned and he thrown to the ground. Two T-34s exploded into fireballs. A T-34 somehow got behind a Tiger and hit it in the rear. The massive explosion that resulted showered Baur with hot steel fragments and bits of Zimmerit.

Baur located the now terrified Bormann and led the remnants of his group into some ruins. The group hid out until the battle between the steel monsters ended. They then proceeded up the Schiffbauerdamm. The Spree River ran alongside, and the group hugged the riverbank. Then someone fired at them. They took cover in a shell hole next to a railroad. An explosion lit up the area. Baur noticed the look on Bormann's face. His fear was unmistakable. Suddenly, Bormann was moving. Baur yelled at him to stop. Bormann kept going. Himmler's words about Bormann were in Baur's mind now. He drew his Walther pistol and aimed it at Bormann. He fired once, and then Bormann was gone in the smoke. Baur got up and went after Bormann, but the man had disappeared.

The following morning, Baur was wounded in the legs. He was rounded up by the Russians and sent to a Russian aid station. He would never know if his aim had been true. If he had hit Bormann, then he settled a personal debt as Baur regarded Hitler as unser vati.

Bormann knew how accurate the shot was as he staggered along the railroad tracks. He knew it led to the Invalidenstrasse Bridge. The bullet from Baur's pistol stung as he wobbled along. He started to gain confidence as he spotted the bridge through the smoky haze. Then there were the voices. Bormann continued forward. He didn't understand the voices at first. Perhaps it was because he had too much liquor still on board. Then it was obvious. They were speaking

Russian and coming his way. They spotted him and advanced toward him. Bormann raised his hands. One of the soldiers drew out a knife. Bormann saw the man's evil intent and decided this is not how he wanted to die. He bit down on the cyanide pill that senior Nazi leaders carried. Seconds later, he lay spread out only yards from his objective and eventual freedom. He had outlived his Fuehrer by less than forty hours, and another lose end was tied up for Himmler.

Schreiber woke up the following morning from a jab in the side. "What's going on?" he wearily asked.

"We've landed and not in the United States," was Dietz's reply.

Schreiber was instantly alert. Although he was inside, Schreiber could tell that they were at least in semitropical waters. It seemed they were at some sort of base. He could hear men walking on the wings of the plane. Soon objects were thrown on the plane. It sounded like hoses. Schreiber went to the cockpit to see what was going on.

Becker was looking at his charts when Schreiber stuck his head inside. "Good morning, Major. Enjoy the flight?"

"What the hell is going on?"

"Refueling. We're in the Canary Islands, Spanish territory, if you're wondering."

"What happened?"

"We sprang a fuel leak. Otherwise, I might have gotten you to North America maybe, but it strictly would be a one-way trip for me. Plus, I didn't want to have a fire on board in the middle of the ocean. This rig was badly shot up and then hurriedly patched up."

"I don't like this. Now the Spanish will know something's up."

"Most of those boys out there are Luftwaffe personnel. We're at a secret base that the Spanish have let us use for refueling and reconnaissance, although I can't say that we are exactly welcome here anymore. We've plotted Allied convoys far out in the Atlantic before for the U-boats using these bases."

"I suspect mainly when we were winning," Schreiber groaned.

"Perhaps. Can we still trust the Spanish?"

"No," was the answer, and it came from behind Schreiber. It was Dietz.

"Then I don't want to be here any longer than we have to be," Schreiber replied.

"Believe me, we won't," Becker replied in an upbeat manner.

"Good." It was Dietz who replied. "The Spanish don't want us around any longer than necessary. If it wasn't for the aide we gave them during their civil war, they wouldn't put up with us for five minutes. I suggest that we stay out of sight with these field jackets."

The two SS officers withdrew into the hold of the plane. Minutes after they did, a Spanish Air Force officer appeared outside the cockpit. Becker watched him with interest. He whispered back to Dietz and Schreiber, "Keep low. There's a Spanish officer outside wearing an Iron Cross, giving us a good eyeballing. He's certainly not sightseeing."

Dietz groaned. Schreiber looked over. "I suspect you know this person."

"If it's who I think it is, probably Colonel Lopez."

"Well?"

"Spanish Air Force intelligence. He flew in support of their Blue Division on the Eastern Front. He is also the arch-intriguer of Spanish intelligence. More so than myself, I might add."

Schreiber whistled. "That I find hard to believe."

"Well, believe me, if it's Colonel Jaime Lopez, he is the ultimate schemer. He collaborated with the SD when we were planning a coup to replace Franco with General Munoz and hopefully bring Spain into the war on our side. Lopez was up to his neck in the plot."

"But it didn't work, I see."

"No, I suspect that Franco found out and thwarted us. Munoz went into nonofficial exile. However, Lopez was never touched and was actually promoted. He is a man to be watched."

"That is saying a lot coming from you."

"Just don't allow those German decorations on his shirt to deceive you. If Franco decided to take action and impound this plane and crew, Lopez certainly wouldn't be very sympathetic to us. Let's find out if it's him."

They listened outside the cockpit. Becker opened the side panel.

The officer made his way outside Becker's position. The Spanish officer was impeccable in his manners.

"Good morning, Señor. This is a very impressive plane. What is KG 200 up to these days so far from home?" His German was as flawless as his manners.

"God damn it, it's him," Dietz cursed softly.

"You're a long ways from home."

"We're still operational until told otherwise. We still do what we do best."

"Such as drop agents behind enemy lines."

"If asked to, yes."

"But there's more ocean around here than land. Plus, a lot of men that could be dropped from a plane that size. There are just a few of the Wiking boats, as I recall."

"Today we were doing some reconnaissance. One of our U-boats sent a distress call, and they were within range."

"So you plan to pick them up?" Lopez obviously did not believe the lie. "Our navy could have done the same and let KG 200 preserve its precious resources."

The two SS officers bristled over that remark. Becker remained nonplussed. "We like to handle things ourselves. That way, it gets done right," he replied.

Lopez ignored the slight. "This is a truly marvelous plane. I would like to take a look at it. I don't recall seeing such a big aircraft when I was stationed in your country."

"Well, nothing is keeping you from motoring around it." Becker was smiling, but his voice had an edge in it. "Just don't think you're going to look inside" was the undertone.

Lopez got the drift and had his motorboat circle the mammoth plane. He tried to find a place to look inside. The windows had been blocked so that if someone turned a light on despite orders, night fighters would not spot them. That lesson had been learned early in the war. Now that lesson served to keep Lopez's prying eyes where they belonged.

"Wonder if someone talked?" Dietz quietly uttered.

"I was wondering the same. It feels sort of like some of the ambushes we ran into on the Eastern Front. I lost a lot of good men that way."

Lopez completed his circle around the plane and approached Becker again. "She's a real beauty. I would like to take a look around inside."

"Sorry, we're on a tight schedule, Colonel. I would like to get to the U-boat and land in Germany while it's still dark."

"A good idea."

"If I'm back this way in a few days to sell this plane, like we are with a lot of other aircraft, you can look at it all you want."

Lopez laughed. He looked at the figure painted on the nose. It was a Valkyrie. "If you're lucky then. Otherwise, this is the last flight of the Valkyrie."

"I've come back from every other flight."

"Well then, good luck and have a safe flight back to the Fatherland. Auf Weidersehn."

"Auf Weidersehn."

Lopez departed. The plane was refueled now and ready for departure. Becker wasted no time in getting airborne. Schreiber and Dietz glanced at each other.

"Think he'll buy that line of shit?" Schreiber asked.

"Probably not. I wouldn't"

"I'll fly northeast so that if they track us on their radar, they won't suspect us of flying to North America," Becker called out from the cockpit.

"Smart pilot," Schreiber muttered.

"He's been at it long enough," Dietz added.

"What about Lopez? Think he's working for the British and Americans. He sure was nosy."

"If it's to his advantage, he's working for them. His loyalty is to Lopez."

Becker flew northeast for one hundred miles and then altered course back toward the coast of Maine. For Becker, this was actually refreshing to be flying in the daylight compared with the stress of the nocturnal flights he had flown. For now, there was little danger of being intercepted by allied fighters. He sat back and relaxed and let his copilot do most of the work for now.

On the morning of May 3rd, Himmler arrived with his SS guard at Flensurg. He was establishing his presence there to maintain his influence. He was attending a conference that Doenitz had called to discuss the military situation. Berlin had fallen the day before. Those assembled suspected that the Western Allies did not want the Russians in the middle of Germany. However, there were no offers from the British and Americans, and so the discussion revolved around whether or not to continue the war from outside Germany. There were sizeable German forces under Himmler's command in Denmark and Norway that had been untouched by the war.

That afternoon, Admiral Friedeberg returned. He had met with Field Marshal Montgomery to negotiate surrender terms. Now he had them. Montgomery would accept the surrender of all German forces in Holland, Norway, and Schleswig-Holstein. Army Group Vistula and other forces in the east would be left to the mercy of the Russians.

The next morning, Himmler arrived for another conference with hopes of a continued struggle. His unscathed forces in Scandinavia were formidable assets. Of course, there was that top-secret mission that he had sent to the United States, which he did not mention to Doenitz. He knew now that the plane had departed. As of yet, there was no confirmation of their landing. However, Himmler was a patient man He would let Doenitz know of his scheme later, maybe.

Doenitz greeted everyone formally. "Good morning, gentlemen. I trust that everyone is familiar with Montgomery's terms."

A quiet murmur indicated they had.

Doenitz continued. "As you are well aware, he would not accept the surrender of the Army Group Vistula. However, a surrender would save considerable bloodshed."

Himmler spoke up. "I don't think that Holland and Norway should be thrown away. Our forces are still strong and well supplied. These are valuable assets and should be used to negotiate concessions."

Jodl joined in support. "The formations in the north are still strong. In addition, fighting in Norway would be very difficult for an invader. An offensive there would not be easy."

"If we fight to the bitter end, Germany will be completely destroyed," Doenitz rejoined. "One of the reasons we agreed to an armistice in 1918 was to preserve the military so that the nation might survive. We should keep that in mind now. We should still resist the Russians to allow as many people to escape to the west that we can. There are also signs of unrest among the military and civilians. There have been thwarted uprisings and mutinies. We do not want anything like the red uprisings we saw in 1918."

"I still think we should proceed cautiously. We still have strong reserves. We should not throw these away. In addition, we do have the werewolf program in place for resisting the enemy behind his lines. Capitulation at this point seems a little premature." Himmler's response was mild.

Doenitz considered the remarks that Himmler and others made. The discussion continued on. Despite the confidence that Himmler and other die-hards exuded, there was no denying the fact that Germany was beaten militarily. Finally, he spoke.

"None of us could have foreseen this moment nearly six years ago. It was inconceivable to us as German officers. There can be no denying the bravery of our nation's young or of the sacrifices our country as a whole has made. Despite the presence of uncounted reserves, we are beaten. We do not have oil to supply our ground forces. We lost command of the air a long time ago. Our navy is mostly on the bottom of the ocean. As hard as it is for me to say this, I see where we have no choice but to accept Montgomery's terms no matter how bitter they may be. Since I am now Fuehrer, it is my unpleasant duty to order our forces to capitulate. I don't like it, but those are my orders, and they will be obeyed."

There was silence as everyone looked on Doenitz. No one spoke. Only he had the terrible burden of supreme command. More remarks were made, but Doenitz had made his decision. He then dismissed the conference.

"Reichsfuehrer, please stay. There is one other thing I need to discuss with you."

The others quickly left the room. They caught the drift of something they did not want to hear. Himmler, they suspected, had come to the end of the road. Now Doenitz was going to deal with him some way.

"Gross Admiral, I think you are making a mistake by not holding out for more."

"Not at all. I think you overestimate your connections in the west. The fact is that Germany is beaten. All we can do is make things worse by continuing the struggle."

"The Allies may not be so understanding if we surrender unconditionally, some of our policies in the east, for example."

Doenitz cut him off. "May invite retribution from the Russians. They have already started in case you haven't heard. Anyway, I see where we have no choice. Some people will be needed to rebuild Germany. As concerns you, we will not longer need a police force to keep order. The victors can do that. There will be no place for you and your organization in the current Germany. As a result, I am abolishing the office of Reichsfuehrer."

Himmler seemed to grasp what was going on. At least Doenitz was not going to have him arrested. But with the dismissal and everything else, Doenitz seemed to be saying, "Sorry we don't want to be associated with you or your dark organization. You are on your own now."

"Grand Admiral, you are being too hasty."

Doenitz motioned for Himmler to remain silent. "No, I'm being rational. Surrender is the only option. And I would remind you that I am your Fuehrer now."

"So this is this end," Himmler muttered.

"It is. I do not mean to sound ungrateful, but negotiation is not an option anymore. Our enemies have refused to grant us that option. However, I have to make my position clear that I am in charge. In that position, I do thank you for your years of devoted service to the Reich." With that, Doenitz offered his hand to Himmler.

Himmler took the proffered hand and then left the building with his entourage. That afternoon he gave a farewell speech to his loyal followers. There was no talk of fighting to the bitter end. Instead, Himmler emphasized survival. He advised his minions to hide out in the Wehrmact under assumed names. Himmler himself had taken the papers of a sergeant from the secret field police. Officially, the sergeant, Heinrich Hitzinger, had been executed for sedition a few months before. He also bore a remarkable resemblance to Himmler. Although one of his closest aides, Gfaf Schwerin von Krosigk, had advised against it, Himmler planned to hide out rather than surrender. Himmler had already made plans for survival and intended to pursue them. His last sentence in his speech expressed his attitude succinctly. "I, for one, will not commit suicide." Himmler would not have been Himmler if he had acted differently.

It was nightfall when the BV 222 landed off the coast of Maine. Becker landed the plane gently in a coarse parallel to the coast. He had taken the precaution of flying a large circle around the area to make sure no ships were in the area to catch them unloading. The ocean was empty. No lights were seen on land either. Slowly, he nudged the huge plane closer to shore.

"Are we there yet?" Schreiber asked.

"Close. I hope the beach is as smooth as is claimed."

"So do I. Hopefully, it's deserted. I've taken off under fire too many times."

"Well, I certainly don't like greeting parties on these outings. They're usually not very friendly."

"They very seldom are when I'm transporting your type. I got a wound badge from one of these outings in Russia."

"Sounds like you have experience with us."

"Plenty. I've had several planes shot up by Ivan courtesy of Himmler and Canaris. Well, hopefully, this one will be just an exercise. Let me check the map one last time." Becker pulled out a penlight and studied his map. Everything looked all right. "We're in the right place. I'll maneuver this big tub around where you can get on the beach."

"We're ready."

"You ready to win the war, Schreiber?" Becker asked as he adjusted power and maneuvered the big plane.

"What makes you say that?" Schreiber was on his guard.

"Well, I know that I'm not inserting a crack commando team into America at the end of the war just for the hell of it. Someone high up has figured there's a way to change the war's course no matter how crazy the idea. That's all."

"I assume that you don't know our plans, but it is crazy."

"I figured as much. Well, we're in place. Whenever you are ready."

"Men, we prepare to invade America. Fouts, you take five men and secure the beach. We'll cover you with machine guns."

"Jawohl."

"One other thing, Fouts, we speak English from here on, or we keep our mouths shut. Understood?"

"Sorry, sir."

The large ramp dropped into the water. Fouts and his men swiftly got their rafts ashore. Schreiber watched the beach intently through his binoculars. So far, everything seemed okay. Fouts gave an all-clear sign with his hands.

"Let's unload. Get the jeeps ashore. Keep your German uniforms on until I tell you otherwise. If something goes wrong, I want to be in German uniform."

Schreiber watched as the jeeps moved ashore. He was fascinated how the canvas flotation devices the Americans came up with worked so well. He did not have to worry about the jeeps sinking, and his men would get ashore fairly dry. He also appreciated the pilot's skill in getting them so close to land. Otherwise, they might not have taken the risk of bringing the jeeps ashore. After all, it was a long walk to New York from Maine.

Finally, everyone was ashore except the last jeep crew. Schreiber was about to say thanks to the pilot when he smelled something strange. Gas fumes. Schreiber hunted Becker up. "I think I smell fumes."

"I know. That's why I didn't want to fly this barge across the Atlantic. It was badly shot up. Probably should have been junked except this mission came up."

The engineer came up. "Fire in the number 4 engine."

"Damn," Becker cursed vehemently. "Can you put it out?"

An explosion from the engine answered the question. Soon another engine was on fire. Soon the whole wing was engulfed.

"We've got to get this plane further out, or the Americans will spot the plane." Schreiber was worrying about mission falling apart just as they were starting.

"This thing could blow anytime."

"Have everyone else get off, and we'll fly it out a few meters. Then we'll let it sink."

Becker thought about it and reluctantly gave the order. Seconds later, only Schreiber and Becker were on board the crippled plane.

"Time for you to get off unless you want to have a Viking funeral."

Schreiber laughed. "Trust me. When you get into the raft, you want two of us because I have more experience with rafts than you."

"Very well." Becker then sat in the pilot's chair and moved the plane forward. He got out to about a hundred yards. More explosions racked the plane. The blazing wing shuttered.

"Time to get out," Becker yelled.

Schreiber didn't argue. He had placed an explosive charge in the bottom of the plane. He gave them five minutes to get away from the plane. It was enough. After five minutes, a coughing sound signaled the last moments of the BV 222. Slowly, she slid under the water nose first. Finally, the wings went under, and the fire extinguished. The sudden absence of light did not permit them to see the tail disappear.

"Think it's deep enough?" Schreiber asked.

"Yes. I just hope the water's not too clear. Otherwise, they could spot it from the air."

"Well, we won't sit around and find out."

The two men rowed their raft to the shore. By now, it was dark again. Fouts was waiting for them when they came ashore. "Thank heavens, you made it ashore. The crew was expecting the plane to blow anytime."

"So did we," Becker replied.

Dietz came forward. "You should quit taking risks like that. You'll live longer."

"I haven't used up all of my nine lives."

"Maybe not, but several of them," Fouts added.

"What about the beach?" Schreiber asked.

"No one around to kill like they should have done in 1942 with Operation Pastorious. We have got the beach all to ourselves. My only concern is about the fire. That would have been visible for miles."

"I know. Everyone accounted for."

"Yes, sir."

"Let's get out of here. Anyone know the way?"

"I found a road. Good shape too." Fouts was proving his worth already.

"Let's get going. We've pressed our luck enough." Schreiber was feeling just a bit uneasy about the plane catching on fire. "Hopefully, if anyone saw it, they'll think they were dreaming or had too much beer."

Within seconds, the beach was deserted as Schreiber's men and the aircrew made their hasty departure. Fortunately, their landing and the plane's mishap were unnoticed. An hour later, they found a paved road and were on their way to make contact with their agent in New York City.

CHAPTER 10

After May 5th, Himmler kept a low profile and moved in with his mistress Hedwig Potthast and their two children in Flensberg along with some of his main satraps. They could all feel the net closing in. In the meantime, Doenitz began to distance himself and the rest of the military from Himmler and his organization. He grandly pronounced, "We have nothing to be ashamed of, and we stand without a spot on our honor." He had letters of dismissal typed up for most of the important politicians that had served the Third Reich. Himmler's name was on one of the letters. Meanwhile, Doenitz continued the painful process of negotiating surrender.

Himmler continued to keep a low profile after Germany's surrender. On May 10, he left his mistress and accompanied by Macher, Otto Ohlendorf, and other prominent SS officers headed south. A series of safe houses and escape routes had been set up all across Germany. The Russian 4th Bureau General Staff had discovered several of these. However, in the south, there was a powerful transmitting station at Sigmarigen. Himmler could maintain contact with Dietz through this station once the war ended.

Despite von Krosigks's advice to go to Eisenhower and surrender, Himmler shaved his mustache and set off with his false identity papers. During this time, British intelligence had heard rumors that Himmler would try to head south. Officers and men were ordered to keep an extra eye out Himmler and his companions as the former Reichsfuehrer was one of the most wanted men in Europe now.

On May 5th, Walter Kohler was returning to his residence in New York City. On April 30th, he sent his last transmission to Germany at the behest of the FBI. It was an unremarkable description of a new army division's patch. Although he had been a spy for twenty-five years, he felt his career in espionage was almost over. He had played his latest double game for three years. He had carried on a pretense of loyalty to the United States now for three years. He had dutifully transmitted everything that the FBI had told him to. Despite their surveillance, he had organized a real German spy ring under the FBI's noses and had scored some major penetrations of the Russian spy rings in the United States. Now his concern was surviving the war and not having the FBI discover his true mission in the United States.

He suddenly found himself facing two men dressed in the uniforms of the army's military police. One was a captain and the other was a first lieutenant. Kohler's heart skipped a beat. Had he been figured out at last? Had someone leaked some information that fingered him? Had the FBI played with him like a cat with a mouse? But why military police? The FBI loved the glory of catching one of the bad guys and the prestige such action conferred.

"Walter Kohler, I presume?" It was the lieutenant who spoke.

"Yes, that would be me."

"Gertrude said you had some interesting recipes. Perhaps you could direct us her way."

Kohler's eyes almost popped at the mention of Gertrude. Only the German intelligence organization used that name if someone needed to contact him directly. He looked around furtively in case the FBI decided to keep tabs with him today.

"Don't worry. J. Edgar doesn't have any of his boys on your tail today. We already checked the area ourselves."

"So Gertrude sent you to collect some recipes."

"Yes. We arrived only a few days ago. We also figured your surveillance is marginal since they figured they've won the war. But you have been in this position before, as I recall, most remarkable even to a man like myself. Your reports didn't get the respect they deserved, particularly on helium."

Kohler was breathing hard. "So my bosses are serious. Why at so late a date?"

The captain answered this time. "It's a desperate gamble for us. Basically, we want to mitigate the terms of unconditional surrender that are being demanded of us. Otherwise, there might be some unpleasant consequences for the country."

"I don't doubt that. I remember what happened after the last war. Starvation resulted when the British refused to drop their blockade."

"This time will be worse," the captain relied. "Unless we do something."

"What is something?"

"Steal this device that is being made."

"You can't be serious. The Americans don't even have one of the bombs ready. They may never. True they have made great strides, but until one is exploded, what are you going to steal?"

"Let's say we'll be in a position to steal it."

"You're asking a lot. For one, penetration of their atomic program. Security is tight, and not very many people are sympathetic to us."

"How do we penetrate it?" asked the lieutenant.

"I'm not the one to ask. If you know anything about me, you know I organized another ring that is based out of Rochester. Here's the address. Tell the owner that you were directed there by Gertrude for clothing alterations."

"This owner, is he—"

"Reliable? Yes. Former naval officer and then did some work for the admiral afterward. He was in some very deep stuff. That's all I can tell you on anything. Good day, gentlemen."

An hour later, a convoy of what appeared to be military police left New York City. Later that evening, the convoy was driving down the main street of Rochester. Schreiber was in the lead jeep. He was studying the addresses of the businesses when Dietz grabbed him by the shoulder and started shaking him. He was pointing energetically at a sign, Waring's Laundry and Alterations. Schreiber saw the address on the piece of paper. It was the same.

"He has a lot of nerve," Dietz remarked.

"Who?"

"You'll soon find out."

Inside the owner was preparing to close when he noticed the convoy. He watched as two officers approached his store. This was late for more business. Well, he would politely turn them away and ask them to come back tomorrow. He noticed with interest that they were dressed in fatigues and not dress khakis. Well, he wouldn't be too rude. He had made a lot of money off uniforms between altering, cleaning, and fitting uniforms. Officers in particular were fastidious about their clothes. As they approached closer, he noticed that one moved like a front-line soldier. Something was not quite right.

As they entered, he remarked, "Sorry, gentlemen. I'm about to close."

"Good. We would like a word in private anyway." It was the lieutenant speaking. "Gertrude recommended you for someone serious about alterations."

The owner maintained his composure. He suspected a trap. "Oh, really. What did you plan to seriously alter?"

"The war." Schreiber was speaking now. "You evidently have some information that might help us out."

"That might be stretching it a little."

"Manhattan is no small thing, particularly if it works."

The owner stared at the lieutenant. "Who are you anyway?"

Schreiber and Dietz looked at each other, and Schreiber answered, "I'm Major Eric Schreiber. I've been ordered to steal the finished product if it is made and works."

"That is a big if, and if it doesn't work, you have wasted your time."

"It seems that the Americans have made great progress. The Russians believe that the Americans will succeed. Captain Wehring."

The owner stared at Dietz. "I see you did your homework, whoever you are."

"Konrad Dietz of the SD."

"What else do you know about me?"

"You are a veteran of Jutland with the Iron Cross, first class. Wound Badge and one of Canaris's greatest agents." Dietz looked around the laundry. A number of cuckoo clocks adorned the wall. Wehring was a master watchman who plied his trade in the Orkneys until Commander Prien arrived and sunk the Royal Oak. "You helped guide Prien into Scapa Flow and then vanished into legend."

"You are a very knowledgeable man, I see. Yes, you are right. I do have some insights into the Manhattan Project. However, I think you are on a fool's errand. Security is tight, and I have penetrated it obliquely. Basically, I penetrated the Communist ring that has been spying for the Russians. They penetrated the Manhattan Project in 1942. I have a source in Washington DC, who I have blackmailed into giving me information that the NKVD provides to Moscow. I transmit what I can but some of the technical information is difficult to communicate."

"Can this source in Washington get us inside the project?"

"Perhaps. However, I will check with him to see and also on the bomb's progress. However, the way the war is going, you might want to see if Germany capitulates. Otherwise, you really are out on a limb."

"Our orders are for us to continue even in the event of surrender," Schreiber interjected. "The Western Allies do not exactly plan to treat our people well according to the provisions of the Geneva Convention. There were already reports of prisoners being systematically being mistreated."

Wehring sighed. "You may have picked a suicide mission. You have no protection after the war if you try to carry this out and are caught."

"Right now, there's not much option," Dietz continued. "Anyway, you have been in the same boat too, haven't you? You were in England for almost sixteen years, as I recall."

"Yes, I was, as a matter of fact. Sixteen too many years. The country and the people sort of grew on me. It was actually hard leaving. And then the sinking was even harder. I knew a lot of the sailors and their families on the Royal Oak."

"Well, if we get the bomb and use it on Manhattan, let's say, you wouldn't know anyone there but Kohler. Ironic if we got to explode the bomb in Manhattan."

"Hopefully, it won't come to that," Schreiber interjected. "But I don't want to see Germany go through what it did after the last war."

Wehring realized these men were not backing down. "Very well. I see you are determined to carry on. All I can say is best of luck. I don't have a plan or idea of how to help you get the bomb. I will try to point you in the right direction. First though, we need to do something about those uniforms. You need to be in dress khakis."

"What's wrong with these?' Dietz wondered.

"Nothing, if you are at the front or in Europe or maneuvers. However, with the war in Europe practically over, there is no reason for you to be dressed like you're headed to combat tomorrow. Some high-ranking officer might see you and demand an explanation. I think we would like to avoid that."

"So would I," Schreiber replied.

"How many of you are there?"

"Twenty-eight."

"That will keep me busy. However, I can manage. Have your men slip around back gradually. I want no lines to attract attention. Also, I need to check your ID cards. You may need new ones if you are to get inside the Manhattan Project. It has its own security service. Otherwise, once you and your men are properly dressed, I don't think you'll have any problems."

Dietz and Schreiber walked back to their jeeps. "Do you get the feeling that we are wasting our time?" Schreiber asked.

"You know the order"

"Oh, I know. But on every other mission, I had a definite target or goal."

"We do here too."

"Not yet. We're waiting for the enemy to build it and hope that he succeeds."

"It will be. After all, the intelligence reports indicated the Americans are only weeks away from testing a bomb."

"How do you know they will succeed?"

"I just do."

Schreiber shrugged his shoulders and continued on. The men were quietly ordered to make their way to the back of the store one at a time to be measured. The rest sauntered up and down the street until it was their turn to be fitted. Each man was taped and measured in seconds. Finally, he was down to the last man when Schreiber and Dietz returned.

"What a distinguished group you have brought across the ocean. As I suspected, everyone needs some khakis. But I should have uniforms for everyone in eight days."

"Can you do that?" Dietz was skeptical. "Plus, that's a wasted week."

"That's why I'm in the business. A certain manufacturer of cloth keeps me well supplied with cloth for uniforms. By being reliable, I've had plenty of customers. Of course, I've picked up a few tidbits along the way. Also, the bomb won't be ready for some time. I guarantee it won't be tested tomorrow. I need time to think on how to get you inside the program."

"Do you have any ideas?" Schreiber asked.

"Not yet. However, your MP status might prove useful. However, I have to look at this closely. The project has its own security apparatus. If you suddenly show up from nowhere, some suspicions may arise. Perhaps some snooping on our Communist friends may give me some ideas. I'll pass word to our operatives."

"In the meantime, we wait for our new clothes." Schreiber seemed impatient.

"Don't complain. Plus, it will give your men a chance to blend in."

"And your business will be overflowing," Dietz remarked. "A bit better than repairing clocks, I suppose."

"It is slightly different from what I did in the Orkneys. However, the basics remain the same. Go into something that no one would suspect a spy in. Then deliver what you say and worm your way into people's confidence at the same time. After all, who would suspect a mere humble laundryman of being a spy?"

"And a very good one," Dietz effused. "One of our last grossagenten."

"Well, gentlemen, I have work to do. I won't dwell on my past accomplishments. In the meantime, enjoy yourselves."

As Schreiber prepared to leave, he noticed that Wehring was trying to get his attention with his eyes. "Dietz, would you make sure that the men are ready to leave? We'll need a place to stay for the night."

"Of course," Dietz replied unsuspectingly.

After Dietz left, Wehring grabbed Schreiber by the arm. "Watch him. He has a hidden agenda, secret orders or something else. You're a regular soldier. I can tell that. He's not. There's a lot more than meets the eye here. He's what, Gestapo?"

"SD."

"Worse. They're the smart ones unfortunately and even more dangerous. That's why I didn't stay in Germany after Scapa Flow. I saw what was going on and asked Admiral Canaris to send me overseas. I was hoping to be left alone this time. Anyway, don't get yourself killed near the end of the war. I know you are a soldier and trained to obey orders. Make sure you do, the right ones anyway or the ones that should have been given."

"I think I understand."

"Really? What are your orders? To explode the bomb in a place like New York?"

"Not really. I am supposed to use it more as a leveraging tool."

"Interesting. Do you seriously think that the U.S. State Department is going to negotiate with you?"

"Not really."

"What are Dietz's orders then?"

"To assist me."

Wehring snorted. "A major like you doesn't need assistance

from a man like Dietz. I've been in similar situations before. Don't let Dietz explode the bomb if those are his orders. No matter how sweet the revenge will seem at the time, it will soon turned bitter. You will only make things worse for Germany."

"I will keep that in mind. After all, I'm not exactly suicidal either."

Schreiber returned then to the waiting convoy. It was time to get the men fed and bedded down for the night. As he settled in his bed, he had to admit that it was tempting to hide out in the United States. *Would his family in St. Louis take him in?* he wondered. Probably. What about his men? He couldn't let them down. Well, things would depend on the orders he received.

On the morning of May 8, Schreiber and Dietz had settled in a small café for breakfast when pandemonium broke out in the streets. They went out into the street to investigate. Schreiber had a premonition that something was not right with people hugging each other.

"What in God's name?" Schreiber asked. If the Americans were celebrating with such spontaneity, then something was up.

"The Krauts have had it," someone shouted.

"The war's over."

Schreiber bought a paper. The headlines hit him like a hammer. His worse fears were confirmed. He knew what his orders were, but still the news of Germany's surrender was a terrible blow. He turned to Dietz.

"We have to contact Flensburg or whoever is in charge. You get on your transmitter tonight and contact home to make sure our orders haven't changed."

"They haven't."

"We will make sure. I am not playing with the lives of my men."

Dietz opened his mouth to say something but thought better of it. He knew what the answer would be and decided not to make a fuss now. He considered carefully before speaking. "We should talk to Captain Wehring and let him do the transmission. After all, he is in this with us, and I'm sure he'll want an independent source other than me."

Clever bastard, Schreiber thought. He already knows the answer. And he's right. If this succeeds, we need Wehring. "All right. Let's go see the good captain. I say we are going nowhere without his help."

"He does have all the names and numbers."

They headed for Wehring's laundry immediately. Several other customers were in the laundry. Everyone was excited that the war in Europe was over. Several women were anxious that their husbands return home. A few looked at Schreiber and Dietz with a gleam in their eyes. The look was not reciprocated.

One woman came over and started pawing Schreiber. "I can't believe it. A man from the front already. I have an apartment with some friends nearby."

A few years before, Schreiber would have enjoyed this. But if there was ever a time to maintain his composure, it was now. "I would love too. But I'm moving out in a few days with my unit. There is, after all, a war in the Pacific. I hope to add a few yellow bastards to my tally before it ends."

The woman blanched at the vulgarity and then laughed. Wehring stopped any further conversation. "Captain, how may I help you?"

"Just checking on the uniforms I ordered. Also, to clarify the details on the insignia. And to get a final tally." At the same time, Schreiber was holding up the paper with the headline. Ever the consummate spy, Wehring showed no emotion.

"Come back at five, and I will have an answer.

At the appointed time, Schreiber and Dietz returned. By then, Wehring was ready to close. He greeted the two men as if nothing happened. "Well, it has been an interesting day."

"Not like I thought it would be in 1939."

"I know it may seem like a long time, but I still remember November 11th very well. Then, I was still a regular naval officer. I thought about my friends who had not made it, of all of the useless sacrifices."

"I can't say I remember it, but I do want to make sure that we still have a mission. I need you to contact Germany," Schreiber explained.

"Don't you have a transmitter?" Wehring queried.

"Yes. However, you are in this too. Plus, you know where to go. This mission goes nowhere without you."

"You do make a convincing point. Come around back, and we'll take a drive and find out if our communications are still intact with the Fatherland."

The three men walked to the rear of Wehring's business. A sleek blue car was parked off to one side. The windows were rolled down.

"She's a beauty," Dietz quipped.

"1942 New Yorker. One of the last few that were produced before all of the auto factories were converted into war manufacturing. I happened to have my connections and greased a few palms and acquired this one."

Schreiber admired the blue soft leather. He noted with approval the smooth ride. Soon Wehring was in rural New York, driving through the middle of a large forest. He took a small dirt road off the main road and approached a farmhouse. The landscape suggested nothing that would betray this as a spies' nest to the casual observer. By now, the sun was starting to set. Wehring set up his set and soon began transmitting his message.

In Sigmarigen, the message was duly received. The Allies prior to the surrender had not overrun the station. Lieutenant Colonel Rauh, the case officer for Kohler and Wehring, read the message. He looked at another message from Himmler. Although he did not know the nature of the mission in question, the instructions from Himmler were succinct: the mission would continue.

"Send this message back. Continue as planned. Will stay in contact."

"Herr Oberst, with the war over, should we make such a decision?" The sergeant transmitting was genuinely concerned about the message he was to send.

"Our orders are plain. Transmit the order."

"Jawohl, Herr Oberst."

Back in New York, the message was quickly read quickly following deciphering. Dietz and Wehring showed no surprise at the response. Schreiber sighed. Inside, he wondered if Skorzeny was still in the loop. But this was no time to express doubt. The order was official.

"I guess it's still on." Schreiber seemed relaxed despite his inner doubts.

"I don't envy you. You're being asked to do the impossible. However, you still have my full support. Be careful. You will need every bit of cunning you have to succeed."

"I believe Major Schreiber can pull off almost anything," Dietz confidently remarked.

"Even the best make mistakes. I constantly review my actions to see if I have let anything slip. In the meantime, I suggest you lay low and have some of your men get to know the country and improve their English."

"You've done well," Schreiber commented sincerely. "I hope I have your luck."

"So do I. Well, it's time to go." The men went to the car. Wehring paused and looked up. "I do love this part of the world. Here it is so peaceful, and here we are trying to change that."

"At least we won't be changing this part of the world," Schreiber quipped.

Wehring smiled slightly and got into the driver's seat. Schreiber and Dietz entered after him. Seconds later, a cloud of dust marked their previous location. Soon the only sounds were the occasional bird or insect.

On May 10th, a group set out from Flensburg composed of fifteen of Himmler's closest aides. The journey was hazardous even for groups and foolhardy for individuals. Lawlessness ruled the countryside they passed through. Armed men took food from the unwary. The roads were choked with war weary refugees and their carts. No semblance of order was seen as communications, and police authority had completely broken down.

Most of the fifteen men were well known inside the SS. Included were Dr. Brandt, Hitler's personal physician, Dr. Karl Gebhardt, Himmler's personal physician, Otto Ohlendorf, Major Heinz Macher, and seven NCOs. All carried papers identifying them as members of the Geheime Feldpolizei. They were posing as demobilized ill members on their way to Munich for treatment. All insignia had been removed from their uniforms. One man wore an eye patch and carried the papers of Heinrich Hitzinger on him.

The group moved slowly south in four large cars and took two days to reach Marne. They abandoned the vehicles at the Elbe. They then took a ferry to Neuhaus. From then on, they were on foot. By May 18th, they had reached Bremervorde on the Oste River. Although they could have forded the river upstream undetected, they inexplicably chose to cross on a bridge guarded by the British army.

The bridge they chose was the eastern bridge. It had been blown up weeks before and had been replaced by a Bailey bridge. The Forty-fifth Field Security Section of the intelligence apparatus had set up this site as a screening and security point with Staff-Sergeant John Hogg in charge. Sergeants Arthur Britton and Ken Baisbrown were assigned to help. All three men spoke fluent German and were keeping a sharp lookout for war criminals on their list of wanted SS, SD, and Gestapo authorities. This had been drawn up by CROWCASS (Central Registry of War Criminals and Security Suspects.). A copy of this list had been obtained by the SD and delivered to Himmler before the end of the war.

The group arrived at the house of Herr Dangers. The man's son noticed an odd behavior among the members. Some of the men seemed to be guarding the others. One member left and asked the local mayor for passes. The mayor, Herr Dohrmann, refused twice to give the passes.

The group, except for three men, decided to cross the bridge despite the risks. At 3:00 p.m., Gebhardt and another man set off to investigate the bridge. Sergeant Baisbrown stopped them. He decided to reassure them and sent two lorries with an escort to pick up the remaining men.

Sergeant Hogg had Dr. Gebhardt brought to him. "Sit down, Doctor, and tell me about this group of yours."

"As I told you before, these are sick men that have been released. I am trying to get them to Munich where they can get better care."

"I see. All of these men are yours?"

"Of course, including three we left at a farmhouse."

"Why do all of the documents bear the seal of the headquarters of the SD?"

"These men are part of the secret field police."

"What happened? Did everyone get sick all at once?"

Gebhardt sputtered. "We have not been able to get adequate food for some time. Malnutrition is quite common."

"Everyone here looks like they didn't suffer too much."

"But I assure you that—"

Hogg cut Gebhardt off. "Bring me the private over there," he ordered Baisbrown.

A younger man dressed in a now shabby uniform of a private of the SD now sat before Hogg. The man's papers were examined. Hogg nodded at Baisbrown and Britton for them to start the interrogation.

"Are you traveling with this group?"

"Not originally."

"Not originally? What's that supposed to mean?"

"I hadn't planned to leave Flensburg and was going to try to go home with the end of the war."

"You were in the SD?"

"Yes."

'What were your duties?"

"I was mainly a clerk. I handled a lot of paperwork." The British NCOs noticed the young German was fidgeting.

"But everyone started out from Flensburg, didn't they?"

"Yes, we did."

"Now I can tell that you are a pretty small fish in the scheme of things. Right? But there are some pretty big fish in this group, isn't there? They just are using you to do their work they're too lazy to do themselves?"

The young SD man looked up; his face was drenched with perspiration. He gave a barely perceptible nod, but it was enough. Hogg had the group arrested. He summoned some lorries and had the men transported to the internment camp in Westertinke. Meanwhile, because of the expressed concerns of Gebhardt and others about the three men left behind, Britton was detached to find them.

However, the three men had disappeared from the farm. Britton found a valise containing a manicure set with the letters RFSS engraved on it. Britton returned back to the bridge in disgust. Hogg immediately contacted his superiors, and the local British forces were advised to keep an additional lookout for the trio.

Twenty-four hours later, the trio suddenly appeared in the middle of Bremervorde. Macher and another man named Grothman were wearing dark green SS overcoats. The third man was dressed in an assortment of civilian clothes, including a blue overcoat. A British patrol noticed them immediately. They assumed that the two officers were in charge of the smaller man. They were immediately escorted back to the mill and were met by Sergeant Britton.

Britton immediately called Staff-Sergeant Hogg. He and Baisbrown immediately went to the mill. The two officers were standing up. The third man was sitting between the two other men. The trio claimed to be NCOs. The third man carried the card of Heinrich Hitzinger. He was searched, and an impressive magnifying glass with eagle wings was removed. That night, the three prisoners slept among some grain sacks.

On the morning of May 23rd, Britton drove the three men to the internment camp. Britton stopped briefly at Zeven and reported to Captain Excel of the Forty-fifth Field Security Station. Excel saw no reason to look at the prisoners and ordered Britton to proceed on to Westertinke.

The prisoners arrived early in the morning and were registered at 9:00 a.m. As soon as they were recognized as former members of the SD, they were transported to a special interrogation camp at Kolkhagen. At 9:40 a.m., the men were loaded up again and were driven to the camp, which was fifty miles to the southeast.

The truck carrying the trio arrived sometime in the evening. Karl Kaufman was next to the barbed wire, watching the truck unload its passengers. The former Gauleiter of Hamburg noticed a man with a black patch and was clean shaven get off. Kaufman looked closely and recoiled inside himself. Was this who he thought it was?

A few minutes later, the man had removed his patch. A few minutes later, Kaufman noticed that the guards had been doubled. The British seemed excited about something. Kaufman had a good idea what it was about.

Shortly after arriving, Hitzinger and his companions demanded to see the commandant of Camp 031. Captain Thomas Selvester had the men brought into his office. Hitzinger walked in first followed by Macher and Grothman. Selvester felt there was something odd about the group and decided to act.

"Sergeant Bedford, take the two prisoners in the green coats and lock them up. No one is to speak to them unless I give permission. Take them now."

"Yes, sir. Come with me, lads. We want no trouble." His stern look discouraged any arguing.

After the two men left, the third man now put on his spectacles. "Heinrich Himmler," he said in a quiet voice.

Selvester immediately called the headquarters of the British Second Army. Major Rice of intelligence was dispatched to verify the identity. Selvester then turned his attention back to his infamous prisoner. Another sergeant stood by. It was time to do a body search.

"Strip," he ordered the small figure.

The prisoner did so reluctantly. Selvester examined each item of clothing and then passed on to the sergeant for a second inspection. In the jacket, a small brass case was found with a tiny glass phial. It was a suicide pill.

"What does this contain?" Selvester asked.

"That has my stomach medicine. It relieves my cramps."

Selvester said nothing and kept on examining the clothing. Another brass case was found. It was empty. Selvester realized his prisoner had hidden the other vial on his body. After the prisoner was completely naked, he was thoroughly searched. His hair was combed, and all of his orifices probed except his mouth. Selvester worried that if the phial was secreted in the mouth, the prisoner would crush it in any attempt to remove it. The search revealed nothing. Selvester then had some cheese sandwiches made while he awaited the arrival of Major Rice.

Rice arrived around 7:30 p.m. He brought with him the SHAEF index card on Himmler. This card contained two paragraphs on Himmler, his party and SS number, date of birth, and a photograph of Himmler in a black uniform. However, he had no physical data such as dental records or fingerprints to aid him.

Rice started immediately. He compared the ear in the photograph with his subject. There seemed to be a match. Then he began the questioning.

"What is your Nazi Party number?"

"In the 14,000 series."

Rice thought about that and continued. "What is your SS number?"

"It is 169 or about."

Rice looked at his card and sighed. "The number on his card was 168.

"What is your birthday?"

"October 7."

Rice looked at his card. It read 7 November 1900. Rice was puzzled but should not have been. The mistake was from SHAEF. Finally, he asked for a signature.

"Only if it is immediately destroyed."

Rice relented and obtained the desired signature. It seemed close enough to be the real thing. He decided he had his man.

"May I see the picture you have of me?"

Rice passed the card over to the man. "It is a rather impressive photograph."

"This must have been taken before the war because I have not worn the black uniform since war broke out. That was most unfortunate, as we did not want war with your country. Now you see what has happened. We now have the Russian hordes in the middle of Europe ready to enslave anyone they can. That is why I must speak to Eisenhower."

Rice made no response to this unwanted diatribe. He called Colonel Michael Murphy, chief of Intelligence for the British Second Army. Murphy immediately set off for Kolkhagen despite an upset stomach from the various victory celebrations. His condition went from bad to worse when his car broke down. Finally, he arrived at 9:45 p.m. Rice was there to meet him.

"Well, what do you have?" Murphy got immediately to the point.

"I'm not sure, sir. He got very close on his Nazi Party and SS numbers. He was off on his birthday. Signature seems to be the same. Facial features appear the same except he's shaved his mustache."

"Let's see him."

The prisoner was summoned. "Strip and put these on." Murphy had not even introduced himself as he threw a set of British battledress into a chair.

"Why? I have already been searched once. And those are not my uniform. I refuse to wear the uniform of the enemy."

"You don't have much choice. You can undress yourself or the guards will do it for you. You are not in a position now to make demands."

Shocked by this language, the prisoner undressed a second time that day. Following the search, he put on a shirt, underpants, and some socks. Someone produced a military blanket, which he wrapped around his shoulders. This search also failed to find the missing phial of poison.

Murphy decided it was time to conduct a medical search. He called his ADC and asked him to have a doctor ready. At 10:40 p.m., the shivering prisoner was shoved into the backseat of a car and was placed between Murphy's second-in-command Lieutenant Colonel Bernard Stapleton and a guard. They drove to 31a Ulzenerstrasse in Luneburg.

Waiting for them was Captain Clement Wells, who was an acting regimental surgeon. He had been trying to arrange leave when he was urgently summoned to the headquarters building. Sergeant C. S. M. Austin then accompanied him. They waited in the road for Murphy to arrive with his important prisoner.

When the car arrived, Murphy got out first. "Are you the doctor?" he arrogantly asked Wells. He noticed Wells's medical insignia and immediately added, "You will search this man for poison."

Wells was simmering now. "I am a doctor, not a detective."

Murphy was not amused by the retort. "You will do as you are ordered."

The prisoner was led into nicely furnished room at the residence. As the group proceeded, Sergeant Austin asked Colonel Murphy for permission to sandbag the prisoner. One prominent prisoner, General Pruetzmann, had already been lost to suicide. The loss of someone like Himmler could only make matters worse. However, Murphy refused to allow Austin to carry out his physical threat.

The room they arrived in had a large bay window that was open. The prisoner was ordered to undress again. He stood shivering from the night air pouring through the window. Wells decided that an audience was not ideal and asked Murphy and the others to leave. Murphy was only too happy to leave as his intestines were acting up, and he retired to a lavatory across the hall.

With only Sergeant Austin in the room, Wells resumed the search. He tried to reassure the prisoner. He started with obvious areas on the man. When he reached the mouth, he noticed a dark object between the lower left jaw and cheek. Wells pretended not to notice and contemplated on how he could get the object out without the prisoner crushing it. He decided to repeat the exam. When he got to the mouth, he asked the man to open it. As soon as he did, Wells put his finger in to try to sweep it out.

The prisoner clamped his jaws on the finger. Wells cried out, "My God, it's in his mouth, and he's done it on me!" They struggled; and, finally, the prisoner wrenched Wells's finger out of his mouth and bit down on the capsule. His face became contorted, and his eyes turned glassy as he crashed to the ground.

Wells called for a cardiac stimulant. As none were immediately available, one of the junior officers went to the hospital. He found the doctors in the middle of a big blowout celebrating the war's end. When he asked for a cardiac stimulant, the resulting laughter was stupendous. By the time he returned, the drama had ended.

Soon senior officers were aware of the evening's debacle, including the senior medical officer present, Brigadier Glyn Hughes. Hughes spent the next few minutes calling a dental officer and pathologist to conduct a postmortem exam. The next morning, he met with Colonel Browne of the Royal Army Dental Corps and Captain M. C. Bond. Browne collected some plaster of Paris for the molds and brought along Major George Attkins, his assistant. Interestingly, Hughes did not call Dr. Ian Morris, a leading forensic pathologist attached to Unit No 2 of the War Crimes Commission.

"Identify the bastard carefully and record everything, including needle marks," were Hughes's final words to the postmortem team before they set about their unenviable task. At 11:00 a.m. they went to work. A death mask was made, the state of dentition was recorded, and even the hair in the ears was commented on. By one 1:15 p.m., the three men had completed their work. A request was made for the Royal Military Police to make a set of fingerprints from the dead man. The request never made it to them.

By now, Murphy realized the implications of the bungled handling of the prisoner. To ward off criticism, he held a hastily convened press conference that lasted thirty minutes. He then allowed the press to view the body. Then he decided to have the body secretly buried and hopefully end any speculation and criticism about his handling of the prisoner.

The following morning, a Bedford truck drove up to the back of the building to pick up the body. The body was wrapped in camouflage netting and bound with wire. A jeep with Whittaker in front led the way. After thirty minutes, they found an isolated spot. The body was unwrapped and kicked into the freshly dug grave. After the dirt was shoveled over the remains, leaves, twigs, and other debris were spread over the site in an attempt to hide it. Although the officers involved thought this had solved their problems, this action only served to arouse the suspicions of the other Allies, as the body was never satisfactorily confirmed to be Heinrich Himmler's.

While the wrath of God, the Americans, and the Russians descended on Colonel Murphy for his handling of Himmler or Hirtzinger, the Russians were busy in Flensburg. They were very interested in Gehlen's Foreign Armies East apparatus and were anxious to get their hands on as many of its personnel that they could find. General Trussov was in charge of a four-man Russian team whose purpose was to root out any threats to Soviet intelligence. Foreign Armies East was foremost on their minds. Trussov soon fastened onto Major Borchers who had been on Gehlen's staff. Trussov had the German brought before him.

Trussov was in an office when the major arrived. "Major Borchers, I presume?"

"That is correct."

"I am General Trussov. I understand that you worked for an organization called Foreign Armies East. Is that correct?"

"At one time, I was assigned to them."

"There are serious questions about your organization's actions in Russia during the war." Trussov let that sink in. He didn't expect a response or get one. "There are some questions about certain activities that might be regarded as war crimes."

"I am not aware of any such activities."

"Then I am sure you could tell me who would know for sure whether any atrocities were committed."

By now, Borchers was sweating. He did not like the idea of turning his men over to the Russians. "The man in charge was General Gehlen."

"Where is he?"

"I don't know. He was relieved of his command in April and disappeared. I had already left Foreign Armies East by then. All I know is what others told me."

"Are there any other members of Foreign Armies East here at Flensburg?"

Borchers hesitated. Trussov noticed this. "Yes, there are."

"I expect you to be here at ten tomorrow morning with these officers for questioning. Otherwise we will be coming for you." With that ominous remark, Borchers was dismissed.

While Borchers brooded over his dilemma, Major General Rooks of Eisenhower's staff got wind of the Soviet interest in Foreign Armies East. He knew he was onto something and made his own inquiries. Despite Ike's insistence on getting along with their erstwhile Allies, Rooks had the officers from Gehlen's organization arrested and spirited away from further Russian interrogation. Soon word passed through the Western Allies: find General Reinhard Gehlen.

Rook could not help but rub Trussov's nose. The next day, Borchers arrived back in Trussov's office, escorted by two American MPs. The startled Trussov raised his eyebrows.

"What is going on here?" Trussov angrily demanded.

"The Americans arrested them yesterday. All of them," Borchers replied smiling. He made no attempt to hide his satisfaction at the way Trussov had been thwarted.

Trussov was furious. He suffered the humiliation of having his prize being taken away from him in the hour of triumph. Soon the OSS and MI6 would be learning everything that Gehlen's group had learned. He also shuddered at the thought of what Moscow would have to say about his failure to apprehend the Foreign Armies East officers at Flensburg.

During this time, the decision was made to dissolve the Doenitz government. The British rounded up the Grand Admiral and his staff in a dawn raid. Everyone, including Doenitz, was stripped and searched in an act of degradation. Then the Germans were carted off in pairs to prison. Doenitz's office was then searched. On his desk were unsigned letters of dismissal for Himmler, Ribbentrop, and other unsavory members of the Third Reich. No papers were to be found on any last-minute missions, including Gotterdammerrung.

At sea, U-234 received news of the capitulation. Captain Fehler knew that he had to surrender soon or he and his crew would be treated as pirates. Discussions were made on what to do and who to surrender to. Fehler had already received instructions to proceed on to Japan or return to Bergen. However, news was picked up that Japan had severed relations with Germany and was arresting all German citizens. In addition, the two Japanese officers wished to be put ashore in Spanish territory. Fehler declined to do this and had the two Japanese confined to their quarters under guard. Later, the Japanese were found lifeless from a barbiturate overdose. The Germans buried the men at sea along with a secret transmitter and radar that had been destined for Japan.

Captain Fehler and his men decided they wanted to surrender to the Americans. A false location was broadcast in case the Canadians were listening. Soon a race was on between the Canadians and the Americans to reach U-234. Technically, U-234 was in the Canadian zone, and Fehler was supposed to set a course for Halifax. However, he played a game of cat and mouse with Halifax by transmitting false locations while heading for the American shore. Soon the transmissions were being jammed, and Halifax ordered Fehler to switch to another frequency. That too was jammed. The source of the jamming became apparent soon as the source of the interference identified itself as the USS *Sutton*.

On May 12th, Captain Nazro of the Sutton received order 121322 from CINLANT to intercept U-234. On the way, Nazro ordered the jamming that prevented Halifax from communicating with U-234. At the same time, his navigator was able to fix the U-boat's present location. Nazro directed his vessel along a course to intercept. Along the way, he intercepted messages from Canadian warships, indicating they had found no trace of the submarine. Nazro knew that they wouldn't.

At 2024, contact was made, and at 2141, it was confirmed to be U-234. Because of the late hour, Nazro decided not to board the submarine until the morning. At 0800, he gave the boarding party its final instructions. "This is the enemy. You will not tolerate anything out of them. On the other hand, they have surrendered. Be careful."

The officer leading the boarding party handed Fehler a letter detailing how he was to surrender. At 1100 that morning, Fehler formally surrendered his U-boat. Tears ran down his face when he saw the stars and stripes flying from the periscope. U-234 was then prepared for its journey to Portsmouth. A skeleton crew of Germans was kept on board to run the submarine. The American sailors then started securing small arms and ammunition. During the course of their duties, one of the Sutton's crew was accidentally shot in the right leg and required evacuation. One of the German officers remarked, "These Americans, when they can't shoot at us, they shoot at each other."

On May 15, the Sutton radioed her position and headed for Portsmouth to rendezvous with the Coast Guard surrender unit stationed there. On May 17, two other ships, the *Muir* and *Carter*, joined the group. On May 19, the group passed by the Isles of Shoals and handed U-234 over to the surrender group.

Aboard the Coast Guard cutter, Argos Commander Alexander Moffat waited in anticipation. He had replaced Lieutenant Charles Winslow because of his experience in handling such tricky matters. Allied intelligence had a good idea of what was on board. Of particular interest was the uranium as the Manhattan Project was desperate for every once that it could find. Moffat was expected to keep things quiet until the U-boats contents were inventoried.

The navy had planned to keep U-234's capture under wraps. However, its own secretary, James Forrestal, sabotaged it. On May 16, he held a news conference in which he described the surrender of the U-boat. While the conference was designed as a public relations ploy, the damage had been done as for as the admirals were concerned. Although some still wanted the arrival of U-234 kept secret, local naval officials recognized the public relations disaster that would follow. As a result, reporters were present when U-234 landed.

The press had been granted access to previous U-boat crews when they landed. Most German sailors had refused to talk. Now the reporters would have to watch as the Germans were led to buses. Fehler was now having second thoughts about surrendering to the Americans. The crew of the Sutton had treated his men with respect. However, the crew of the *Argos* had been abusive to his crew. As Fehler left the *Argos*, he started to complain to Winslow about the treatment he and his men had endured. Seizing his chance for publicity, Winslow told Fehler to "get the hell off my ship." The reporters on the pier caught this and promptly wrote Winslow's remarks down. Among the reporters was a man on good term with a man named Kohler, who lived in New York City.

Wehring had the uniforms ready on time as he had promised. Schreiber had used the time to let his men blend into American society. An English speaker was present with every group when they went into town, and so far, no questions had been asked. As before, Schreiber's men went into the store at closing time.

"Good evening, gentlemen. I hope everything is satisfactory." Wehring was playing his role to the hilt.

"Impeccable," Dietz remarked as he slid the dress uniform on.

"Not quite," Wehring remarked. "Everyone will need some ribbons. If nothing else, some campaign ribbons are useful. I would be careful about any decorations for valor. It could lead to some embarrassing situations that I think you want to avoid."

"I second that," Schreiber conceded. "By the way, any additional thoughts on our mission?"

Wehring sat down. "Gentlemen, you are in an unenviable position. Of course, as I told you before, I have been there myself. I understand the reasons for your orders. Now if you are going to proceed, some interesting developments have occurred that you might be able to take advantage of."

"Improvising is second nature for my men," Schreiber remarked.

"Good. As you may have seen in the newspapers, all U-boats have been required to surrender. Only a few days ago, one that was headed to Japan with a special cargo when we surrendered pulled into Portsmouth. Among the goodies on board was uranium-235."

"I suppose that somehow could involve us, although I'm ignorant of the finer details of this kind of bomb."

"So am I," Wehring continued. "The importance is that the Americans need every bit to build their bomb. The quantities on board might be just enough to finish it."

"What if we stole the uranium?" Dietz asked.

"You could, but then you would blow your cover. It would just take the Americans longer to make more uranium. I suggest that you make use of your uniforms as MPs and escort the uranium to its various destinations. Otherwise, I suggest everyone call it quits and hide out in Mexico."

"What about the security?"

"The uranium itself is not under the control of the Manhattan Project yet. You're also in luck here as well. The head of security for the entire project, Lieutenant Colonel John Lonsdale, happens to be in Europe now, looking for Germany's supplies of uranium."

"So if we want to get inside the project, now's the time while the chief watchdog is away."

"Precisely. After all, who would expect a bunch of Germans to deliver some badly needed ingredients for their most important weapons projects?"

"Where is this material?" Schreiber asked.

"Right now, it is at Portsmouth, New Hampshire. However, it is supposed to be moved soon. That information is key. Right now, security is tight around Portsmouth because U-234 was carrying a lot of interesting gadgets and people."

"Such as?" Dietz was asking now.

"A Luftwaffe general, a disassembled 262, and V-2 among other things. Nothing that will help you on your mission. The main thing is to penetrate the Manhattan Project. And it has been penetrated, I might add. What I know is superficial. However, not everyone working for the project is a star-spangled banner American. A good many of the scientists have leanings to the left. In fact, many are actively passing on information to the NKVD. So we will not actively get any help from any of these disloyal Americans. However, by keeping tabs on these underground Communists, I have got an overall view of the project. In addition, the Communists have infiltrated the War Department. It happens that one of these individuals is in charge of overseeing the bomb's development. He is also a pervert. I have the proof on film."

Dietz smiled deliciously as he thought about the implications.

Schreiber whistled in amazement. Dietz gave unrestrained praise. "It's obvious that neither Himmler nor Canaris fully recognized your special abilities. I doubt you would be here working on this if they had."

"There's a lot luck involved in successful espionage, Dietz, and being in the right place at the right time. I would also remind you that the bomb has not been exploded, so you don't know if it's going to work."

Schreiber spoke up now. "But at least we can be in position to take possession of one if their tests are successful."

"I agree, gentlemen. However, give me a few days to verify my information. Ultimately, you will need to get to the facility at Los Alamos. In the meantime, I will collect the appropriate ribbons for your uniforms and other documents. Otherwise, your cover will be blown before you get a chance to cross the Mississippi River."

Ten days after the capitulation, Otto Skorzeny decided it was time to surrender. He sent three letters to the Americans, offering to turn himself in. He had no idea the reputation he had made for himself across enemy lines. As a result, the Americans did not believe that Hitler's D'Artagnan would give himself up so easily. Finally, Skorzeny and Radl left the mountain they had hidden on and descended to the plains. They came across a Texan who gave him a lift.

As they drove along, they chatted casually. The Texan asked, "So you really are Skorzeny?"

"That's what I told you."

The Texan reached under his seat and handed Skorzeny a bottle of wine. "If that's right, you'll hang tonight. So enjoy it."

Skorzeny laughed. After all, the war was over, and he had committed no atrocities. However, he underestimated the extent to which Allied intelligence had inflated his image, although he would soon find out. The Texan drove them to Salzburg. He dropped Skorzeny and Radl off in front of a hotel. An American major met him and took him to a villa outside the town. Skorzeny still had no concerns as he walked into the villa's fine dining room. He had just entered when doors were flung open. Machine guns were at each entrance. Both SS officers were manacled like wild beasts and then were unceremoniously driven off to prison cells. Skorzeny endured the ride with a pistol stuck in his chest by the American MP sitting next to him. By now, the fate of Schreiber was pushed to the back of his mind as Skorzeny began to comprehend what might lie in store for him.

The first week of June, Schreiber felt that things were coming together. Wehring had dressed his men up where they would pass as genuine MPs. Every ribbon was explained to the men. Schreiber went over the men personally to make sure nothing was amiss with the new khakis. Wehring also suggested that they make a trip to Washington DC.

"We need to talk to a certain man in the War Department. First, we need to be sure where the uranium is being stored. Then you need orders to transport the uranium to Oak Ridge if my information is correct. By the way, do you have your new identity down?"

"Captain Lawson Ford, of the 223rd Military Police," Schreiber replied.

"Good. Then we're set for now. Let's go to Washington."

Meanwhile in Portsmouth, unloading of U-234 continued. Lieutenant Pfaff had been retained by the Americans to unload the vessel since he had supervised its loading. His presence was especially requested at the unloading of the uranium. The cylinders containing the precious ore were gently lifted out of the submarine one at a time. Then the sealed containers were placed on trucks bound for Indian Head, Maryland, home of the U.S. Navy's Ordinance Investigation Laboratory and the Naval Powder Factory.

Schreiber's team and Wehring arrived in Washington around noon the first week in June. By now, it was fairly warm, and Schreiber was thankful for the new khaki uniforms that Wehring had provided. Otherwise, he would be burning up. Only two jeeps drove up to the War Department. Schreiber, Dietz, and Wehring got out and went into the building. A guard who examined their ID cards scrutinized them. He waved them through.

"Who are we meeting?" Schreiber asked.

"The man's name is Wheeler. Paul Wheeler, but I call him Squealer."

"Squealer Wheeler, huh?" Dietz snickered.

"Partly out of the way, he squealed when I showed him the compromising picture. Then also the way he squealed on his fellow Communists when I turned on the heat."

They arrived outside Wheeler's office. A pretty secretary was out front. "May I help you gentlemen?" she said sweetly.

"We need to see Mr. Wheeler."

"May I ask who you are?"

"Mr. Waring."

She picked the phone up, spoke briefly, and hung up. "I'm sorry, but he has a meeting in fifteen minutes."

"We'll only take five."

"I'm sorry but—"

Wehring said nothing but went to the door to Wheeler's office and slid a manila envelope under it. Wheeler opened the door immediately.

"I figured that would have the desired effect," Wehring caustically remarked.

"Come in," Wheeler squeaked, trying to maintain his composure. "What do you want?"

"Let me introduce you to Captain Lawson Ford and First Lieutenant Rodney Hughes. I understand there is some uranium that needs transporting to Oak Ridge."

"Yes, but do you know how sensitive that project is?" Wheeler hissed.

"Of course, I do. However, these gentlemen could use a rest from their experiences in Europe. I would like for them to be assigned to a peaceful area to finish out their service."

"Lonsdale won't like this."

"What's there to worry about? Germany has surrendered, and Japan doesn't stand much of a chance. Anyway, Lonsdale is in Europe. Now if you're worried about the Russians." Wehring gave a sly smile, while Wheeler sweated.

"Okay, you win. There will be orders for Captain Ford this afternoon." Wheeler took a pad out and wrote down the information he needed. "Be here at 1600."

"We'll be punctual."

As they left the building, the three men chuckled. It wasn't just because Wheeler was the enemy. All three relished seeing someone so exalted being cowed by previous indiscretions. "Some rather strong pictures if I may say so myself," was Dietz's sardonic remark.

"I still prefer women," Schreiber remarked.

"I certainly hope so, or you'll be wearing a pink triangle with an A on it in one of Himmler's special cells."

"I thought we read about his death."

"Well, you know what I mean."

The men got into their jeep and drove out of Washington. They stopped by a hotel where Wehring had left his blue New Yorker. He shook hands with Dietz and Schreiber.

"Gentlemen, this is where we part for now. Tomorrow we will see how this works. I'm not worried about Wheeler tattling. He's too chickenshit as the Americans put it. Well, good luck."

"We'll hold our breath. Keep low yourself." Schreiber almost felt like saluting the old spy but instead went back to the jeep. "Well, Dietz, let's go to Indian Head in the morning. By this time tomorrow, we're either inside the Manhattan Project or in one of Truman's padded cells instead of Himmler's."

"Believe me, I don't want to be in either one."

At 0800, Schreiber's men arrived outside the main gate at the Indian Head Naval Base. Schreiber noted that the marine guards were a no nonsense lot. The marines were well built, and most showed campaign ribbons from the Pacific. Most also wore a Purple Heart."

"Your papers, sir." A marine corporal took Schreiber's ID and orders. He made a phone call. "Sir, please report to Captain McGhee."

"Can you tell us how to get there?"

After the marine gave him directions, Schreiber continued until he reached the headquarters building. He went in asked for Captain

McGhee and was directed through a maze of rooms and halls until he was face to face with Navy Captain McGhee.

"Captain Ford reporting, sir. Here are my orders." He handed his orders to McGhee.

"Have a seat, Captain. I must say the Manhattan Project didn't waste time homing in on this cache of uranium. Well, your credentials are impeccable." McGhee picked up a phone and called an officer in. "Lieutenant Jones here will escort you to the uranium. Have a safe trip to Oak Ridge."

Schreiber went with Jones to the storage area where the uranium was secured. A marine gunnery sergeant Red Crawford was in charge. He gave Schreiber a good looking over.

"You'll have to excuse the gunny for giving you a hard look. He's very particular about his work," Jones remarked

"I wouldn't want him any other way."

"Damn right you wouldn't. That's why I'm alive, and this country's on the winning side, both this war and the last one." Crawford was crusty marine of the old breed.

"You were in the first war?."

Gunny Crawford looked down his nose at Schreiber. "While you were still wet behind the ears, I was killing Krauts at Belleau Wood. Got my share of Japs in the Philippines too."

"I thought the Philippines was mainly an army operation."

"I was there in '42 when the little yellow bastards invaded, and McArthur bugged out. We surrendered at first, but after the first killings, my CO led a group of us into the jungle. We fought the Japs until dugout Doug returned." Crawford then spit contemptuously on the ground.

By now, the uranium was loaded. Schreiber turned to thank Jones. Crawford was looking Schreiber's men over. Schreiber suppressed a shudder. He remembered his father talking about fighting the legendary devil dogs the Americans threw against his position in 1918.

"Let's get out of here," Schreiber told his driver. "That marine sergeant is making me nervous."

"Me too. I'll get us out of here."

Seconds later, the convoy was almost out of the gate. Crawford had lit a cigar and was chomping on it. As one of the old breed of marines, he despised cigarettes. He seemed puzzled. Jones wondered what was going on in that jarhead mind.

"Something bothering you, gunny?"

"Yeah. I've seen plenty of army guys before and beat the hell out of them. Just a bunch of women with some balls. Those guys. See the scars? Particularly the ones without Purple Hearts."

"Can't say that I did."

"Well, why are a bunch of guys like that shoveling shit instead of killing little yellow bastards? They look like marines in army uniform."

"Come on, gunny. Just your imagination."

"Maybe so. Something just ain't right."

Schreiber finally relaxed after they left Indian Head. He turned to Dietz. "That marine was starting to worry me."

"Relax. We're in now."

"Not quite. We'll find out for sure at Oak Ridge."

"I suspect that once we're in, then we're in."

"I hope you're right."

Two days later, they convoy pulled up to the entrance to Oak Ridge in Tennessee's Blue Ridge Mountains. It was already warm in this part of the country. Schreiber was trying to remain calm. Today would be the ultimate test of his and his men's training. If they got inside the, camp then they were inside the Manhattan Project. Since the uranium was not in big containers, Schreiber decided to only bring twelve of his men through the gate. Hopefully, he would not attract a lot of attention this way as a larger group might. The others would blend in until they moved on.

It took a few minutes to find the entrance to the facility as Oak Ridge had limited access. Schreiber finally drove toward an area that appeared to be a farm with all of the buildings that one would expect. As he looked closer, a silo appeared to have antiaircraft guns. He had found it.

They proceeded cautiously down a road and ran into a checkpoint. Several guards appeared, rifles at the ready.

An army sergeant appeared. Schreiber handed him his orders. "Sergeant, I do have load of uranium to deliver. All I know is it's important. I would appreciate not having those rifles pointed at me."

"Sorry, sir, but I must verify your story."

"Please do."

The sergeant made a call. He soon returned. "I'm sorry about your reception, Captain. No one expected you so soon. Everyone is excited that you arrived so early."

"When I have a job to do, Sergeant, I don't take my time about it. There is a bomb to be built after all."

"Yes, sir. Someone will come and take you where you need to go."

A green staff car arrived shortly after Schreiber's arrival. "I'm Lieutenant Adams. Captain Ford, would you please follow me."

Schreiber motioned for his men to follow. He followed the staff car to a plain building. More guards and some anxious scientists greeted him.

"Easy, gentlemen. I think we have something very important for you. Bring the containers in."

Some technicians went out and brought the containers in. Schreiber handed the inventory to a scientist. The man read the inventory and smiled; he was pleased with the contents. He passed it around to the others. They too smiled.

"So this is the German uranium. We're indebted to you for bringing this to us," one of the scientists spoke. The others nodded in agreement. "We heard that the Germans had some good stuff, but we weren't expecting this. We need to get this enriched."

Schreiber had some idea the remarks had to do with the bomb. "Lieutenant, would you take me to whoever is in charge of the MPs here. I would like to get my men settled for the night and next few days."

"That might be difficult if you haven't been cleared for the project."

"If the War Department thought I was qualified to deliver this material, I'm surely qualified to get some place to stay."

"I agree, sir, but it's not my call. I'll take you to the man in charge."

As Dietz and Schreiber followed the staff car, they admired the size of the buildings. One building was half a mile long. Schreiber tried to make note of his surroundings. Even though the bomb was not being built here, Schreiber wanted to be familiar with his territory in case he needed to make a quick escape.

"All of this to build one bomb," Schreiber muttered to Dietz.

"We did underestimate the Americans badly. Obviously, the Russians haven't," replied Dietz. "Perhaps the Americans have underestimated us."

They arrived at the office of the head of security. Captain Ted Baker was inside when Adams walked in with Schreiber and Dietz. "Sir, Captain Ford has just delivered the uranium from that German submarine. He and his men need a place to stay."

"What are your orders, Captain?"

"Deliver the uranium as soon as possible and await further instructions."

"This is a little out of the ordinary."

"As I told the lieutenant, if the War Department thought I was safe enough to deliver this material, then certainly I can spend the night here.

"Well, you do have a point. If you and you're men could help on security around here for a few days, that would help. I have a few men on leave plus a few that are in the hospital."

"I would be delighted to help."

"Good. The lieutenant will show you to your quarters."

Over the next few days, the uranium was enriched. Meanwhile, Schreiber and Dietz came to the conclusion as had Wehring that no bomb would ever be made in Oak Ridge. Another problem arose, which was how to get inside Los Alamos.

Schreiber pulled Dietz over a few days later. "The uranium is almost ready to be shipped. The want to test the bomb in the middle of July, and they want to ship the material in ten days."

"How's it supposed to get there?"

"I found out that a courier takes the finished product by train to Chicago. Then he takes another train to Santa Fe."

"What if the courier ends up ill or whatever?"

"It might arouse some suspicion. Plus, they could pick another courier."

Dietz leaned back. "We need to act soon, I gather."

"Correct."

Dietz straightened up. "Accidents do happen on trains and railways, don't they?"

"Yes, they do. What are you suggesting?"

"If a train breaks down or the railway needs repairing, the courier is going to be stuck awhile, isn't he?"

"And they will need another way to get the uranium to Los Alamos. With the current guard situation, we're the only ones they could spare to transport the uranium."

"Exactly."

"Well, be careful, Dietz. Don't get caught."

During the last half of June, several boilers exploded between Chicago and Santa Fe. Some problems with the rails were found in Tennessee requiring repairs. As a result, rail travel became disrupted and was unreliable for several days. By the end of the month, the enriched uranium was ready for transport.

Schreiber walked into Baker's office during the rail problems and heard him talking on the phone with someone about the rail problem. "I can only provide security here at Oak Ridge. No one has even suggested sabotage on the railroads, and it's out of my control anyway." He was becoming exasperated by the conversation. He looked up and saw Schreiber.

"Perhaps I could be of help. After all, I brought the stuff here from Indian Head."

A sigh of relief escaped Baker's lips. "Are you sure? I don't want to dump on you." His eyes told another story.

"Get me the paperwork to refuel along the way, and we will be there before the rain arrives."

The relief was such that Baker hardly knew how to act. "It is a tight schedule, and they want the uranium as soon as possible. The railways have been unreliable because of maintenance and engine problems. Since you and your men are the nearest thing to excess I've got, it would be great if you drove it to New Mexico. You need to leave today."

"That won't be a problem once you get the orders drawn up."

"They'll be ready in an hour. We owe you big on this one, if you ever need a favor."

"Don't mention it. There is a job to be done and a war to be finished."

"Exactly. Have a good trip."

That afternoon, Schreiber's orders were ready. He drove out to get the finished product. He couldn't help but marvel at the antiaircraft guns near the enrichment plant. Who was going to bomb this area anyway? He picked up the uranium in its sealed containers and after signing a receipt for the material headed out of the complex. The rest of the evening was spent crossing the state of Tennessee. By now, the state's vegetation had put out its summer foliage. The heat was also oppressive. Some of the men who served in Africa thought the Dark Continent was more tolerable. That evening, they stopped outside Jackson.

The following day, they crossed the Mississippi River at Memphis into the Arkansas delta. North of them was a railway bridge. Schreiber wondered why the uranium had always gone through Chicago. The men marveled at the size of the Mississippi. Only the Rhine and Danube even approached its size.

"I had forgotten how big the United States really is, even though I spent some time in St. Louis," Schreiber remarked to Dietz.

"It is huge," Dietz conceded.

"We shouldn't have fought the United States and Russia at the same time."

"We'll know for sure in a few weeks."

"I guess we will."

The convoy continued along a two-lane highway between Little Rock and Memphis. They reached Fort Pike in North Little Rock at midday and stopped to refuel. As they ascended the plateau, a fleeting view of Arkansas's capital city revealed itself to the south.

"Nice country except for the heat," one of the men complained.

Schreiber agreed whole heartily. Then his eye caught sight of something else. He spotted German POWs. He clenched his jaw. They had obviously been well taken care of and appeared fit. Most, however, had the look of men who were homesick. War was far from their minds now. Schreiber had a twinge of doubt in the back of his mind about carrying on but suppressed the thought.

Refueling proceeded without a hitch. Then he crossed the Arkansas River and headed toward Ft. Chaffee outside the town of Ft. Smith. By now, his men had found out how hot the South could be. Their main relief was that the vehicles were open. They arrived late that afternoon at Ft. Smith. The ground was gently rolling and wooded. Barracks dotted the open areas. Schreiber watched as recruits marched back to their barracks at the bark of their drill instructors. Also, the rumble of tanks was heard in the background. Schreiber recalled this was an armored training center. The Americans obviously were preparing for an invasion of Japan despite their efforts on the bomb.

Schreiber's men again entered the base without a problem. Overnight accommodations were arranged. The following morning, they awoke to a blazing Arkansas morning. In addition to the heat, they endured swarms of mosquitoes. They cursed the pesky insects to no avail. After breakfast, they left Ft. Chaffee and headed into Oklahoma. By now, the foliage was shorter and vegetation more sparse. Finally, the ground consisted of sagebrush and sand.

The convoy continued west through Oklahoma City and into the boot heel of Texas. Finally, they reached the New Mexico border. Schreiber halted his men for a few hours before proceeding on to Los Alamos. He wanted to arrive in the evening when they would have no choice but to let him stay overnight. In addition, he wanted to talk to his men one last time.

"We are near our destination. Soon the Americans will have their bomb ready to test. I do not understand all of the mysteries of science. If it works, we will steal one, and hopefully, someone can renegotiate the terms of surrender. That is all there is to be said on that. If it doesn't, then we are going to simply disappear. The Americans will never know that we were here. Remember, we are still in enemy territory. We must use all of the tricks we learned to survive, mainly act like Americans. Those of you who were with me in the Brandenburg Division don't need to be reminded. Deutschland uber Alles."

After they resumed their trip, Schreiber thought of how this reminded him of Maikop. Only this time, he was in charge and not the audacious Baron. Would he measure up to the Baron's abilities? He knew he would soon find out.

The convoy proceeded on through Santa Fe and turned northwest to begin its entry into Los Alamos. As they moved toward the entrance, Schreiber noticed his surroundings. To the west were the Jemez Mountains. The Rocky Mountains were east. The Rockies descended to form the Sayre de Cristo. The land between was one of stark, harsh beauty. Only a few cacti and spindly shrubs interrupted the endless sand and rock.

They drove up to the gate; this was the moment of truth. If they got in, then they were in. Still Schreiber was nervous. Even though his orders were legitimate, Schreiber hoped that he would genuinely worm his way into the project.

An army corporal greeted him. "I'm Captain Ford; delivering a shipment of uranium from Oak Ridge."

"I need to call. You aren't expected until tomorrow."

"I was instructed to deliver this as soon as possible, not be as inefficient as possible."

The corporal stiffened. "I still need to call my CO."

Soon a jeep with a captain arrived. He got out and approached.

He looked at Schreiber's orders. He looked at the containers. "Follow me, Captain Ford."

Schreiber's jeep followed the army captain. As they drove to their destination, Schreiber noted the cheap barracks buildings that had been hastily erected and housed military and civilian personnel. Few sidewalks were on the spartan compound. The area was not designed for comfort, which meant people were supposed to work.

The convoy proceeded on to the delivery point. They were stopped outside a more substantial building where Schreiber suspected the bomb was put together. It certainly wasn't for living in. Schreiber's men were asked to form a cordon around the entrance while the material was taken inside. Schreiber deducted that they had delivered a crucial amount of uranium and that if the bomb was being built inside this building, then something almost as important was going on.

The unloading was uneventful and swift. Obviously, they were in a hurry here in Los Alamos. Some more scientists showed up to examine the cargo. They were obviously satisfied with what they saw. When the loading was complete, Schreiber asked the captain about billeting. He also needed to ingratiate himself with this man. Wearing insignia of equal rank would carry some weight.

"Captain, I need a place for myself and my men. We have been driving like hell to get this stuff here on schedule."

"Actually, you are ahead of time. It isn't exactly within the rules, but they have been having a fit around here with the delays. I think I can let you slide under those conditions."

"We are just doing our job."

"Well, thanks again. By the way, name's Smith. Come with me and we'll get some rooms for you. By the way, how much do you know about what's going on here?"

"Enough to keep my mouth shut and not ask questions."

"Good. Well, you know this is very secret. I know very little details. If this works, then it will save us the trouble of invading Japan and God knows how many casualties. Right now, I could use a few extra men. The bomb will be tested in a few days at Alamogordo. Everyone could use a break from the strain."

"If you could use us, we would be happy to help. Since you know the area, I certainly don't plan to pull rank. I just want to get some sleep for my men and myself tonight. Tomorrow we can call about assignment here."

"Great! I could use the extra men."

Schreiber and Dietz got individual rooms. Later that night, they met.

"Well, we're in," Dietz remarked.

"Yes, but everything is up to the Americans now. We do need to note the landscape, routes out of here, and so on if we have to make a run for it."

"That can wait until the morning."

"For once, Dietz, I agree completely with you."

CHAPTER 11

By the end of the first week in July 1945, Otto Skorzeny had been in Nuremburg prison for almost a month. He was resting in his cell when he heard the jingling of keys and then the door opened. Sergeant Rufus Johnson, his black guard, stood at the door. Ironically, the two men had developed a mutual respect for each other despite the intentions of the prison's commandant, Colonel Andrus. Andrus was a Lithuanian who had worked his way up through the ranks to his current position. He hated Germans in particular and had placed Negro guards over the SS in a move designed to demean Hitler's former elite. His plan backfired, as it didn't work on Skorzeny and most of the others. They had already learned the idiocy of the racial theories on the Eastern Front when so many of the untermenschen had buried their comrades. As it turned out, the SS and blacks were in the same boat. A friendship developed between Skorzeny and Johnson. The big black would slip Skorzeny candy, cigarettes, and whatever else he could. He and other blacks despised Andrus as much as the Germans, and this was his way of defying his superior. It wasn't much, but it was more than Skorzeny could do in return.

"Don'ts worry about it, Colonel. Ah's never saw a white person worse than us po black folk until now. I figure's must be something good bout you if dey's treating you like me." Although a simple person, Johnson retained his humanity despite his inferior status in the U.S. Army. Skorzeny could respect that.

Johnson's face didn't reveal anything today about his entering. "Someone to see you, Colonel. Some general," he said in his southern drawl.

"Well, who might that be?" Skorzeny say up on his cot.

"A Gen'ral Donavan."

"General Donavan of the OSS?"

"Beats me, Colonel. Dey's just tells me to come and get you."

Skorzeny smiled. Johnson didn't have a clue. At least he was nice enough. Skorzeny wished there were more like him. He followed Johnson to the room where he would meet with Donavan. Along the way, Skorzeny tried to recall what he knew about Donavan. He was basically Skorzeny's opposite number in the American Army as head of the OSS. However, he had more support during the war than Skorzeny had ever dreamed of. Skorzeny wondered if this was social call or to be a deep interrogation. He gritted his teeth as he thought of last month and the degradation he had been through.

Skorzeny was led to the office of Colonel Andrus. Donavan had used his rank to appropriate the office and kick the little prick out. Skorzeny considered that a good sign. As Skorzeny entered, he recognized Donavan from photographs and sized the man up. Donavan was an older man, well built, and wore the uniform of a two-star general. Skorzeny recalled bitterly when he had his collar patches ripped off by the Americans.

He also noted a chest full of medals above the man's left pocket. He noted a pale blue one with five stars, the Medal of Honor. It was probably more difficult to receive than the Knights Cross had been. He knew Donavan's medal dated back to World War I when he had earned the name "Wild Bill." Hopefully, Donavan would be a kindred spirit."

Donavan did not disappoint him. "Colonel Skorzeny, it's good to meet a worthy opponent even if we didn't directly butt heads during the war. Please sit down."

"Thank you. Your own feats were legendary as I recall, more so in the last war."

"I was much younger and able to dodge bullets better. I see that you have a souvenir from combat on your face there."

Skorzeny grinned about the dueling scar. "It's from my student days as you probably know. Another student and I fought over a dancer. Then a month later, she married someone that neither of us knew about.'

Both men laughed at that. "The battlefield isn't the only place where one can get hurt."

"I understand that you got your nickname for exploits on and off the battlefield as well."

"I see that you are as well informed as I have been most of the time. You did surprise us at the Bulge though."

"That almost didn't happen after Keitel's letter circulated."

"We messed up royally on that. Then we overdid it in response. We still don't know how many GIs killed each other in the resulting confusion. Best of all, one of our men shot out Montgomery's tires when he tried to run right past one of our checkpoints. At least you did one good thing for the Americans."

Skorzeny had good laugh at that one. "I had similar problems locating Mussolini. At times it seemed like someone was feeding information to you. I was almost shot down over the Mediterranean during one of my aerial reconnaissance flights."

"That was probably your greatest exploit, getting Mussolini off the Gran Sasso."

"Probably so, but Admiral Horthy required more finesse.

"I could see that. You had other projects in mind as well as I recall."

Skorzeny went on to describe his attacks at Remagen, plans to kidnap Petain, and other little schemes. They continued their discussion for two hours. Finally, Donavan popped the critical question.

"What mission had the biggest potential to influence or did influence the war."

"That would have been Operation Gotterdammerung."

Donavan held his composure. He had not heard of this one. *Why?* he thought. "Tell me about this operation."

"I have to as nothing was ever written down. It was one of Himmler's madcap schemes as far as I'm concerned. At the end of the war, Himmler wanted me to send a commando team in to steal one of your atomic bombs if you ever developed it."

"What was the purpose of this?"

"If you developed the bomb and we somehow got hold of it, then you might have reconsidered your terms of our surrender. Plus our POWs might be getting better treatment than what they are."

"I'm afraid that's outside my control as much as I do disagree with what's being done. I thought Ike had better sense." Meanwhile, alarms were going off inside Donavan's head.

"How did Himmler get hold of the information about the bomb?"

"From General Gehlen, head of Foreign Armies East. He had a spy in Moscow who had access to the most sensitive NKVD operations. One of these involved your Manhattan Project."

Donavan groaned inside. He had warned FDR on several occasions that the United States needed to set up a spy ring in the Soviet Union. This only served to confirm Donavan's suspicions. "Any idea where or who this source is?"

"Not at all. Schellenberg would be the one to ask."

"So were you going to lead Gotterdammerung?"

"I wanted to, but Himmler forbade it. There was no discussing the matter."

"So who was to lead it?"

"Major Max Schreiber."

"Tell me about this Major Schreiber. I had not heard of him."

"Nice to know we had a few secrets. Schreiber was probably the best officer under my command. He rose through the enlisted ranks and received the oak leaves to the Knights Cross."

"There were only about eight hundred of those awarded as I recall."

"Something like that." Skorzeny proceeded to give Donavan

more details of Schreiber's career and came back to what he knew had transpired at the end of the war. "The last I knew, he was at Flensburg where KG 200 had its flying boats. I never got to talk to him again, although I gave him code words in case I cancelled the mission. I felt that Himmler was willing to sacrifice people needlessly for whatever ulterior aims he had in mind."

The conversation drifted on for a few more minutes. Donavan got the code words on whether to cancel the mission from Skorzeny. Also chilling was the order Himmler gave the men to continue even with the cessation of hostilities. Obviously, Skorzeny thought that Schreiber had been rounded up after the surrender. Donavan wanted to be sure of it. Before he left, he asked Skorzeny, "Is there anything I can do for you?"

"Anything you can do about our POWs?"

"It's completely out of my hands. I will bring it up when I can, but Eisenhower is running things. I can't lean on him directly. I will have to work behind the scenes if I achieve anything. I can't promise you any results, but I'll try."

"I can't ask for more."

With that, the two former enemies shook hands, and Skorzeny was led back to his bleak cell. Later that day, Donavan made it a point to dine with his aide Major Parker. He told him about the conversation with Skorzeny. "I doubt that he's making it up, but we need to verify that Schreiber is not out there somewhere. He is an old Brandendurger, and they were good. Let's not get caught with our pants down on this one."

"Well, surely the end of the war would make them stop."

"Evidently, Himmler gave orders for this to continue even if the war ended. Make sure they didn't fly out of Flensburg at the end of the war. KG 200 had the planes to do it with. Unfortunately, Skorzeny couldn't stop it because he was in southern Germany."

Two days later, Parker had the information that Donavan wanted. "Sir, I checked out Skorzeny's story. On May 2 or 3, it appears a flying boat took off from Flensburg. It had almost thirty men aboard. Most were SS with Major Schreiber on board. The plane took off. It never returned. There were no distress calls and no record of them saying they made it. A Spanish agent reported a visit in the Azores by a flying boat in May, but he provided no details."

"However, the calls would not necessarily come to Flensburg. We need to check their station in Hamburg and locate any other stations in operation then. Handle this quietly, Parker. This may be nothing. Get the files on Schreiber to make sure he existed. It may be that the OSS has an urgent new mission."

"Yes, sir. I'll get on it right away."

Damn, Donavan thought. *I thought I could relax. Now I have to contact General Groves and tell him a threat may exist. Too bad Skorzeny didn't stop Schreiber, that is, if he tried anyway. But Skorzeny's believable. Hopefully, we will wrap this up with a minimum of fuss.* Later that week, Donavan met with General Leslie Groves and informed him of the possible threat. Groves sat patiently listening to this improbable tale. After all, he had more important things to take care of, mainly build an atomic bomb. After Donavan finished, Groves looked at him blankly.

"You mean to tell me that a bunch of renegade Germans have flown across the Atlantic and are preparing to steal the atomic bomb from us once we make it. This is utterly ridiculous. Do you know how much security I have in the Manhattan Project? Lonsdale has run a tight ship from the beginning. They are not getting in. That's it."

"I just wanted to warn you. I don't think the group will get far if the plane didn't crash in the Atlantic. They may call it quits once they're here. But I do have to tell you this, just in case. I have to do my job."

"And let me do mine. If they're out there, you get them."

"I plan to. I would like to remind you these are combat veterans. Some of them have six years of experience."

"I don't care if they have ten or twenty years of experience. They're not getting in. Anyway, if they do get in, they aren't going to move it far. Indications are that the smallest size bomb will be five tons. That is a hell of a lot of bomb to move. Frankly, I would be surprised if they all didn't call it quits and disappeared into our society."

"If they're here, I hope that is the case. I will keep you informed General."

"Thanks for the heads up, Donovan. I'll talk with Lonsdale when he gets back from Europe."

"What's he doing over there?"

"Looking for additional uranium stores that the Germans gathered up."

Groves didn't need to say another word. Donovan realized that no one was watching the house with the head of security out of the country. Parker had better be wrapping things up soon.

While the Manhattan Project moved forward in the dusty plains of New Mexico, the invasion of Japan was being planned in Washington. The recent bloodbath at Okinawa filled the civilian and military leaders with apprehension about the proposed invasion. President Truman met with Secretary of War Stimson, Secretary of State Designate James Byrnes, to discuss the invasion and use of the bomb.

Truman got down to business. "We are facing a big decision. We must prepare for the invasion of Japan. The thought of so many American boys dying at this stage of the war sickens me. We can only hope that the atomic bomb, if we are able to use it, will bring the Japanese leaders to their senses."

Stimson had been down this road before. The dignified elderly statesman had the annoying habit of pointing out the downside to any proposal. "No closure or end to this war will be easy. The best outcome will be if we use the bomb and the Japanese surrender. The other is obvious. Hopefully, the destruction of an entire city will get their attention. However, we may get the attention of a lot of other nations as well. They may not be pleased that we have chosen to use a weapon of such mass destruction. We do bear a certain responsibility when we prepare to use such a weapon, a weapon that potentially has the ability to wipe out human kind."

Truman was quick to respond. Anyone else would have received a good tongue lashing if not an outright cussing as a measure of Truman's contempt. However, Stimson had good judgment and insight that was to be respected even by the president of the United States.

"I respect your opinion, but the idea of butchering American boys does not appeal to me. Look at our recent losses on Iwo Jima and Okinawa. I have a letter hear from a marine sergeant who was busted from gunnery sergeant to staff sergeant because he went AWOL in Hawaii for two weeks. Do you know why he went AWOL? It was because of all the dreadful casualties he witnessed on Iwo Jima. He states that most of the veteran officers and enlisted men have been killed or wounded. The new troops don't really have experienced men to lead them on a local level. This poor marine sergeant was tired of seeing inexperienced boys sent to the meat grinder because the leadership was inexperienced. I'm sorry, gentlemen, if there is any way this bomb can shorten the war and save American boys, the decision is easy for me."

Stimson persisted. "Mr. President, I share your sentiments exactly. I don't want to see more war dead, but we should think about the precedent we're setting. The fact is we still don't know that the bomb will work."

"I know. However, we will know in a few days. If it does, I will use it to save us a million casualties. I am also considering a blockade. I am ready for this war to be over, however."

"We all are. I feel that I should point out all relevant facts as I see them. I know that it is not an easy decision. I want to make sure that you have heard all sides before you decide."

"I fully appreciate what you have to say. Byrnes, you may have to deal with the Russians over the matter. We're having enough friction with them already. I don't know what they'll think when we drop it. That's for you to handle."

"I'll get working on it, Mr. President."

General Donavan met with Major Parker later that week. He told him of his meeting with Groves. "Basically, he pooh-pooed the whole thing. I can't exactly say that I blame him. My problem is this isn't exactly under my domain. However, if I go to Hoover and the FBI, they would be sure to bungle it up as usual. Imagine a bunch of Hoover's G-men up against a platoon of seasoned Waffen-SS troops. It would be over in seconds. If Schreiber is loose, I want him taken care of quietly out of the public eye. Understand, Parker?"

"Yes, sir. Too bad General Groves didn't pay attention to you."

"Well, he's more interested in building this bomb. That's what he's being paid to do. We'll try to smoke out Schreiber ourselves. No big investigation. I don't want the FBI snooping around and hindering development of the bomb. That's why I don't want a big to do of the sort that Hoover likes. Who do we have that's good?"

Parker started thinking aloud. "Most of our people are trained to fight in small units against regular forces. No one is really trained to fight another commando group, except marines or rangers. We have Major Ortiz, but he is still hospitalized after being freed from a German POW camp."

"Anyone who performed their mission while wearing the enemy's uniform?"

"Very few and most of those are in units outside our control." Parker paused. "Wait a minute. There was that marine major we picked up who refused to surrender in '42 when McArthur left. He actually passed into Japanese towns wearing Jap uniforms. Who was that?" Parker thumbed through some files and handed one to Donavan.

"Roger Bennett, quite a character it looks like." Donavan started thumbing through the file.

"Actually, it's Benedetti or something like that. His father was Italian, and his mother is Mexican. Evidently, that gave him enough of an oriental look to fool the Japanese. He slipped into the apartment of the head of the Kempetai in Manila and tried to assassinate him. Instead, he killed an aide. The Japs put quite a price tag on his head after that exploit. He went on to blow up supplies and a few ammo dumps. The Japs called him the Ghost of the Jungle. The Filipinos called him one-shot because he never missed. He did similar things like our friend Schreiber did in the Brandenburg Division. Finally, he came back in '44 after the liberation of Manila."

"Sounds like our man. Where is he?"

"Here in Washington at the training ground we have outside town. He's been recuperating from malaria."

"Two navy crosses, silver star, and three purple hearts. Brazen, ruthless, and self-confident, I like this man." Donavan closed the folder and handed back to Donavan. "Bring him in."

"Yes, sir. Using a rogue to catch a rogue, sir?"

"If that what it takes, yes."

Major Robert Bennett walked into Donavan's office at precisely 1600 hours. He was in the khaki service dress of a marine officer. The globe and anchor stood out on his garrison cap and lapels. In addition to his medals for valor, he wore a Pacific campaign ribbon with two stars and good conduct medal from his enlisted years.

Donavan was casual. Before Bennett could come to attention, Donavan ordered him to sit down.

"Thank you, sir."

"You've had quite a career, Bennett."

"Tried to survive."

"You seemed to go on the offensive enough."

"I always heard the best defense is a good offense."

"Gave the Kempetai a run for the money it seems."

"Well, their boss was breathing down my neck. I thought if I killed him, it may take some pressure off my guerillas."

"Instead, they sent more reinforcements. At least they didn't come and interfere with our landings elsewhere, one unexpected benefit of your action."

Both laughed lightly, then Donavan got down to business. "I imagine you're wanting to get in on the invasion of Japan."

"If there are going to be marines, there I want to be there."

"Suppose I told you I had other plans."

"Not interested. I would like to get back to the Corps."

"Maybe later. Right now, something has come up that is right down your alley. Are you aware of the atomic bomb?"

"Never heard of it."

"Understandable given your career. Well, this is basically a super bomb. It works it could wipe out a whole city."

"That's some bomb."

"Well, I have a job concerning this bomb for you."

"What is it?"

"Ever heard of Otto Skorzeny?"

"No."

"The Brandenburg Division?"

"Definitely not."

"Then let me educate you. The Brandenburg Division was a German unit trained to operate behind enemy lines in enemy uniforms. They would worm their way inside headquarters; supply dumps much like you, and then do their dirty work when it was time. Skorzeny was head of the SS commandos. He recruited a lot of men from the Brandenburg Division."

"I think I know where this is going."

"Well, at the end of the war, Himmler may have sent a commando team over to try to snatch this device of ours and use it for blackmail."

"I thought the Germans called it quits in May."

"Evidently, Himmler gave orders for the team to continue in the event of surrender. We don't know if the group made it or not. We're still looking through their transmissions to see if they made it. All we know is that the plane took off with a platoon of Waffen-SS and never returned."

"Skorzeny didn't stop this."

"He figured they never left Germany with all of the confusion. He gave the leader some vague instructions about dropping the project, but we don't know what has exactly happened. Skorzeny felt it was one of Himmler's crazy schemes. However, the British intercepted Himmler on his way south before he committed suicide. There is some thought that he was trying to get to one of the last transmitters still functioning before we took over. He could have been trying to get hold of Schreiber's group."

"What about the people running this operation? Don't they have their own security?"

"Yes, but their head of security is in Europe, looking for uranium, and General Groves thinks this is a figment of our imagination. So it needs to be handled quietly."

"So what I'm supposed to do is hunt down these bad Germans in SS uniform and prevent them from rewriting May 8?"

"No, they will be wearing American uniforms. Somewhat like your wearing Japanese uniforms in the Philippines."

"Let me tell you about the leader, Major Schreiber. He started out as enlisted man like you and fought his way up to his current rank. He received the Knights Cross with oak leaves. That's about like our Medal of Honor. A little over eight hundred were awarded. Oh, here's a folder on him. Sorry there's no photograph."

Bennett read through the file. The exploit at Maikop was fascinating. Then he received a battlefield commission. That was perhaps an even more rare event in the German army than in the U.S. Army or Marine Corps. Then there was the breakout from East Prussia. The man takes care of his men and knows his business. *The kind of man I would like to have even if he is German*, Bennett thought.

"Where do I start?"

"Oak Ridge. You'll need these." Donavan handed him a special I.D.

"What's this?"

"The right to pry around the Manhattan Project without being detained. See where their weaknesses are. How could someone penetrate the different plants? Hopefully, this is all just an exercise in futility. But don't treat it as one."

"Understood. I just hope the surrender took the fight out of these men."

"Be careful. I know this all sounds ridiculous. Sometimes the ridiculous gets serious."

"I know. That's why I'm still alive."

"And why I picked you. Good luck."

Schreiber and his men insinuated themselves deftly into the

security at Los Alamos. They were shocked at the laxity of the security inside the compound. Secret documents were left unattended on desks overnight. The Germans often purloined these, and Kohlman got a handle on how the bomb was to work

The problem was how to get the bomb out with no Americans tagging along. It was no problem for individuals to get in and out of the perimeter that existed around the compound. Local Indians had regularly come through the fence to graze their goats. Plus, Schreiber was already behind in some ways. The components for the bomb called Little Boy had been shipped out on June 27 to San Diego and then to an island called Tinian. Groves and J. Robert Oppenheimer felt comfortable enough about the upcoming tests to ship the bomb parts overseas in anticipation of its eventual use. Schreiber thought about stealing the test bomb, but if it didn't work, then they had a lot of useless metal to hide.

Schreiber chatted with Dietz about their predicament. "You know that one bomb's already on its way and so is part of the second."

"Which leaves the test bomb and possibly a third. There appears some question whether they will be able to build a third one soon."

"We need to let them fire the test bomb to make sure it works. Otherwise, we could be bluffing with nothing to back it up. If we tried to make off with the test, I'm not sure we would get very far. They are keeping a close eye on this device as they are putting it together."

"Certainly a lot tighter than they do their papers. I'm aware that security is going to be tight for the test. If we tried to make a run, they could close off any roads with ease. Plus, it would be hard to hide from the air."

"And if we blow up part of New Mexico, who will ever care?"

Both laughed. Dietz concluded, "I think you are right. We'll go after the third bomb."

The evening after meeting with Donavan, Bennett went to a bar in Washington to think things over. As he sat sipping on some beer, he thought about his meeting with Donavan. He wondered if there were ulterior motives. Some in the Corps were upset with

Donavan because some politicians had wanted him to be in charge of the Marine Raider program. Although Donavan remained in the army and got the OSS, the idea had still rankled even now. Was this Donavan's way of playing ball in return? He didn't know. It didn't seem like Donavan. Well, he would drive to Oak Ridge tomorrow and begin his investigation.

About that time, he heard a commotion and a voice he had not heard in a long time. Only one man could talk and fight like that. Bennett had not seen Gunny Crawford since they had been sent back to the States. Bennett walked over to where Crawford had knocked not one but two sailors down. Someone was yelling for police.

"Break it up," Bennett's voice was hard.

The three men looked at Bennett. The sailors noticed his major's oak leaf and left without a word.

"Damn, sir, you just broke up the beginnings of a good bar fight. Do you realize how hard it is to find one of those anymore?" Crawford stood up and straightened his uniform.

"With you around, it should be easy. Come on over, gunny, and I'll get you a drink"

"What are you having, sir?"

"A beer."

"Couldn't you get something better than that horse piss?"

"I never developed a taste for anything else."

"How can you be a marine officer and not like anything else? Let me have some Bourbon."

"What are you up to these days, gunny?"

"Shoveling the horse shit over at Indian Head."

"The naval ordinance headquarters?"

"Something like that."

"Sounds boring."

"It is. The most excitement we had is when a group of army guys showed up to pick up some uranium off a captured U-boat to transport to someplace called Oak Ridge. Only thing odd about that was the army guys looked more like marines. Except, of course, they were in army uniforms."

The effects the alcohol had on Bennett evaporated when he heard Oak Ridge. "Did you say Oak Ridge?"

"Yes, I did. Anything special about that?"

"I'm going there tomorrow."

"Well, ain't that grand."

"You're coming with me."

"What do you mean, sir? My orders are for me to be at Indian Head."

"I'll get those changed immediately. Like within the hour."

"Is something up?"

"Maybe. I've been asked to investigate an irregularity. I want someone that I can depend on in a pinch. You know how I think and I know I can trust you in a tight situation."

"This is crazy. Here in the United States."

"Finish your Bourbon, you fish. Then we're leaving."

"Damn it. A man can't even go to the bar anymore without his work following him. What's this all about?'

"I'll tell you about it later."

Bennett got Crawford out of the bar and found a phone to call Donavan. He explained the situation and ended, "Either he comes, or you get someone else to do this. I need someone I can trust. Have orders for the gunny sent to Indian Head."

There was no argument. They made the drive to Indian Head that night. The gunny stared in disbelief as Bennett told him the story. "You actually believe this. Sounds like the army has gone off in la–la land."

"Maybe so. But don't forget the crazy shit I did in Japanese uniform."

"Boy, do I remember. I thought you had punched your ticket in many at time."

"Almost did too, didn't I? Still I wish I had killed that bastard Colonel Nagahama at Manila. The Kempetai would have gone apeshit with the death of its Manila chief. Only thing better would have been better would have been a bullet into General Baba."

"That would have been a hornet's nest then."

"Well, we may have one on our hands now."

They arrived back at Indian Head late that night. Crawford's orders were ready when he arrived. Bennett decided that they would start out in the morning. They had a little too much alcohol on board.

"Will you be ready at 0600?"

"If I have to."

"You have to."

Two mornings later, the two marines were at Oak Ridge. It was obvious that the bomb wasn't being built here. Bennett talked briefly with the head of security.

"Anything unusual."

"Not really."

"No new faces," Bennett persisted.

"Just the guys who brought the uranium from Indian Head here. Then they were out of here in no time it seemed. Why all of the questions?"

"Possible irregularities. I've been asked to check out the truth. Sort of an independent thing."

"Okay, but everything has been fine around here. Like I said, nothing new except those guys with the uranium."

"Nothing else?"

"These guys still around?"

"No. After the uranium got enriched, they drove the stuff to Los Alamos. We had to have them do it since the railroads have had some problems. Normally, a courier takes the stuff to Santa Fe. However, there were too many breakdowns a week or two ago."

"What did the leader look like?"

"He was young with some European campaign ribbons. He was very well built."

"Thank you, Captain. That has been informative."

The marines left Oak ridge empty-handed. "What do you think, Major?"

"We certainly are not going to find a bomb here and neither are the Germans. New Mexico is where our answer's going to be. Let me pull over later and talk to Donovan when we come across a phone."

"What about that captain transferring the uranium?"

"Probably okay. But it does seem odd that the problems on the railways happened all of a sudden. I wonder if that was convenient sabotage."

"Dunno, Major. Maybe we're losing our touch since the Japanese aren't chasing us anymore."

In New Mexico, progress continued on the bomb. Some faulty castings were improved while plutonium hemispheres were cast. Then everything was prepared for transport, including the core."

However, a tropical air mass moved inland on July 10th and forced cancellation of the planned test. It was decided to test the bomb on July 16th, a Monday. Truman was in Potsdam at the same time, and Groves wanted to be able to reassure Truman that the bomb worked while he was meeting with Stalin.

In anticipation of the test, the army began moving the bomb components to the test site. The plutonium core left for its final destination on July 12th in an army sedan. A carload of armed guards preceded it, and technicians followed behind. That night, it was guarded in an abandoned ranch house. For security reasons, the majority of the bomb's parts, including the high explosive, were transported at night. For good luck, the trucks carrying the bomb's very components started leaving at 12:01 a.m. on Friday the fourteenth.

Schreiber had arranged for some of his men to be part of the group leaving after midnight. He sat next to one of the scientists named Kistiakowsky. The five-ton truck with the high explosive was right behind Schreiber. A dark tarpaulin hid the contents from any prying eyes. As the convoy entered Santa Fe, the sirens were turned on in an attempt to dissuade any drunken drivers from ramming into the precious cargo. Kistiakowsky woke up during the drive through Santa Fe. After leaving the town, the scientist went back to sleep. Schreiber dozed intermittingly during the eight-hour trip himself.

When they drove through the gate at the test site, several prominent people had already arrived. Brigadier General Thomas Ferrell, Graves's deputy, was there to ensure smooth preparations.

Oppenheimer was there as well. In addition, many of the bomb's key components including the plutonium hemispheres, the beryllium detonator, and the eighty-pound plug of tamper had arrived previously.

Schreiber's group delivered the explosives to a test tower. Then Schreiber and his men received some time off since they had been up late. Schreiber realized that they were very isolated. The idea of making off with the bomb resurrected itself briefly, but Schreiber just as quickly put it out of his mind when he saw the size of the components. At 1300, the explosive complex was prepared for hoisting. Schreiber and some of his men formed the security detachment as the technicians made their final preparations. Some of his men were called over to assist taking the crate apart. The two tons of explosive were taken off the truck and placed on asphalt under the tower.

Even Schreiber's men who were present seemed to be infected with the spirit of the moment. This was going to be big whatever it was, and the feelings of anticipation were contagious. Mild panic occurred they went to insert one of the plugs, and it would not fit. Finally, someone realized that the plug was hotter from being out in the heat and had expanded, while the recently arrived explosive was still cold from storage. The technicians took a break, and after an hour, the plug slid right in.

On Saturday, the project's preparations continued. The openings for the detonator were bandaged to keep dust out. Then the U.S. Army men strained to lift the explosive device to the top of the tower. The heat made them sweat profusely. When the explosives were fifteen feet off the ground, Schreiber assisted his men and the other GIs in placing mattresses beneath it to cushion any fall. Then the men strained to lift it to the top. Finally, it reached the top without mishap where the technicians gently inserted the detonators one at a time.

Prior to this, the parts of Little Boy were shipped out to Kirkland Air Force Base bear Albuquerque. From there, the parts were flown to San Francisco and then Tinian in anticipation of a successful test. The actual dropping depended on the next few hours' events.

During the last-minute preparations, some doubt arouse about the explosives needed to set of the detonator. Schreiber picked up on the gloom that started to spread among the scientists. Oppenheimer sought relief in the Bhagavad-Gita. During this time, another physicist, Hans Bethe, reran the calculations and concluded there was no cause for concern about the explosion occurring.

Oppenheimer breathed easier after Bethe's conclusions. However, the weather continued to be fickle and threatened to delay the tests more. The tropical cell did not budge in its location over the tests site. In the meantime, everyone continued to broil.

"What's going on? Why haven't they fired the thing?" Fouts asked him when they were alone.

"The weather's the reason. They need for it to clear up. That's all. The scientists have been griping constantly about it." Schreiber knew he needed to reassure his men.

"This is as bad as North Africa."

"I was never there. But if you were right, I can't say I envied whatever you did."

"It was hot. The northern part wasn't so bad. But when we headed south, it was like this."

"So you were in the group that went looking for the legendary railway."

"That was us."

"Ever find anything?"

"Nothing, I don't think it even existed except in the minds of the high command. In fact, there was much to prove that no humans were around. We did run into an isolated French outpost. They must have been sent there on punishment duty."

"No doubt." Schreiber laughed.

At 1600 on Sunday, Oppenheimer, Groves, and Ferrell met with an army meteorologist at the farmhouse to discuss the weather predicament. They decided to schedule a weather conference at 0200. If the weather showed improvement, then they would proceed with the detonation at 0400.

That afternoon, Schreiber observed Oppenheimer making some last-minute checks on the device on top of the tower. Even from the ground, Schreiber could make out a jumble of wires running from the device to a junction box. With nothing for him to do, Schreiber decided to catch some rest before things began in earnest.

At 2200, an MP sergeant woke the scientist responsible for the main sequence timing switch. In the tower, another physicist was reconnecting the capacitors used for practice runs to the real thing. A makeshift weather station was also in operation now. At 0200, black thunderclouds unleashed their contents on the barren desert below. Some feared that an electrical discharge could set off the bomb before they were ready. Gusts of thirty miles an hour swept the area, and the blowing rain stung men's faces as they worked to complete the preparations.

It was obvious that the 0400 detonation would not be made. However, the meteorologist predicted a window of opportunity between 0500 and 0600. Groves was very agitated by now with all of the delays. With difficulty, Oppenheimer calmed the general down. Finally, a time of 0530 was decided upon for the detonation. After this decision, Groves called the governor of New Mexico and advised him to be prepared to declare martial law.

At 0440, the meteorologist presented his final forecast. A detonation would be feasible. although the weather would not be ideal. Different teams responsible for various sections made their way to their stations.

Schreiber went with the firing party. They arrived at the concrete control bunker at 0508. The master switch was unlocked, and the countdown began at 0509:45. Oppenheimer was there to watch as usual. At various times, different colored rockets were fire from the control bunker. At 0525, a green rocket was fired. A siren began its sharp wail. A two-minute rocket and then one-minute rocket were fired. At the control bunker, a more precise time was kept on special sensors. One scientist watched a switch and monitor to disconnect the firing sequence if need be. Four red lights flashed on his console thirty seconds prior to detonation.

Throughout the countdown, Oppenheimer was a bundle of nervous energy. A gong went off at ten seconds. The tension was unbearable. At 0529:45, the detonation was initiated. A series of reactions occurred in milliseconds. This started when the firing circuit closed leading to the detonation at thirty-two separate points simultaneously. This led to a series of reactions leading to the compression of the plutonium core. This led to the mixing of polonium and beryllium atoms. The resulting free neutrons crashed into the plutonium core resulting in a massive chain reaction.

Schreiber and the other guards did not understand the principles behind the bomb, but they soon understood its power. At first, no one realized what had happened. A tremendous flash of light illuminated the desert landscape. To those standing outside, it seemed somehow that the flash passed right through them. Those ten miles away felt a massive heat wave immediately. As everyone watched in fascination, the explosion gave birth to a bright mass that seemed to grow out of the ground. From this materialized a column that rose into the dark clouds. Schreiber watched in a mixture of horror and fascination as this mushroomed in a mixture of spectral colors. The clouds were tinged with red initially but turned an eerie purple as the cloud evolved.

Slowly, the scientists recovered from the shock of what they had done. Schreiber watched as Kistiakowsky slapped Oppenheimer on the back. "You owe me ten dollars," he shouted regarding a bet the two had made on the bomb's power.

"You'll have to wait. My wallet is empty."

Schreiber knew the ride back would be an anti-climax. He was absorbed deep in thought. German patriot that he was, the recent test had been sobering and was deeply disturbing. Thank God the Americans never got a chance to use this on Germany. Did he really want to carry out his orders and steal the bomb and then detonate it if ordered? But who was giving the orders? Himmler and Hitler were dead. Was someone still operating underground who could guide him?

When he got back to Los Alamos, he pulled the radio operator aside. "Contact home. I want to know if we still are to proceed."

"Yes, Major. What do you think they will say?"

"I hope they cancel this mission, but we'll see what they say."

"If no one replies?"

"We'll worry about it then. After all, the Mexican border is only a few miles from here."

Monday night, a former SD Rottenfuehrer set at a transmitter flanked by an army sergeant and first lieutenant in intelligence. They were trying to help track down any rogue agents or shut them down. The officer, Paul Chambers, was anxious to prove himself as he had missed most of the war. He watched as the former SD man received and transmitted messages back.

Most traffic evaporated at the end of hostilities. Chambers had been instructed on the basics of Operation Gotterdammerung. Mainly, he was to transmit the word Tag back to cancel it. However, the OSS officer had mentioned that nacht would mean for the group to continue.

The rottenfuehrer began receiving a message. "It's regarding Gotterdammerung," he said.

"Finally," the sergeant commented. "Now we can close this one out."

Chambers remained silent and then spoke, "Transmit nacht."

"But, sir! The orders are."

"Sergeant, I am an officer, and I can make decisions on my own. If there are some rogue Germans still operating, don't you think that we should try to catch them?"

"We can't make that call."

"You can't. I can." Turning to the German, he ordered, "Transmit nacht."

The former SD man trembled as he typed out a reply. He had seen things during the war, heard screams during interrogations and had survived bombing raids. However, he had never feared for his life as much as he did now after hearing the exchange between the two Americans. He knew how dangerous it had been in the years before to be an unwanted witness.

On Thursday, Major Parker walked into Donavan's office. The

general looked up and by the look on Parker's face knew something was bad wrong.

"What is it, Parker?"

"Snafu. Shouldn't have happened. Schreiber transmitted back Monday after the bomb test."

"So he's still out there."

"Apparently, sir. Anyway, the intelligence officer who received the message got ambitious and decided he knew more about the situation than we did. He gave Schreiber the code word to go ahead. We just found out today. His commanding officer was out on leave and didn't find out until today."

Donavan barely controlled his anger. "So we gave him the green light to go ahead. It means he's inside or he's got a good source inside the project. I suspect a source. When Bennett calls in again, I want to speak to him. Schreiber appears to be better than we ever thought. Where is he anyway?"

"Headed to Los Alamos."

"When he calls in, tell him to speed it up as well. Also have someone get to Skorzeny. I want a letter from him canceling Gotterdammerung."

The day after the explosion, Schreiber met with Dietz, Kohlman, and his NCOs. "Well, there is no doubt now. The Americans were successful. In addition, our contacts with the Fatherland have told us to proceed. The bomb they call Little Boy has already been shipped off. The Fat Man is on its way. There are parts to a second Fat Man being readied for shipment. There are no other bombs ready. The question is what we do with the bomb if we get it. There are no large cities nearby to threaten. If we make off, we could be easily isolated."

"Perhaps we should see if we can get it." Dietz spoke slowly but carefully. "They do have a tight security. Obviously, we are not going to take this through the fences as big as this thing is and then reassemble it at our leisure. Once we get the bomb, we need to be able to move it fast."

"Are there any planes nearby to transport something this big?"

"Not here. There is at Wendover, Utah. They have a squadron there dedicated to delivering these bombs."

"If we took a bomb, we need to get it there. Better yet we need orders. This might work." Schreiber felt that he finally had his answers.

"We need Wehring's help."

"You handle that. You seem to be good at that."

The following day, Wehring arrived in Santa Fe. Schreiber and Dietz met him that afternoon. Wehring showed no emotion as he listened to the two men recount the previous day's events. Wehring nodded perceptively as he listened.

"I'll have a little talk with the squealer. You had better hold fast. The first two bombs are out of your grasp. The third bomb will not be ready for two weeks. So any orders to move it will have to wait until then. Oh, this came for you." Wehring handed a sealed envelope to Dietz.

Dietz opened the envelope. He kept the contents to himself. He recognized the familiar handwriting with notes in the margins. There was no signature, but Dietz didn't need one. He knew the handwriting only too well. It gave him his orders, and that was all that he needed. He folded the paper and placed it in his pocket.

As they walked alone, Wehring pulled Schreiber over. "Your friend has orders to use the bomb. I opened the letter and resealed it. Hopefully, he doesn't catch on."

"Who gave the order?" Schreiber bristled.

"Unsigned. But you can bet Dietz knows whom. Did you see his face? And he didn't throw the letter away. Remember my previous admonition."

"I will. However, I will still get the bomb in an attempt to ease the conditions of surrender. If we can get it on a plane, I need a place to land it. Some of Becker's men need to find a place to land it on the east coast."

"That may be difficult on short notice."

"Just have them find some smooth ground. Tell Becker the bomb's weight is about 4,500 kilograms."

"That's a big bomb."

"After he finds a spot, have him meet us here, and then we'll worry about flying this thing out."

In Nuremburg, an OSS officer visited Skorzeny in his cell. "We need to talk."

"What about? I talked to your boss a few weeks ago."

"One of our people gave Schreiber the green light to carry out Gotterdammerrung."

"You're kidding."

"Do I sound like it?"

"No. So what do you want?"

"To stop it."

"How?"

"Write out an order to Schreiber to stop."

"Is that all?"

"That's all."

Within minutes, Skorzeny wrote an order ordering Schreiber to stop trying to obtain the bomb. The OSS officer also made sure that a surprised Doenitz put his signature on the document without explaining the meaning behind it.

Bennett arrived at Los Alamos two days after the bomb was exploded. He and Crawford were coolly received. "There are no irregularities here. The bomb went off without a hitch. The other two bombs are already on their way to the Pacific." The head of security was in no mood to tell these two marines anything even with their clearance.

"Are there any other bombs?"

"Yes, there are two, but those were taken out of here before the test."

"Where did the bombs go to from here?"

"Not that it's any of your business, but it doesn't make any difference. The bomb parts were flown out to San Francisco. Most of the parts are either on some God–forsaken island or on a ship in the middle of the Pacific."

"Anything else unusual? New faces?"

"Just the men who brought the uranium from Oak Ridge. And if they hadn't done that, we still might be twiddling our thumbs because of delays."

"Where are they now?"

"Still doing guard duty as required. And they are very good at it."

"Could I speak with their commander?"

"Okay, but watch your step. You're not part of the project, so you don't need to need to know anything. This is a courtesy."

"I'll keep that in mind."

The captain made a phone call. Schreiber arrived shortly.

"Captain Ford, meet Major Bennett of the OSS and marines."

"Good morning, Major. How can I be of help?"

"I want to ask you some questions. How long have you been with this project?"

"Since the first part of June."

"I see you have some campaign ribbons from Europe. Did you see much action?"

Schreiber wondered if he was being baited. Were the Americans onto him? "What a military policeman usually does, breaking up fights in bars, escorting prisoners, and so on. The Bulge was really a challenge with the confusion with the Germans wearing our uniforms."

"Do you speak German?"

"No."

Bennett looked at the man's face. *Was this the man?* he wondered. Too bad there was no picture. Was this a wild goose chase? Donavan was sure the man was loose.

"You didn't offer to take the bomb on to San Francisco?"

The head of security became aggravated. "That was not even a consideration. Plans had already been made for the transfer of the bombs, and there are none here now. Do you have anything of substance to ask?" These two jarheads didn't need to know about the other bomb that was being assembled here at Los Alamos.

"No, I think that will do it."

"Good, if you have any other questions, you can go to San Francisco. Everything is fine here."

"We're on our way now."

As Bennett and Crawford left, Bennett asked, "Is he the one you saw at Indian Head?"

"That's the one. What do you think?"

"If Ford really is Schreiber, he's one cool customer. Trouble is if he's supposed to steal a bomb, why is he still here and not in San Francisco?"

"Doesn't make sense does it, sir? You have to admit that he looks like a marine in army uniform."

"You do have a point. But does it mean anything? We'll call Donavan. Have him check on this, Captain Ford. We better get to San Francisco and make sure that we haven't been fooled."

"As long as we get our whiskey tonight."

"You certainly have your priorities straight, don't you?"

Meanwhile, Schreiber chatted with the head of security. "What was that all about?"

"The OSS sticking its nose where it doesn't belong. Imagine them sending a damn jarhead on top of everything else. Lonsdale will have a fit when he gets back from Europe."

"The sooner the better."

"You got that right. Don't worry about this marine snoop."

"I noticed you didn't mention the third bomb we're making."

"It's none of his damned business. In fact, you don't tell him anything if you see him again."

Schreiber smiled inside. However, he would need to discuss this with Dietz later. If only they had reliable information from home.

As expected, Bennett found nothing unusual in San Francisco about the loading of the bomb parts. There had been no evidence of sabotage or attempts to tamper with the bomb parts. Security had been tight.

"I think we have been had," Crawford remarked to Bennett as they left the San Francisco Naval Base during the first part of August. "Everything seems to be in order."

"That's the only problem. These guys were good about laying low until the right time. I wonder if that is what is going on?"

"Something should have happened by now."

"Perhaps they just didn't get a chance. I won't complain if that was the case."

On August 6th, a B-29 named the Enola Gay took off with the bomb called Little Boy aboard. The plane arrived over Hiroshima at around 0800. A bombing course was set, and then the bomb was dropped. At 0816, Little Boy exploded at 1900 feet above the city. The events of July 16th were repeated except that humans were now unwilling participants. Thousands were instantly reduced to ash. They were the lucky ones. Countless others were badly burned to varying degrees. Many were would suffer lingering deaths.

Schreiber read the accounts of the bombing as soon as it hit the newspapers. So they did it. They actually dropped the damn thing. A shudder ran through him as he thought of the results should he get a bomb and have to use it.

August 9th would see another atomic bomb being dropped. Fat Man was loaded aboard a B-29 named Bock's Car and was delivered to Nagasaki. Another blinding flash signaled the end of tens of thousands of Japanese as the city disappeared in a mushroom cloud.

Also on this day, General Groves informed General Marshal that he had gained time in the manufacturing process and would be able to send a core and initiator to Tinian the following week. As soon as he confirmed the third bomb was nearly ready, Schreiber devised his plan. Since the next bomb was a Fat Man, safety was not as big a concern as Little Boy was more temperamental. Fat Man was more forgiving. If they could get Fat Man aboard a plane, then they could fly it away for safekeeping.

On August 9th, an urgent call was received at Los Alamos that another bomb was needed in the Pacific. The military wanted to keep the tempo up. Meanwhile, some questioned the wisdom of putting any bomb parts aboard ship after the fate of the USS *Indianapolis*. Schreiber mentioned taking the bomb to Wendover as they had planes to fly a whole bomb. Here planes dropped 10,000-pound pumpkins as the fake bombs were called. Pits had been dug along the runway to allow for the loading of the practice bombs. Schreiber pointed out that by taking the whole bomb to Wendover a lot of problems would be solved. The bomb stayed together and if flown out would negate the problems of ocean travel. Since it was Fat Man they would be delivering, there was less worry about an accidental explosion.

On Friday, August 12th, Secretary of War Stimson had decided he wanted no more bombs dropped. Truman wanted to continue, as he was concerned about the fate of countless American soldiers. That afternoon, he had second thoughts. After meeting with his cabinet later that day, the decision was made to prosecute the war at the current pace, but no further use of the bomb was planned.

At Los Alamos, a mild epidemic of dysentery broke out. Several of the security was hit by the infection. While Dietz said nothing about this turn of events, the look on his ace told everything. The evening of the eleventh, Schreiber cornered Dietz. "Tomorrow is probably now or never. While the guards are down, they will have to send us. We just need orders to get it to Wendover."

"Yes, and before the Americans go all out in launching an atomic campaign against Japan. Otherwise, there won't be any bombs to steal."

"Plus, if we can get the bomb out tomorrow, no one is likely to suspect anything until Monday. Remember how Hitler liked to strike on weekends. Plus, the Americans think they have everything under control now."

"Going now would be the best time. I'll see if the squealer can't oblige us one more time. Have you thought about just driving off with the damned thing instead of going to Wendover?"

"Quicker delivery to where ever we want to threaten. Anywhere else they could easily isolate us. Remember our trip out here. If we blow up Oklahoma City or Little Rock or Amarillo, who'll ever hear of it or care."

"Good point. Perhaps we ought to pick a target so that we can place the bomb nearby. Otherwise, we'll have the FBI down our backs in no time."

"Where do you suggest?"

"Why not Washington. It's the capitol, and we can land the plane in Virginia and transport the bomb from there for future use if need be. Becker should be able to find a suitable landing strip somewhere in the area."

Schreiber thought about that. "Sounds reasonable. Just get us some orders."

On the evening of August 12th, orders from the War Department arrived at Los Alamos for the second Fat Man to be delivered to Wendover as quickly as possible. The desire was for the bomb to be sent to Tinian as quickly as possible.

The head of security swiftly summoned Schreiber. "We need the second Fat Man in Wendover as soon as possible. They want to have it ready to fly as quickly as possible if the Japs don't surrender. You've shown that you can move fast, and since so many of my men are ill, I need you to be in charge of the convoy."

"This is quite unexpected."

"Just get the bomb to Wendover."

At 1700, Schreiber led his convoy through the main gate, with the second Fat Man loaded on a truck and covered. They paused briefly to pick up Becker and members of his crew. He headed the convoy north into Colorado and then toward Salt Lake City. They saw little of their surroundings as they traveled much of the night. They reached Salt Lake City at midday. The wide streets made travel easy. Their route took them past the gray gothic Mormon temple and the neighboring tabernacle. A few made remarks about blowing up such a forbidding structure. Schreiber reminded them they had more important things to do than improving the architecture of western America.

On leaving Salt Lake City, north of their route was the Great Salt Lake. The terrain was remarkably flat until the neared the border between Utah and Nevada. Finally, some signs appeared announcing the presence of Wendover. They found the town. As they proceeded to the entrance of the base, Schreiber noticed a woman with a young girl in tow. As he thought about the child's innocence, he had second thoughts about the bomb. After they left the main road, Schreiber realized just how isolated the area was. The total population was nearly twenty thousand, although the local civilian population was much smaller.

They entered the airbase without incident. They noticed the security was extremely tight on Wendover. The security under Tibbetts had been oppressive. Letters had been opened and two officers who had made indiscreet remarks were shipped off to Alaska for the war's duration. After Tibbetts had flown out to Tinian to pilot the Enola Gay, the men of the 509th composite group had relaxed.

Schreiber's men used Sunday to get familiar with the base. He visited the base commander who was unaware of Schreiber's mission. Schreiber used the code word silver plate to confirm the importance of his mission.

"I'll have to detail someone to fly the plane tomorrow. This is most unusual. But I see your credentials are impeccable. Have your men guard the plane."

"Those were my plans."

Afterward, he approached Dietz. "They plan to have a pilot ready in the morning. In the meantime, we provide security."

"What about Becker?"

"Let's let their pilot get this thing off the ground. Becker's good, but I would hate to crash at this stage of the game. Have the men assemble the bomb except for the detonators."

"I believe the Americans are fixing to have a big surprise."

"Let's hope so."

Bennett and Crawford were kicking up their heels in San Francisco Saturday after being through what they considered an exercise in futility. Bennett made one last call to check in with Donavan. "This seems to be a waste of time. Surely you have something better for me to do."

"One last thing for you to check, and we'll call it quits and assume Schreiber's headed to Mexico. Check out Wendover Air Base in Utah. There is supposed to be a bomb delivered there this weekend."

"I thought there were only two. At least that's what they told me at Los Alamos."

"Probably didn't like you snooping around. Anyway, check it out. I'll call the base commander and Groves again, although that may stir up a storm. If you need anything from the commander there, use the word silver plate. It's a very special word, if you know what I mean."

"Where to now, sir?"

"Some shithole called Wendover in Utah."

"I almost wish we were back in the Philippines."

"I know, gunny, I know."

Bennett and Crawford arrived early Monday morning. As they entered, they noticed a B-29 backing up over a pit. Several MPs formed a security perimeter around it. *There it is*, Bennett thought to himself. *We'll wrap this up in a hurry.* He went in to talk to the base commander, Colonel Townsbridge.

"This is most unusual, Major Bennett. What in the hell is an OSS officer and a marine at that nosing around this base asking questions about the bomb?"

"I've been wondering the same thing myself, sir." Bennett tried to gently defuse the situation. "General Donavan has expressed some concern about possible irregularities that may have occurred inside the Manhattan Project."

"Then why in the hell isn't he working with Tibbetts and Lonsdale on this instead of hiring his own private eye?"

"It involves renegade Germans who may have tried to penetrate the program."

"Oh, give me a break, Major."

An aide walked in. "Major Bennett, this just arrived for you."

An envelope marked top secret was handed to him. Bennett handed it to Crawford with the remark, "Go ahead and open it."

Bennett and Colonel Townsbridge continued their conversation, while Crawford struggled with the envelope. "I see you trust your aide here."

"We went through a lot in the Philippines."

Crawford finally opened the envelope. He pulled out a photograph and a short letter. He exclaimed "Jesus fucking Christ."

"What is it?" Bennett asked.

"You'll see for yourself." He handed the sensitive material to Bennett with trembling hands.

"Gentlemen, just what in the hell is going on?" Townsbridge demanded.

Bennett looked at the letter from Donovan. He mumbled the words, "We finally located a photograph of Schreiber. Also a signed order from Skorzeny telling him to cancel the operation." Bennett looked at the photo. It was good quality picture from the waist up. It showed him with all of his medals. There was no mistaking the face. Schreiber and Ford were the same. "Did the man who delivered the bomb go by the name of Captain Ford?"

"Yes, as a matter of fact, yes. Now are you ready to explain some things to me or not?"

Bennett handed him the letter and photograph. "Take a good look."

Townsbridge took the documents and went pale. "My god, is this true?"

"I'm afraid so. I thought I had been chasing a ghost for a while. That is until I got this."

"We can't let him leave," Townsbridge blurted out.

"Have many of your men have seen ground combat?"

"None," Townsbridge meekly admitted.

"How many people in the area on and off base?"

"Twenty thousand. Twenty-two at most."

"So if they blow the bomb here, they would kill off all those people."

"Also these B-29s are the only ones equipped to deliver atomic bombs. If they wipe this base out, then we don't have any nuclear capabilities. Except for a few planes at Tinian, these are the only B-29s that can carry an atomic bomb."

"Where are they supposed to be going?"

"Eventually, Tinian. What do you have in mind, Major?"

"Colonel, to be blunt, those army troops there around the plane are seasoned German soldiers. If your men take them on, they'll just have a good target practice. If they explode the bomb here, then you know what'll happen. If we let them take off and I'm on it, maybe I can stop them with this order. At least I hopefully keep anything catastrophic from happening. Crawford, get on the phone with Donavan. Colonel, could you cut me some orders for Tinian?"

"Major you're the greatest hero or the biggest fool I have ever met."

"Possibly both, Colonel. Can you get me those orders?"

Schreiber was with his men as they prepared to load the huge bomb. The detonators had been kept separate for safety. The huge plane had been backed into position over the deep pit that held the bomb. When the plane was in place, the bomb bay doors swung open. Then platform the bomb rested on was elevated until the bomb fit inside the modified bomb bay. Finally, it was secured and the bomb bay closed.

Schreiber motioned for his men to leave except for those to accompany him. At this time, a jeep arrived. Colonel Townsbridge arrived with Bennett. "Here we are. Captain Ford, Major Bennett will be aboard for the flight. He has special orders to fly to Tinian immediately. As you are eventually headed that way, he needs to be aboard."

Schreiber and Dietz looked at each other. "Not my concern. I'm not flying this thing"

"Let's get your bags, Major," Colonel Townsbridge said trying to be helpful. "My god, you were right," he whispered to Bennett."

"I wish I wasn't, Colonel."

"Over here, Major." One of Schreiber's men motioned for him to bring his bags to the ladder that led into the plane. A pair of hands reached down and grabbed his bag. Bennett then entered into the cabin and seated himself. A genuine Army Air Corps pilot was in the pilot's seat. Soon Schreiber climbed in with Becker and Dietz behind him. Schreiber's explosive expert Kohlman was last. Kohlman had always been in the background, but soon he would have an important role to play. Finally, the cabin was full. Bennett sat on the left side in the seat at the rear of the cockpit.

The army pilot was surprised when Becker sat down next to him. He called the control tower for verification. The pilot was surprised when he was told there was no problem. *Good for Colonel Townsbridge,* Bennett thought. *I bet he's about to shit in his pants though and with good reason. If this goes wrong, he'll be the one alive getting his ass chewed. I'll be well.* Bennett closed his eyes on that thought.

When the pilot received permission to take off, he instructed the crewman in the tail gunner's position to switch the battery on so he could start the engines. With a cough and puff of smoke, the big bird came to life as the other three engines kicked on. Soon all four engines were alive.

"This is the part that makes me nervous. This is a lot of weight even for this plane." The B-29 lumbered down the runway gathering speed. The pilot was only too well aware of how many planes had crashed on takeoff. Landing was a lot easier. However, landing was going to be something else he realized.

"Pull back," he yelled at Becker. "I want to clear the runway and not end up in the scrap heap."

With great effort he lifted the B-29 in the air. "Set a course for." He never completed the sentence. One of Schreiber's men was behind the pilot. Then he walked back. The pilot was slumped over. The plane was heading east now with no indication that it would turn. Bennett pretended not to notice that anything was wrong. He would wait before opening the can of worms.

"Odd that a marine major would be out in the desert." Schreiber opened the conversation.

"The OSS doesn't necessarily send you to where you think your skills are most useful."

A warning bell went off in Schreiber's head. The OSS was roughly similar to Skorzeny's organization. Was this fixing to be commando versus commando? "Nice array of ribbons you have there, Major. Were you mainly in the Pacific?"

"All of it. Stayed in the Philippines but never surrendered. After witnessing a Jap atrocity when we were going to an appointed surrender site made me change my mind. Not quite like dealing with the Germans where there was at least a Geneva Convention."

"At least while there was a war on."

"Not a bad bunch of medals yourself."

Schreiber laughed. "Just some campaign ribbons. Means we were there."

"I was talking about your regular uniform." Bennett handed him the photograph and orders from Skorzeny.

Schreiber cautiously took the photograph. All eyes were on him. He couldn't help but smile when he saw the picture of himself in Waffen-SS uniform. He read the note signed by Skorzeny and Doenitz. He leaned back and sighed. "You're good, Bennett. Damned good."

"I don't know about that. After all, you did get the bomb. Maikop wasn't bad either."

Schreiber smiled again at the mention of the exploit. "I wasn't in charge then, just a sergeant."

"But the baron was a good teacher wasn't he. Still one hell of an exploit."

"It was indeed."

"What's going on?" Dietz asked.

"We've been found out." Schreiber was matter of fact. "This gentleman has obviously been tracking us."

"I should have killed you at Los Alamos," Dietz snarled.

"Then you would have given yourself away. I didn't know until this morning when I got your picture that I knew for sure. If you had killed me, then intelligence would have been swarming all over the place. You probably would not have gotten the bomb."

"By the way, Major Bennett, let me introduce you to Major Dietz of the SD."

"No one said anything about you. What's your role watchdog?"

"I think it's obvious that Schreiber is quite capable without me. I possess certain matters of intelligence that helped make things go smoother."

"The SD. Was that like the Gestapo?"

Dietz bristled at that. "No. We were smarter. We did foreign intelligence and the like. The Gestapo was like your FBI."

"Does that include ineffectiveness?"

Dietz smiled at that. "Perhaps it was. We did refer to the FBI as the American Gestapo, perhaps with good reason."

Schreiber handed Dietz the letter with Skorzeny's and Doenitz's signatures. "It's over, Konrad. Straight from the top."

Dietz looked at the document. "No, it's not."

"We've got our orders."

"And I have mine.' Dietz pulled out his Walther P38. "The mission continues."

"For God's sake, Konrad?"

"I have a little piece of paper for you." Dietz handled Schreiber a piece of paper that he had received through Wehring.

Schreiber read the letter. The letter was unsigned. However, the there were notes in the margins and other distinctive traits. Dietz was instructed to carry out the mission at all costs and explode the bomb if there was danger of being caught or losing the bomb. He would disregard all other instructions from others.

"Pretty potent letter. Too bad they didn't' have the guts to sign it," Schreiber commented.

"Didn't have too. He knew I would recognize the handwriting with those notes all over."

"Who's he."

"Himmler."

"He's dead."

"Rubbish, probably his double. He had one, you know. The man was officially executed months ago, but I knew better. Himmler probably used the same threat on him that he did me."

"What's that, firing squad?"

"No, my family"

"How's that?"

"Himmler felt that families of traitors should be held responsible.

If someone failed, then one's family might be executed. In my case, my wife is half-Jewish."

"Skorzeny warned me you might have a secret agenda. But this is beyond belief."

"Is it? How long have you been in the SS? Two or three years. You didn't get your hands dirty with shooting hostages?" Too bad. There is little room for failure."

Bennett spoke up. "It's not too late to turn back now. As long as you don't explode the bomb, no one will ever know this happened."

"How chivalrous, Major Bennett. However, there is no honorable surrender for Himmler or me. For me it's my wife. For Himmler he's an out and out scoundrel. I am curious how you found out about us? Nothing was ever written down about this."

"Yes." Schreiber agreed. He seemed to be in a type of inner turmoil.

"Skorzeny told us. He never felt this mission of yours would get off the ground. He was surprised to learn that you left the country."

"We also got a message to proceed twice after hostilities were over."

Bennett groaned at that. "We know. One of our ambitious lieutenants decided that we really needed to catch you and gave you the word to proceed. I imagine he's cleaning latrines now."

Dietz burst out laughing at that. "We just thought the FBI was incompetent. Sounds like the OSS was as well."

"Just our military intelligence people. So you were blackmailed into doing this?" Bennett directed his remarks at Dietz.

"In a way. I was willing in others."

"I heard some of the rumors about you," Schreiber said. "Like the king of Bulgaria, the duke of Windsor, and a few others."

"All on orders. Some of it is buried deeper than the bodies, I'll admit. However, I've got plenty of blood on my hands. It looks like there will be a lot more."

"It doesn't have to be this way." Bennett thought desperately of what to say.

"I see no other way. My instructions are clear. I might as well go out with a bang. Oh, by the way, keep your hands where I can see them."

Meanwhile, Schreiber gritted his teeth in frustration of coming this far through a series of errors and goof ups on both sides of the game.

As Schreiber's men made their way back to Salt Lake City they ran into a roadblock. As they slowed down, men raised up alongside the road. Obviously, they had run into an ambush.

"Get out with your hands up. We're not fooling around. Anything funny and we open fire. Understood?"

Without a sound, the men gave up. Because of the sensitivity of the situation, they were driven to Fort Douglas in Salt Lake City in covered trucks. A cellblock was made off limits to restrict access to them until a decision was made about their future.

Meanwhile, Donavan called Groves about the developing situation. Groves was stunned by the bad news. "I didn't think this was even possible. It would have been nice if I had been called last night, for example."

"If I had known last night, I would have called. Meanwhile, we need to know where he's going. He disappeared once he crossed the Rockies." We'll look for him. We need to get some planes in the air. What happens if we shoot him down? Could be one hell of an explosion."

"Don't shoot it down over a populated city. The big question is whether they've been able to arm the thing."

"Main thing is finding them. Is there anything else?"

"Battery on the thing has to be recharged periodically, or it won't explode."

"How long can it go without charging?"

"No longer than seventy-two hours."

"I'll keep you informed."

Groves slammed the phone down in disgust. Now the United States was facing the prospect of having Hiroshima and Nagasaki repeated on its own soil. He hadn't heeded Donavan's warning. True Lonsdale was in charge of security and had been out of the country.

Now the enemy had a bomb and a B-29 to carry it in. What would they do?

Meanwhile at thirty-five thousand feet, the men aboard the renegade B-29 traveled in relative comfort. The pressurized cabin allowed the men to do their duties without wearing pressurized suits. Bennett looked his situation over. He was in the radar operator's seat at the left and rear of the cabin. Schreiber was in the flight engineer's seat, while Dietz was in the radio operator's seat on the right. Above Bennett's head to the right was a pistol flare.

"Ready for a ring-side seat, Major Bennett?" Dietz was cold.

"You're mad."

"Probably so, but I don't have a choice. And do keep your hands where I can see them."

"Washington's in sight," Becker called out.

"Tell Kohlman to get the bomb ready."

On the ground, Donavan paced relentlessly until he got report of the B-29. Parker came rushing into his office to give him an update. "Sir, I think we've located them."

"Where are they?"

"About thirty minutes from here."

"Oh my god. Call the president. Have the air raid sirens sounded."

"That probably won't work. People will think it's a drill the way the war is going."

"Sound them anyway." Donavan felt sick. Even if people had time to evacuate, it would not be enough. Then it dawned on him: seventy-two hours. What the Germans wanted to do was blackmail them. "Get me connected to the B-29."

A few minutes later, Bennett heard a familiar voice calling for him. "Answer it carefully," Dietz ordered. "I'll be watching."

Becker handed him earplugs. "Bennett here."

"How are things at thirty-five thousand feet?"

"Pretty comfortable, General. You should fly one of these. Pressurized. No need to suit up. Quite nice even with my coat. If only I didn't have a major of the SD pointing a gun at me right now, I would be perfectly happy."

"SD you said?"

"An unexpected twist."

"There is some good news. Find out how long it's been since they charged the battery?"

"On what?"

"The bomb. If it hasn't been charged in seventy-two hours, it can't detonate."

"That's enough," Dietz said. "What was that you were talking about anyway?"

"Some matters of nuclear physics that neither of us quite understand."

"Sit down then." Dietz looked back into the bomb bay area. "Is the bomb about ready?"

"Jawohl, detonators are in place." Kohlman remained out of sight.

"How close are we?

"Five minutes."

"Get up to the bombardier's seat," Dietz ordered one of Becker's crew.

The man went to the station and peered down the Norden bombsight. "I've never done this before."

"There's always a first time," Dietz sneered.

"Is the battery charged?" Bennett asked.

"What battery?" Kohlman asked.

"Never mind."

"What battery?" Dietz asked suspiciously.

"You'll find out soon enough, you Aryan superman."

Dietz gripped his pistol. "I've shot people for less."

"Almost there," Kohlman called out.

"Drop it."

"I have to open the bomb doors."

"Open them!"

"Bomb bay doors open."

"Drop it."

Kohlman pulled the release for the bomb. The plane jumped up several feet because of the lightened load. Dietz was thrown off balance. Becker pulled the plane up to the left to minimize the sudden weight loss. Bennett used the opportunity to grab the flare gun. Mustangs closing in on the bomber reported a large object falling from the plane. Donavan overheard the report. He stepped outside.

"Shouldn't we be heading to the bomb shelter?" Parker asked.

"If it explodes, it means I have failed miserably. Better to die doing my duty than to live with this. Parker, you go on to the shelter."

Donavan looked up at the sky. The B-29 was barely visible like a small silvery dot in the sky. Fighters were catching up to him. Donavan looked at his watch and after several seconds went back inside.

"Parker, organize a search for the bomb."

Aboard the B-29, everyone waited for the explosion.

"What did you tell everyone about your plans, Dietz?" Bennett asked.

"Only what they needed to know."

"Or what you wanted them to know."

"Same difference. They were expendable."

"Was that the philosophy of the SD?"

"Somewhat. If something needed to be done, we got it done no matter what."

"What about the crew now?"

"They're still expendable. Don't look so shocked, Schreiber. You Brandenburgers didn't exactly have lily-white hands either. As I recall, some of your combat training involved the use of concentration camp inmates. Several of you were detached to the SD at one time or another by Admiral Canaris to assist us in carrying out the dirty work."

Schreiber sucked in his breath. He knew Dietz was cold-blooded but not this cold-blooded. He regretted not getting rid of Dietz sooner. If the bomb went off and the crew survived, then it would be only if Dietz wanted them to for now. Schreiber wondered if they would still be loose ends. *I need to get my men through this,* he thought. *Then by God there is a score to settle.*

"Fighters closing in," Becker called out.

"That's one mistake that was made a long time ago. Two-ton Herman should have been removed from head of the Luftwaffe after Dunkirk. We might be flying home now instead looking for a place to land. At least we got rid of Canaris." Dietz was obviously feeling good.

"Don't forget Himmler," Schreiber retorted. "He was also removed for treason."

"Even the Fuchrer made some mistakes. It's true. However, I don't have Himmler in my sights now, do I? Should be showtime any second now." Dietz glanced at his watch.

Kohlman had delayed dropping the bomb as he was inexperienced and normally was not a bombardier. He had aimed the bomb for the middle of the Potomac. Down below in the middle of the river, Leroy Johnson was enjoying an afternoon fishing. Things had been rather peaceful, and the fish were slow to bite. Suddenly, a tremendous splash of water drenched him and swamped the boat with water. He struggled to keep the boat afloat and finally upended it to have something to hang on to. He looked up into the sky to see where the object had come from. The afternoon remained as peaceful as before. Only the drone of faraway planes hinted at the cause of his current predicament.

"It hasn't exploded!" Dietz exclaimed.

"And it won't." Kohlman was talking. "The battery wasn't charged. In addition, I reversed the male and female leads for safety. Two reasons it won't explode."

"You little shrimp." Dietz aimed the pistol at Kohlman. A wrench flew through the air and hit Dietz's wrist. The rear gunner had climbed through the tunnel, saw what was going on, went back for a wrench, came back through the tunnel, and disrupted Dietz's plans. Meanwhile, Bennett pulled out the flare gun and aimed it at Dietz.

"I've had enough fun for one day. Dietz, take a good look. This may not kill you when I fire, but you know that you will want to be dead when I get through with you. Understood?"

Dietz bitterly nodded his head in assent.

"Good boy. Becker, tell the controller you want directions for landing. Oh, and make sure the mustangs know we're surrendering before they blow us out of the sky."

"Well done, Bennett. This would have been a Knights Cross for you in Germany."

"I'll take that as a compliment. By the way, Kohlman, why did you do what you did?"

"Major Schreiber was in charge no matter what. Dietz was just excess baggage as far as I was concerned."

"That's the best summation I heard in a long time. You would go far if not for this."

"I'm afraid the best we have to look forward to is a decent death by firing squad." Schreiber was numb.

"Perhaps. You do have some outs."

"Really, the electric chair instead."

"I'll talk to Donavan. There is a respect for fellow commandos, even those on the other side."

Becker was directed to an airfield outside Washington. The security was tight. Jeeps followed the plane as it taxied. The mustangs circled until the plane came to a stop. Schreiber and his men offered no resistance as they were led away. Dietz had a look of defiance on his face. Bennett felt exhausted from the mental strain. What he had just been through was catching up with him now. Bennett went to the officers' club and collapsed into a chair.

Donavan walked in thirty minutes later. "Well done, Major. I don't how you did it, but congratulations."

"None needed. The Germans didn't explode it themselves. One of their people set it so it wouldn't explode. Give him credit."

"Well, I want a full report later. I bet you could use a rest."

"I could use a drink first."

"I'll get that drink for you."

August 10, 1945, Konan, the province of Korea

Captain Minoru Yamagata watched as the scientists worked long hours to perfect the bomb. The device, genzai bakudan, might yet change the course of the war. Trucks rumbled in and out of the cave where he was in charge of security. Finally, the last of the bomb's components left the cave, and Yamagata went with the scientists to view the test. A small islet in the Sea of Japan was chosen as the test site. That morning a launch with the bomb left for the islet. Several small vessels and junks had been assembled. The scientists waited in anticipation as the launch reached the test site. A timer had been set to coincide with the sunrise. At that moment, a tremendous flash lit up the sky. The fireball was estimated to be one thousand yards in diameter.

Yamagata smiled inside as the fireball rose. Hiroshima and Nagasaki would be avenged. When the foreign devils landed on the beaches at Tokyo Bay, they would be in for a rude awakening as the deployed genzai bakudan vaporized the invading forces.

That was not to be. Yamagata's superior called him immediately after the test. "The Russians are advancing faster than we believed. We must destroy the remaining bombs. Then we will seal the cave."

Yamagata forced back the tears. They were so close. If only the Russians had not proven to be so treacherous, then the war might still be won. He went about his work methodically. He helped the scientists destroy important papers. Destructive devices were placed on the remaining bombs, and then the cave's entrance was blown up.

Hours later, he was with a convoy trying to evade the onrushing Soviets. Later in the afternoon, the small group of scientists and soldiers stopped briefly. Yamagata walked into the woods to relieve himself briefly. He heard foreign voices and a large commotion. He walked carefully through the woods and peaked through the foliage. To his horror, the Russians had arrived and surrounded the convoy. The Russians had moved faster than expected. With a sick feeling, he watched as the scientists were rounded up like cattle and marched into captivity.

Yamagata made his way along paths and side roads. Fortunately, it was getting dark, and he was able to make good his escape. He avoided the main roads and the long Russian columns. After five days, he entered the zone allocated to the Americans. He learned of the emperor's surrender decree and with a heavy heart turned himself in to the conquering Allies.

October 1945

Wild Bill Donavan had been having a difficult day. In fact, he had been having a difficult three months. He had hoped that things would settle down after the Japanese surrender and Schreiber's neutralization. President Truman had even signed a presidential order abolishing the OSS. A new organization, the Secret Service Unit had come into existence. Donavan's second in command Brigadier general John Macgruder had taken command of the new entity. As a favor Donavan was attempting a smooth transition. However, events in the world were contributing to an ongoing headache. The French had a full-scale insurrection in Indochina. Contributing to Donavan's difficulties, many of his OSS officers supported the Viet Minh under Ho Chi Minh. Donavan sympathized with his men since the local French bureaucracy had collaborated with the Japanese. Now the United States had decided to back the French, and experienced agents were being pulled from the area. It would take time to rebuild his organization there.

Other thoughts were on his mind when Major Parker walked in. "Have you come with some names for the replacements in Indochina?"

"Still working on it, sir."

"What about Schreiber?"

"Still in isolation. The best thing is if he could just vanish."

"I know. No one wants a trial. If that happened, then the public would be in an uproar. Secret executions are legal since they did this after the end of hostilities. However, tongues would still waggle and probably more so. With secret trial or secret executions, word still tends to get out. At least J. Edgar still doesn't have a clue about what happened. This could be useful since he has been on the defensive since Elizabeth Bentley's revelations."

"I gather we will save that for later and the fact that he never figured out Kohler was still Canaris's agent."

"Exactly."

Parker knew how much Donavan had been unsettled by Bentley's disclosures to the FBI. A NKVD agent for years, she had become disillusioned with the Communist ideology. Although her details were sensational, they were also true. As a courier, she knew who had been a supplier of information to the Soviets. She supplied the names of eighty people who had worked in the OSS, the War Department, the Commerce Department, and the Department of the Army. Several OSS officers were suspended and under investigation as result. Most galling to Donavan was the fact that Duncan Lee, his protégée from his New York law firm, had been in league with the NKVD. Donavan had acted swiftly, but Hoover had suggested that the FBI investigate the OSS. Fortunately, Donavan had many times urged that agents be used to penetrate the Soviet Union, but Roosevelt had declined the requests every time. After meeting with Truman and reminding him of these recommendations and mentioning Hoover's failure to unmask Kohler, the OSS was still abolished but the Secret Services Unit was formed out most of the OSS personnel.

"What about Korea, General?"

"You mean the reports about the Japanese bomb?"

"Yes, sir. The implications are big."

"I know they are."

Both men knew the stakes were high. Everyone thought that America was the only nuclear power and probably still was. However, the defection of Gousenko proved that the Soviet Union regarded the United States as its next enemy. The further discovery of certain atomic scientists passing on secrets to the NKVD had served to turn Donavan's world upside down. If the Japanese had developed the bomb and failed to destroy them, then Russia might actually have the winning hand if a showdown occurred now. The refusal of the Russians to return some of the B-29s that had landed in Siberia now took on a different light. The idea of the Russians dropping a dozen bombs on allied forces in Western Europe was a frightening possibility.

"That could be our biggest problem, and we don't have any agents inside the Russian lines. Nor do we have anyone qualified to penetrate the Soviet apparatus. What a nice combination to have on our plate. Schreiber, Indochina, and worse of all the Russians may have the bomb." Here he was the former head of the OSS and couldn't help General Macgruder because they weren't prepared.

"Help me out, Parker. I need some answers. Give me a solution, someone to do the job,"

For a minute, Parker drew a blank. Then his face lit up like a lightbulb. "I think I have an answer to all your problems." Parker leaned over Donavan's desk and whispered. "Schreiber's the answer."

"What? Schreiber?"

"Think about it, sir. He's perfect. His Russian is good. Remember the episode at Maikop. He's trained and has done this already to us. We could send him into northern Korea posing as NKVD. If he's captured, we could deny he even works for us. If you think about it, he's perfect in every way. If he doesn't want to cooperate, we can even draft him since he has dual American and German citizenship. He could also be useful later in Indochina as some of the Brandenburgers were trapped there after the surrender. Evidently, some of them have joined the French Foreign Legion. They could be a good source of information."

"So Schreiber goes to work for us like nothing happened. That may not make some people happy."

"Stage a bus accident and officially kill him off. Accidents happen all the time, don't they?"

"By God, I've underestimated you. It's crazy, but it's beautiful.

Everything. The pilot is good. Even Dietz could have his uses. I would take a harder line with him."

"Of course, sir."

"Do you think that he would work for us, especially knowing what we were doing to their POWs on the Rhine?"

"Schreiber's the linchpin. If we get him, the others will blindly follow him. If we have to, we can draft him. We've done it to other German POWs to fulfill their military obligations. Also, we might make use of General Gehlen while he's in the country."

"Have Schreiber fulfill his military obligations to the country. This is so absurd it's funny."

"I am serious."

"I know you are. And you are so right. If we use Schreiber, this will be perfect. It solves a lot of problems. It helps the story about the bomb parts being damaged on their way to Tinain. Schreiber could be used to give credence to the story. I'll have a talk with Gehlen. As I recall, he hates the Communists with a passion."

"I believe so."

"You know, this is a big relief. This decision is nothing short of Solomonic. We need to do something about the color of those oak leaves on your uniform. This sort of thing deserves to be rewarded."

Parker beamed. "Thank you, sir."

"Get everything arranged. We want Gehlen around when I talk to Schreiber. Let's do this within three days."

"You can count it being done, sir."

That night, Donavan slept the best sleep in three months. Although nothing was guaranteed, he now had a workable plan that had a good chance of success and not leave General Macgruder with an unmitigated mess.

Two days later, the cell to Schreiber's cell was thrown open. Parker was there to fetch Schreiber. Marines on the naval base were guarding him and his men. Schreiber didn't even know where they were.

"Major Schreiber, would you come with me?"

So this is it, Schreiber thought. *They're going to give us the bad news.* "Sorry, we respect you, but you're not entitled to even a trial. Orders from above." Parker was unusually jovial for someone leading another man to his doom.

One of the guards roughly manhandled Schreiber. He started to fight back when Parker intervened. "You will treat the man with respect, or you will lose your stripes and find yourself shoveling shit in the Philippines or whatever God-forsaken place I can find. If you think that because you're a marine and I'm army that I can't touch you, I assure you the SSU has no problem working around that."

The guard apologized. Schreiber wondered just what was going on. This was really the first time he had been mistreated by the marines. Still, why Parker's instant defense? There was more than just the courtesy accorded a defeated foe.

As they approached Donavan's office in the prison, Schreiber noticed Dietz being led away. Only now he was wearing an American uniform. Schreiber's men had been allowed the decency of wearing their national uniform again in prison. He even had been allowed to keep his insignia and decorations. Why was Dietz wearing an American uniform? Had he been a traitor all along?

Parker noticed Schreiber's look. "It's not what you think."

"What am I thinking?"

Parker ignored him and motioned him inside. "Major Schreiber, sir."

"Have a seat, Schreiber. Care for a drink, Major?" Donavan asked. Macgruder remained in the background.

Schreiber was suspicious. "If it's going to be my last one, yes.'

"That will be up to you. I suggest you take one. We may be here a while."

Parker closed the door and stood in front of it. *Why the hell is his face so aglow?* Schreiber wondered. *Is he a sadistic bastard?*

"Parker, are you still wearing your gold oak leaves?"

"Yes, sir, haven't had time to get them changed."

"Well, that can wait. Well, Schreiber, I wanted to meet you personally. Quite a record you have. One hell of an exploit. I doubt we have a group of men who could have cleared Maikop out like you did."

Schreiber went alive inside. While he expected some sort of condemnation or faint praise, the mention of Maikop made him instantly alert. If Donavan didn't have his attention initially, he did now. This was not going to be an ordinary conversation. "Sir, I had a good commander. Baron Foelkersam was an outstanding leader."

"Maybe he had some good men. Some of them are with you in this prison that are veterans of that adventure."

"Several are." Schreiber was confused. *What the hell was this all about? There was no malice in the man.*

"Your latest adventure has got to be one of the great exploits of the war. Trouble is no one will ever know about it. The trouble for you is you did it after the war was over. That puts you in a very precarious position, you know."

"I understood that before I took the assignment."

"You understand you have no protection under the Geneva Convention. However, standing you and your men up in front of a firing squad is not going to accomplish a lot, is it now?"

"Not from our viewpoint."

"You demonstrated that you're a man of considerable talent. Skorzeny feels you were his best man after losing that baron you mentioned. I feel executing you would be a waste of talent."

Here it comes, Schreiber thought. He had an idea where this was leading. *From the pan into the fire?* He understood he was being offered a way out. *Just what was the price?* he wondered. "It sounds like you're offering me a bargain."

"Yes, as a matter of fact, I am. I'm glad you're no fool, or I wouldn't waste much time with you. Colonel Parker made an interesting proposal to me the other day after reviewing the current world situation. Several more people have come to the conclusion that the Communists are not such nice people after all. I recommended under the previous president that we place some agents in Russia, and I got turned down. However, that good will was not reciprocated as you well know."

"I'm listening."

"What I need is a troubleshooter. Someone who knows these people we're dealing with. At the same time, we can deny any knowledge of that person if they're caught. You fit the bill."

"In other words, I'm expendable along with my men."

"To be blunt, yes, but I don't' send my people out to get killed just for the hell of it. If they go out, then there should be a good chance they can accomplish the mission and come back. You are too valuable to waste so keep that in mind. Keep in mind, I read your file. What you did in the Brandenburg Division was incredible. There are not many of you left in the world like that anywhere. I can't waste people like you."

"You must have something big in mind."

"As a matter of fact, yes." Donavan fingered a file with Top Secret written over it. "I am going to let you read something. Once you read it, there is no turning back. So are you with me or not?"

"If it will save the lives of my men, I accept."

Donavan looked at Parker, who breathed a sigh of relief while Macgruder appeared to be deep in thought. He handed the file to Schreiber. It described the results of interrogations of Japanese refugees from Korea. The inescapable conclusion was that Japan had detonated an atomic bomb. Several more, perhaps a dozen were buried in the cave. There was doubt about whether the Japanese actually destroyed the bombs since no one actually witnessed the bombs' destruction. The conclusion was that if the Soviets got hold of intact bombs, it would speed development of their own nuclear program and allow them to launch a nuclear surprise attack in Western Europe. No one had to say the results would be more catastrophic or just as shocking as Pearl Harbor had been.

"I don't know what to say. This is incredible."

"I know. I wish it were just a bad dream. But there is too much smoke here to be no fire. We need to know if those bombs were destroyed. If not, they need to be. Keep in mind the only place the Russians could really use those bombs now is in Western Europe, mainly in Germany. I personally do not like the idea of one million or more Americans being vaporized at once by Stalin. I don't think what you like the idea of that many Germans suffering the same fate either."

"Neither do I." A third man had entered the room. "You will be fighting for Germany still. That is the main thing."

"I believe you know of General Reinhard Gehlen. He commanded Foreign Armies East."

Schreiber figured there would be no end of surprises now. "I suspect you had something to do with my current situation."

"One of my agents did penetrate the Soviet High Command and provide the information that led to Operation Gotterdammerung. I'm glad things ended the way they did. No doubt you're confused but consider what General Donavan has offered you. No firing squad and a new start. Currently, we are trying to insert agents back into Russia. The Americans need our help since we have had considerable success in the past. We in turn need the American's help."

"I said I'd do it. I agree for the sake of my men. No more or no less and no apologies."

"I didn't expect anything less. You maybe relieved to learn that the conditions in the POW camps have improved. Some of us have had to work behind Eisenhower's back to do it. Some of us feel that we should be rearming your people, but we are in the minority still."

"I can't ask for more. Perhaps my mission resulted in some good after all."

"Perhaps," Gehlen responded. "Even though Germany is a conquered and occupied country, you will still be fighting for her. None of us want to see the Communists stronger. I myself was disaffected with Hitler and thought about joining Stauffenberg's plot. However, when he wanted to include Communists in his government, I said no as did a lot of other senior officers. Working with them was not and is still not an option."

"I have no qualms with that." Schreiber was breathing easier.

"Keep in mind there is still a war on. It is a war in the shadows now. There may be no shooting between armies but there is a war on. You are a vital part of it now." Gehlen put emphasis in his words.

Donavan spoke up. "I think that's enough for Major Schreiber to take in. Colonel Parker will take you back to your cell for now. He'll arrange better accommodations for you." Donavan then got up and shook hands with Schreiber. "Welcome to the SSU, Major Schreiber."

"Thank you, General." He didn't know what else to say.

"One other thing, Schreiber. I'm offering your men equivalent rank and pay. I think it's better than unemployment in Germany. And the bomb, it never ever happened, and you were never at Los Alamos."

"Understood."

As they left, Schreiber told Parker. "I guess I'm supposed to thank you for coming up with this harebrained plan that keeps me away from a firing squad."

"Not at all. Just doing my job like you did yours. You have to admit you're perfect for the job. I have to say good luck, though."

"I'm flattered. I knew war was crazy, but this is beyond belief."

Donavan and Gehlen continued to chat after Schreiber left. "The only bad thing about this now is that that bastard Himmler got away. Now with trouble with the Russians brewing, no one will give a rat's ass about him now that the British have declared him dead. And their own damn reports indicate that it was probably a double that committed suicide."

"There still may be a chance to get him. Too bad you didn't deal with him during the war."

"I know," Donavan continued. "Still to send men like Schreiber to do his real dirty work."

"This can be done quietly. You know he's gone underground."

"Yeah, probably living a life of luxury in a quiet villa with scarcely a concern now that he's officially dead."

"That will be the time to deal with him," Gehlen quietly replied.

"Perhaps you're right, General. Well, I think I've had enough for now. Good day, General Gehlen."

"Auf weidersehn, General Donavan.

Later that afternoon, Schreiber assembled his men. Parker was by him to prevent any action by the guards as much as anything else.

"Men, you have a choice. The Americans are having second thoughts about their Russian Allies. They need men to do what we have been doing for four years. The only ones they have are us." He knew his men. Although they showed no emotion, he knew they were perturbed inside. "As a result, the Americans want us to work for them. The past few events have never happened as far as they are concerned if we accept. Although I am tired of war, the Communists are enslaving our people in the east. Because of this, some of our former intelligence people are actively helping the Americans. They beg for your help. I will only take this offer for you, my family, and Germany. Only under these terms can I do this under a clear conscience and ask you to join me."

The men did not say a word at first. They quietly came up to shake hands or hug Schreiber. Some one muttered, "We knew you'll get us out." Soon they surrounded him and broke out cheering him. Every man agreed to join.

Parker then did something that surprised everyone. He saluted Schreiber. Schreiber in turn came to attention and gave Parker a proper military salute.

"Surprises never cease today."

"You may earn this and more before this is all over with."

Parker went back to Donavan, well pleased with himself. "They all agreed to sign up."

"All of them."

"Any hesitancy? Questions about anyone?"

"No. They all seem sincere. They do appear to hate the Communists."

"They may get to hate them a lot more and us as well."

"Well, you have made my day. Why don't you take tomorrow off? What you have done probably deserves more than one promotion, but I can only give you one now."

"One other thing, sir. Bennett wants to go back to the marines.

He's already turned a request in for transfer back. He's also made calls down to Quantico also."

"Can't say that I blame him. However, we could probably still use him."

"Particularly with Schreiber. You recall he's an old China hand."

"I see where you're going. I need to speak with him and Vandegrift."

Bennett walked into Donavan's office the following day. "You wished to see me, sir?"

"Sit down, Major. We need to talk."

"I guess you heard that I requested transfer back to the marines."

"Request denied."

"Sir?"

"We still need you here at the OSS. Read this." He tossed Bennett the file on the Japanese atomic bomb.

"This sounds crazy."

"I wish it was like the Schreiber thing. Unfortunately, there is good corroborating evidence. Worse still, we don't know for sure that the Japanese destroyed the bombs they made. They set destructive charges and then blew the cave. If the Russians find the bombs intact, it could help their nuclear program or give them nuclear superiority."

"That doesn't sound good."

"It's not. That's why I still need you."

"Sorry, but I don't speak Russian. I do speak some Chinese."

"Well, I realize that I did have someone else after all. I need you to be in charge. Read this." He handed him a summary on Maikop.

"Schreiber was there as I recall."

"Which is why he's perfect for this operation. He speaks Russian and has done this before. And if he gets caught, we can deny he's ours."

"But he's in prison. He has no protection from us under the Geneva Convention for what he did. I thought he was awaiting punishment."

"For what?"

"Stealing the atomic bomb. I thought everyone wanted his head over that."

"That never happened. It's hard to execute someone for something he didn't do, isn't it?"

"But the man is extremely dangerous."

"What's your point?"

"I guess I don't have one."

"No, you don't. But I do. My job is to protect this country from any threats I detect. Right now, the Russians are not exactly getting along with us. Now I have identified a potential threat that could that could make us wish for Pearl Harbor again. If the Russians find these bombs and drop them on our forces in Europe, they could kill a million men before we realized what had happened. Now if I shoot Schreiber to satisfy the bloodlust of some politician and allow a million men to die, then am I not guilty of dereliction of duty."

"I guess in way, yes."

"I guess you think Schreiber ought to be shot?"

"I didn't say that. I do have a problem with what he did."

"Even with us starving German POWs."

"Well, it is a little unsettling."

"Then get over it. If there are bombs out there, I want them neutralized at all costs. This is as important as stopping Schreiber. Make sure the Russians do not find them. Understand?"

"Yes, sir."

"Dismissed."

November 1945

One month later, Stalin was in conference with prominent intelligence officers. Included were Beria, Sudoplatov, Makarov, and others. Sudoplatov was rising in prominence as Russia pursued nuclear power. Makarov was well known now as Sudoplatov's right-hand man. He had seen Korotokov banished to obscurity at a border guard post for bungling the Scherhorn operation at the end of the war. Had it been earlier, he probably would have been shot.

Stalin opened the conference. He was in an exuberant mood. His victories in Europe and Asia had reaffirmed in his mind his abilities as military commander. He was setting up puppet governments in the conquered countries and crushing any signs of democracy fom rivals of the Communist groups. His confidence from the victories and plans for the future had led him to tell Beria to make an atomic bomb in five years or face the consequences.

"Comrades, the year has ended with us victorious in Europe and in Asia. Now we are in an ideological war with the west. This will be more decisive than the last war. We must be better prepared than we were for the last war. The Americans have dropped two bombs on foreign soil. I have no doubt they would use one against us if they felt it necessary. We must be prepared to strike back. I'm pleased with the progress Department S has made. However, this story about the Americans having an atomic bomb stolen intrigues me."

Makarov knew he needed to answer the unasked question. "We have researched this as best we can. Since Elizabeth Bentley talked to the FBI, we have lost several couriers, and the information is sketchy. It does appear that a group of renegade Germans penetrated Los Alamos and stole a bomb. They transported it to Utah and got it aboard a B-29. The plane came down close to Washington. We believe the Germans are being held in a secure facility. There is no report of their execution. The Americans are keeping very quiet about this. No accounts have appeared in the newspapers, nor do I expect them to admit that something like this happened."

"I agree. It certainly would not be in Pravda if it happened to us," Stalin commented. "Who was the leader?"

"A man named Schreiber. He was in the old Brandenburg Division. He went over to Skorzeny later. He also participated at Maikop." Makarov had hesitated to bring up that sore point.

"We last traced him to Flensburg. We think his team flew out near the end of the war in a flying boat. He was highly decorated. Anyway, we came across a series of messages sent back to Germany after the war regarding an operation called Gotterdammerrung. Our review of KG 200s records shows no other long-range flights in Western Europe."

"There may be some good in this after all." Stalin was enjoying the story. "Please continue.

"Other inquiries show that Werther did not inform us about this as he did other planned operations. It may be that he was not informed. We feel that Himmler kept this too himself as we can find no written records regarding this project. Only a few members in the SS knew about this, as we have found no one who knew anything about this. Even torture has failed to help us. The Americans had some clues late in July that something was wrong, but they continued believing their security was foolproof. In July, one of their intelligence officers had a chance to cancel the mission but actually gave the Germans the order to continue. He was ambitious and wanted to catch the Germans."

"We would have strictly dealt with such a person in our usual way. This is all very good." Stalin was cold now.

"I don't understand," Makarov replied.

"It shows that the American's security is sloppy and that the bomb could be neutralized on the ground. It shows that many options are open to us. Who was Schreiber's commander?"

"Otto Skorzeny."

"What has become of him?"

"Currently, he's imprisoned at Nuremburg. The Americans wanted him very badly and want to put him on trial for war crimes."

"A man like that could be useful," Stalin replied. "We do have sympathizers among the Polish guards, don't we, in Nuremburg?"

"I believe so. I will check that out."

"I believe you should. Have an offer made to Skorzeny. A glowing fate would await him if he taught us the tactics he used against the west. He performed quite well as I recall."

"He rescued Mussolini and carried off Admiral Horthy. He may have destroyed the bridge at Remagen."

"Quite impressive," Stalin remarked. "We need to keep tabs with this Schreiber. We will hear from him again."

"If he did this at the end of the war, he's subject to execution without trial. The Americans are quite touchy about those sorts of things."

"They may officially execute him, but I doubt that you will see anything in the papers. Keep a watch for him. Wiser heads will prevail and use him against us. Comrades, we must be prepared." With that, Stalin concluded.

Fortunately, no one has wondered how the Germans figured this out, Makarov thought. Hopefully, Skorzeny will tell the Communists to get lost. Meanwhile, Makarov knew he would need to make sure his tracks stayed covered. For now, his secret seemed to be safe.

1990

"So you actually had the bomb. This happened." Eric Schreiber had a hard time absorbing what he had been told.

His father looked up at the sky. The sun had passed its zenith and was starting to set. "You understand some things now, don't you?"

"It's so fantastic. But I remember how certain senior officers gave me weird looks."

"You should see the ones they give me. Well, I wanted you to know why certain things are the way they are. What I did was for you, your mother, and the Fatherland. I don't know if what I did was right, but I did it."

"I think you did right. If you kept the Russians where they're at, you did the right thing."

"Perhaps, but at what cost?"

"We're still free."

"Yes, we're free."

"That's what's important. We're still free."

"I guess it is. Shall we call it a day?"

His son nodded. For a moment, Max Schreiber looked at

the purples and reds from the sunset. For a few seconds, he was transformed back to a younger man in July 1945, watching the red and purple mushroom cloud spread across the desert sky. Then he was back to 1990. "It's time we call it a day, son."

As they walked back to the car, Eric asked his father, "The bombs in Korea, did you find them?"

"Of course. That was my job."

"What happened?"

"That is another story another day."

The following day, Becker summoned Eric Schreiber to his office. "Quite a story, isn't it?"

"Fascinating."

"You figured out my father was the pilot."

"Naturally. It is so unreal. But it explains a lot of things now."

"Yes, it does." Becker opened a drawer and handed Eric the newspaper clipping he showed him yesterday. It gave details about the wreckage of a German floatplane that a fisherman had pulled up off the coast of Maine. "Just so you know, your father is not off in his head."

"I know. I just wish I knew. About this, about Korea."

"He mentioned Korea?"

"He briefly mentioned it. No details. He said it was another story another day."

"He's right. It is another story another day."

The end.